SORRY
I
MISSED
YOU

ALSO BY SUZY KRAUSE

Valencia and Valentine

SORRY I MISSED YOU

a novel

Suzy Krause

LAKE UNION
PUBLISHING

Text copyright © 2020 by Elena Krause
All rights reserved.

Published by Lake Union Publishing, Seattle
www.apub.com

Amazon, the Amazon logo, and Lake Union Publishing are trademarks of Amazon.com, Inc., or its affiliates.

ISBN-13: 9781542010207
ISBN-10: 1542010209

Cover design and illustration by Liz Casal

Printed in the United States of America

To my mom and dad
I'm sorry that people were concerned about my
upbringing after reading that other book I wrote. For
what it's worth, I think you did a great job.

GHOSTING STORIES

Maude and Richard

It was Maude's wedding day, and she looked awful in her dress. It bunched and sagged and pillowed and bulged. It washed her out while somehow also accentuating what was, in Maude's mind, her worst feature—her face. Richard wouldn't care; she knew this because she looked awful in everything, and he never cared, or even seemed to notice. He didn't really talk about how she looked, but he wasn't one of those skeezy older men who talked about how *other* women looked either. Instead, he laughed hard at her jokes, engaged her in enriching conversation, made her extravagant meals, and held her hand proudly in public. He absently played with her hair while they watched movies as though it were long and soft rather than short and wiry. He touched her face affectionately when he told her he loved her, and his eyes crinkled at the sides, like he couldn't believe he was so lucky. When this happened, she always felt her eyes do the same thing.

Maude smiled into the full-length mirror, aghast at all those lines. It was definitely harder to look good in fancy things when you were in your sixties—not impossible, just harder than it was when you were twenty-five. You could do all the squats you wanted, walk ten miles every day, apply moisturizer with a fire hose—didn't matter: you'd lived in your body, and it showed. For the first time in her life, Maude wished she'd gotten married in her early twenties—this dress was meant for *that* bride. But then she thought about the kind of man she would've chosen back then, and she laughed out loud and decided not to worry about her face or her bulging midsection and enjoy the fact that she was in actual, mutual love. Maybe deciding not to worry was one of the few things that came easier when you were in your sixties.

And so, gathering up her courage and multiple layers of tulle and satin, she boarded a bus to the park beside the courthouse downtown, where they were to meet their photographer before the ceremony— Richard's idea. The people on the bus stared at her curiously, and she smiled back, unbothered. *Maybe they think I look beautiful,* she thought, and before she could dismiss the notion, she put it on like another dress and wore it all the way to the park.

The photographer was already there when she arrived, and he didn't notice her at first. He was taking pictures of a tree for some reason— circling it slowly like *it* was the bride, rotating the camera and fiddling with it, spinning the little dials, stopping every so often to frown with consternation at the sun like he hadn't expected it to be out at two p.m.

He wasn't a professional photographer, just a friend of Richard's who had always enjoyed taking pictures. This meant that his services were going to be cheap, and that was the most important thing. Maude and Richard's wedding album would not be passed down from generation to generation; it would merely sit on a coffee table for a few years until Maude and Richard were gone, and then someone would take the pictures out of it and throw them in the garbage, and the album, if it was lucky, would end up in a thrift store with a twenty-five-cent sticker on it. This was Maude's first marriage, Richard's second, and neither of them had children. Their relationship wasn't the start of anything but itself.

"Hi, Maude!" said the photographer.

"Hi," said Maude. She couldn't remember his name.

"You look beautiful," said the photographer.

"Liar!" said Maude, laughing. "Take lots of pictures of us kissing and from behind. More of him than me. Maybe we could do a few of those funny ones where the bride holds her bouquet in front of her face."

"Okay," said the photographer, looking uncomfortable. "Speaking of, why don't we start with some bridal portraits? I read that lots of brides like to have just a couple—"

"No, thank you," said Maude quickly. "None of just me."

"Oh, okay, sure, no problem, sorry," said the photographer. He took another picture of the tree.

"I'm just going to sit over there on that bench until my groom arrives," Maude said, giddy at the thought of Richard walking down the tree-lined path toward her, dressed in a suit, looking at her in that way he always did, like she was an angel *and* Jane Fonda *and* the only woman left on planet Earth.

She arranged her pretty dress around her on the park bench and patted her hair and ran her ring fingers under her eyes to check for stray flecks of mascara and then she sat—and sat, and sat—until she began to wonder if she had misunderstood Richard when he'd said they should meet at this park. But the photographer was here; what were the chances they'd both gotten it wrong?

"Excuse me, uh . . . Mister . . . Photographer," said Maude, a little embarrassed that she couldn't remember the young man's name. "I'm going to find a pay phone. I'll be right back. If Richard gets here before I do, make him feel bad for being so late, will you?" She smiled to show she wasn't serious.

"Okay," said the photographer, who did not appear to mind being called "Photographer." It even seemed to puff him up a bit. "Are there working pay phones, still?"

"Of course there are working pay phones!" Maude chuckled. "Not everybody has a cell phone in their pocket."

The photographer mumbled something about thinking that everybody did, actually, have a cell phone in their pocket, and Maude went off to find a working pay phone.

She was right; there was one just around the corner, and she punched Richard's number into it, feeling conspicuous. A wedding dress was, by design, a conspicuous thing to begin with—but usually if you were wearing one, it meant that you did not have to be conspicuous all by yourself. Usually.

The phone rang a few times. She wasn't upset yet, just a little concerned. If he answered, that would be bad; he lived twenty minutes out of town, and he was already late. If he didn't answer, though, that might be worse because, well, where *was* he?

"Hello?"

Okay. Bad but not worse.

"Richard!" Maude exclaimed. "What are you still doing at home?"

"Maude! Oh, Maude." He sounded surprised to hear her voice. Who did he think would be calling on the day of his wedding?

She was quiet as she waited for a wave of emotion to pass. It was fine; everything was fine. It was her wedding day! But then, Richard wasn't *here*, so . . . "Did . . . did you forget our wedding, Richard?"

"Mm . . ." His voice rumbled over the phone line. "See . . . yes. No! No, I didn't. No, I was . . . I'm all . . . I'm trying to think of that . . . saying . . . cold something. Cold . . . ?"

"Richard. Are you okay?" He sounded off. His speech was slurred, and he seemed confused. She tried not to panic. "Richard? Richard!" What were you supposed to ask if you suspected a person was having a stroke? There was an acronym for it. *FAST.* That was it. Face. Arms . . . something, something. It would come to her; time was of the essence. "Okay, Richard, *face*—"

This caused Richard to break into laughter. "Cold face? No! Cold *face*?" He laughed so hard he struggled to form sentences. "Cold *feet*! That's what it is. But no, that can't be it either. That's just ab . . .

absur . . ." A gurgling sound traveled through the receiver, followed by an emphatic belch. "Cold feet! Ha! 'Maude, my feet are too cold to get married. My feet—'" He was laughing too hard to finish his sentence.

"You're drunk," Maude said, surprising herself. She'd said the words before they'd even crossed her mind. She wasn't mad, not yet; she wasn't even sure she was awake. It could have been a dream, one of those ones where you're naked in front of a lot of people. Only she was the opposite of naked; she was overdressed. And her inebriated fiancé was laughing much too hard at an unfunny age-old idiom that meant he didn't want to marry her. At any moment, she would flap her arms and fly away in the phone booth, and then she'd wake up on her wedding day and chuckle about it to herself, and maybe she'd tell Richard all about it later—on their honeymoon. They were going to Canmore. They had a honeymoon suite. They were going to drive into Banff one day and take a cableway ride to the top of Sulphur Mountain.

"No!" yelled Richard, laughing again. "Well . . . yes. Yes. That *is* true." He was hysterical. "I have to go, Maude. This whole thing . . ." He hung up.

So there stood Maude in a phone booth on Scarth Street, utterly confused and abruptly overdressed. She was not heartbroken, but that would come when the shock wore off.

This whole thing . . . absurd.

Well said, Richard.

It was not Maude's wedding day after all.

She sent the photographer home and canceled the ceremony, and then she went home, too, and changed out of that stupid dress—as embarrassing a thing as it had been to put on in the first place, taking it off and trying to fit it back into its pretty box were downright humiliating.

Then there was nothing to do but wait for Richard to sober up and call her with an apology and an explanation for his bizarre behavior, but he never did. There would be no cableway ride to the top of Sulphur Mountain.

She knew she wasn't the first person to be left like that; leaving was what people did best and most often. But the abruptness of this leaving, the unexplained nature of it, was torture, and it came as close to killing her as anything ever had. Her body became bloated with questions; she felt them in her feet when she walked, and they flowed through her veins and whispered in her head at night. She couldn't eat, couldn't sleep, couldn't concentrate. It was strangely—punishingly—similar to being in love. It was awful, and it made her awful.

~

Mackenzie and Tanya

"But it's my birthday." Mackenzie stood in the bedroom doorway. She was trying to feel angry so she wouldn't feel hurt.

"Was. Yesterday." Tanya's voice floated in from the tree just outside the bedroom window. She'd been on her way down when Mackenzie caught her and now she was perched on a branch, her bone-white skin glowing in the moonlight so she looked like a ghost hovering there.

"That's not how it works."

"That's exactly how it works. It's two in the morning. It's not anyone's birthday."

"Pretty sure it's a bajillion people's birthday."

"You know what I mean. Not yours." Tanya glanced down the tree, not to see who was down there but to indicate to Mackenzie that she wanted to join them.

"You just don't want to admit you're ditching me to go hang out with someone you like more on my birthday."

"Again: your birthday was yesterday. Go to bed."

"*Wow.* Thanks." Mackenzie tried to look hurt without pouting.

But Tanya could only care about one thing at a time, and right now, Mackenzie wasn't it. "Kenz. Chill out. We had a party. We had fun. That was your birthday, this is something else. We don't have to share everything."

"I'm sorry you've had to share anything with me. I'm sorry that's been so sucky for you."

Tanya smiled impatiently. "Mmmkay, well. We gotta go. You're not going to tell, right? Be cool." Tanya was always telling Mackenzie to "be cool." Like it was something she had control over. Like she'd chosen, at birth, to be a loser.

"*Obviously* I'm not going to tell," said Mackenzie, trying to appear indifferent rather than devastated.

"Awesome," said Tanya, indifferent without even trying.

She whispered something down the tree, and a whisper came back up to her. She twisted her body toward the tree trunk, reaching in the dark for an invisible branch, trusting it would be there even though she couldn't see it. Mackenzie realized in that moment how familiar this escape route had become to her sister.

"I don't think you should go," she said quickly. One last attempt.

Tanya drew in an exaggerated breath.

"Mom would hate it if she knew you were going off with some guy you barely know."

This got Tanya's attention. She changed direction and hauled herself back in through the window, climbing over her dresser and jumping onto the floor in front of Mackenzie. She landed without a sound, somehow, like she was a shadow instead of a person. If Mackenzie were to attempt the exact same thing, everyone in the household would wake up and come running to see if a tree had fallen on the roof or if there had been an earthquake.

"What do you know about it?" Tanya wasn't indifferent anymore.

Mackenzie knew she had the upper hand now. She didn't *want* the upper hand, though; she just wanted to be invited. Not because they were threatened by her or because they felt like they had to invite her, but because they wanted her around. She stared at her sister, her eyes welling up with tears, trying to decide how to play it. Should she mention the things she'd read in her sister's email in-box? The *crazy* amount of money she knew Tanya had in her purse right now? The fact that she knew exactly where Tanya was going and who she was meeting? "Nothing," she said finally, staring at her purple toenails.

"Why'd you say that then?"

"It was a guess."

"You *guessed* that I was going off with a guy I barely know?"

"You're always going off with guys you barely know. You're always going off with everybody, and you never take me with you." She didn't want them to invite her because they felt sorry for her, but maybe that was just what it was going to take.

Tanya relaxed. Her eyes became bored again. She was neither empathetic nor concerned. "Later, Mackenzie."

She climbed up onto her dresser and slipped out the window into the dark, and that was the last time Mackenzie ever saw her in real life.

But she showed up in Mackenzie's dreams almost every night after that and often began to materialize in her periphery in public places, looking just as ghostly and shadowy as she had the night she disappeared, only to vanish when Mackenzie turned her head.

~

Sunna and Brett

The stove might as well have blown up. The bathtub from the apartment above might as well have fallen through the ceiling and onto the dining table with a naked neighbor in it. The chicken they were eating might as well have reassembled itself and run screaming out the front door. The fight had had that kind of quality to it—it was shocking, surreal. Unprecedented. Something they never thought would happen to them—and it did feel like something that had happened *to* them, not something in which they had agency. They'd been having supper together, and then they were yelling at each other, then screaming. Who had started it? Who had become angry first? And why? Neither party could remember afterward.

Two words ended the fight, one on each side. Brett called Sunna jealous, and Sunna called Brett fake, and though both women had used many worse words than those throughout the course of the fight, those were the ones that rang in the air like gunshots. As the saying goes, the truth hurts.

Maybe the fight would've been the end of their relationship, but they'd been at Brett's house, and when Sunna stormed out, she forgot to take her jacket. It wasn't a special jacket, but it was a jacket—and this was Toronto, and it was January. Sunna had been angry enough to make it home that day without it, but she'd had to make a sheepish phone call the next morning to arrange a time to pick up her coat—"When's good for you? Sorry I flew out like that. Sorry for everything, actually . . ."

She hadn't meant to apologize and didn't mean the apology; it had come out of her mouth like someone else had commandeered her voice box. She realized then that she was opening a door that had been a relief to slam shut.

Of course, then, Brett had no choice but to apologize back. "I know—I'm sorry too. I was out of line . . ."

And Sunna hated herself for saying the next thing and for how whiny and pleading her voice sounded when she said it. "Can we please just forget that happened? Like, all of it. I want to be friends again, like we were before all of this."

"Yes. Me too." Brett sounded sincere, but Brett was a good actress.

And then they sat there on the phone, and Sunna knew both of them were thinking the same thing.

How do adults end friendships?

Sunna and Brett had known each other for over a decade, had been each other's only support through all the usual twentysomething milestones and heartbreaks. They'd gone to school together, worked together, lived together. They had *history*. Why would anyone want to end that kind of friendship, the kind only lucky people even got the chance to experience in the first place? It was almost ungrateful, wasn't it?

But Sunna showed up at Brett's apartment that afternoon, and they hugged and said how relieved they were not to have lost each other, and Sunna even found herself tearing up and then wondering, *Do I mean all of this? I must! I'm crying . . .*

She got her coat, said goodbye, and felt a little better as she closed the door behind her. Everything was okay. This friendship was far from over.

The cautious optimism lasted all the way to Ossington station, where she stepped onto a subway car and sat ruefully beneath a massive banner that read *The 30 Under 35 Initiative—the Future of Toronto Is in Great Hands!* It bore the radiant image of none other than her now unestranged friend, Brett. Toronto's most notable up-and-coming VIP golden child. A role model for anyone even a second younger than her, an inspiration to everyone else. The ad spoke to Sunna; it said, "Look at this woman. Look at you. The friendship *is* over."

But they'd disrupted the natural progression of things. That stupid jacket. They were "friends again," and now they met for coffee every week because they didn't know how adults ended friendships.

The relationship was on life support. The coffee dates were torturous: Sunna would ask, politely, about Brett's latest campaigns and sponsorships and speaking gigs. Brett would, in turn, lean across the table and lower her voice and put on her concerned face and speak to Sunna the same way she spoke to her massive Instagram audience.

"Sunna," she would say, scrunching her forehead up like she was working hard to select every word that came out of her mouth, "I know your job makes you money, but does it make you *happy*? Are you in your BLZ?"

That was Brett's problem. She couldn't even drop her act in casual conversation. She was always on, always Brett Lynn Zaleschuck, creator of the social media empire Best Life Zone. Always there to help the commoners in their pathetic attempts to be like her. Sunna hated it, but in the name of "friendship," she would smile stiffly and assure Brett that she was in her BLZ, a statement that made her want to pour her hot coffee directly onto her own face.

Occasionally, the women would reminisce about college, or one of them would share something hard or sad and the other would comfort her, and they'd both remember that this relationship, though now strained and warped, was important to each of them, and that it wasn't going away. They were like family.

At the end of each appointment, out of some kind of weird, polite, mutually shared impulse, one of them would say, "I'll see you next week?" And they'd make another date.

Sunna was early today; she snagged the last free table in the small coffee shop / cocktail bar on Mutual Street and sipped a black coffee. Brett was fifteen minutes late, then twenty, then thirty. Sunna felt irritated. It was just like Brett to forget; she'd probably had something come up that seemed more important. Next time they got together Sunna would tell her off. This was the nice thing about crossing over from the carefulness and politeness of friendship into familial territory: Sunna could always say how she felt.

But, as it turned out, there would not be a next time. Brett didn't call to explain why she hadn't shown up or to offer any kind of apology. She didn't call at all. Their weekly coffee dates ceased, and a few weeks later, Sunna noticed that Brett had unfollowed her on Instagram.

The finality should've made her happy. But you don't get to choose your feelings, just like you don't get to choose your family.

THE LAST WILL AND TESTAMENT OF REBECCA FINLEY

Larry

Larry Finley was not supposed to sell the house on Montreal Street, but he couldn't live in it either. It said so in the will:

To Larry Finley I give my house on the condition that he does not (a) sell it or (b) listen to any music produced after 1952 in it or (c) paint it or (d) plant flowers anywhere in the front yard or (e) go into the attic or allow anyone else to enter the attic or (f) . . .

The will went on and on like that, almost a full alphabet of strange, mostly unexplained rules.

Larry thought the whole thing was stupid. If he couldn't listen to his music in the house, he couldn't move into it. And if he couldn't live in a house or sell it, and if parts of it were off limits, and if the house came with more rules than a cult, what good, exactly, did it do him to inherit it? At first, a free house had sounded great, but now it just made him cranky.

On his way home from the lawyer's office, he stopped by the deli counter at the grocery store for potato wedges. This was what he always did when he needed cheering up. It worked for two reasons: one, he liked potato wedges, and two, he liked Ang, the motherly cashier who always magically seemed to be working when he needed cheer-up wedges.

"Hey there, Larry. How'll you be paying?" Ang always smiled at him like she was relieved to see him, like she'd been waiting for him and was worried he wouldn't show. It made him feel like his presence, all by itself, was a good deed. He felt the same way about her and always kind of wished he could tell her that. "Cash?"

"Hey, Ang," he said, digging into his pocket for his wallet. "Yeah, cash."

"You okay, Larry?"

"Yeah, just . . . a little bit . . . grouchy. Sorry. I inherited a house today."

Ang laughed through her nose. "Hate it when that happens."

"Yeah, no—the house is fine. It's nice. It's that big one on Montreal? With the turret thing on top? They were gonna make it a historical site or something back in—anyway. It was my aunt's, and it just comes with a lot of . . . unreasonable obligations. She was kinda . . ." He made a pained face.

Ang nodded. "I see. Well if you want to off-load it . . ."

Larry laughed. He knew how he sounded. She had a way of making him hear himself. "Thanks, Ang. I'll keep you in mind."

Someone placed a box of Cheerios on the conveyor belt at his elbow, and he turned. A woman stood there, carefully moving groceries from the basket slung over her arm onto the counter like she was putting a puzzle together. She had small, close-set brown eyes and frizzy chin-length hair, dyed bright blue—the color of five-cent candy whales. Her face was decorated all over with tiny silver hoops and studs, and she was wearing army boots. She was perfect. She looked up and caught his eye. "Sounds like you come here often," she said, then smiled at Ang.

Larry knew he had no business looking at beautiful people because he wasn't one of them. He was a thin man—fast-food, fast-metabolism thin, not gym-and-protein-shakes thin. He had acne scars all over his face and a goatee on his chin and an instantly discernible penchant for '80s- and '90s-era punk rock. He still wore a wallet chain. He was forty-three.

He had no business looking, but he was looking anyway—he realized he was even staring—and interrupted himself with a nervous laugh that sounded, unfortunately, like a squawk. "Every day," he said, and then he felt embarrassed about admitting he was the kind of person who went to the grocery store every day. The squawk was not good either.

Ang rescued him—and whether it was on purpose or not, he loved her for it. "Larry's my favorite customer," she said. She probably said this about all her customers. "He always brings me the most interesting coins."

Larry tucked his chin into his chest and cleared his throat. "Ang collects coins," he explained. "I don't know anything about coin collecting. I just bring her anything that looks old or different. Oh! Speaking of . . ." He reached into his coat pocket and pulled out the nickel he'd been saving for her. "This one's cool," he said, forgetting about the beautiful, beautiful woman standing just inches from him. "Look at the edges—squared! It has twelve sides. Have you seen one like that before?"

Ang nodded, grinning appreciatively as she tucked his potato wedges into a bag and traded them for the nickel. "Thanks, Larry! I'm excited to take a look at it."

As he turned to go, the woman behind him cleared her throat, and he glanced back at her. She was looking at him in a funny way, like she'd made the noise to get his attention but now didn't know what to do with it. "I like your shirt," she said. And though Larry was wearing a shirt and though the woman was looking straight at the shirt he was wearing, it seemed impossible that she was saying this *to him.*

He looked at Ang for help.

"Descendents," Ang read, picking up on his distress. "Is that . . . a . . ."

"It's a punk band," said the woman. Then she looked Larry straight in the eyes and added, "*Milo Goes to College* is *such* a great album."

Larry had never fallen in love before; he'd always thought that would be an intentional, gradual process that could take weeks, months, or even years. He was well versed in physical attraction and had had a thousand crushes, meaningless and otherwise, but couldn't fathom what it would take to decide you *loved* someone.

But, as it turned out, falling in love was exactly what it sounded like. Love was like a sewer: something you knew about but didn't think about until someone left a manhole cover open and you just tripped right in and your stomach dropped like you were on a roller coaster and you felt thrilled but also like you were going to barf. Messy, painful, disorienting. Amazing.

It happened to Larry when he looked into her eyes. He got distracted, didn't watch where he was going, tripped over his feet, and plunged, face first, straight into love.

He nodded, unable to tear his eyes away from hers. "Can I have your phone number?" he asked breathlessly.

The woman burst out laughing, which was good because Larry couldn't have recovered from such a massive gaffe if she thought he wasn't joking. But his relief lasted for only a moment. Then it occurred to him that laughter wasn't a great response to a request for a phone number if it was not followed by a phone number.

His phone started to buzz in his pocket, and again, he couldn't decide if that was good or bad. *Good, probably.* He needed to get away. It was over; he'd messed it up. He glanced down at the screen. *Glenda.* His older sister, returning the call he'd made on his way to the store to complain about the house and the will; their aunt had left *her* a 1974 Lincoln Continental with no stipulations whatsoever. She could sit in it, she could drive it, she could look in the glove box. She could plant flowers in the trunk for all anyone cared. It wasn't fair.

"Well," said Larry, holding the phone up, "I have to take this. It's the sister. I mean, it's *my* sister. Not . . . some random nun." He cleared his throat. "So. Nice to meet you guys. I mean, not you, Ang."

Ang looked like she wanted to save him again, but they both knew it was too late.

He turned and walked away fast, holding the phone to his ear and clutching the potato wedges like a purse, thinking to himself that, while he had enjoyed his brief encounter with love, he was probably going to need to avoid it from here on. It had taken everything out of him, and he'd come up with nothing in the end. He felt sorry for himself. First the house, now this.

"Hey, Glenda," he said.

"How was it?"

"Weird. I got her house."

Silence.

"But, Glenda, listen, it's not just simple like that. There are a whole bunch of really weird rules that I have to follow if I want to keep it. Just ridiculous rules. Is that even allowed?"

"Is what allowed?"

"To, just, to make such strange, specific rules and requests in your will. That can't be allowed, can it? Legally?"

Glenda paused, the way she always did before she was about to play devil's advocate. Larry hated that pause. "Well, I read somewhere that Napoleon Bonaparte's will said to shave his head and distribute the hair among his friends. If that's not strange and specific, I don't know what is. You could probably look into it, though—ask the lawyer how much of it they can make you follow. What kind of rules did she put in there?"

"Well, I'm not allowed in the attic—"

"Larry. You don't even want to go into the attic, do you? Not after what happened up there."

"No, I don't want to go into the attic. I want to be *allowed* to go into the attic. That's different. But here's another one, Glenda: I'm not allowed to plant flowers in the front yard."

"*You* were going to plant flowers?"

"Again: I just don't want to be told I couldn't if I wanted to. Glenda, I'm not even allowed to *live* in the house."

"What?" Glenda sounded either skeptical or giddy. "She *said* you can't live in it?"

"Well. She said I can't listen to my music in it."

"That's . . . not the same thing. At all."

"It is to *me*," said Larry solemnly.

"Don't whine, Larry," Glenda said in a voice all warbly and choppy. She probably had him on speakerphone. She couldn't just sit and take a phone call; she had to be doing something else at the same time. "She left you a *house*."

"I'm not whining, and she didn't leave me a house. A house, you can live in—comfortably. You can listen to whatever you want in it. You can decorate it how you want and go into all the rooms. When you're done with it, you can sell it. She basically left me a really, really big box I can't get rid of. A box that people died in. A two-thousand-square-foot *casket*."

"Why don't you rent it out?"

Larry leaned against his car. Why hadn't that occurred to him? The upside of such specific rules was that there wasn't a lot of guesswork to be done. The rules did not state that someone else couldn't live in the house. It was a big house; lots of people could live in it. He could stay where he was and collect enough rent to cover his living expenses and then some. He could even quit his job. *Huh.*

"I could maybe do that," he mumbled.

"It's a big house," Glenda said. She liked to read his mind and repeat his thoughts out loud like a psychic parrot. "You could fit lots of people in it. You could stay in your crappy little apartment and collect enough rent to quit your job." He couldn't be sure, but he thought his sister sounded mad now. "She always did like you and Jim best."

"Why, what did she leave to Jim?"

"She gave him those paintings of Uncle Garnet's—the landscapes. I mean, they're not going to make anyone rich, but they're nice. They'll look nice in his house. Meanwhile, *I* will drive my newly acquired boat straight to the dump because Aunt Rebecca, apparently, didn't like me."

"Glenda . . ."

"Larry . . ."

"Well at least the Lincoln isn't haunted."

"Larry."

"Glenda."

But Larry was right. The Lincoln didn't have ghosts in the glove box. The house, however, was widely known to have at least two—one being, presumably, the ghost of his uncle Garnet, who'd dragged a chest into the middle of the attic floor, climbed up onto it, and hanged himself over two decades ago. The second being his business partner, who'd done the same right next to Uncle Garnet.

Over the years, Aunt Rebecca had gotten used to the ghosts. She was always telling people what they wanted and what they didn't want, who they didn't want around, what kind of music they wanted to listen to, etcetera. They didn't like Larry's uncle Ronny, for example, so Ronny was not allowed to visit. They were picky ghosts, she said, always shrugging apologetically. "*I* like you, Ronny," she said when she told him the bad news, "but *they* make the rules in this house."

Larry hadn't believed in the ghosts until the fall of '93. All the Finleys had been gathered around the dining room table, and someone had turned on the radio, and Celine Dion had started caterwauling like a banshee. Aunt Rebecca shook her head disapprovingly and said, "That woman is caterwauling like a banshee. The ghosts won't like *that*," but no one turned the radio off. Then the door to the attic started to open and close, and open and close: Bang! Bang! Bang! Bang! Aunt Rebecca made a face at her peas like, *I told you so*. "AM 1190," she said, looking bored with their insolence.

So someone turned the radio to AM 1190, where the Blue Jays were playing the Phillies. The banging stopped. The ghosts, it would seem, liked baseball. Sports ghosts.

Aunt Rebecca sat back in her chair, smug and knowing, and said, "The ghosts *hate* Celine Dion." From that point, all the Finleys believed in the ghosts. *Larry* believed in the ghosts, and he presumed now that the suicides and the subsequent ghosts were the reason he wasn't allowed in the attic, and they probably also had something to do with him not being allowed to sell the house or plant the flowers, if he were the kind of person who wanted to plant flowers. And they were the reason he would obey the orders in the will to the letter, even though the average person might choose to ignore them if they legally could.

But the ghosts had not said he couldn't rent the house out.

~

So Larry hired some contractors and turned the house into three separate suites. Basement, main, second floor. The ghosts left everyone alone during the process, though one worker claimed to have heard singing when everyone else had gone for their lunch break and he'd been there by himself. Larry took this to mean that they were happy with him for obeying the rules, and though Larry liked to give the impression that he disliked authority, he was actually an incurable people pleaser. (In this case, an ex–people pleaser.)

On the last day of renovations, he checked the door to the attic, which was accessible from the second-floor suite. It was locked, and the one key he'd been given—the key to the front door—didn't fit the lock.

That was that, and it was fine with Larry. In fact, now that he was face to face with that door, remembering that day in 1993 and all the other incidents that had happened since, he only felt relief. He couldn't have slept in the house, even if he was allowed.

He knew he wouldn't have a hard time renting the suites out. The neighborhood was established, safe, well located. A short walk northwest to the downtown area, a shorter walk in the opposite direction to Wascana Lake. Montreal Street was quiet and wide and lined with old trees, and the house itself was pretty: light blue with white trim, a big wooden porch, an enclosed widow's walk on the roof, and a fifty-foot Manchurian ash in the front yard, the roots of which were beginning to break up through the city sidewalk. No flowers, just like the ghosts wanted.

As he hammered a For Rent sign into the lawn, Larry thought about the woman from the grocery store. Maybe she needed a place to live? Just as quickly, though, he remembered her laughter. As though the mere thought of someone like her giving someone like him a phone number was so ludicrous it didn't even warrant an actual response, and they both knew it.

The first renter called within a day and wanted to move in immediately. She was not the grocery store woman; her name was Maude. She was crispy and angular and partially obscured beneath a big floofy hat. She took the suite upstairs, 2139A. She looked old enough—but not sweet enough—to be his grandmother and brought with her a cat and a couch (she called it a chesterfield). She seemed fragile and weepy and said these were the only possessions she could still look at without crying, that she'd finally just sold everything else. Larry didn't ask why, even though this statement seemed a bit leading, especially the way she whispered it into the air and then looked sideways at him to gauge his response.

Before he left, she complimented him on his Hogan's Heroes T-shirt and said something about "TV back when it was good," and he didn't have the heart to tell her that he'd purchased the shirt at a punk show, that the Heroes were a band he liked, that he had never seen a single episode of the ancient sitcom.

A week later, a university student named Mackenzie moved into the basement suite, 2139C. Mackenzie was tall and bold and athletic and she had purple-black hair and a colorful, fine-line tattoo that ran from her elbow up her arm and into the sleeve of her T-shirt like dyed spider veins. She almost—but not quite—looked like someone who could've belonged to the beloved punk scene of his youth, though her tattoo sleeve was too delicate, her whole aesthetic too clean and polished and new looking. (It was a shame, what had happened to punk. He tried not to be that guy who constantly thought about it, but he was.)

Mackenzie had even less furniture than Maude, like any kid who'd just moved out of her parents' house, but she had a ludicrous number of suitcases, like she needed a different shirt for every hour of every day. She and another girl around her age pulled up in two separate cars, hauling Mackenzie's stuff up the porch steps and down the basement stairs like two picnic ants, and then they stood on the porch talking and laughing for what must have been an hour as Larry awkwardly stood by, waiting to hand off the door key.

When the other girl finally left, she took a couple of empty suitcases with her. She also took Mackenzie's quiet confidence, and suddenly Mackenzie was only quiet. She no longer seemed like she fit in her own clothes and skin, like someone else had inhabited her body, dressed her and decorated her and then left her, bewildered and lost, standing in someone else's ripped skinny jeans in front of someone else's house.

She stuttered an almost-inaudible thank-you to Larry, took the key, and hurried into her apartment. Larry heard the door close and lock and bolt behind her.

2139B, the entire main floor, remained vacant for almost a month before it was occupied by a woman named Sunna. She had long shiny fingernails and short shiny hair and white shiny teeth lined up neatly in a mouth that smiled without alerting the rest of her face. She was extremely beautiful, but in a different way than the grocery store woman. Where that woman could grace the cover of Larry's favorite punk magazine, *Razorcake*, Sunna was someone you'd see in a commercial for perfume or playing a lawyer in a TV drama.

He and Sunna hadn't gotten off to a great start—when he'd showed up to give her the house key, she'd grasped it gingerly between her thumb and middle finger like it was dirty, said a curt "thank you," and opened the door without even looking at him, though he continued to babble on about keys and mailboxes and the other women living in 2139A and 2139C—but still, every time his phone rang from that day forward, he hoped it was her asking him to come fix the dishwasher or something. It wasn't love, but only because he was being more careful about love these days.

He didn't mention the ghosts to any of the tenants. They'd find out soon enough.

A LETTER ARRIVES AT 2139 MONTREAL STREET

Sunna

Sunna had been transferred, and she was still trying not to take it personally. It wasn't that she wanted to stay—she wanted to leave more than anything—it was that she didn't want to be sent away. Leaving should be her idea, and people should beg her not to go.

But Fire! Fitness was expanding, with new locations in Saskatchewan and Alberta, and sending Sunna to one of them made the most sense, logistically, so Sunna had to act sad (to be leaving) but not too sad (lest they reconsider and decide to send someone else), when all she really felt was relief. She needed to be out of this city, where everyone knew Brett but not Sunna, where Brett's face grinned from billboards and signs in the subway and from the stages she graced when she was asked to emcee fancy events and charity dinners. This was Brett's city, and while Sunna had long wished she didn't have to live here, she'd never had a good enough reason to leave.

So Sunna flew west, and she spent much of that flight contemplating all the usual things people worried about when they were leaving anything for anything else—whether she was running "away" or "toward," whether she had failed or outgrown, whether she was being stupidly impulsive or thrillingly spontaneous. By the time she landed in her new home—Regina, Saskatchewan, the Queen City, the Actual Center of the Middle of Nowhere—she'd landed on all the most unflattering conclusions. She was running away from Brett, she had failed at everything she'd ever attempted, and accepting this transfer was one big fear-and-failure-fueled mistake.

But just because you knew you'd made a mistake, that didn't mean you knew how to fix it, and the cab from the airport to her hotel was only fifteen bucks, where a flight back home would've been several hundred. And maybe there was something for her in this tiny city. Maybe it would be easier to find because it had so few places to hide.

Within days, she'd found a more permanent temporary place to live and was accepting a house key from a scrawny guy dressed like a fourteen-year-old who couldn't look her in the eye but wouldn't shut up about keys and mailboxes and the other tenants living above and below her. When she'd seen the listing for this gorgeous, mansion-like home, he was not the sort of landlord she'd pictured greeting her at the front door.

The letter came a week later, and she didn't think for one second that it was meant for her because she didn't have friends who communicated by snail mail. More accurately, she didn't have friends.

When she left Toronto, there had been a going-away party, put on by a group of people she had once called her friends. They'd acted sad and said they'd keep in touch, but Sunna didn't expect them to and wasn't bothered by the thought that they wouldn't. Her moving away wasn't the real end of those friendships, but it was tangible and easy for everyone to point to. As though she'd begun to dematerialize during a dinner party and no one had noticed until a voice from a seemingly empty chair said, "Well, I guess I'll be leaving now."

So this letter wouldn't be for her; it would be for one of the other renters. The landlord had mentioned that he planned on installing separate mailboxes and doorbells for each of the suites as soon as he could; he said he simply hadn't thought of it before and then apologized and apologized and apologized. People who apologized like that, like they were begging for reassurance, drove her nuts.

She reached into the mailbox, rolling her shoulder up so her purse wouldn't fall to the porch. The envelope, along with a grocery store flyer and a door hanger advertisement, was sitting in several inches of rusty water.

"Oh, gross," she said, holding the soused papers in front of her with the tips of her acrylic nails. There was a clucking sound behind her.

"That mailbox is awful. We need to speak to Larry about it. Every time it rains, it fills up like a bathtub and wrecks my coupons."

Sunna looked up. An older woman stood there, shaking her head and cradling a grocery bag like it was an infant. She wore glasses on a beaded chain around her neck and a ridiculous Kentucky Derby–style cocktail hat on her head. The hat had a veritable bouquet of feathers and flowers on the side and would've looked festive except for the fact that it was all black, which meant the feathers looked like they'd come from a crow, and the flowers looked like they'd come from a funeral scene in a Tim Burton movie. Except for that strange gothic hat, everything about her was sharp and no nonsense, from her nose to her collarbones to the pleats in her pants.

"Larry?"

"The *landlord*," said the woman. Her voice was sharp too.

"Oh. Right, yeah, Larry," said Sunna, embarrassed.

"I'm Maude," said the woman. "I live above you." Her tone also seemed to say, I *am* above you.

"Right. I'm on the main floor. I'm Sunna."

"Oh." The woman's lip curled disdainfully, as though she didn't like names that couldn't be found in very old Canadian phone books.

Sunna looked down at the mess in her hands, holding it out so as to not drip rusty mailbox water on her shoes. "You're right though. This is . . . *oh*. What—"

"Mm?" said Maude, her eyes not moving from Sunna's. The wind moved the feathers in her hat so they waved like wispy black fingers.

"Look at this," said Sunna. She peeled the soggy envelope out from the folds of the grocery store flyer and held it up so Maude could see. "Half of this is gone—it's been ripped right off. I can't find the other half. What happened to . . . ?"

"I can't imagine," said Maude.

"A dog?" mumbled Sunna.

"Well, *obviously*," said Maude, who only a second before had not been able to imagine a dog or anything else. She snatched the flyer out of Sunna's hands, disinterested in the letter. She turned to the page with the coupons, and her face collapsed into a heavy frown. "Look at this." She held it up, and Sunna saw that the flyer had suffered a similar fate to the letter. "We need to talk to Larry about this. They can't scan those coupons after they've been in water overnight, or after the barcode's been ripped off like that. Happens at least once a week. I've had to pay full price for several items I had a coupon for. In fact, I think Larry owes me money."

"I'm not sure that's how it . . ." Sunna swallowed the words. It wasn't her business, and she got the feeling she didn't want it to be. She held out the sopping letter. "Here. I think this letter is for you or the other tenant. It's not for me."

"Why wouldn't it be for you? Because it's *dirty*? Because it's *ripped*?"

"No. Just because I don't get mail. Ever."

"Whose name is on it?" asked Maude.

"No one's. See? Half of it's gone. The address was probably on that half."

"Then how did the mailman know to put it in our box?"

"I guess . . . it must have happened after it was in our mailbox." That was frustrating. No dog could get into a mailbox and mangle the contents and then put some of it back. Was this the work of a mentally unhinged neighbor? Annoying teenagers thinking they were funny?

"Oh," said Maude. "Well then."

"Yeah," said Sunna, and she felt like she'd won some kind of silent fight.

Maude scowled at Sunna and at the ash tree and the sky. A car pulled up behind her with its radio blaring. It parked, and she turned and scowled at it too. A girl with short hair slid out of the car. At first, she looked surprised to see people on the porch, then excited. She jogged up the sidewalk, stopping short at the porch steps. Her body was tall and wide, and she carried herself athletically but self-consciously, eager but full of nervous energy. She offered a funny little wave and smiled, oblivious to the tension between the other two women. "Hi," she said. "I'm Mackenzie Simons. Are you the neighbors? I'm really happy to meet you; I've been wondering who else lived here. It's weird not knowing who all's in the same house as you, you know? It's . . . strange . . ." She trailed off, and her smile wavered slightly.

Sunna smiled back, trying to shake her annoyance with Maude. "Hi, Mackenzie. I'm Sunna. I'm on the main floor. This is Maude—she's upstairs."

Maude nodded. "I wondered if I'd ever see either of you, and now here we are, all at the same time." She sounded like she'd been waiting for this moment for a while, like she had something to get off her chest. "Good. I needed to talk to you both about your *hours.*"

"Our—"

Mackenzie's smile didn't falter when Maude cut her off. "Yes, *hours.* You leave and come back at strange *hours.* The doors in this house are *loud.* It wakes me *up* when you *slam* them." She kept nodding emphatically as though pointing out the important words with her head.

Sunna opened her mouth to defend herself. She'd only been here a week and hadn't gone out except to get groceries or go to work—though she did leave very early for work. She taught classes at the gym as early as five a.m. That wasn't all that unheard of, though, was it? Lots of people had to leave early for work. And she didn't slam the door on her way out or anything. She wasn't a person who tiptoed around, but she wasn't inconsiderate.

Mackenzie, however, was earnestly apologetic. "I do, don't I?" she said. "I'm really sorry. I have early-morning classes, and I usually work quite late. I'm *so*—"

"It's not a problem," Sunna interjected. "This is just how it is when you rent a suite instead of buying your own whole house. You're not loud, and you have as much right as either of us to close doors whenever you feel like it. You pay rent too."

Maude gaped, and Sunna felt like she'd won again.

"Anyway," said Sunna, "we were just talking about this." She held up the dripping letter, still pinched between her fingernails. "Found it in the mailbox; half of it's gone. Weird, right? I don't think it's for me, and I thought I should check if either of you were expecting something before I read it."

"Huh." Mackenzie was polite but unconcerned. "I'm not expecting anything, and honestly I don't know who'd write me a letter. Probably not mine." They both looked at Maude. They were likely both thinking the same thing: *Old people still write letters.*

Maude clucked her tongue again. "And I'm in the same boat as you two. Why don't you just read it? Then we'll know who it's for."

"Okay," said Sunna, unfolding the sopping paper.

"Well?" said Maude.

Sunna frowned. "Short and sweet," she said. "Really short, actually, since half of it's missing. See?" She held it out. The ink on the right side of the letter was bleeding and barely legible, but the left side of the letter was gone. "I can't tell what all of it says." Sunna held it closer to her face.

"Read it," said Maude. "Out loud."

"I literally just said I can't read it," said Sunna.

"I just meant," said Maude, her voice taut, "that I want you to read whatever of it you can make out. You *literally* just said you can't really tell what *all* of it says. That *literally* means you *can* tell what *some* of it says. Maybe even *most* of it. If we are, in fact, being *literal*."

The women exchanged withering looks, and Mackenzie became singularly focused on a hangnail on her thumb.

"Fine," Sunna said, trying to sound nonchalant. "Half of it's missing, but . . ." She cleared her throat and held the paper close to her face, squinting more than necessary. "Okay, so the letter, what's left of it, says—"

"Is there a name? A salutation?" Maude interrupted.

"Doing the best I can here, Maude," Sunna said, pressing her teeth together. An ache bloomed behind her ears. "No, there's no salutation. That would've been over here." She pointed at the air where the left side of the letter would've been.

"Annoying," said Maude.

"Okay, I'm going to read this, here, Maude."

"Yes, fine," said Maude, like she couldn't understand why Sunna needed to spell it out like that. "Go on."

"Okay," said Sunna, shaking some new tension out of her shoulders. "Here it is:

> "orry I missed you—I swung by on my way to
> if you'd be here but that was a long shot.
> such a long time, and I'm sorry for that too. My
> ave some time that afternoon and maybe we could
> Cup? It's the one by the airport. If you were free—"

Sunna stopped. At the bottom of the letter, instead of a signature, there was a tiny letter *B*. Could it be for her after all? She remembered the way her stomach had dropped every time her phone beeped for months after Brett disappeared on her, with some mixture of hope and preemptive disappointment and anger. She remembered it vividly because, for the first time in a while, she was experiencing it right now.

"Keep going," said Maude. She sounded anxious all of a sudden.

"I can't. That's all there is."

"A little water isn't going to make a whole letter illegible," said Maude stubbornly. "Are you sure there's not more there?"

"No," said Sunna. Her anxiety was making her even more irritable. "Maude. *Half* of the letter is missing. Gone."

Mackenzie's face bore the same eager expression as Maude's. "Can I see that?" she asked.

But before Sunna could hand it to her, Maude reached forward and snatched the letter, almost dropping her groceries on the ground. A little more of the paper tore off, but it was so soggy it made no sound. "I have an inkling this was meant for me," Maude said. She spoke in a reverent whisper and moved toward the door, fumbling with her keys, the letter pinned between her elbow and her body, a damp spot growing on her coat.

"Maude, I was trying to hand that to Mackenzie."

Mackenzie smiled gratefully.

"Well, it's not *for* Mackenzie," said Maude. "It's for me. I know exactly who wrote it."

"You *think* you know who wrote it," said Sunna. "But maybe Mackenzie does too. You can't just declare that it's yours and not let her look at it."

Maude glared at Sunna. She looked Mackenzie up and down. At last, she sighed. "Fine, then—come inside. It's too cold out here for this."

~

The shared entryway was a small room with three locked doors: behind one was Sunna's apartment, and behind the other two were staircases to Maude's and Mackenzie's. Maude unlocked the one on the right and tromped up the stairs clutching the letter; Mackenzie and Sunna followed at a safe distance, like Maude was a bomb.

At the top of the stairs was another door, and behind that, a living room with big naked windows and gleaming hardwood floors. Maude's square heels echoed throughout the room. A blue-and-white floral couch rested against the far wall, looking crumpled and out of place. A cat perched, statue-still, on one of the cushions, contemplating the visitors. There was a TV/VCR combo on the floor with several precarious stacks of videocassette tapes on either side. This was what there was and nothing else, not even a speck of dust.

"You're not moved in yet?" asked Mackenzie.

Maude didn't seem to hear the question. She had already disappeared into the kitchen. Sunna and Mackenzie stood at the top of the stairs, unsure if they should follow.

"Come!" Maude barked, her voice reverberating off the walls, and they scurried after her. The kitchen, like the living room, looked empty and unused. It smelled like bleach and lemons. The appliances and cupboards, at least, took up a little space, but the countertops gleamed, and the open shelves had nothing on them but a plastic salt and pepper set and a couple of plates. There was a dining table with four mismatched wooden chairs, and the bag of groceries Maude had been carrying was now on the floor by the refrigerator. Maude was already seated at the table, the letter in front of her, wrinkling up as it dried to match the hands holding it.

"Sit down," she said to Mackenzie. Hunched over her dinner table with her black blouse and sharp chin, she reminded Sunna of a vulture. "What are *you* doing here?"

The question was for Sunna.

"You said to come inside."

"I said for Mackenzie to come inside. This isn't your business."

Sunna sat down defiantly. "It's my mailbox too. Possibly my letter."

31

Maude frowned but didn't press the issue. She set the letter in front of her and fixed her eyes on Mackenzie. "I need to put my groceries away—goodness knows everything's going to melt in there—but first we need to sort this nonsense out. Read it again."

Sunna picked the letter up. "I already read everything I could—"

"So read *that* again."

"Stop talking and I will." Maude looked wounded and Sunna couldn't make herself feel bad about it. She cleared her throat, drawing it out until she noticed the look on Mackenzie's face—not quite impatient, but silently pleading with her to hurry—and felt guilty. She read what she could once more and then added, "And there's a *B* at the bottom."

Maude almost jumped out of her chair at this. "A *B*? You didn't say that before."

"I'm saying it now. I didn't realize I hadn't said it out loud before. I'm sorry."

"That's a pretty important detail to just leave out." Maude took the letter back again, searching for the *B*.

"Right there." Sunna pointed. "I'm pretty sure it's a *B*." *B* for Brett.

"May I?" Mackenzie held out her hand, and Maude reluctantly gave her the letter.

"I don't think that's a *B*. I think it's a heart. Tipped over on its side a little," Mackenzie said, excited. "This looks like it was written by a woman. It's very pretty handwriting."

"Some men have pretty handwriting," said Maude, staring past Mackenzie at the clock on the wall behind her. "I've known a man with gorgeous penmanship." She plucked the letter from Mackenzie's hands and squinted at it. "Like this. It looked just like this. I'm almost *certain* . . ." Then she seemed to reconsider her tone. She handed the letter back to Mackenzie. "You have younger eyes than Susan. Could it be an *R*? An *R* could look like a *B* or a heart, couldn't it?"

Sunna opened her mouth to correct Maude but closed it again. Maude could call her whatever she wanted. It wasn't like they'd be talking much after today, but she'd have to talk to her more now just to say that her name wasn't Susan.

Mackenzie shrugged. "I'm so sorry, Maude. I wish I could read more too. But what's not there just . . . isn't."

Maude pressed her lips together and raised the forehead where her eyebrows presumably once were. "Okay. Well then."

Sunna took the letter back again. "Actually, that's not entirely true. That what's not there isn't, I mean. There's enough here to assume a few of the words that aren't, right?"

"True," said Mackenzie, leaning in. "Oh! Like, that 'Cup,' there—that's Paper Cup. It's a coffee shop. It's by the airport, like it says. Just on the other side of the Lewvan. It's cute. They have good pastries. That's what it was supposed to say."

Sunna nodded. "Yeah, like that. Great. I don't know this town well enough to know stuff like that. Maude, you got a pen? And paper?"

Maude made a stern face and shook her head.

"Whatever. I was just going to . . . never mind. Whatever. Someone wants to meet someone at Paper Cup in the afternoon on an unknown day. And their name starts with a *B*," said Sunna.

"Or it's a heart," said Mackenzie.

"Or it's an *R*," said Maude.

"That"—Sunna folded the letter and set it in the middle of the table—"is all. I *literally*," she looked straight at Maude, "can't read another word."

"You've forgotten the most important part," said Mackenzie.

"Which is?"

"The person they want to meet up with is either me or Maude."

"Or me," said Sunna.

Maude frowned. "Since when?"

"It just could be," said Sunna. "Why not me?"

"Because you said yourself it wasn't."

"No, I didn't. I just never said it was. I said I was waiting to see."

"You said you don't know people who mail letters."

"Yes, and then I actually read it. It says this person 'swung by.' So it was a hand-delivered note; that's different." Sunna was swinging wildly from one hope (that the letter was from Brett) to another (that it wasn't) with no pause in the middle. Brett traveled a lot; it wasn't a stretch to think she'd gotten Sunna's address from a mutual friend and stopped by. *Sorry I missed you.* Would Brett be sorry to miss her? That was the part more likely to be a stretch. "Anyway," she said, standing, "guess we'll never know. Too bad." *Was* it too bad?

"I guess we're done here, then," said Maude, though for all her subtlety she might as well have shooed them out of her house with a broom. Her cat jumped up onto her lap, and she gathered it into her arms and stood. The two stared at their unwelcome visitors, a unified front.

Mackenzie leaned over the table like she was ready to grab hold of it and hang on if someone tried to make her leave. "Okay," she said. "The things we don't know are the day, the exact time, and who is meeting who. So . . . let's figure it out. We'll go together."

"What?" Sunna was confused. "Go where?"

"To Paper Cup. Starting tomorrow. From twelve until close, to cover all our bases. Every day until someone's person shows."

Maude sat back down, and her chair squeaked beneath her. She rested her hands on the cat's back, but the cat didn't relax under them. "Someone's person? What do you mean?"

"We're all thinking of at least one person, aren't we?" Mackenzie looked from Maude to Sunna and back again. No one said they were not. "I can tell. Someone important, I think. Right?"

Maude conceded with a nod. "Why twelve until close?" She looked at Mackenzie suspiciously, as though she'd found something in the letter that she was keeping from them.

Mackenzie shrugged, still smiling at Maude, and if she felt irritated, she didn't show it, even for a second. "It said afternoon. Which works out well for me—I have classes in the morning and work at night, but I spend my afternoons writing and studying anyway. Might as well be at Paper Cup."

"Oh," said Maude. "All right, then—and that will work for me as well—I'm retired."

Sunna backed away from the table. She could go, too, if she wanted. She worked the coveted morning shift at Fire! Fitness and was always out of there before noon (one of the perks of seniority was getting first crack at the work schedule). She traded sleeping in for free afternoons, and for her it was a worthwhile swap. She wasn't about to give up those afternoons for any number of consecutive coffee dates with Vulture Maude. "No thanks."

"Why not?"

"Because it's a massive waste of time."

"No way! It'll be . . . fun." Mackenzie seemed to think this was a big adventure. "Besides, what if Maude and I go, but the letter's for you, and then we don't know when it's safe to stop going?"

"I don't know . . . I'm sorry? I just can't. Don't want to." The kitchen, which had initially smelled so strongly of bleach and lemons, now also smelled like thinly masked cigarette smoke and vinegar. The combination of nicotine and cleaning supplies began to make her nauseated.

"Well, I'm going to, anyway," said Mackenzie, her eyes big and serious. "I can think of people who might've written this letter to me, and I don't want to miss them if they show up."

Sunna tried to quell her irritation. "So *call* them or *email* them. It's not 1997. Ask them if they left you a letter in your mailbox. And tell *them* it's not 1997 while you're at it."

At this, Mackenzie's eyes glazed, but she kept smiling. "Would if I could."

Sunna knew she'd said something wrong but didn't know how to fix it. She was being a hypocrite, anyway—she sure wasn't going to call Brett and ask if she'd sent this letter. She looked down at her hands and then over at Maude, who was nodding so furiously that Sunna pictured her head rolling off her shoulders and under the table. "I'm going to come too. You're a smart girl. *I'm* certainly not going to be the one to call—" Maude stopped herself and cleared her throat. "I'm coming too."

Sunna considered this. Say Brett was in town for work, what then? Why wouldn't she just call like a normal person? Or, better yet, stay gone? And who cared, anyway? This was part of growing up; she'd known it for a long time. Sometimes you got closure, but most of the time you didn't. People who sat around pining for it were desperate. Her old friends in Toronto were like that, always wanting to discuss their feelings about incidents that had happened years before. Always wanting to rehash breakups, to get together with friends who weren't friends anymore to see if anything could be salvaged. "Yeah, well," she said. "You guys go do that. I have a life."

This wasn't true, but she looked at Maude when she said it and smiled.

EX-PUNK

Larry

The phone call woke Larry from a midafternoon nap.

He'd fallen asleep in front of his TV watching a homemade "documentary" about a local punk band from the '90s. The video was objectively awful. The picture was grainy, the camerawork jerky and headache inducing; it had been shot by a couple of the band members' girlfriends, years before quality recording equipment was available to people who didn't make movies for a living. But the DIY nature of it reminded Larry of the good old days—listening to lo-fi recordings with a sense of nonironic superiority, of going to shows in buddies' basements, where he thrashed and moshed and gave himself piercings and stick-and-poke tattoos without flinching. It reminded Larry of being young and feeling—not *cool*, but like he was something even better. He was *better* than the cool kids; he was an angry straight edge punk, a misunderstood misfit, and he belonged to a small, tight-knit group of other misunderstood misfits. They crashed together in time with their discordant, four-chord punk songs, took shoes to their faces, and generally danced like they were trying to beat the snot out of each other. They felt everything. It had been glorious.

And now, it was so long ago that the fuel for the movement, and for his involvement in it—angst, depression, rejection—had become romanticized and idealized, and he thought he kind of missed it. He missed the sharp, all-consuming feelings and their urgent and immediate call to action. He missed pain that proved something—not like this dull back pain that came from being on his feet so much at the art gallery, forcing him to wear orthopedic shoes at forty-three. Nowadays, negative feelings just pooled in his gut and made him lethargic. Nowadays, all he had were these VHS tapes and old band T-shirts.

"Hello?" he mumbled into the phone.

"Hello, um, L . . . Larry?"

Larry sat straight up. "Yes," he said, his voice cracking though it only had to deliver that one syllable. He tried another one with only slightly better luck. "Hey." It was Sunna. He knew right away. He hadn't thought she'd call so soon. He hadn't thought she'd call at all. This was the best thing that had happened to him in a long time.

She paused, and he considered all the different directions this conversation could take. It was a delight at first and then excruciating. He stared at the wall, which was plastered with signed gig posters, like somewhere in the hand-lettered band names he would find clues about what Sunna would say next. Time slowed; he couldn't wait to hear what words would come out of her mouth.

"Um, hey. This is Sunna. I . . . this is really embarrassing . . ."

He was dreaming. He had to be dreaming.

"I locked myself out of my place . . . can you come by and—"

So, okay. It was not quite flirtatious, but it was her saying something directly to him, and that was great. Almost miraculous.

She stopped speaking before she'd even finished asking the question, and this perplexed him until he realized that it was because he'd shouted "Yes!" as she was still talking. It rang in his ears now, and he worried his enthusiasm might be off putting.

She paused again. "'Kay," she said. "Thank you. I'll just be in Mackenzie's apartment—the basement suite—when you get here."

She hung up without saying goodbye. Or maybe she had said good-bye. Maybe he was too far up in the clouds to notice.

PICAROON PIZZA AND THE DREAD PIRATE HAIRS

Mackenzie

Picaroon Pizza was, as the name implied, a pirate-themed pizza parlor owned by Randall Hairs, a middle-aged Scottish man who had only ever wanted to be a pirate when he grew up. Very few people only ever want to be one thing, and fewer actually become that thing in the end, but Randall Hairs was living the dream: he was a pirate—or at least he got to dress and talk like one every day. It was as close to his dream as he needed it to be.

The quality of the food served at Picaroon was such that one could tell he was in it for the flair, for the ability to wear an eye patch to work every day, not his love of the culinary arts. He drank like a pirate, too, starting first thing in the morning and carrying on until closing time, and to him, this was just another perk of owning Picaroon Pizza. He sauntered through his restaurant like Johnny Depp, singing *Yo ho ho and a bottle of rum*. The customers couldn't tell whether it was an act or not. Maybe Randall didn't even know anymore. It was one of those things that was funny to witness until you witnessed it more than once, and then, if you really thought about it, it was downright depressing.

The restaurant was on the second floor of 1305 Hamilton Street and shared the space with Café Flash, which was not actually a café at all but a kitschy gift shop. The first floor housed Reggie's Shoes, and it was hard to tell whether the overall smell of the building was of feet or pizza or the perfume worn by the owner of Café Flash. It all mingled together into a salty, flowery, pizza-saucy potpourri.

Mackenzie had started work at Picaroon two days after moving to Regina. Her parents hadn't wanted her to go to the city. They seemed to be rooting for her to struggle financially so she'd have to move back home. It felt like fate, then, that Grant was the first person she met at the university. He was smart, friendly, and helpful—he helped her find her first class, and when she mentioned she was looking for a job, he told her that Picaroon Pizza, where he had been employed for three months already, was hiring.

She would soon realize that Picaroon Pizza was always, always hiring, *urgently* hiring, and at first she would wonder why. The job interview was theatrical and hysterical and exciting. It was more like going to a play than interviewing for a food service position. Her uniform came complete with a stuffed shoulder parrot and papier-mâché sword. Mackenzie thought, at first, that Randall was hilarious, and she smiled enthusiastically at customers and said, "Polly want a drink with that?" just like she'd been instructed to in her offbeat training session, but after only a month of watching Randall Hairs sway and flail around the kitchen like he was on the deck of a ship instead of in a busy workplace, Mackenzie began neglecting her *AAARRRR*s when she thought Randall might not notice (he did not care about health-code violations, but he absolutely hated it when his employees broke character).

The day the letter arrived, Mackenzie considered calling in sick. All the little absurdities of Picaroon Pizza—the decor, the uniforms, the lingo—were irritating on a normal day. On *that* day, she wondered if she could stand them at all.

She went back to her basement suite after they read the letter. She locked the dead bolt on the door at the top of the stairs, like always, giving the handle an extra tug to make sure it was secure, and tucked a chair under the handle of the door at the bottom of the stairs. She walked around the perimeter of her space, checking the windows, the closets, the corners, under the bed, under the table, behind the couch.

Satisfied that she was safe, she made some coffee and sat at her table. Maude had insisted on keeping the letter, which had enraged Sunna (Mackenzie couldn't decide if Sunna was an angry person in general or just an angry person at Maude). Mackenzie hadn't cared at the time who kept the letter, but now, back in the quiet of her own space, she wished she had it. She'd thought she wouldn't forget the few incomplete lines, but they had already become foggy and pixelated, like the fragments of a dream. She wanted to read it again, to examine it for any kind of familiarity that might tell her who wrote it. She felt sure it was meant for her but was increasingly unsure about who the author was. She saw two faces in her mind's eye, two people who could've written a letter like that, but when she tried to picture either person saying the words, she just heard Sunna, her voice hard and thin and irritated.

"Sorry for disappearing," Mackenzie whispered. "No . . . sorry I missed you." She tried to hear her sister's voice, and then Jared's. Now she could only hear herself. If she had the letter, she could see if there was a comma in that sentence. Was it *Sorry* and *I missed you*, or was the sender just sorry they had missed running into her?

She wandered into the living room, clutching her mug with both hands. The floor snapped above her head—likely Sunna, or just the sound of the wood shifting as the weather grew colder—and she jumped, spilling hot coffee over the sides of the mug and onto her hands. This, the thing that should've made her flinch, barely registered; it was like her nerve endings were turned off, like her body was spending all its energy being afraid. She set the cup on the coffee table and wiped her hands on her shirt. She wondered if she would ever stop being afraid.

Rain began to hit the windows, and she heard a soft but powerful crack of thunder, like a car crash very far away. The lights flickered, and the ceiling above her creaked again. This made her decision easier. If the power went out, she'd rather be at work. Being annoyed was better than being scared, and she was scared enough with the lights on.

She changed into her uniform and made herself a sandwich, suddenly anxious to leave the fidgety old house. As she finished the last bites of her meal, she heard a shuffling sound on the landing upstairs and paused midbite. There was a knock, and she swallowed, the bread suddenly dry, like a chunk of wood scraping down her throat. "Hello?" she rasped.

"It's me." *Sunna.*

"Come in," she called, slightly louder, relieved and embarrassed. Who else would it have been? Why did her body still react to everything like it was an emergency situation? She stood and brushed the bread crumbs off her ruffled Picaroon shirt, grimacing at the thought of Sunna coming in and finding her dressed like this.

"Can't. It's locked."

"Right." Mackenzie moved the chair, opened the door, ran up to the locked one at the top of the stairs, slid the dead bolt out of its track, fiddled with the lock on the handle. A humiliating process when someone else was waiting and witnessing it, like she was making performance art of her paranoia. When she opened that door, Sunna surveyed her with a mix of judgment and amusement. "What're you doing down there? Moving furniture around?"

Mackenzie blushed. "No."

"And you're . . . dressed like a pirate?"

"Yep." She shifted, and her oversize black boots squeaked. Randall was too cheap to order new costumes for new employees, so she had inherited one from a guy a couple of sizes bigger.

"You weren't dressed like a pirate before."

"Sure wasn't."

Sunna's forehead creased. "Uh, so I got locked out of my apartment when I went to check the mail. The landlord is coming, but I was wondering if I could stay in here for a few minutes. He's taking forever, and this entryway isn't heated, and it's kind of cold out here. This city is cold. It's colder here this time of year than it ever was in Toronto." Sunna said this accusingly, like Mackenzie was in charge of the weather.

"You've just been standing out here all this time?" Mackenzie asked, forgetting her embarrassment over the chair and the door and the pirate costume. "I'm so sorry; I didn't realize. You could've come in here sooner."

"I wish I had. Looks like I missed the pirate party."

Mackenzie was terrible at being cold to people. She gave up. "It's for work," she said.

"You work . . . on a ship?"

"Picaroon Pizza."

"Oh yeah. I've seen the sign for that place. On Hamilton, right?"

"Yep."

"Ah. I work around the corner, actually. At Fire! Fitness. I'm a trainer."

Mackenzie stepped back and motioned for Sunna to follow her. "Sorry, come in. Sit down. Coffee?"

"Great. Thanks." At the bottom of the stairs, Sunna studied Mackenzie's kitchen. "It's nice down here. Bright, for a basement."

"I'm enjoying it. Lots better than living in my parents' house— here." Mackenzie set a half-full mug in front of Sunna. "Sorry, that's all that was left in the pot. I can't even make more; I need to go out and buy beans."

"No, this is great. Thanks." A car drove by, its wheels sloshing through a puddle. The furnace clunked and settled into a hum. Maude may have been antagonistic, but at least she kept awkward silences at bay. Sunna sipped at her coffee, staring absently at the two intricate poppies inked just above the crook of Mackenzie's arm. "I like your tattoo."

"Thanks." Mackenzie worried Sunna was going to ask her to explain the meaning behind the flowers. She touched them instinctively.

"I'm curious," Sunna said. "Who is it?"

"Who?" Mackenzie asked cautiously.

"You said before that you knew who might have written that letter. Seemed kinda urgent about it, I guess."

"Oh. I don't know. It could be lots of people." Mackenzie placed her hand over the flowers protectively. Sunna had asked the question Mackenzie expected, just in a different way.

"An ex?" Sunna pressed, oblivious to Mackenzie's discomfort.

"Maybe." She pictured Jared writing the letter. Driving up to the house in his old blue pickup truck with his grandmother's necklace hanging from the rearview mirror. Walking up to the house and slipping the envelope into the mailbox, thinking of her but too afraid to face her just yet.

Sorry, I missed you.

Or maybe he'd come to the house *to* face her, but she had been at the university, and he'd sat on the front porch and written the note.

Sorry I missed you.

"Or friends. Or other people." She laughed, like she hadn't given too much thought to the whole thing. "I feel like everyone has a list of people who could send them a letter like that, right? People they wish would come and explain things to them. Apologize to them. Probably another list of people we need to explain and apologize *to*." She smiled weakly and pretended to take a drink from her empty coffee cup.

Sunna raised her eyebrows a little, but everything else on her face stayed perfectly still. Mackenzie wondered if she did Botox. *Did* Botox? *Used* Botox? *Had* Botox *done*? At nineteen, Mackenzie was too young to know the terminology of the unhappily aging.

"But is there someone in particular you hope it is? I mean, you said so, earlier."

Mackenzie grimaced. "You know what, Sunna, I'm actually going to be late for work. Could you just lock the handle on your way out when Larry comes?" Mackenzie stood, towering over Sunna. In her ruffled shirt, a tricorn on her head—a *tricorn!*—she didn't feel like having a heart-to-heart. She hunched forward, trying to make herself a little smaller. "But hey, I would be more than willing to continue this discussion if you find yourself at Paper Cup tomorrow." *I'll be more prepared at least.*

Sunna snorted. "Yeah . . . I don't know. I don't think I care enough."

"About who wrote the letter? You don't *care?*"

"Nope. I don't care. Just straight up don't care." Sunna shifted in her seat and began to rub at something on the hem of her shirt. There was a loud thud above them, and both women glanced at the ceiling. Sunna rolled her eyes and mumbled something under her breath about Maude.

"Well . . . if you decide to come for the company, you know, I'll be there anyway. Just come for coffee."

"Oh," said Sunna. She looked surprised and then guilty, like she was just now realizing she'd been rude. "I guess it could be nice to go for coffee with someone. I don't really know anyone here yet, and I can't even remember the last time I went for coffee with someone. And, I mean, most of my friends back home had babies; it was all they talked about. Parenting. Diapers. Babysitters . . ."

"Well, I don't have a baby," Mackenzie said, grabbing her Velcro parrot off the counter and stuffing it into her purse. "Just this dumb parrot and this dumb shirt and these dumb boots. And I don't want to talk about any of it."

"Okay." Sunna shifted in her seat. "I mean, Maude will be there, though. So. Probably won't."

"Fair enough. But if you end up coming, I'll be there too. You can sit with me. And I promise I won't be dressed like this."

"Good," said Sunna. She looked embarrassed again, and Mackenzie felt sorry for her. It was like she couldn't help herself. "I mean, but if you did, that would be totally fine too. You look . . . you don't look *bad*. I mean." She took a long drink of coffee and chuckled. "For a pirate."

Mackenzie smiled. "Well, thank you."

~

When Mackenzie opened the door upstairs, Larry was there, his hand in midair as though he'd been about to knock. He looked excited and then disappointed when he saw her. She smiled at him anyway, putting the pieces together easily enough. That look of excitement was not usually for her. Sunna probably saw it a lot. "Hi, Larry."

"Hey," he said, trying to peer around her without being obvious.

"How's it going?" Mackenzie asked when he didn't move to let her pass. She wasn't good at asking people to move, and he didn't appear to excel at picking up on social cues, so they could be stuck here for a while.

"Great," said Larry. "Yup. Good." His head bobbed forward on his giraffe-like neck.

"Good," said Mackenzie.

Larry cleared his throat. "You going out? Costume party?"

"No, to work."

"Ah, yeah. Of course." He seemed embarrassed to have suggested she might be wearing a costume, and Mackenzie was too tired to explain.

He considered her big black boots. He shifted, and she thought he was moving out of her way, so she took a step forward, but he hadn't been, so now she was just closer to him.

"The Planks used to dress like pirates," he said, almost to himself.

47

Mackenzie tried not to look confused. She nodded, hoping he would think she knew what he was talking about and let her go. No such luck.

He chuckled, as though she'd asked him to explain himself. "Local band. Called themselves the Planks. They all wore pirate boots just like those." He stopped short, like he realized he'd put his foot in his mouth. "Not that *your* boots are pirate boots," he began.

"No, they are," she said.

He nodded. "Cool," he said. Nodding, nodding, nodding. "Yeah, the Planks. I used to go to all their shows. If they were playing, I was there."

Mackenzie was going to be late for work. She looked longingly over his shoulder. "Yeah? What kind of music?"

"Punk," he said. He was still looking over her shoulder too. He looked supremely sad. "We had a good scene back then. There weren't a lot of us, and"—he cleared his throat again—"no one big ever came here, but the local guys were great. Played in basements and garages mostly, and at the Underground. It was the best. Used to be a German restaurant called the Schnitzel Haus, and it was owned by people who didn't even like punk music; they just liked people, so they let the punks play there . . ." He was talking fast, and he had a distant look on his face, like he was telling her about another country, a place he'd lived once but could never go back to. He ran a hand through his hair, looking lost, and she felt sorry for him.

A silence followed, and it was even more awkward than the long-ing-filled conversation. She grasped for something to say. "Do you go to shows at the Exchange often?" Grant had asked her this very question earlier in the week, and she'd changed the subject fast so she didn't have to admit that she didn't go anywhere after dark except work, that the only shows she'd ever seen were ones uploaded onto YouTube.

"Oh!" His eyes lit up. "Well . . . no. I haven't been to a show in . . . years . . . I mean, but maybe I should?"

He seemed to be asking her for permission. Far be it from her to tell him he couldn't go to a show if he wanted to. "Yeah, you should, Larry. It's on the website, ticket prices and concert listings and stuff. So." They both let out a big breath in unison. She smiled. "Anyway, are you here to let Sunna in?"

"Oh! Yeah," he said, suddenly nervous again. "Is . . . is she . . . ?"

"Yep," said Mackenzie. "She's down in my apartment. You can just unlock her door, and I'll let her know it's open."

Larry's face fell. "Oh," he said. "Don't let me keep you! I can—*I* can go down and . . ." He trailed off, clearly realizing that he was offering to go into Mackenzie's apartment without her, and that this was kind of a strange thing to do. "No," he said, almost to himself. "You're right, that is better. If you go. I'll just unlock it for her and be off . . ." He gestured at his truck. He might as well have shown up in a tux with flowers and some kind of romantic declaration written in the sky behind him in the smoke of a small airplane.

They were finally able to synchronize their movements; they each took a step to their right. He unlocked Sunna's door, and Mackenzie decided to wait a moment before calling down for Sunna to come up— it felt like a small favor Sunna would never know about. Larry seemed harmless enough, but still.

Mackenzie watched Larry walk down the sidewalk, a heavy wallet chain slapping against his leg with each step, and something occurred to her. Her heart sank. "Oh, hey Larry, one thing."

He turned.

"There was a letter in the mailbox this afternoon; it was pretty mangled, and we don't know who it's from, but I just now realized it's probably for *you*—Maude has it."

Larry shook his head. "Wouldn't be for me. I don't"—he looked down, embarrassed—"have a lot of friends. And the ones I do have would never try to contact me here, let alone by mail. I've never lived here. Maybe it was for my aunt? But she's dead, so you can just chuck it. Unless it seemed important?"

Mackenzie shook her head. "No, just someone writing to say they missed someone else." She felt deflated. The more possible recipients the letter had, the less likely it was that it was meant for her—and that was already pretty unlikely.

It made sense that the letter would be for Larry's dead aunt, way more sense than it being for one of the current inhabitants of the house. But when you're really hoping for something, and when that hope takes up so much space inside your rib cage that it's hard to eat or breathe in, you have to dismiss the things that make sense to make room for it. It's a survival thing.

LARRY, THE VERY GOOD LANDLORD

Larry

Going to a punk show was not the same as going to the bank, or going to the grocery store, or going . . . anywhere else in the entire world, actually. Going to a punk show meant you were going to be seen and subsequently labeled either a punk or a poseur, and your self-worth hinged on that label, but you had to act like you didn't care at all, not even a little. You had to dress like you didn't care, but you had to get it *right*.

Larry had all his clothes laid out on the bed like he was a teenager getting ready for the first day of high school. He was worrying that people would be able to tell just by looking at him how much work he'd put into this. But he had to put enough work into it that it looked effortless.

He turned the CD player up and let Jello Biafra's quavering baritone voice fill the room until he could hardly hear himself think. *This is what this music was invented for.*

Music was the only override button for Larry's brain. It was like a bubble in the ocean, a place for him with none of the stuff inside of it that filled everything outside of it. It was just notes and chords and percussion. When he listened to punk music, his mind, which never stopped running, stopped running. This was why he couldn't have lived in that house—his mind would've run him to death in that silence. What was the cutoff date in the will? 1952? The earliest punk band Larry knew of was Los Saicos, and they didn't come along until the '60s.

At Mackenzie's suggestion, he'd gone onto the Exchange website and saw that there was a show tonight. *Tonight.* The headliner was a local band called Jet Leg. There was no picture of them on the site, and when he tried googling them on his phone, Google asked him if he would like to search instead for jet *lag* and then showed him 76,800,000 search results for *jet lag* anyway. Still. Jet Leg. Sounded punkish. The gig poster on the website was messy and cheap, like someone had given a ninth grader a Sharpie marker and two minutes, which was promising. That was what gig posters were supposed to look like. He couldn't wait to once again be shoulder to shoulder with other people, in a room too loud for conversation.

But a bad thought burst his bubble: What if this show was *new* punk? He'd gone into CD Plus way back in the day—what, 2006?—and asked the kid working behind the counter to show him some new punk, and the kid had given him a whole stack of terrible, terrible CDs and said they were great. Whiny children playing fast and calling it punk. They weren't fooling anyone. What if that was what he was walking into tonight?

Or worse: What if all his old buddies were there, and they thought he was a poseur now? None of his clothes fit right. He didn't know what was going on. What was worse: being the only punk in a room or being the only poseur?

He was drowning in the ocean now, and not even Jello Biafra could save him.

He didn't hear his phone ring, but he looked down just as it lit up with a call from an unknown number, and he scrambled to mute the music.

"Hello?"

"Hello, Larry." Larry sat straight up and looked around even though the voice came from his cell phone; his blood cells were like Pop Rocks.

"Aunt Rebecca?" He gulped. "Is that . . . you?" Aunt Rebecca had been dead now for six months. Or seven. Or—what day was it? What month? He'd never heard of the dead communicating this way, but then, all the good ghost stories were from a time before smartphones. Were smartphones *that* smart? He pinched the skin on the back of his hand to see if he was dreaming.

"No, Maude here," said the voice.

Right. Maude. He laughed out loud.

"What's funny?" Maude sounded like she didn't appreciate funny things.

"Nothing," said Larry.

Maude cleared her throat. "We need you to come fix the mailbox, Larry. As soon as possible, please."

"Oh, right—"

"Does tonight work for you?" She didn't wait for him to reply. "You need to take care of it before it rains again. We're having such trouble with water getting into it—and dogs or mice or something, too—and ruining the coupons. I've spent a *substantial* amount of money on full-price items that I should've gotten for at *least* ten percent off. Also, I'm going to need you to come look at, I don't know, the radiator or something in my suite. It's making a racket. And is there something you can do to make the other tenants' doors less *squeaky*? They're always going in and out of this place in the middle of the night, and it wakes me up." She started hacking into her phone, and he held his away from his ear. "Also, *Larry*"—she started speaking again before she'd fully recovered—"there's a—ahem—*eck*—excuse me—strange sound coming from the attic. A scraping kind of noise; you should look into that, too, while you're here."

She finally seemed to be done. He looked at the calendar hanging on the wall; it was still on August. Of the previous year. Who was he kidding, keeping a calendar, as though he needed help keeping track of a schedule? He had no schedule. He had exactly one activity, besides his night shifts at the art gallery, planned for this whole month. Luckily, it fell on one of his nights off.

Tonight.

"Yeah," he said. "I can't come tonight; I'm . . . going to a show. A punk show." That felt great to say. Like he'd been in a coma for years and years and tonight, for the first time in a long time, he was going to open his eyes and walk around. But it was also becoming more terrifying by the minute. The clock on the wall ticked loudly, and it seemed to be chanting at him, like an angsty mosh pit full of zit-faced sixteen-year-olds.

Po-seur. Po-seur. Po-seur.

Was there anything more pathetic than a grown man who worried about teenagers thinking mean thoughts at him?

Maude interrupted his frantic thoughts. She didn't know what a punk show was and asked him to explain.

"It's a genre of music," he said, his mind still racing. "Like rock, but faster. More political. It encompasses a lot of subgenres—you've got your tamer stuff, your punk rock, your cowpunk, your—"

"Larry, can you go to . . . that . . . another night? This is important."

"Okay," he said, surprising himself. But what else could he say? He wasn't chickening out on the punk show; the old lady needed him. He was being kind. He wasn't washed up or lame or intimidated—he was kind. He was being a good landlord.

"Thank you," said Maude, without sounding overly thankful. "And . . ."

Larry waited. "And?"

"No, that's it," said Maude. "Thank you."

Click.

∿

So that night, instead of going to a punk show, Larry went to the Montreal house and replaced the one existing mailbox. He installed two more, one for 2139B and one for 2139C; he brought stickers to mark them and used a ruler to make sure he applied them straight. No one answered when he knocked, so he let himself into the small entrance. The smell of Aunt Rebecca still clung to the walls of the old house, enveloping him as he stepped inside just like she used to. He'd always loved Aunt Rebecca, but he'd never loved the way she smelled. He gagged a little. Moving quickly, he opened each door and applied WD-40 to all the hinges, even though they didn't strike him as being all *that* loud. What was the other thing? A noisy radiator? Noises in the attic? He glanced up the stairs to Maude's part of the house—toward the attic—and shuddered. He would tell Maude, if she called back, that radiators were noisy, and so were old houses, and he couldn't do anything about it. Old houses were full of screeching door hinges and banging radiators. She'd get used to it.

He locked all the doors back up and left, stopping when he reached the sidewalk to admire the old house. If nothing else—if not a punk, if not a member of anything elite or particularly cool—he was a good landlord. He smiled and enjoyed a rare moment of satisfaction.

He began the short walk to his car. Across the street, an old man in a black sport coat made his way down the sidewalk with small lurching steps, out for a leisurely stroll around the neighborhood. Larry smiled and nodded courteously at the man, who disregarded him entirely.

As Larry turned back for one last look at the house—hoping, perhaps, that he would see Sunna coming out of it—his eyes were drawn up toward the attic window, almost involuntarily, as though they'd been caught by a sudden movement. But it was too dark, and he couldn't have seen anything really. Not even if there had been something to see.

Which, Larry knew, there was.

BRENDA'S VERY EXCITING MORNING

Sunna

Regina was a funny place. People referred to it as a city, and it technically was, but it was a city in the same way an eighteen-year-old was an adult: just barely, and unconvincingly so. The skyline resembled the mouth of a six-year-old in the middle of losing his baby teeth—just a few scattered stubby towers. Traffic was sparse, and the downtown area was quiet.

It was nice, though. Sunna was pleasantly surprised by both the size and location of the suite she could afford. There was a library only a few blocks away. Her bedroom was bigger than her whole apartment in Toronto, and the walk to work took ten minutes.

The short journey took her through a quiet neighborhood full of mature trees and colorful homes and then onto Broad, a busy street lined with offices and hair salons and coffee shops.

On October 1, the day of the bomb threats, Sunna didn't have anyone scheduled until eight a.m., so she was taking her time, enjoying the few other people she saw. She craved social interaction, even if it was just a thank-you wave to someone in a car who stopped to let her cross the street.

She first registered the sirens as she passed the blood bank, a choir of alarms coming from the direction in which she was headed, growing steadily louder. She waited for a line of emergency vehicles to pass by, but they stayed where they were. She walked faster.

A few blocks from her gym, she was met with tape and police cars; she couldn't get closer. She followed the barriers for a few blocks before realizing the entire downtown area was taped off. Hordes of people lined the perimeter, talking loudly and trying to see. There was no smoke, but flashing lights reflected off every glassy surface. What could possibly have happened?

Retreating from the chaos, Sunna turned onto a quieter street and pulled out her phone. She tried calling the gym, but there was no answer, so she scrolled through her address book, looking for someone who didn't belong to her past life in Toronto. Lee. Iryn. Lawrence. Abe. Nicole. Nope, nope, nope, nope. *Wow.* There was nothing more life affirming than scrolling through an address book full of people who'd forgotten you the second you left their city. There was only one relevant name now, and it wasn't a name that sparked joy: *Brenda.* Brenda was the receptionist at Fire! Fitness. She was a jarring, desperate person with sleek blonde hair and a fluffy clump of 1992 bangs—she looked like a Yorkie-poo. She cared very little about other people except if they liked her or not, though it almost felt, at times, like she was actively working to make sure they didn't. She talked over people and laughed too loud, expelling warm blasts of mint gum and halitosis so pungent it almost tricked you into thinking you could see it, like smog. Sunna had not anticipated actually ever calling Brenda, but here she was.

"Hello?"

Sunna could tell by the noise in the background that Brenda was in the middle of a crowd. "Hi, Brenda—"

"Hi! Sunna! Is that you!"

"What's going on, Brenda?"

"Just a moment, Sunna! I have to walk over here a bit! It's noisy!" The crowd sounds lessened, but Brenda still shouted into the receiver, her voice distorted like music from a blown speaker. "Sunna! Good heavens! What's that?"

"I asked what's going on. Where are you?"

"Oh dear! So much! So much is going on! The SWAT team is here! And the bomb squad! And *firemen*! Where are you, dear?"

"I'm . . . I don't know." Sunna looked around for street signs. "The corner of Thirteenth and Rose. Why is the SWAT team there? What's going on, Brenda?"

"Bomb threat!" Brenda yelled, her voice crackling and fuzzing out. She shouted something else that sounded like *Can you believe it?*

"Can't understand you when you shout, Brenda."

"Sorry!" Brenda shouted again, slower and louder. "Bomb threat! There was a bomb threat! Can you hear me now? I said—"

"Yeah, I *hear* you, Brenda; but when you shout, it's actually harder—"

"I've lived here for thirty years," Brenda carried on, "and this is a first for me!"

"What building? Is anyone still inside?"

"Well, I don't know," said Brenda, as though the thought hadn't occurred to her. "I sure hope not. Yikes *bikes!*" Brenda liked pseudo-swears and half-baked expressions that made no sense and used them when there were plenty of existing words and phrases that would've done just fine.

Or no words at all, Sunna thought. She wished she hadn't been curious enough about the fire trucks to call this woman. It wasn't worth it.

Brenda had quieted and sounded frightened now, like the thought of a bomb was so abstract and movie-like that it hadn't caused her any real alarm before this conversation. "Oh dear!" she shouted. "Oh dear! I'm coming to find you right now, Sunna!"

Sunna groaned. "No, Brenda, you stay where you are. I'll come find you."

Then she hung up before Brenda could call her bluff and fled Thirteenth and Rose.

"What's going on over there?" The question came from a delicate old man with cloudy eyes. He'd been leaning casually against the brick walls of an old apartment building, and she hadn't noticed him until he spoke.

"I have no clue. I mean"—she waved a hand in the air to indicate she'd misspoken—"I mean, I've heard there was a bomb threat. But I don't know anything beyond that."

The man smiled. "Which building?"

"I don't know."

"The art gallery, I bet." He yawned and stretched like bomb threats were boring. "That's in the dead center of downtown, and it's run by a bunch of—" He checked himself. "Makes sense why they'd have to evacuate all the buildings. Biggest thing to happen in this city in a long time, I must say. We don't have a lot of action around here." He paused to catch his breath. "But you—you're not from around here, eh?"

Sunna found herself shrinking from the man. He'd seemed innocuous at first. Now it felt like he might be enjoying her discomfort.

"Yeah, actually, I am," she lied.

But he knew. She could tell by the look on his face.

"Sunna!"

Brenda. Almost on top of her, Brenda came to a halt, patting her hair, adjusting her jacket, hiking up her leggings. "I went to Thirteenth and Rose, but you weren't there! This is *Fourteenth*," she brayed, gesturing at the sign above her. "Of course, I may have misheard you, but . . . I don't think I did." She giggled like they were sharing a joke. "Isn't this just crazy? They're trying to get everyone to go home, but people want to know what's going on! It's like a big party!"

"It's not like a party at all," snapped Sunna. What was with these small-town people and their giddiness over crime? "People should go home. They could get hurt. Let the police do their job."

"Well, *you're* here. We all have as much right to be here as you." Brenda was indignant.

"I just got here. And I'm leaving. You should leave too."

Sunna glanced back to where the old man had been standing, but he was gone, as though he'd melted into the wall behind him or vanished into thin air.

THE COFFEE SHOP BESIDE THE CREMATORIUM

Sunna

Sunna walked home slowly, past the hair salons and the blood bank. Her neighborhood was oblivious to the drama downtown, and the silence was downright eerie. She stopped just inside her front door. It felt wrong in her suite, and she couldn't figure out why. Had she left the curtains in the living room open like that? She didn't think so. When those curtains were open, she could see into the neighbor's house, and presumably they could see into hers, too, so she never opened them—but they were open now.

Even after she closed the curtains, the feeling persisted that something wasn't right. She looked around the room, but there was nothing else out of the ordinary. Maybe it was just *her*, being home when she should be at work. Being in Regina when she should've been somewhere else. Done something else. Become something else. Maybe it wasn't the curtains that were wrong; maybe it was her whole life.

She stood in the arch between the kitchen and the living room and stared at the navy tea towels draped neatly over the oven door handle, at the bare fridge, at the dirty dishes and pots piling up in the sink, as though she had something better to do than wash dishes.

The old her always had something better to do. The old her had stuff stuck all over the fridge door—ticket stubs from movies and concerts, four-frame photo booth pictures, tacky souvenir magnets from a friend who traveled a lot. When had she become this version of herself, the one with no hobbies or social life? She walked over to the counter and picked up a faded-pink pottery mug, still half-full of cold coffee from a day or so ago. Even coffee used to be a social thing, but now she just had a caffeine addiction. She drank it alone and out of necessity.

Sunna was officially lonely. She thought of Mackenzie's invitation. *You can sit with me.*

But *Maude* would be there. The question was, Did she not want to drink her coffee alone more than she did not want to drink her coffee with Maude?

~

Paper Cup was not a place Sunna ever would've stumbled across on her own. It was a narrow building stuck between a ratty-looking tattoo parlor and a sad gray crematorium. An ancient pay phone stood beside the door, and a woman in an oversized denim jacket leaned against it, staring across the parking lot like it was an endless desert. She half smiled when she made eye contact with Sunna, then turned and disappeared into the crematorium—at which point her bleak expression made perfect sense. Sunna shuddered. She wouldn't mind being cremated next to a coffee shop, but she disliked the idea of drinking coffee next to a crematorium.

A bell jingled over Sunna's head as she entered the coffee shop, and suddenly, she felt like she was back in Toronto, but ten years earlier.

Where the bigger city's coffee shops had moved on to more modern—Instagram-worthy—design trends and oat milk lattes, this place still had the chalkboard menu behind the counter, a plaque on the wall with a quote about not being able to function without coffee in that once-trendy bridesmaid font. A soft folk song played in the background, and the baristas laughed together as they made drinks.

What were the chances the mysterious letter writer was there already? First day, first hour? The skin on the back of her neck lifted at the thought of hearing the door open behind her, a familiar voice calling out her name—

"Sunna! You came!"

Sunna jumped and spun, fully expecting to see Brett standing there, and when she saw that it was only Mackenzie, trailed closely by Maude, she wasn't sure whether she was relieved or disappointed. Adrenaline traveled up her arms, and she tried, subtly, to shake it out.

Mackenzie couldn't read Sunna's expression either. "You don't look happy to see us," she joked. She carried an overly full backpack that made it appear as though she intended on camping at Paper Cup until the mystery person showed up. Maude stood close behind her, looking bewildered, like she'd never been out in public before. She was still wearing that ridiculous hat, and it looked even more bombastic in this granola coffee-shop setting.

Sunna felt a twinge of sympathy. "Hey. How are you guys?"

Maude scowled. "It's too busy in here. Too loud. Why would anyone come here to *talk*?"

"Because the crematorium doesn't serve coffee?" Sunna said.

Maude stared at her blankly. "What crematorium? What are you talking about?"

Mackenzie laughed. "I'm going to go dump this stuff at a table before there are none left. Would you order me a large black medium roast? Here, this is exact change." She pressed some coins into Sunna's hand, separated into two little groups. "That pile's for the tip."

"Wow. Come here often?"

"I'm a university student. I *live* in coffee shops." She started toward an empty table, then spun around, her backpack swinging into a man seated at the table behind her. Sunna cringed. "Oh, Maude, what do you want? My treat."

"I want to go home," Maude grumbled.

"No, you don't. Come with me. Sunna, grab Maude a tea or something; I'll pay you back."

Maude snorted. "I don't drink tea. Get me coffee. *Nothing in it.* Just plain black, fully caffeinated coffee." She said it like she thought Sunna might try to sneak something into her drink.

~

When Sunna arrived at the table, Maude was staring into space and Mackenzie was awkwardly smiling at her hands in her lap. She looked relieved to see Sunna. "Thanks for picking those up," she said. "This is for Maude's." She handed over another pile of change.

Maude nodded, and the dark bouquet in her hat bobbled. Sunna had a hunch this was as close as the woman ever got to saying thank you.

"No worries," she said, carefully setting the cups down. The three sat in silence for a minute. Sunna scratched her arm. Why was she still here? Why had she come? Loneliness no longer seemed like a good enough reason.

"So. You came," said Mackenzie again.

"Yeah," said Sunna, realizing she was actually excited to share the morning's events with someone. "Oh, you'll never guess what happened downtown—"

"The bomb threat," said Maude.

"Yeah," said Sunna. She slouched back into her chair. "How did you know about it?"

"We heard about it on the radio. Biggest thing to happen to this town in *eons*. It was at the art gallery downtown—did you know *that*?" Maude had the same thirsty look on her face as Brenda. Like this was the only interesting thing that had ever happened in close proximity to her and she wanted to be part of it somehow.

"I can't believe this city even has an art gallery," Sunna mumbled.

"Of course we have an art gallery," said Maude indignantly. "A very nice one. And now, we've also had a heist. Our first art *heist*."

"It wasn't a heist," said Sunna, trying to quell her irritation. "It was a bomb threat."

"Means something," said Mackenzie.

"What does?" Maude asked.

"This morning when I woke up, I just had this feeling that something big was going to happen today, and then *that* happened. And I thought it wasn't the Thing at first because usually when I have that feeling, it's for something that affects me directly, but now Sunna's here, and she was there when it all happened, so, you know. It's adjacent to me, anyway. So it's not just a thing that happened; it *means* something."

Maude stared at Mackenzie like she'd turned blue. "What on earth are you talking about? What does it mean?"

"I don't know," said Mackenzie. "You don't always know what it means when something means something. You just know that it means something. That it *has meaning*."

Maude widened her eyes much more than necessary—or even, one would think, possible—at Mackenzie. She made an overexaggerated, incredulous face at Sunna. *"Oh,"* she said, sipping her coffee. "You're one of *those* people."

Mackenzie appeared unbothered; she sipped at her coffee. "Sure, Maude. Not sure what you mean by that, but okay. I'm intuitive. I pay attention."

Maude grunted.

"How was work last night?" Sunna smiled politely, addressing Mackenzie and changing the subject.

"Good."

"Cool."

They all stared at each other, and Sunna wondered if everyone at the table was trying to come up with an excuse to leave. But suddenly, Maude was noisily scooching her chair forward, her eyes fixed on Mackenzie. "So?" she said when she finally appeared happy with the distance between the table and herself. She leaned in. "Who are you waiting for?"

Mackenzie looked surprised. "You mean . . . like, who, specifically? Now?"

"Of course. Who do you think wrote that letter? Who do you think is going to come here today?"

Mackenzie looked around the crowded shop, her eyes resting on the mother and daughter at the next table. She watched them so intently and for such a long time that Sunna wondered if she'd heard the question.

"You said yesterday that you were thinking of an important person," Maude persisted.

Mackenzie nodded slowly, her eyes wandering back to the table. "I did, didn't I?"

"You did." Maude's eyes gleamed, and Sunna could tell she was hoping for something really juicy.

"Okay. Sure, I'll bite. His name's Jared."

"An old boyfriend?"

"Yep. He graduated about a month after we started dating. We were together that summer and all of the next year while he lived in another town, working for his uncle. I was in grade eleven."

"A year is a long time for a relationship at that age," said Sunna.

As the words left her mouth, she worried they sounded patronizing, but Maude saved her by being downright condescending. "It was high school," she muttered. "Those don't count."

Mackenzie looked truly offended for the first time since Sunna had met her. "What do you mean, they don't count? Of course they count. You can't go around telling people their feelings don't *count*."

Maude looked kind of sorry but didn't retract her statement. "Well." She waved a hand, dismissing Mackenzie. "They didn't in my day. I went out with a lot of boys back then, and I don't carry a torch for any of them." She held her cup to her face and guzzled loudly.

Sunna turned to her. "You're also not nineteen. Or . . . twenty?" She glanced at Mackenzie, who nodded.

"Nineteen."

"Yeah." She angled her body away from Maude. "How long ago did you break up?"

"That's just it," said Mackenzie. "We didn't break up. He ghosted."

"Pardon?" Maude said. "What do you mean, 'He ghosted'?"

"Oh, like, he disappeared. From my life, I mean. We didn't have a talk about breaking up—he just stopped calling, stopped coming home on the weekends to see me, stopped answering my texts. It was like we'd never met, like he'd never existed. I guess he just decided it was over and was too cowardly to tell me about it."

"I see," said Maude. She tilted her head to one side, and the feathers in her hat seemed to wilt.

"It was really weird, because things had been going well, I thought. I know it's not an uncommon thing; I've seen it happen to other people. I'd just never had it happen to me. I still have a bunch of his stuff; he's still got a bunch of mine . . . anyway. It would just really make sense if he'd written the letter. He owes me something. An explanation or an apology. And I don't know where he's at now."

"Did you love him?" Maude asked.

Mackenzie glanced at her suspiciously. "Uh . . . it wasn't, you know, like I thought I was going to marry him or anything, but . . . we went through a lot together. And I think that pushed our relationship to a deeper place. And I don't know what else to call it . . . yeah. Love. Like. Codependency. Infatuation. I liked how he smelled. Honestly, though, I could've hated him and I'd still want to know why he just stopped talking to me."

In a surprising show of empathy, Maude rested a hand on Mackenzie's shoulder, and Sunna twisted her mouth into a sympathetic smile. Mackenzie thanked them for listening and said she needed to get to her homework.

The writer of the letter did not come that day.

GHOSTS IN THE
GALLERY

Larry

Larry didn't like telling people he was a custodian. It wasn't that he felt ashamed to be a custodian; it was that other people felt ashamed *for* him, and he could tell. It was uncomfortable having people pass judgment on you in such a subtle way. If someone would just say to him, "I think less of you as a person because of your job," he could at least hate them for it without feeling guilty or wondering if he'd misunderstood.

But it was strange that people felt that way about his work. Being a custodian was an important job—it required attention to detail, good work ethic, care. And the building he took care of was a very important one: it was the largest and most prestigious art gallery in the province. His uncle, who had been an artist himself, had always dreamed of having his pieces displayed here. (Aunt Rebecca had said once, years after his death, that she blamed the gallery in part for his suicide—for "passing over him" for so many years, for refusing to support a local artist and excluding him from the arts community. But Larry, who felt a certain sense of allegiance to the gallery—he'd been employed there for almost twelve years—tried not to think about that.)

No. Larry wasn't ashamed of his job; he just didn't like it. Didn't like the messes in the bathrooms, didn't like the starched coveralls he had to wear, didn't like Benjamin, the crabby, sluglike night watchman who slept his shift away behind his desk and didn't *watch* anything but the backs of his own eyelids.

Most of all, he didn't like the dark. He didn't like the gallery *in* the dark.

The old building was massive and his shift started when it closed to the public for the day. Eight p.m. Eight p.m. in the summer was one thing. Eight p.m. in October, when the sun went down hours earlier, was another. He had to enter an aphotic building with shadows bunching up in the corners, seeping across the floors like oil. Trees scratching at the windows with sharp, spindly fingers. A sleeping watchman at the door.

He always worked silently, worried that if he put headphones on while he mopped the floors, someone would sneak up behind him and bludgeon him to death. He knew it was a silly fear—what would make him a target of such a senseless killing in the first place?—but silly fears were just as scary as rational fears. Besides, just as darkness made it hard to tell the difference between a mannequin and a real person, it made it hard to tell the difference between a silly fear and a rational fear.

And now there was this bomb threat business. Larry didn't like it at all. He'd come into work oblivious because he didn't listen to the news, didn't watch the news, didn't even read the news. Benjamin had to tell him about the phone call. "I'm going to blow the art gallery up!" the caller had said. "I'm going to blow it up! You believe it! You better get out of there, or I'll blow you up too!"

Poor Ai Fen, everyone's favorite receptionist, had been the one to answer that call, and they'd given her the month off because it had affected her so much. Larry wondered why everyone wasn't getting the month off—how sure were they that there was no bomb? And even if there wasn't, did that mean the threat meant nothing?

But no. He hadn't even been given one day off. There had been a major threat only that morning, and here was Larry, less than twelve hours later, mopping floors that might explode beneath him like an erupting volcano, tearing him into a million pieces and showering him like bloody confetti onto the art gallery's front lawn.

He mopped fast. Would anyone notice if he didn't do every room? If he just did a spot clean, just tonight?

The first time he heard the sound, he told himself it was Benjamin. He said it out loud to make it true.

"Hey, Benjamin!"

His voice echoed around the large wooden room. There was a painting in front of him of a woman with a cone-shaped face. She examined him critically. His heart started clattering around in his chest, like a frightened cat in a cupboard full of pots and pans.

He heard the sound a second time, and even in his fear he found himself straining to understand it. It was unearthly. A whispery shuffling sound, something that came from everywhere and nowhere at the same time. The cat in his chest froze.

"B-B-Benjamin?"

Silence.

He was losing it. Imagining things.

They should've given him a month off.

Like Ai Fen.

And now, what was this? Did he hear . . . singing? Far, far away, it sounded—probably not in this building.

Of course it's not in this building. Outside. Some kid's just singing on the street.

But no. It was in this building. And it wasn't a kid. He realized that now. It was a woman's voice, singing the national anthem in sharp, over-exaggerated falsetto. The voice was coming through the vents, louder and louder, bouncing off the walls so that it could've been coming from anywhere but sounded like it was coming from *everywhere*. If he were not a man who believed in ghosts, he might have had the wherewithal to talk himself down.

"Benjamin!" he yelped. "Benjamin?" As he spun on his heel, his mop slipped from his hands and fell against a painting on the wall. Had he scratched it? He leaned in to check, but—there was that sound again. He straightened up and ran from the room.

THE CASE OF THE MISSING CHEESE

Mackenzie

When Mackenzie opened her door at 11:51 a.m. the next morning, Sunna was standing there with Maude. "I took a bus to the Paper Cup yesterday, and it was a pain," said Sunna. "You mind if I hop in with you guys?"

Mackenzie nodded, but Maude glowered at her. "My fridge was empty this morning," she said.

It took Mackenzie a moment to realize that it was an accusation. "What?"

"My fridge! Somebody broke into my apartment and stole everything out of my fridge. My cheese and my leftover Chinese takeout."

Mackenzie looked at Sunna, who shrugged. "We've already had this conversation," she said. "I asked if she just didn't have anything in there in the first place, and she bit my head off."

"*Bit your head off*—please, I did no such thing," said Maude. "And *excuse me* for being angry, but groceries are expensive—no thanks to Larry and his coupon-eating *mailbox*. And I wouldn't forget that I didn't go grocery shopping—I *went* grocery shopping. You saw me carrying my groceries *in*."

"I'm sorry, Maude," said Mackenzie. "Is there for sure no chance that . . . you . . . ate your cheese?"

Maude's scowl turned into a pout. "I'll call the police," she said. "And if they find out it was either of you, you'll go to jail."

Mackenzie and Sunna exchanged glances. "Come on in," said Mackenzie, retreating into her bedroom. "I'll be ready in a sec. I'm just trying to find my shoes . . ." She thought she heard a sigh from the door but couldn't tell if it was a Maude sigh or a Sunna sigh. "Sorry!" she called.

Mackenzie had packed suitcases and suitcases full of clothes in advance of her move to the city, but she'd accidentally left one behind: the giant black duffel bag full of shoes. So, at the moment, she only had two pairs of shoes—the black canvas sneakers she'd been wearing on moving day and those too-big boots from the Picaroon uniform. And now the sneakers were missing.

Her suite didn't have many hiding places. She'd been wearing them yesterday. Where could they possibly have gone?

When she came back into the kitchen, Maude was examining the pictures on the fridge. "Who's that?" she asked, jabbing a crooked finger at one of Mackenzie with her arm around a girl in a sparkly pink grad dress.

"My best friend, Celeste."

"How come she never comes over here?"

"She moved to Edmonton for school."

Maude moved her finger to a flowery save-the-date postcard. "And these people?"

"My cousin," said Mackenzie absently. "How does a person lose *shoes*? They were literally tied to my feet all yesterday."

"Their wedding invitation doesn't have the address or the time of the event."

Mackenzie glanced at Sunna, who looked like she'd already had her fill of Maude for the morning.

"Well, yeah. It's not an invitation, just a save the date."

"A save the date. What is *that*?"

"It's just . . . it tells you when the wedding is."

"An *invitation* tells you when the wedding is. Why would you spend all that money on stationery and postage to do the invitation in two parts?"

"I don't know, Maude. It's just the way they're doing it. I've never planned a wedding before. I don't know." Mackenzie stuck her head in the closet. The shoes weren't there, same as the last four times she'd checked.

"That's the traditional way to do it," said Sunna.

Maude was unimpressed—and fully invested in the wedding proceedings of these two perfect strangers. She looked down her nose at the picture of the happy couple and spoke as though directly to them. "Just because something is a tradition doesn't mean it's a good idea. In fact, it seems to me that the traditional way to do something is often the worst way. Especially when it comes to weddings."

"Maybe you're right," Mackenzie said, and she noticed Sunna's look of disgust. *I'm not a pushover. I just don't feel like getting into it.* Sunna struck her as the kind of person who liked getting into it. Maybe where Mackenzie got lonely for people to confide in and share her life with, Sunna needed people to fight with. Maybe that was why she was here even though she'd insisted she didn't want to be. Maybe Maude was fulfilling her need for a good rivalry.

Defeated, she pulled on the pirate boots. "Okay, I'm ready."

Sunna tipped her head to the side. "You're wearing your pirate boots?" Like if the choice was between wearing pirate boots and staying home, she would obviously stay home.

Mackenzie sighed. "I'm wearing my pirate boots. Let's go."

The women piled into Mackenzie's car, a black two-door 1998 Chevy Cavalier that had belonged to one of her older cousins. Maude made a show of standing in front of the car to indicate that she would be sitting in the front seat. Sunna, to her credit, ducked into the back without complaint.

They pulled up to Paper Cup fifteen minutes later, and Maude and Sunna noisily unfolded themselves from Mackenzie's car as though it were a shoebox instead of a vehicle. The air was sharp and the trees were already half-bare, though it was only the beginning of October. It made Mackenzie sad. Winter always came before its turn.

In the weeks and months after she'd watched Tanya slip out the bedroom window, she'd felt about evenings the way she now felt about winter, and she'd felt about mornings the way she now felt about spring. She'd wake up each day, and everything was far too still and quiet to be her family's new reality, and she felt like maybe she was back at the beginning of *that* day, like she only had to get out of bed and make a few different decisions to change everything. But then the day would unfold, and it was, despite its initial appearance, a different day. A day in which nothing could be done to fix what had happened.

That feeling had mostly gone away over time, but it still came back at the beginning of every spring, when the first buds appeared on the ends of the branches and the air warmed up and Mackenzie felt vaguely hopeful and then crushed as she understood where the feeling was coming from.

"You okay, Mackenzie?" Sunna was holding the door for her; Maude was already inside, standing in line.

"Yep," Mackenzie said, embarrassed. "Was just trying to decide what I wanted to order. You two go ahead and sit; I'll grab our coffees."

Mackenzie followed them inside and watched them walk off to find a table. A funny pair. Sunna turned heads for one reason and Maude for another. Mackenzie, with her tattoos and large frame, was also used to being stared at in public. Maybe that was their one commonality. That and this letter—until whoever had written it showed up and sent two of them back to their wondering while one of them got closure.

The door opened behind her, and a cool breeze brought a fusty, acrid smell, like a roomful of cats and couches but no windows. Mackenzie sneaked a peek over her shoulder at a woman behind her who was almost certainly the source of the offensive fragrance. The woman smiled, but it was a pinched smile, and the eyes above it, caked in bright-blue shadow, looked off at some distant point.

She was like a painting, the woman: her makeup thick and heavy, her features large and sharp and beautiful, her jewelry showy. Her eyes drifted down to meet Mackenzie's, and she turned to face forward. The smell settled in Mackenzie's nostrils like smoke.

It was not only a terrible smell but a familiar one. She couldn't place it. It was like hearing a song you knew from a scene in a movie but not anywhere else, and not being able to remember which movie it was, or even what kind of movie it was, or whether the association was positive or negative. You just knew that it had stuck out to you the first time you heard it for some reason, and that alone made it important.

Maude? Yes, Maude smelled like this; it just wasn't as strong with her—more like an aura than a scent. But if they let Maude sit alone in that room up there, windows closed, cats multiplying, someday Maude would walk into a room, and her loneliness would be a smell that people would think about long after she left.

BRETT, THAT JERK

Sunna

"Is there cream in it?" asked Maude.

"No," said Mackenzie. "It's black like you wanted."

"You didn't ask me if I wanted it black."

"Well, no, but I remember you telling Sunna yesterday that you wanted it black."

Sunna watched the exchange with fascination. Mackenzie was so even keeled, so calm in the face of unnecessary hysterics, like a kindergarten teacher or a skydiving instructor.

"I *did* want it black yesterday," said Maude. "But what if I wanted cream today? Sometimes I change my mind. It's my prerogative. Who only ever feels one way about something?"

"Okay, well, I'll go get you some cream."

"I wasn't saying that I *did* change my mind; I was saying that I *can*, that sometimes I *do*. That you should have *asked*."

Mackenzie nodded, like a saint. Like an angel. Like, yes, she should have asked, it was entirely her fault and so totally okay for someone to speak to her like this after she'd paid for their coffee. Sunna was about to chastise Maude, but before she could utter a word, Maude drooped, her hat obscuring her face, the crow feathers threatening to dip into

Sunna's coffee. "I'm sorry, Mackenzie. I think I'm more tired than usual today. I haven't been sleeping much since that letter came. And I didn't really sleep much before *that*."

Mackenzie looked surprised by the apology (but not as surprised as she should've, Sunna thought). "No, no, I get that," she cooed. "It's all good." She looked, for a moment, like she might reach out and pat the top of Maude's head, but she folded her hands in front of her on the table instead. "Speaking of . . . that letter . . . can I ask who you think wrote it?"

"No," said Maude softly. "You can't."

Mackenzie looked at Sunna pleadingly, and Sunna realized that she wanted help changing the subject. To take the focus off Maude, as though Maude deserved a reprieve. Sunna pretended she didn't understand and took a sip of her coffee.

"Sunna?" Mackenzie wasn't going to let her off the hook.

"What?"

"Who do you think wrote it?"

"I don't know. It's like you said—could be anyone."

"Well yeah, but we're here for a few hours, and we've got nothing better to do. And you wouldn't be here if you didn't have someone in mind."

Sunna shrugged. "Okay, fine," she said. "You're right; we've got nothing better to do. If it's for me, it's probably from this chick I knew named Brett."

Mackenzie nodded. "So spill. The whole story."

"Okay." Sunna felt eager, all of a sudden, to get to tell her side of the story to someone—to talk about Brett with people who didn't know her, who weren't enamored of her. Far from Toronto, far from Brett's awards and billboards. She pulled her phone out and opened Instagram, tapping through to Brett's profile. The profile picture had been taken from the cover of a women's magazine. Her bio read: *Making a Difference/Looking Pretty*. She had three million followers but only followed four hundred herself. "So, this is her." She turned the phone toward them, hoping Mackenzie would say something about how smug Brett looked.

But Mackenzie only looked impressed. Too impressed. "Brett *Zaleschuck*? You know Brett *Zaleschuck*? Brett *Zaleschuck* ghosted you?"

"You know this woman, Mackenzie?" Maude had forgotten her pity party and was now holding her glasses slightly away from her face, simultaneously leaning toward the phone and stretching her neck away from it in a contortion that seemed difficult and counterproductive.

Mackenzie laughed and shook her head. "No way. I mean, not personally—but I definitely know who she is. All my friends basically worship her. She's . . . kind of a big deal." Mackenzie must have noticed that Sunna was glaring at her because she looked down at her hands and added, "In some circles. To certain kinds of people."

Disappointed, Sunna examined the screen. "Brett was my best friend—we went to the U of T. We both wanted to, like, change the world . . ." Saying that out loud felt funny all of a sudden. Embarrassing. Like she was a child sitting with two adults, telling them she wanted to be a princess when she grew up. She'd never been shy about her aspirations before; when had this happened? Probably when she'd failed at everything. Telling people you'd always wanted to be a princess wouldn't be embarrassing if you were one now, or if you were, at the very least, dating a prince. "We met in the student lounge on our first day of classes. We were sitting at separate tables, facing each other and reading the same book. I looked up and realized it a fraction of a second before she looked up, and I said, 'Good book?,' and she laughed and came over to sit with me. It was one of those moments where you feel like you're in the pilot episode of a super cheesy sitcom. We became instant friends."

Mackenzie was good at listening to other people talk. She nodded a lot and had expressive eyes that said, *Go on, go on, keep going—this is all so interesting.* But Maude drifted away as you spoke to her, fidgeted, studied the clock like she was pleading with it to go faster. Her eyes said, *Shut up, skip this part, you're wasting my time.*

She had a point, though—or her eyes did, anyway. Sunna could skip the years of university, the nights spent planning and brainstorming and dreaming, the friendship with Brett that was more like a marriage in its exclusivity and future-focused energy. This was good, actually, because it made Sunna sad to talk about that time. Too bad how the end of something could ruin the beginning and middle of it.

Sunna's high school years had been full of dysfunction—parents who couldn't get it together, abusive and disappointing relationships— so the combination of Brett's friendship and the promise of something big ahead had made the university years like a second chance at family and healthy relationships and future plans. She was homesick for those years now. She'd never been homesick for her actual home for a single second in her life, but this version of that sickness was worse—she knew it was—and she resented all the kids she'd ever known who'd been sad at sleepovers and summer camps because they wanted to go home. After all: in the end, they *could*.

"So you found out you liked the same books," said Maude, yawning (more of an insult than an involuntary reflex). "And then what?"

Sunna studied Maude's pinched face. "We finished school," she said, trying to keep it together—like Mackenzie, "and moved in together, and neither of us could find jobs in our field, so we both got jobs at this gym down the street from our house—Fire! Fitness. She started a blog about it."

"A blog?" Maude looked skeptical, like she thought Sunna might have made the word up.

Sunna pretended not to hear her. "It was 2006. Blogs were kind of a niche thing, something only really nerdy or really emo people did. They didn't make anyone any money; they were just this strange, vain hobby. And there wasn't even, like, connective tissue—Twitter was, I can't remember, either really new or nonexistent. Same with Instagram,

Facebook, all that stuff. Blogs were just chunks of ice floating around in the internet ocean."

"I have no idea what you're talking about," said Maude, louder this time. "The internet ocean and *blogs* and *emo* people."

"A website," said Sunna. It was mind boggling that a person, any person, even *this* person, didn't know what a blog was. "A website where Brett wrote diary entries about the ridiculousness that went on at the gym, people using equipment wrong or obnoxiously checking themselves out in the mirrors, whatever. But sometimes she had these little inspirational stories—cute write-ups about clients who were doing really well or who told her she'd changed their lives or whatever. No one read it but me—until, somehow, people started stumbling across it, and it started getting hits." Sunna glanced at Maude. "People started clicking on and reading the entries."

Maude shrugged, as though she knew exactly what *hits* meant.

"By around 2010, her blog was getting popular, and then Instagram came along—"

Maude clucked and shook her head, giving up on the conversation altogether.

"It's the thing I just showed you, Maude. It's a place on the internet where people share pictures with each other. And you can get famous on there if you get enough followers—"

"*Followers,*" said Maude. It wasn't a question; she just thought it was funny. "*Famous.* But you don't mean *actually* famous."

"I do," said Sunna, almost protectively. "You saw. She has millions of fans."

Maude was unimpressed. "*Angela Lansbury* is famous. Everyone knows who that is. This Brittany person—I've never heard of her."

It was Mackenzie's turn to look lost.

"Anyway," said Sunna. "At first it was fine. It was 2010, and influencers hadn't yet become the social disease they are now—"

"*Influencers?*"

"Social disease?"

Maude and Mackenzie both gaped at her.

Sunna was exasperated with her audience; she hadn't anticipated having to explain such obvious things to them. "Social media influencers," she said to Maude, "are privileged, vapid, beautiful people who make a living dispensing common sense on social media like it's groundbreaking wisdom. And it's a social disease"—now she looked at Mackenzie—"because it pumps up the ego of the influencer while tricking the influencees into thinking it's for *them*. So now we have all these egomaniacs quitting their normal jobs to go on free vacations and give business advice while not only contributing nothing of actual use or value but encouraging everyone else to do the same. They live gorgeously and effortlessly and make normal people jealous and dissatisfied with real life."

Mackenzie seemed to be holding back some strong opinions, but Maude still had no idea what Sunna was talking about, and it appeared to have had a humbling effect on her. She went back to looking into her coffee cup. A comforting, familiar black hole.

"So anyway, Brett became an influencer. Fitness brands started reaching out to her, sending her free gear—"

"Why would they do that?" Maude looked like she didn't believe this story at all anymore.

"Because that's how it works. Brands send you free stuff, you wear it in pictures on your blog, you link to it—"

"Oh," said Maude. "Advertising. Brett was a model?"

"Sort of," Sunna said. "Like a model slash billboard. And over the years, the whole thing *swallowed* her. Everything she did was for that blog, for her Instagram account. She quit working at the gym. She began to think she was smarter than everyone else because people asked her for advice on everything from relationships to clothes to music, even though she'd only ever claimed to be a gym rat. She thought she was prettier than everyone else because people were constantly telling her that she was. She thought she was better than everyone. Than me."

Maude started clicking like an old furnace in a cold house.

"What?"

"I didn't say anything."

"You made that noise."

"What noise?"

"The one that means you have something to say and it's going to be rude."

"It wasn't going to be rude," said Maude. She looked hurt.

Sunna waited.

"I just understand now. She thought she was better than you, but you don't think anyone is better than you. So you had a fight."

"See, that's a rude thing to say."

"Well, I just mean, knowing you—"

"But you don't know me." Sunna was more tired than angry now. "We met a couple of days ago."

"I just wonder"—Maude paused, considering—"if her side of the story is different."

"Of *course* her side is different. I'm not dumb enough to think she's not the hero of her own story. But listen, if you want to hear *this* story, you have to stop clicking at me like that."

Maude peered into her cup again.

Mackenzie spoke, her voice warm in the chilly silence. "That makes sense, though," she said. "I have friends like that—on a way smaller scale, obviously. Internet fame does 'swallow people.' But, I mean, how could it not when you're *Brett Zaleschuck*?" Mackenzie forgot to act unimpressed this time.

"Yeah." Sunna had been naive to think she could escape Brett's reputation simply by moving a few provinces away. She was like all those wives in '90s sitcoms who stormed off to sleep on the couch when they were mad at their husbands but were still married to those same husbands in the morning.

Mackenzie looked sympathetic. At least that was something. "So . . . if you think she wrote you this letter, you're obviously not speaking anymore . . . ?"

"We had a fight. She'd moved into her own place; we'd been drifting apart for a while, and she could suddenly afford to live in a better neighborhood, in a better apartment, but we were still hanging out a bunch. I was over there for supper; she asked me what I was thinking, and I told her. I told her I was sad about who she was becoming, and—" Sunna felt her voice shake and quickly took a sip of coffee. She didn't want to feel sad. Angry was fine; sad was embarrassing. "And then, I don't know, it just blew up. We started yelling at each other. Screaming at each other. I've never been so upset with someone, and I've never had someone so upset with me. And the fact that it was *her* . . . I called her—well." Sunna's face turned bright red. "I called her awful names. She called me worse names, for the record."

Maude looked like she was actually biting her tongue.

"She said she thought we'd only become friends in the first place because it was convenient. Right place, right time. We both needed someone, and she wasn't being picky, or she would never have chosen *me*. She said I was using her to get somewhere because I wasn't going anywhere. I said she'd become someone else, that she was fake, and she said I was jealous."

"And you haven't spoken since?" Mackenzie asked.

"No, we have. We hung out a lot after that fight, actually."

"Why?" Maude clearly couldn't handle being confused. She was hunkered down in her chair, arms crossed. This whole conversation was one big confounding mess to her. "I would never stay friendly with anyone who said that to *me*."

Sunna sighed. "She was my family, you know? She was one of those people who can say the most hurtful, ridiculous, horrendous things right to your face, and you just, you still love them."

Mackenzie nodded gravely.

"But I guess she didn't feel the same way, because a little while later, after we'd kind of made up and were 'friends' again, she"—Sunna pointed at Mackenzie—"she ghosted. She didn't show up for coffee one day, and then she just never called me again. And it was her *turn*, you know? The ball was in her court. And now she's vapid and rich, and she's the queen of the internet, and everyone *licks* the ground she walks on . . ." Sunna shook her head and shrugged a few times. "I get so worked up talking about it. Sorry."

"No worries," said Mackenzie. "Question, though. What would Brett Zaleschuck be doing *here*? And how would she know where to find you?"

This was the question Sunna had been stepping around in her mind. But why? Why couldn't she just admit that this was a long shot, that the letter was most likely for Mackenzie or Maude, definitely not for her? For whatever reason, she didn't want to yet.

"I don't know how she'd know where I live—maybe she got the address from a mutual friend back home—but she travels a lot for work; brands fly her all over the place, gyms fly her in for motivational—" Sunna froze and racked her brain, trying desperately to remember what was in that letter. Could Fire! Fitness have flown Brett in to give a presentation to the Regina team or to do some kind of promotional video for the new location? Would the receptionist there have given out her address? Not for just anyone, of course, but for Brett Zaleschuck . . . maybe?

Sunna truly hadn't believed the letter had been for her until this moment. She knew because she'd been pretending the heaviness in her chest was nervousness at the thought of seeing Brett again, but it was actually sadness at the thought that she never, ever would. And now it was just full-blown anxiety. There was a chance, a legitimate chance, that this letter was for her.

"Motivational *whats*?" said Maude.

"Speeches," whispered Sunna, sure there was not a single drop of blood left in her head. But now she felt stupid. It was a lost friendship, not a death or a divorce. She had no right to be on the verge of tears over it. She made herself smile, blinking furiously. "Okay, that's me," she said lightly, though she still sounded like she'd been punched in the stomach. "Now it's your turn, Maude."

Maude's eyes flashed. "I already said *no!*" she screeched, rising from her chair with unexpected speed and force. Sunna pictured giant wings unfurling behind the woman, accompanied by operatic music and lightning strikes. "I said *no*, and I meant it. My life is not some dramatic story for your entertainment. It is my *very real life*." People at the tables around them were staring. Maude's face seemed to melt around her beak-like mouth, her eyes glassy and red. She noticed a little boy gaping at her and straightened up. "I am going to sit over there," she said, her voice tight. "Thank you for the coffee, Mackenzie." She marched to a spot by the window, plunking her body down on the chair like it was a sack of something that disgusted her.

Sunna didn't know what to say. She wanted to throw a fit like Maude, but she wanted to be sweet and angelic like Mackenzie. She wanted to be nineteen again and make different choices so she would end up anywhere but a coffee shop in a town-city with these strange women. She wanted to know what she wanted. She wanted to unzip her skin and evaporate from inside, separated into particles of steam and air. That was when it hit her, really hit her: she wasn't just unhappy or discontent; she was downright depressed.

"You okay?" Mackenzie asked.

"Does it bother you, drinking coffee right next to a crematorium?" Sunna replied, fighting tears again. "It bothers me so much."

AN INVESTIGATION IS UNDERWAY

Larry

When Larry arrived at work, Benjamin was not the only one at the front desk—Marilyn, the art gallery facilitator, was there, too, along with an intimidating policeman. Marilyn didn't look happy to see Larry, but it didn't worry him at first because she never looked happy to see anyone.

Benjamin snuffled a hello and ducked his head down, intent on some papers, and this was what set Larry on edge. Larry had never seen Benjamin intent on anything before.

"Larry," said Marilyn, her usually unsmiling mouth even more unsmiling than usual, "I need to ask you to take a few days off."

"A few days . . . off?" This wasn't computing. They didn't want him, the person who cleaned the bathrooms, to come to work?

"Yes, a few days off. Maybe quite a few."

"Uh . . . okay." He glanced again at Benjamin who was working so hard on his "paperwork" that his face was red. "Obviously I want to know why . . ."

"Of course. We all have lots of questions."

Well, Larry wanted to say, *I think I'm mostly the one with questions.* "Is this because I left early the other night?"

Marilyn frowned.

Larry knew he shouldn't say anything more. He did anyway. "There was a woman *singing,*" he said. "In the main gallery. In the vents . . ."

It was Marilyn who tried to make eye contact with Benjamin this time, but Benjamin was obviously determined not to make eye contact with anyone.

Marilyn continued. "You know what, Larry, I'm simply here to ask you to leave your uniform with Benjamin and to please leave the premises until the investigation is over—at which point we will figure out whether or not you still have a job."

Larry gulped. "The investigation? Marilyn, all due respect, I have no clue what you're talking about."

Marilyn smiled without smiling, somehow. "Like I said, I'm not here to have a conversation. In fact, I think I'm not *supposed* to." She sighed and glanced at the uniformed officer by her side, who had still not said anything. "Honestly, if we were at my gallery in *Calgary,* this would've all been handled much differently. They have, perhaps, a little too much faith in people here."

Larry was well aware that he was being insulted, or maybe it was his city being insulted, maybe it was even the officer being insulted, but he had no context, so he couldn't defend himself. He just nodded. "They do," he said. He smiled at the officer so it would be known that *he* was not the one trying to insult the police or the city. He liked faith.

"Officer, I believe you have some questions for Mr. Finley?"

The officer nodded. "Just a few."

Marilyn dipped her head and gave a great dramatic sigh, as though she had just done something very brave and hard and scary. "Okay," she said. "I'd love to stick around, but I need to pick up my daughter, and I've already had to stay much later than usual, unfortunately." She looked hard at Larry so he would understand that this was his fault. "You understand. Thank you for your service here, Larry. We wish you all the best."

"It kind of sounds like you're firing me?" said Larry.

"No," said Marilyn. "Not yet."

MAUDE THROWS YET ANOTHER SUBSTANTIAL FIT

Mackenzie

The next three afternoons at Paper Cup were quiet. Mackenzie, feet still clad in enormous buccaneer boots, was working on an essay. Maude passed the time staring out the window from the solitude of her own table, and Sunna read paperback novels, one after another, like she was chain-smoking.

On the fourth day, Maude joined the other two at their table but warned them not to pry into her affairs—as though she had not traveled to and from the coffee shop in the same vehicle as them for the past few days without being asked any invasive questions. She seemed jumpy.

They'd been there for an hour before she pulled her purse onto the table and unzipped the middle compartment. "I brought this," she said, extracting the letter, which was now wrinkly and brown. "I thought someone else should take care of it."

Sunna frowned. "Why the change of heart?"

Maude frowned back, and Mackenzie felt herself do the same.

"I just don't want it in my house—in my part of the house. What if I die? Wouldn't you want it, then?"

"I'll break down your door and get it," said Sunna.

Maude brought her hand down on the table with a loud thud. "Just take it and stop being an idiot!" she shrieked.

Sunna sat up straight.

Maude sighed and became sad Maude, a Maude who broke Mackenzie's heart just as much as mad Maude infuriated her. "I just don't want it near me. I can't stop reading what's there and trying to fill in the blanks. I wake up at night and read it. I wake up in the morning and read it. I've strained what's left of my eyes trying to see what's not there. It's not good for me to have it. Not healthy."

Sunna looked annoyed. "Well, I tried to take it from you in the first place—"

"Sunna!" Mackenzie yelled, surprising herself. A woman at the next table who had been watching YouTube videos on her iPad shot a disapproving look at their table. Mackenzie lowered her voice. "If I could see it just one more time, I'll take a picture of it with my phone, and then, Sunna, you can take it home with you, and everyone will be happy. How's that?" She sounded like her mother.

Maude nodded and started to give the letter to Mackenzie, but her hand froze in midair. "Oh my," she whispered.

Mackenzie followed Maude's gaze to the door of the coffee shop, where a man stood. He was handsome, balding slightly, in good shape. There was a woman by his side. It was raining, and the couple was soaked; they were flapping their jackets and laughing at the water droplets on her glasses. He reached up and rubbed his thumbs over them, imitating windshield wipers, holding her face for a moment longer than necessary. She admonished him playfully, taking off her glasses and rubbing them with a cloth from her pocket.

They were adorable.

Maude was furious. She withdrew the letter and shoved it back into her purse.

Sunna wasn't seeing any of it. "Maude," she began, "what are you doing? I thought you didn't *want* the letter—"

Maude whirled around and hissed at Sunna. "It's my letter! It's not yours! It's not *yours! Mine!*"

Sunna pursed her lips; she was used to mad Maude, bored with her. "Really, Maude? This is just stupid . . ."

But Maude was already stalking across the coffee shop. She looked like something dragged from a swamp, something that had been killed and brought back to life to avenge itself. She looked like she was going to destroy the man at the door. He didn't see her coming, and Mackenzie felt as though she should call out a warning.

Sunna watched her go. "That was so weird. How's she going to get home? Bus?"

"Sunna. She's not leaving. She's going over there to talk to that guy. Do you think that's who wrote the letter?"

Sunna saw the man just as the man saw Maude, and just as the woman saw the man see Maude. Mackenzie felt—and it might have been her imagination, but she often felt this way—as though she were seeing everything a few seconds before anyone else.

Maude stopped in front of the man, burst into tears, and walked right back to the table. But when she reached Sunna and Mackenzie, instead of sitting, she puffed out her chest and announced in a voice much louder and higher than her own, "I have to go to the bathroom! I'll be back in just a second!" She took a long, dragging sniff, fixed her mouth into a firm line, and stomped to the bathroom. Unfortunately, it was a one-room, wheelchair-accessible bathroom, and it was occupied, so she had to wait for someone to come out before she could stomp into it. The room held its breath, trying not to stare but a little too obvious in its collective attempt to look at anything but the lady crying at the bathroom door. The person inside, when he emerged at last, was flabbergasted to find the entire coffee shop staring at him as he exited, and he turned crimson as he slunk away. Finally—*finally*—Maude entered the sanctuary and slammed the door behind her.

The man who had started the whole thing looked appalled, the woman at his side equally so.

He whispered something to her, gave her a squeeze and a firm kiss on top of her head, and started toward Mackenzie and Sunna.

Sunna gasped. "Oh. Oh. Oh no. Oh *no*! He's coming over here. What do we say? This is so awkward."

"Sunna, calm down. It's not the end of the world."

And then the man was there, looming over them.

"Hi, ladies." His forehead was creased with concern. "Is everything okay here? Is that woman a . . . friend of yours?"

Sunna began to shake her head no, but Mackenzie kicked her under the table. She nodded reluctantly, pouting.

"Is she all right?"

Sunna snorted. "Clearly not."

"Sunna!"

"Well. You saw it too. She's insane. She's actually, literally insane."

"*Sunna!* That's so offensive. You can't call—"

"Do you know her?" Sunna asked the man, ignoring Mackenzie.

"Me?" The man looked startled. "No, I can't say that I do. My wife is terribly upset over this. Would it help for me to talk to your friend, or should we just leave?"

Mackenzie felt sorry for the wife, who was now standing by the door looking like she might also burst into tears. "It's fine; neither of us are sure what's going on either. You do whatever you were going to do—"

"Wait," said Sunna. She was eyeing the man suspiciously. "First. Have you written any letters lately?"

The man's face was blank. "I'm sorry?"

"Letters. Have you written any letters to anyone lately?"

"Uh . . ." The man shot a pleading look at Mackenzie. "As in, *paper* letters . . . ?"

"No. Plastic. Yeah, paper. Obviously, paper."

"Sorry, sorry, of course. No, I haven't. I do most of my communicating over email these days . . ."

Sunna pursed her lips. "Yeah. Whatever. If I were you, I'd probably leave before Maude gets back. Unless you have something to say to her. Do you have something to say to her?"

The man's expression changed from confusion to frustration. "No," he said shortly. "Thank you." He turned on his heel and stalked away, muttering under his breath, then gathered his wife at the door and ushered her out. Mackenzie felt sad for them and their spoiled coffee date.

"How much you want to bet that guy does know Maude? He totally wrote that letter. I bet he cheated on her and broke her heart, and that was the other woman. He was acting so suspicious. And that would explain Maude's . . . you know . . . how she looks . . . how she looks so *haggard* and why she acts so insane—"

"Sunna! Stop! Seriously." Mackenzie picked up her pen and began sketching stick figures on the side of her loose-leaf. Sunna took a swig of coffee and resumed her novel.

Maude came back twenty minutes later, her face in its usual dour expression. She lowered herself into her chair and glared at Sunna and Mackenzie, who were too terrified to say anything.

Finally, she spoke.

"That wasn't him," she said, and her voice was like a still pool of water, with no undercurrents or living things in it. "How embarrassing."

Mackenzie prayed Sunna wouldn't say anything.

"I got right up to him," Maude continued, "before I realized it wasn't him. And the funny thing is, he didn't even look like the person I thought it was. But I just saw him with that woman and reacted. I thought he'd married someone else, and I think that made me too mad to see clearly . . . because if he married someone else when he wouldn't marry me, it would mean that he didn't like *me*, not that he didn't like *marriage*, you know?" Maude's mouth bunched up under her nose for a moment as she looked at Mackenzie, who did not know but nodded anyway. Maude was ignoring Sunna. "Do you want to see something? I'll show you what I have in here. It's not like I have any dignity left to preserve at this point." She paused to glare at the gawking iPad lady, who blushed and turned her eyes back to her screen. Then she unzipped her purse and pulled out a ring box from beside the crumpled letter. She set it on the table. There were three gold rings inside: a large, thick wedding band; a smaller, thinner one; and a pretty diamond engagement ring.

Sunna whistled, and Maude gave her a withering look. Mackenzie was tempted to kick her again.

"It's my turn," Maude said, clearing her throat. "I can see how it would be good to talk about it. You've both told yours."

Mackenzie looked down at the table. She felt a twinge in her stomach, like something had pinched her from the inside.

Maude pulled a Kleenex out of her purse and blew her nose. She spent a lot of time dabbing at all the dripping parts of her face and then folding the damp tissue into halves and halves and halves. "I've been single for most of my life. Not because I was adamant about being single; I just never met anyone I wanted to marry. I dated a bit when I was younger but gave that up by the time I was thirty. I thought men were idiots—I ended up being right about that, by the way. That's the cruel irony in all of this. I should've kept right on living the way I was . . . anyway.

"I was a florist—I owned a little shop on Thirteenth, started that business myself and grew it into something really wonderful. When I turned sixty-four—four years ago now—I had to close down my flower shop—the neighborhood changed and the rent went up and it was just, it was just *time*, you know?—and suddenly—" Maude made a motion with her hands like something had blown up. "Everything, you know?

96

Just—" She made the motion again, and Mackenzie and Sunna nodded earnestly even though Mackenzie was sure neither of them really understood what, exactly, Maude was trying to say.

"I became very aimless for the first time in my life. I was set to retire, so I wasn't worried—I was just . . . aimless. I had been so busy running a business, and suddenly I was, you know, walking around downtown on a *Thursday afternoon*." She looked like she was disgusted by Thursday afternoons. "Just walking around. I had money I could spend, but on what? I thought I had friends from all those years running the flower shop, but suddenly I had no place for them to pop in and visit me, and *that's* how I realized they weren't *friends*, they were *customers*." Maude had to spend a bit more time dabbing at her face.

"I knew I was too late to have a family—kids, I mean—but I thought I might like a companion for the last few decades of my life, someone to go on walks with and eat supper with once I wasn't going to a job every day. Someone, you know, *attached* to me. So I went to a senior's speed-dating event at a library. Sounds ridiculous, doesn't it?" She shot Sunna a look that said, *Don't.* "Well, it *wasn't*. It was a lovely evening. I met three decent men: one named Ken, and one named Richard, and one named Morty. I thought 'Maude and Morty' sounded stupid, and he didn't have a sense of humor, so I didn't call him afterward. Ken was shorter than me and fourteen years older, and he told me the only thing he wanted in the whole world was to move to Florida or Arizona and golf all the time, so I didn't call him either. Richard Payne was nice, tall, young—around my age—and he seemed respectable and kind. So I called him. We dated, and I fell in love with him. He was a widower. He had money, and that didn't hurt—I wasn't after it, but it didn't hurt. He was the funniest person I'd ever met. He proposed to me. I accepted. Everyone—the caterer, the lady who signed our license, all of them—thought it was hilarious that I was getting married at my age. It was rude of anyone to let me know they thought that, but young people don't seem to think they need to be polite to anyone over the age of forty." She looked pointedly at Sunna again. "But he left me standing at the altar, and I haven't heard from him since. I tried to keep on the way I was, but it wasn't working for me. It was like everything he'd touched—every piece of furniture, every knickknack, the very *walls* of my *house*, everything—was spoiled. Finally, I sold most of my things and moved into this house with . . . the two of *you*." She snapped the ring box shut and pulled the letter out of her purse. "So this probably isn't for me after all. What explanation could he possibly have to give that would make me feel better? There is nothing in the world that could excuse what he did, and I'm sure he is *well* aware of that." She handed the letter to Mackenzie and cleared her throat, looking embarrassed. "And now, here I am in a coffee shop with a couple of kids, acting like a sixteen-year-old who just had her first real breakup. Which, I suppose, I have. Nothing else counts. To me."

She added the "to me" for my sake, thought Mackenzie. *So as not to discount my high school boyfriend.* She laid her hand on Maude's shoulder the way Maude had done to her the other day. She'd heard somewhere that people often gave or expressed love in the way they'd like it given or expressed to themselves.

PAPER GHOSTS

Sunna

It rained for the next two days straight, and Sunna began to feel like she'd been without light and warmth for years. It made her feel like she couldn't push past her melancholy even enough to smile a little at the baristas when they made her drink orders. But when, on the third day, the sun finally bloomed in the sky again like a blinding yellow daisy, she forgot to be grateful for it, and it didn't help her mood anyway. It was just the sun.

The baristas must have been starting to wonder about the three women who sat in the corner, sometimes yelling at each other, sometimes stomping into the bathroom in tears, sometimes moving to different tables but always grudgingly gravitating back toward each other. Sunna saw them looking and whispering, and she enjoyed it. She never minded having people talk about her.

Mackenzie hated it. "They're talking about us again." She was locked into a stare-off with one of the baristas. "They need to mind their own business. We're paying customers. I come here all the time."

"Yeah," said Sunna, "but you don't always come here with *Maude*."

Maude scowled. She was bent over a newspaper, her sharp nose inches from the table. Despite having declared the letter "not for her," she kept coming to Paper Cup with the other women, and even Sunna understood that she shouldn't question it.

"Speaking of Maude," said Sunna.

"Please don't," said Maude without moving.

"Don't what?"

"Speak of me. Or to me, for that matter. I'm too tired for you today."

"Then go home. Anyway, speaking of you—and speaking of you being tired—what were you doing last night?"

Maude frowned and sat up straight. "How is that any of your business?"

"Because you kept me up until four a.m."

The lines in Maude's face deepened. "I was asleep by nine," she said. "So, no, I most certainly did not keep you up until any time past nine. And even when I was awake, I was just watching TV—a few episodes of *Diagnosis: Murder* with the volume at a reasonable level. Then, *oh right*, I sat there petting my cat for a while and thinking about how rotten and miserable my life is. And then I went to sleep. I'm not sure how that could have kept you up. Could you *hear* me petting my *cat*? Or was I *thinking* too loudly? About how—"

Sunna rolled her eyes. "Whatever, Maude. I heard you moving something heavy around for *hours*. Do you sleepwalk? Were you pushing your couch around your living room?"

Maude's frown shifted to a smirk. "Ah," she said quietly.

"'Ah' what?"

"The ghosts." Maude sipped her drink, chuckling dryly. Sunna could see Maude was withholding information, so she sipped her drink, too, and hoped her message was clear: *I'm not going to ask. I don't care enough to ask.* She had never denied herself more than she had since meeting Maude. She was basically a monk now.

Luckily, Mackenzie was curious. "What ghosts? What do you mean?"

Maude made an annoyed face. She'd clearly wanted to make Sunna ask.

"The ghosts in our attic. It was in the newspaper."

"No one reads the newspaper," said Sunna, ignoring the newspaper spread out in front of Maude.

"Plenty of people read the newspaper, or they wouldn't bother printing it," said Maude, pounding an open hand on the table in front of her. "*I* read the newspaper. That's why I know about the ghosts."

"Why were the . . . the ghosts . . ." Mackenzie faltered. "Why would a newspaper . . . ?"

"When the landlord's aunt died, there was a little write-up about her—well, really it was about the house and her family. Her father was a Mountie, her late husband was an artist, and their house, *our* house, is one of the oldest in the city. It's on the holding list as a heritage property. There was something about it being known to have ghosts—apparently there was a double suicide in the attic. *I* haven't heard them yet. Interesting that they chose to make themselves known to you first, Sunna. You know what *that* means. Can't be good." She sat back in her chair, smug, and brushed the table as though there were crumbs on it.

Sunna didn't know what *that* meant. She stared at Maude. "Maybe the ghosts stole your takeout and cheese."

Maude shrugged. "Make fun, I don't care. You don't have to take my word for it. It doesn't matter if you believe or not. But you can't blame me for the noises. I go to bed at nine. All I have is a chesterfield, a table, and chairs; I'm weak and I intend on leaving them right where they are. If you hear sounds coming from above, I'm telling you, it's not me."

"Okay . . . ," said Sunna. She wasn't afraid of ghosts in the attic, but the thought of this woman living above her was a little unsettling.

～

When five o'clock came around and the barista switched the Open sign off, Sunna stretched her arms behind her. "Well. That's that for me."

Mackenzie frowned. "Huh? What do you mean?"

"I mean I'm done. I've given enough time to this, and now I guess if Brett comes, she comes. This was her window, and it's officially shut—I'm *okay*," she said emphatically, giddy at the thought. "I don't need this. I don't need her. I'm okay."

"Look at this," Maude said, seeming to have heard none of Sunna's declaration. "The art gallery has issued a statement about the bomb threats. The police have a suspect! Oh. Boo. That's all. This whole useless article is just to say they have a suspect. The *janitor*, it says. Fat lot of good that does me. Doesn't say his name—the ethics there seem a bit dicey to me in a small city like this, though. Say his name or don't, but don't tell people who he is and then pretend you've taken the high road by not saying his name outright." She moved her face closer and closer to the newspaper as she spoke. "Why would you make bomb threats to your own—oh, actually that does make sense, doesn't it? He probably hated his boss, or another employee. Maybe he just wanted some time off—oh, *maybe* he was in love with someone there, and they spurned his advances—"

"Excuse me, ladies?" The barista smiled apologetically, but her coworkers were glaring from behind the counter. "We're closed, I'm afraid . . ."

Mackenzie nodded. "We're going. So sorry."

Maude gathered the paper and folded it into quarters as she stood to leave. "Well," she said to Sunna, "it's better than nothing. And just think: we wouldn't have known there was a suspect if it weren't for the newspaper."

"*Okay*, Maude." Sunna opened the door for Mackenzie and Maude and followed them through it. "Next you're going to tell me you still use pay phones," she said, motioning to the old telephone booth they passed on their way out.

"When I need to," Maude mumbled into the collar of her coat.

"Actually?"

Maude stopped walking in the middle of the parking lot and stomped her foot like a child who was about to throw a temper tantrum. "Well, *yes*, Sunna. Not everyone has a cell phone in their pocket."

Sunna shook her head.

"What? Pay phones are fine. Have you honestly never used one before?"

Sunna shook her head again.

"Mackenzie?"

Mackenzie's eyes widened. "Uh . . . well, yes . . ."

Now Sunna stopped walking too. "What? People *actually* use those things? Like, other than Maude and people committing crimes? There's a comedian who has a whole thing about how criminals are the only people who use pay phones."

Mackenzie had that dazed look on her face that she got sometimes, a look Sunna couldn't quite figure out. Was she sad? Worried? Simply lost in thought? If Sunna didn't know better, she'd think the look was a guilty one. Sunna smiled at the thought of Mackenzie committing a crime. Maybe she had Mackenzie pegged all wrong. She seemed like such a quiet, polite person. Maybe it was all an act. Maybe she was exactly the kind of person who used pay phones.

FLOWER CRISIS

Larry

"Hello, Larry, Maude here. There is definitely something in the attic, and it sounds very large. I'm going to need you to call an exterminator, please. As soon as possible. Thank you."

"Hello, Larry, Maude here. Did you get my last message? I left it about ten minutes ago. Let me know if you got it and also when the exterminator will be here. Thank you."

"Larry, where are you? It's Glenda. I've been calling and calling and calling . . . you're all over the news! I mean, they haven't said it's you, but *I* know it's you, and I'm just . . . I'm so worried about you, Lar. Call me."

"Hello, Larry. Maude here. I'm sorry for calling twice in a row, but the noise just started up again, and I wanted you to hear it." Silence. "Okay, so that's what we're dealing with. Please call an exterminator as soon as you can. Thank you."

"Larry! What's going on? Do you need me to come check on you? I know you hate when I do that, but . . . I'm really worried about you. Can you please call me?"

"Larry, it's Glenda again. Where are you? Call me. *Now.* Please."

"Hello, Larry. Maude here. I am beginning to wonder if this is not your number anymore. If there is a better way to reach you, please do let me know as soon as possible. I am having trouble sleeping with all this racket in the attic—oh! There it is again! Listen!" Silence. "Thank you."

~

Larry sat on his couch and watched his phone buzz and buzz and buzz with each successive phone call.

He wasn't ignoring phone calls because he was depressed; he was avoiding them because he felt like he was *allowed*, not that this distinction would make a difference to anyone but him. It was a conscience thing. Surely you were *allowed* a grace period when you were going through something this big, to be reclusive and socially inept. It was almost required. A week or two (or six?) to sit on your couch and wallow in your misfortune, to think about how far your life was from what it was supposed to have been. You were supposed to spend this time in boxer shorts, unshaven, growing a bigger gut. So not answering the phone? Tame. Expected. Allowed. And not really that different from how he normally lived his life, aside from the not answering phone calls and not leaving to go to work.

The phone buzzed for the hundredth time that day. He held it up to see whose number was on the screen. *Glenda. Again.* He set it on the coffee table and watched it skitter toward the edge of the uneven surface.

"I'm being investigated by the police for making bomb threats at my place of employment!" he yelled at the buzzing phone. "I need time to process this, Glenda! Leave me alone for once!" He grabbed the phone and stuck it under the couch cushion he was sitting on.

The cop at the art gallery had asked him only a few basic questions and sent him away infinitely more confused than he thought he should be for someone who was being investigated. What was the logic there? he wondered. Maybe they figured that if he was guilty, he'd already know what had gone on, and if he wasn't, it wasn't any of his business.

They'd told him only that he was under investigation, that they'd used call-detail records and "triangulation" to place the cell phone used to make the bomb threats at or near his place, but that those records were "not precise," and they would, therefore, need to pull a warrant for further investigation. Larry hadn't understood any of it. Should he be worried? You didn't have to be worried if you were innocent, right?

All things considered, Larry was actually doing quite well. He was going to use up his grace period and do his wallowing, and then, when his good name was restored, he would resurface and answer his phone and go back to work—just until he'd paid for the renovations to his inherited mansion, and then he'd quit. Who wanted to work for someone who believed you were the kind of person who made bomb threats?

He looked around the room at the posters, the TV. The remote control on the coffee table beside an empty bowl from so long ago he couldn't remember anymore what he'd eaten out of it. He picked up the remote and pressed "Play." The TV blinked at him, and Nikola Sarcevic's face came into view. He'd been watching his favorite music video compilation before heading out to work the other day. This was good. He could do his wallowing to old punk videos. He dug in the couch cushion for his phone but came up with the latest issue of *Razorcake* instead. Even better. VHS tapes and magazines—he could pretend he was back in the '90s or the early '00s. Simpler times.

He flipped the magazine open to the album reviews, where some new band called Flower Crisis had a three-column write-up and a full-color photograph splashed across the top of the page in which four out of four band members had their tongues out of their mouths for no good reason he could see. *"Flower Crisis,"* Larry mumbled. "Terrible name."

The review began with a question, which Larry hated. Reviews were for telling the audience something. Interviews were for asking the band something. At no point should the writer be asking the audience anything.

Do you long for the heady glory days of old-school punk? Larry nodded to the empty room. Dumb question. Of course he did.

Look no further than this year's breakout punk outfit Flower Crisis. If you were into Simple Plan back in the day and miss the—

Larry frowned. "How could anyone have been into Simple Plan *back in the day?*" he asked no one, loudly. "They didn't exist *back in the day.*"

He flipped to the next page to see who had written the offending sentence. A young man with brown hair parted neatly on one side smiled up at him with a face that clearly said, "I liked Simple Plan back in the day."

"*You* didn't exist back in the day," Larry told the kid.

He sank back into the couch. It wasn't the kid's fault. He looked like he was born well after many of the great punk rockers had already passed on. How was he supposed to know he'd missed it all?

But now this baby and all the others like him would be in charge of the magazines, the show reviews, the band write-ups. Thanks to people like him, the next generation would look back at Simple Plan and think that was where it all began. They'd think "punk" was sticking your tongue out.

It felt like a superhero-origin-story kind of moment. Like future generations of music lovers needed a hero who would help them understand what had gone on before them so they could really appreciate what they had now. And he, Larry Finley, could be that hero.

He had nothing else to do.

He smiled at the thought of his own little picture in *Razorcake* or on a music website, at the bottom of thoughtful articles and critical reviews, dissecting and promoting the music he loved, analyzing its evolution and critiquing its existence in 2020. Finding the really good new bands—he believed they were out there somewhere—and giving them to their audience, giving their audience to them: musical matchmaking. But how did one go about getting his opinions printed and endorsed and then distributed to the masses? How did one gain favor with the editor of *Razorcake*?

He turned the page to the articles section. Another piece about another new band he'd never heard of. He looked at the picture—another kid. Only this one looked familiar. He sat up. It looked like the girl from his basement suite, the one with the dainty tattoo. He held the magazine up to catch the dim light from the bare bulb in the ceiling. It *was* her, for sure—he distinctly remembered the two poppies inked on the inside of her arm. Only, the name in the byline was Kate Weiss. He was sure that wasn't the name of his tenant. A pen name?

He suppressed a shout of excitement. He had an *in*! He could talk to her and ask if she'd put in a good word for him or, at the very least, show him how to send his work to the right place. After he sharpened his pencil and figured out how to write a music review, of course.

Wallowing time was over; Larry Finley had a new lease on life!

(If he didn't have to go to jail at the end of all this.)

He looked around and realized he didn't own a laptop on which to write a music review. He realized he didn't own paper, a notebook, anything.

Incredible.

He would start from nothing at all. Just like Ken Casey of the Dropkick Murphys, who played his first two shows to no fans, only a few friends who were there expressly to make fun of him. *I am just like Ken Casey.*

Larry had some shopping to do.

THE SMELL OF
IMPORTANT EVENTS

Mackenzie

It wasn't the thought of ghosts that kept Mackenzie up late that night—though she couldn't help but think of them every time she heard a strange sound, and there were a lot of those—it was the feeling that something was about to happen. She lazed around, staring into space, because she had a feeling that even if she tried to be productive, she would just be interrupted by the thing that was going to happen anyway.

It was the way the air smelled—the same way it had the night of the birthday party. Mackenzie hadn't been able to sleep that night either. She'd sat up in bed, next to an open window, looking out at the nebulous outlines of the spruce trees that lined the edge of the farmyard. When it was that dark, looking out the window was like looking into a cave. The trees were like giant stalagmites. The black sky could've been stone.

The air that moved her lacy curtains smelled different. Important.

Back then she hadn't known about the way the air smelled when something big was about to happen—because, as far as she was concerned, nothing big had ever happened before that night. But now, a few years later, a few big things later, she knew. It was like the smell before rain but sharper and thicker, a smell that triggered some kind of confoundingly pleasant chemical reaction in her brain but also made her want to cry. She tried to remember if the air had smelled this way the last time she'd talked to Jared and decided it hadn't—which may have meant that he had never been as important as she'd once felt he was.

When she met Grant, the air had smelled like sweat and french fries. (They'd been in the university food court.) What did that mean? He'd mentioned the Exchange again at work the other night, and this time he'd asked if she wanted to go to a show there with him and some of his friends that Sunday. She should've said yes—she'd wanted to. She didn't even have a good reason to say no, and she'd taken a million years to get back to him, not because she was checking her agenda like she'd said, but because she was trying to think of a good way to admit to him that social gatherings caused her excruciating anxiety, especially ones that happened at night. That if she was not at school or at work, she just wanted to be home, barricaded in her suite with a chair under the door handle.

She stared out the kitchen window. It was high and small, but she could see the sidewalk in front of the house and people, when they walked past, from the waist down. Someone with baggy jeans rode by on a skateboard.

Her phone rang. *Here it is.*

"Hello?"

"Mackenzie." Her father. He said her name like it was a touchstone, like he was doing one of his grounding exercises where he looked around the room and said the names of things he was sure of. *Table. Lamp. Window.* It made her nervous.

"What's up, Dad?"

"Well," he said, and there was a pause. She felt frustrated with the pause. Why hadn't he thought about what he was going to say before calling so she didn't have to sit here and listen to him pause?

"What, Dad?"

"Sorry. I'm trying to think of how to say this."

"You could've thought of that before you called," Mackenzie said. She wrinkled her nose. She sounded like Sunna, or even Maude. "I'm sorry," she said.

"No," he said. "I don't blame you. I'll get right to it. I just got some news and called you without stopping to think." He cleared his throat. "So, the police just called. Oh—your mom's here, too, on the other phone."

"Hi," Mackenzie's mom said. "How are you, baby?"

Mackenzie dragged a finger across her forehead to her temple, pulling the skin taut. "I don't *know* how I am, Mom. I have a feeling that however I am, I'm going to be different after you say whatever you're going to say. How about you tell me how I am?"

Her father cut in again. "I'm sorry, Mackenzie. We're sorry. I'll get you up to speed. The police just called, and they're reopening the case."

Mackenzie had wondered if this would be the thing. She just hadn't thought it would happen so soon.

"Why?" she asked.

Her voice was so soft she could barely hear it over the sound of her heartbeat. She looked down at herself, and it was like she'd floated right out of her own body and was looking at someone else's. It seemed tenuous, like a stilt house, like a strong enough gust of wind could blow it over. "Why?" she asked again.

There was a pause, and she realized that someone had been talking and she had interrupted. "Sorry," she said. "I think the connection is bad. Can you start over one more time?"

Her voice sounded strange. She didn't feel frantic, but she sounded frantic. She sounded like she was about to cry even though there was nothing to cry about.

"You okay, Mack?" Her father sounded concerned. "Do you need a minute? I know this is very overwhelming. Your mother and I feel the exact same way. It's okay, Mackenzie; this is a very normal reaction to stress."

Mackenzie's father had spent a lot of time with his therapist after their familial tragedy. Now, whenever anyone around him reacted to anything, he switched into therapist mode and began to recite the things he'd learned there like he was in a school play—and this was one of his favorite therapyisms. *This is a very normal reaction to stress.* He said it about every single thing Mackenzie had done since that summer. She could've snapped and gone on a killing rampage, and she pictured him in the courtroom, tenting his hands and furrowing his brows at the judge and saying, "To be fair, Your Honor, this is a very normal reaction to stress."

Her mother said he liked feeling helpful. She said she and Mackenzie should let him feel helpful even if he wasn't.

"I'm good," said Mackenzie, though she was very far from good. She was far from bad too. She was so far from everything she might as well have been sitting on another earth in another galaxy, listening to someone tell her about the inconsequential goings-on over on this one. "Why? Why are they reopening the case? I thought they said they couldn't do anything more." This time, her voice sounded strained and angry, like someone had their hands around her throat. But she didn't feel angry.

I started this. This was what I wanted.

"They said they have new evidence." His voice broke on the first word, but he pushed through. Mackenzie recognized this version of his voice, because it was the only tone he'd used for months after that awful night.

"Did they say what it was? The new evidence?"

"Well," he said carefully; then he paused again, and she wasn't sure, but she thought she heard him mumbling under his breath: *Chair. Carpet. Clock.* "They're not telling us much at this point. Which . . ." He cleared his throat for a while. *Shoes. Shirt. Belt.* Mackenzie felt vaguely sorry for him, in the same abstract way she'd felt sorry for that jello-y, uninhabited body beneath her a moment earlier. "They received an anonymous tip. And they'll update us as soon as they can. And then we will *absolutely* call you, okay? The second we know anything."

Mackenzie said okay and goodbye, and she hung up the phone and then warmed up a frozen pizza and ate the whole thing by herself. It was, she figured, a very normal reaction to stress.

ATTIC GHOSTS

Sunna

Sunna didn't sleep well that night either.

When the women arrived home from Paper Cup, she said good night, slipped into her suite, and slid down against her door, her knees crackling like tissue paper, like she was a thousand years old instead of thirty-four. The old house was too quiet. The street was too quiet. The *city* was too quiet. There was nothing to drown out her thoughts.

Toronto had been good at distraction; it was loud. Belligerent, like Maude. It didn't wait for your thoughts to settle before it interrupted you, yelled at you, made you feel like you were losing your mind—but at least you had a good, extraneous reason to lose your mind. Sunna's last Toronto apartment had paper-thin walls, and the couple next door fought all the time. Someone in the complex had loud parties on weeknights, and someone else kept their television blaring. Toronto allowed a person to feel superior and self-righteous. *I'm trying to sleep! I have a job! I have people in my life with whom I have civil, indoor-voice conversations!*

Regina was like Mackenzie. It smiled at you politely, waiting for you to say something. It never interrupted. It let you explore every single what-if and mull over every worst-case scenario and even venture into self-loathing, only interjecting with a faraway siren or distant, screeching tire here and there. It forced you to be the noisy one and left no room for you to be upset with anyone other than yourself. It was so polite you caught yourself wishing it would be rude.

Sunna had complained about the midnight furniture moving the night before, but she almost wanted it now. She wished Maude were the type to bang pots and pans as she prepared a meal, had a hard-of-hearing husband who turned his television up too loud, had noisy little grandchildren running around. For the first time, it dawned on her that Maude probably wished for some of these same things.

She would've felt sorry for Maude had she not felt so sorry for herself—it was just too much like looking into her future. Someday she, too, would be sixty- or seventy-whatever and living in a house with two young losers, selling her furniture because it made her sad, and freaking out on strangers in coffee shops for having wives. She would be angry and rude, and she wouldn't brush her hair anymore.

She went to the bathroom and examined her face in the mirror as she washed her hands. Did this face have the potential to look like Maude's? She frowned as severely as she could and pinched her lips together. Yes, she could see some Maude in there. When she unpuckered, the lines stayed. Faint, shallow ditches surrounded by several finer ones that had appeared over the past couple of years, scratched into her face by some invisible hand while she slept.

She thought of a friend back in Toronto who'd mentioned one day that she'd started going in for "some nonsurgical tweaks." She'd called them "injectables." She'd said, "They can change the shape of your nose, create symmetry, give your jaw more definition. That kind of thing."

A few months later, the friend was saving her money again for "just a little more work."

And then came the second bank account, a secret from her husband, to pay for Botox treatments every four months and a series of plastic surgeries that were obvious but never acknowledged.

Sunna had thought her friend was being silly. They'd been, what, twenty-seven at the time? What did anyone need a perfectly symmetrical face for? Why would someone pay thousands of dollars to have a differently shaped nose? And why, after all that, couldn't her friend look in the mirror at that million-dollar person she'd designed and paid for without sighing and poking and grimacing?

Extreme vanity, Sunna had thought.

But now she wished she could apologize to her friend for her judgment, even if that friend had been unaware of it. Sunna had been vain, too; she'd just not yet experienced dissatisfaction. Besides, maybe it wasn't vanity at all—maybe it was actually something closer to fear. Not fear of being ugly but of mattering less than someone who was beautiful. Or successful. Or—she thought of Mackenzie—*good*.

She wandered back into the living room and sat on the couch.

She opened Instagram. Ex-friends smiled from the screen. Their kids were having birthdays and going to school. They were having endless—almost frantic—professional family photo shoots, like they were afraid that one of them was going to die or be disfigured beyond recognition at any moment.

Brett had been one of the only other women in Sunna's small university friend group whose ultimate goal *wasn't* to be a wife and mother; the rest of them, in recent years, had formed couples, become families, amassed little armies of whiny, constantly ill children and banded together in solidarity. The women who had once been so reckless and fun now called each other "Mama" in the same soothing, patronizing voice they used with their children. They got together before the sacred afternoon nap, during the morning hours while Sunna was at work. She was left out of their jokes and wasn't invited to the kids' birthday parties, and she was never sure if she should invite her friends to hang out with her in the evenings because they were always talking about how tired they were. If she mentioned a promotion or told a funny story about a night out, she was most often met with blank stares or, worse, pity. Looks that clearly said, *Isn't it sad that this is what makes you happy?* And then they'd talk about what their two-year-old had accomplished in the bathroom that week and expect her not to make the same face back at them.

Still, none of these flawless photos sparked jealousy in her, even though she knew that at her age, with her relationship status, they had the potential to—were basically designed to. The kids, she knew, were messy and prone to vomiting on airplanes and in cars and talking too much and ruining plans and never sleeping.

She hesitated for a moment, then navigated to a page she knew *would* make her jealous.

Brett Zaleschuck, she typed, and the familiar page loaded onto her screen. This had begun as a once-or-twice-a-month thing, checking in to see what Brett was doing, what people were saying about her. Just out of curiosity, Sunna told herself. *What has she accomplished? Who are her friends now? Where is she traveling?* Now Sunna automatically navigated to Brett's page every single time she went online. Wisdom said this behavior was unhealthy, but did wisdom actually stop anyone from doing anything? No. People stopped doing stuff when they wanted to.

Sunna touched the pink circle at the top of the page, and Brett's face materialized.

Brett paused before speaking to tuck a glossy strand of hair behind a dainty ear adorned with tiny gold hoops and diamonds the size of pinpricks. In that moment, Brett looked so impressed with herself, so fond of the face she saw in her screen, that Sunna felt vaguely voyeuristic, as though she were intruding on something romantic. She checked the background to see if there were any clues to Brett's current location—Regina?—but there was nothing to give it away. Brett didn't use Instagram for vignettes of her day-to-day life the way other people did; these were pep talks. Advice. Encouragement. Dressed up as things Brett was learning right alongside her audience so that people would call her generous and humble instead of a know-it-all.

"Hey, guys," Brett said, flashing a smile and cutely tilting her head. "I just wanted to pop in and say a word of encouragement. I know it's a super busy season; I know we're all running around like chickens with our heads cut off, but I wanted to remind you that the work you're doing is not wasted, because nothing"—here, she slowed down so even the pauses between her words were like whole sentences—"is, ever, wasted." She looked off-screen for a brief second like she was gathering her thoughts, playing with a gold chain around her neck, and then zeroed back in on her reflection. "And I just wanted to say that no matter where you are or who you are or what you're working toward, you're *essential*, babe—"

Sunna snorted and threw the phone on the couch, hard, knowing the cushions would soften its landing.

Brett's voice floated up, unaware of her angst. Unaware of her, period. "The world *needs* your unique talents, your drive, your story—"

Sunna was not an irrational person, given to fits of anger or violence. She was easily irritated and, yes, at times, *snippy*, but it was not like her to, say, throw a phone through a window.

That's how she knew the Brett thing was really getting to her.

It felt good in the moment, exceptionally good, and then immediately and disproportionately terrible. She regretted it the second her phone hit the glass, maybe even the second before. She stared with horror at the hole in the window.

She thought of her dad then—or, more accurately, she thought of her mom talking about her dad to her aunt Denise.

"He doesn't think about us," her mom had said, speaking as though her seven-year-old daughter were not sitting right there at the kitchen table, staring at her. "He just thinks about the things he wants, and he goes and gets them. Actually, no, that's not right; he doesn't think about *them* either. He just goes and gets. He's a go-getter." Her mom had laughed and laughed and laughed, but Sunna had understood that she was angry, and for years after that, she thought it was a bad thing to be a "go-getter."

"You almost can't blame him," her mom had continued. "I don't believe he actually has any control over his actions. I'm always afraid Sunna's going to take after him. She's already so much like him." She'd glanced at her daughter, snapping her fingers and pointing to indicate that Sunna needed to take her fingers out of her mouth.

Of course, Sunna's mom didn't really mean you couldn't blame him; she blamed him all the time, for everything. But that little snippet of conversation stored itself away in a corner of Sunna's brain, and she heard it play like a recording when she did impulsive things. She didn't have any control over her actions. You almost couldn't blame her.

~

It was already getting dark and cold outside; the air was wet. She closed the front door behind her and creaked across the porch, making her way down the stairs and around the side of the old building. An old man passing by on the sidewalk nodded in her direction, and she mumbled a greeting. He went slowly, choosing carefully where every step would land, like an insect making its way across a gravel road. She waited until he was out of sight before she got down on her hands and knees to feel around in the damp grass.

As she made her way around the shadowy yard, Sunna began to second-guess her decision to quit going to Paper Cup. Maybe she wasn't okay after all. You didn't throw expensive things through expensive windows if you were okay. If you were okay, you thought about your actions, and you only followed through on the right ones.

You almost can't blame her, she heard her mother say from way off in the past. *She's just like her dad.*

~

Sunna found her phone in a bush just outside the broken window, miraculously undamaged. She used packing tape left over from her move to temporarily patch the glass. She'd call Larry in the morning.

For now, a book, she thought as she sat, once more, in her living room. She swung an arm over the back of the couch, reaching for the tote bag containing her latest collection of library books, but her hand came up empty. She peered over at the vacant space on the floor. Was she losing her mind? Or—no, she'd forgotten the tote bag at Paper Cup on her last visit. She'd have to go back and pick it up. At least she had an excuse. She could tell herself—and Mackenzie and Maude—that she wasn't really going back because of Brett. That she was still okay—she just didn't want to pay for all those library books.

~

Sunna woke up around midnight to a loud scraping noise. The sound of something tremendous being dragged across the floor above her.

It began directly above her head and moved toward the kitchen. There was a slight pause, and then it started up again, coming back toward her. Another slight pause, more scraping.

"Maude!" she shouted. The scraping continued.

She stormed into the kitchen and grabbed the broom from its nook between the fridge and the wall. She climbed onto the couch and began to slam the broom into the ceiling—she was mostly a live-and-let-live person, but she'd done this a few times in her Toronto apartment when the man who lived above her had his friends over to watch football games. It was harder to live and let live, for some reason, when someone's very existence set your teeth on edge.

The scraping continued.

"Fine," Sunna shouted at the ceiling. "I'm coming up!"

She stomped to the vestibule and tried Maude's door—locked. She knocked with the side of her fist. "Maude!" she yelled and banged again.

Finally, she heard footsteps on the stairs and the sound of a chain being removed from the back of the door. The door cracked open, and Maude peered out suspiciously. "What?" she spat. "What could you possibly want at this time of night, you stupid girl?"

Sunna crossed her arms, sputtering. "Excuse me? At this time of night? At this time of night, what could *I* want? Excuse *me*, Maude?"

From above them, the scraping sound took up again, the familiar grinding noise making its slow trip from one end of the house to the other. Sunna glanced up, but Maude kept her eyes on the younger woman, her sharp chin tipped up.

Sunna's skin prickled, and the inside of her head felt cold. She gulped. "Uh . . . I . . ." She looked back at Maude, to confirm that she was, indeed, standing in front of her.

"I told you," said Maude, her voice flat and matter of fact. "We have ghosts. And I don't think they like you." She slammed the door in Sunna's face, and Sunna heard her feet on the steps again, angry and slow and deliberate.

Sunna went back to her apartment but couldn't fall asleep even after the noises above her had stopped. She couldn't stop thinking about everything—about Brett, about Maude, about the ghosts, the friend in Toronto with the plastic surgery. In the dark, Sunna touched the furrows in her forehead, the craters left by acne, the swell in the middle of her nose that should've been a cute little indent. She couldn't shake the idea that she somehow mattered less than she had even a year ago. That she would just keep on mattering less and less until she no longer mattered at all. She would end up as much a ghost as the ones living in the attic of this old house.

Go to sleep. They're quiet.

They. She'd laugh at herself for being stupid if she weren't so scared.

DETECTIVE MAUDE

Sunna

Mackenzie looked surprised. Maude looked furious. They weren't happy to see her, but Sunna didn't care. "Can I get a ride, Mack?"

"Her name isn't Mack," said Maude. "She's not a middle-aged truck driver."

"I didn't say can I get a ride, middle-aged truck driver," said Sunna. "I said can I get a ride, *Mack*."

If Mackenzie had an opinion about her nickname, she didn't show it; she didn't appear to be paying attention at all. She still looked surprised, but Sunna was beginning to wonder if the surprised look had been there before her arrival and if it wasn't meant for her or caused by her after all.

"So . . . can I?" Sunna said again, irritated at having to ask twice. She watched Mackenzie's eyes focus; the girl's head began to move up and down with clear effort. She wasn't surprised, Sunna realized. She was stunned. She looked like she'd been shot, or witnessed somebody else being shot, or been told she was pregnant with ten babies all at once.

"Yep, hop in." Mackenzie exhaled the words.

"Hop in, Sooooons," said Maude in a screechy bird voice that seemed to wake Mackenzie up. The three stood on the sidewalk in front of the house they lived in, and the trees rustled above their heads. Maude moved to the car and began to peck at the window with a bony fist. "Okay. Let's go. Mackenzie, let us in." Tap-tap-tap-tap-tap . . .

Sunna felt as irritated as if those knuckles were meeting the bone of her skull.

Mackenzie unlocked the doors, walking slowly to the driver's side like she was wading through knee-high water. She dropped her keys twice, and each time she stooped to retrieve them she paused, contemplating them as though she wasn't sure they were worth bending over for.

The drive to Paper Cup was silent. Sunna was irked that no one had asked why she'd come back after giving that big speech about how much she didn't care if she received an apology from Brett. The truth was that she did care—a lot. That was allowed, wasn't it? She could care about something and then not care about it, could be angry and then sad and then neutral, okay and then not okay, could throw things in the privacy of her own living room and tear the pictures of Brett out of her yearbooks and cry and then go to work and feel very indifferent to the whole thing and maybe even remember something that she and Brett had done together that made her smile. That was the truth, whether Maude and Mackenzie understood or not. *Who ever felt only one way about something?*

Mackenzie parked the car twice—it was crooked on the first attempt, and Maude announced that she wouldn't get out until it was corrected. When they'd come to a complete stop the second time, Maude peered out her window at the yellow lines painted on the ground. "Well, it's better, but it's still crooked."

Mackenzie was clutching the steering wheel so hard that her knuckles were white.

"Just get out, Maude," said Sunna. "It's fine."

"Fine for *us*," chirped Maude. "*Less* fine for the cars who want to park *around* us—"

"If only you showed that kind of consideration for the people trying to exist around you," said Sunna.

~

Sunna asked at the counter if a tote bag full of library books had been recovered, but the barista shook her head. "Leave your number, and I can call you if something turns up?"

Sunna sighed, calculating her overdue fines in her head. "Okay," she said.

They sat at their usual table with their usual drinks—for all Maude's righteous indignation at not being asked for her drink order each and every time, she never changed it.

Maude spread her latest newspaper on the table, glancing obnoxiously at Sunna as she smoothed the middle so it would lie flat. "Does it feel, to anyone else, like this whole bomb thing is just dragging on for entirely too long? Why doesn't that guy just blow the place up? Or why don't the police arrest him? What are they *waiting* for?"

Sunna was tired of the bomb threat conversation. It was all anyone wanted to talk about at work—when work wasn't canceled because of bomb threats. "I don't know if anyone noticed, but I'm, you know, *here*."

Mackenzie stared at her blankly, and Sunna felt unnerved. She thought she had Mackenzie figured out: Mackenzie was the nice one, unless you gave her a good reason not to be. Mackenzie was supposed to smile and be interested and ask questions and appear to enjoy the answers. She was supposed to say things meant to make you feel good even if they were untrue, and she was supposed to grab the wheel and swerve the conversation away from wrecks without making you feel like she was, in fact, grabbing the wheel. She was what Sunna had always thought a good mom was supposed to be like.

"Good for you; do you want a medal?" Maude said.

"I just *mean*"—Sunna had to avoid looking directly at Maude—"that I said I wasn't coming back, but here I am." There was a long silence. Mackenzie was drawing figure eights in her coffee with a plastic stir stick.

Maude leaned forward. She was jiggling her feet on the floor so the table shook as she put her weight on it. "Yay," she said. "Yahoo. I'm so glad you could join us. Yippee. Alert the press, Mackenzie. Oh, wait, I forgot—you girls don't believe in newspapers."

"Never mind," said Sunna. "You know what? Maybe *I'll* go sit at a different table today." She didn't move, though. She was still waiting for Mackenzie to try to stop her, but Mackenzie just continued to drag the stir stick through her coffee in slow circles.

"What's *wrong* with you today?" Sunna's voice was shrill, louder than she'd meant it to be. Mackenzie's head snapped up. She wasn't wearing her usual black eyeliner, but there were dark smudges and black flakes beneath her eyes from yesterday's makeup. "Sorry. That came out wrong. I mean . . . what's wrong? Something seems wrong, that's all. You're not . . . happy."

"I got a weird phone call last night," said Mackenzie dully.

"From who?" Maude asked.

"My dad."

"What was weird about it?" Maude asked, her chin moving forward like a chicken pecking at grain.

"Wow, Maude," said Sunna. "All you need is a little room with a two-way mirror and a light to shine in her face."

"So you're allowed to ask her questions, and I'm not?"

Sunna rolled her eyes.

"It seems to me," said Maude, "that there are a bunch of things you're allowed to do that I'm not. I find it hypocritical."

"I asked how she was. You're interrogating her like she's done something wrong."

Mackenzie shook her head. "It's fine. It's fine. I . . ." She let her head loll back, and she examined the ceiling for a moment. Then she sat up decisively. "There's someone else that I've been thinking could've written the letter. Besides Jared, I mean."

"And they called you last night?" Maude's face was impossible to read. She was either angry or excited.

"Her dad called her last night," said Sunna. "She just said that."

Maude sucked her lips into her mouth.

"Yeah, my dad called. To say that they're"—she looked down at her hands—"reopening my sister's missing person case."

Sunna had been lifting her coffee cup to her lips, but her hand froze in the air.

Maude blinked. "Your . . ."

"Sister is missing. Yep. Has been for . . ." Mackenzie paused. "Six years now? Name's Kate. She disappeared from her bedroom one night. On my birthday, actually."

"She ghosted too?" asked Maude.

"Yeah. I guess so. Though that makes it sound like she disappeared on purpose."

"Wow," said Sunna. "They don't think she ran away?"

"They don't think anything anymore," said Mackenzie. "The police investigated it as a missing person case at first. My mom felt like they weren't taking it seriously. We—my family, I mean—knew she wouldn't run away. Or we knew it at first. But then I think my dad hoped she'd run away, because that was better than the other things that could've gone down. He wanted to believe she was in control of whatever happened to her, if that makes sense. And he convinced himself that they'd had a weird exchange the day before and that she'd run away because of him. And then—" Mackenzie stopped talking abruptly and began picking at a hangnail. "Yeah," she said finally. "That's all."

"Wow," said Sunna again, aware that *wow* was wholly inadequate. "But you must think she ran away, too, if you think she wrote you this letter. You think she's coming home."

"She's not, of course," said Maude.

"Maude!" Sunna glared at her, and Maude shrugged.

"What? It was six years ago!"

"Stranger things have happened."

"To *whom*, Sunna?"

Mackenzie cleared her throat quietly. She took the lid off her coffee cup and put it back on. She smiled at a woman walking past, toddler on hip, coffee in hand. When her eyes focused again on Sunna, they were clear, and she almost looked as though she'd forgotten what they were talking about, except for a funny rash-like redness on the tops of her cheeks. "Well," she said carefully. "That was why my dad called last night—to let me know they've reopened the investigation. They got a phone call from someone with an anonymous tip."

"And you're upset? Shouldn't you be happy?" Maude was relentless.

Mackenzie seemed to be fighting back tears now. Sunna could tell there was more, but she felt guilty enough for forcing Mackenzie to say anything at all. She hoped Maude would leave it alone.

But it was not in Maude's nature to leave things alone.

"Oh, I see," said Maude. "You think it's going to be another run-around from the police and that you'll get your hopes up again and they won't find anything?" Maude leaned back in her chair and studied Mackenzie, who was still not responding, then brought both hands down hard on the table with an incredible crash. The man at the next table jumped and knocked his coffee over. "I've got an idea!" she cried as he hurried past, headed for the napkin dispenser, glowering at the back of her head like he wanted to pluck it from her shoulders and crush it like a pop can. "Let's solve it."

"What?" Mackenzie was flustered. She looked to Sunna for clarification—or maybe help.

"Who knows how long we'll be sitting here waiting every afternoon. We have nothing to do but listen to Sunna squawk at everyone about how they're doing everything wrong." Sunna's mouth dropped open. "Let's solve the mystery! *Before* the police!" Maude's eyes were wide, and she smiled with all her teeth; she looked terrifying. "Mackenzie. You're the sister of the victim. That means you know all of the clues, all of the, you know, circumstantial evidence. We could, we could interview you, and you could bring us, uh, her, her diary, her . . . her stuff. Clues." Maude hit the table, over and over, like she was a contestant on a gameshow hitting a buzzer. The man who had spilled his coffee paused midcleanup to utter something uncouth in their general direction.

Mackenzie appeared to have frozen into a chunk of granite.

"Easy there, Sherlock," said Sunna softly. She was trying to figure out the expression on Mackenzie's face.

"I prefer Hercule," said Maude.

"Who?"

"Poirot," said Maude, touching her upper lip in a gesture Sunna didn't understand.

Mackenzie shook her head. "My sister," she said, speaking from the bottom of her register, "is not entertainment either. Just like your fiancé who dumped you at the altar. Just . . . like . . ." She stopped and shook her head again. Like she had wanted to be angry but was too depressed. "I have work to do."

She pulled her laptop out of her backpack and cried unsubtly at the screen for the rest of the afternoon.

~

When Sunna arrived at the house that night, she was exhausted. She had been awake since four thirty and had not slept well before that. She had spent so much emotional energy simply being in the same room as Maude all day that all she wanted was sleep. She staggered into her suite without turning the light on, preferring the soft glow of the streetlight just outside the window. It shone around the edges of the packing tape and the surrounding cracks in the glass, creating the body and legs of a large translucent spider.

Her foot met something soft but with little give, and she pitched forward onto the floor. She rolled over and sat up, checking to see what had tripped her, and there, in the middle of the floor where she could not possibly have missed it before, was her bag of library books.

OLD FRIENDS, NEW SUSPECTS

Larry

"Hello, Larry. Maude here. I've figured it out, the noise. I think you have a tree branch scraping the roof of your house. I'm fairly confident. Oh, oops!" Silence. "Sorry, Larry, Janet needed my help there for a minute. Please call me back at your earliest convenience, and I will advise you as to what I think should be done."

"Larry, Maude here. Hi. I'm not sure what recourse I have if the landlord refuses to return my calls. I suppose I could climb onto the roof and chop this branch off of its stupid tree *myself*, but I presume that it would be awful for you if I were to *fall* . . . you'd have to clean me up, wouldn't you, and I wouldn't want to be that kind of *hassle*. Please call me back, or I will . . . go . . . I will . . ."

"Larry. Hi. Are you *dead*? Call me back." Silence. "Maude here."

Larry knew he was being a terrible landlord, but he was pretty sure she wanted him to do something about the ghosts, and he didn't know how to tell her there *were* ghosts in the first place and that he could do nothing about them in the second place and that if she had a problem with ghosts, which most people did, and who could blame them, she would have to move.

But she was persistent, if nothing else (and he was beginning to wonder if she literally *was* nothing but persistent, if she did nothing else with her free time but persist, specifically with him), and eventually, she wore him down.

He had been sitting at his kitchen table listening to his favorite CDs and tapes, watching his favorite videos and recorded live shows—even the local bands only people from Regina had heard of—and writing practice reviews. It was harder than he had thought it would be, but it was fun. He had purchased a laptop and a thesaurus—you could only describe someone's voice as being "raw" once, and then you couldn't use "raw" to also describe the production and the guitar tone. He had the sound cranked all the way up so he could catch all the words, all the background noise, every detail. He'd never listened to music this way before, so critically; it was like hearing it all for the first time. But the phone calls kept pulling him out of his writing zone. He no longer felt like he should completely ignore them—after all, what if, one of these times, it was the police?

Finally, he put Maude on speakerphone and set her in front of him on the table, resting his chin in the crook of his arm and mumbling a reluctant "Hello?"

"Larry!" Maude clucked. "I was beginning to wonder if you were dead."

"I know," he said, feeling more assertive than usual. "You said so in your last message. The fifteenth one you've left today."

"I feel as though you want me to feel bad for calling fifteen times, when I feel like *you* should feel bad for not *answering* fifteen times."

Larry nodded, ashamed.

"Larry? Are you still there?"

"Yes," he said. "You're right. I'm sorry."

She didn't acknowledge his apology. "Larry, I was calling about those noises—"

"Oh, hey, Maude, before you go any further, I had something I needed to ask *you*." Anything to avoid talking about those noises.

"Yes?"

"Uh . . . so, you know Mackenzie? Who lives in the basement? I mean—*do* you know her? Have, have you *met* her?"

The woman took the bait eagerly, which surprised him. "Yes, I do. What about her?"

"Uh . . . do you know, is she, like, a journalist or something?"

"A journalist?"

"Or . . . you know, does she write? Like, articles? In newspapers and magazines?"

Maude sounded disappointed now and more than a little impatient. "I don't know, Larry. Why's that?"

"Oh. It's not important. I just saw a picture of her in one of my magazines, or, you know, I thought I did. But this girl's name was Kate Weiss, the one in the magazine, so . . . probably wasn't her. Thought it could be a pen name. I just had some questions for her about—"

"You say the girl's name was *Kate*, Larry? Kate? Kate what, again?"

"Uh, Weiss?"

"Are you sure?"

"Uh . . . yes?"

"Hmm. Thanks, Larry. I have to go." Her voice moved away— "Janet! Stop that!"—and abruptly cut off. She'd hung up. *Huh.* He thought he'd have to work a lot harder to get out of that phone call.

Back to work.

～

He was taking a leisurely spin through his Bouncing Souls discography when he realized that the slightly off-time drumbeat was actually a fist on his door. Glenda? Most likely. He hadn't even listened to the last few messages she'd left yet; he'd been completely consumed by his new passion. He turned the music off and opened the door, expecting the disapproving face of his sister.

But there were two disapproving faces, and neither belonged to Glenda.

Police officers. He hoped they hadn't been waiting there for long. He hoped they weren't here to cart him off to prison. Had they "obtained their warrant"?

"Hi," Larry squeaked. "May I help you?"

"Larry Finley?" asked the taller of the officers.

He nodded. Did a double take. "Shelby?"

"Yep." The officer grinned at her partner. "We went to high school together. Campbell."

"Oh. Okay," said the partner, unimpressed. "Hi, Larry."

Larry nodded. "Hey. You're probably not here to invite me to the class reunion."

Shelby laughed. "No, no, I'm not."

"Uh—should I have a lawyer?" The thought had not occurred to him before this minute.

Shelby might not have heard him. "We just have a few questions to ask you, Larry."

Larry nodded. "But should I have a lawyer?"

She shrugged. "Don't see why you'd need one."

"I mean, isn't that why you're here? Aren't I a suspect?" As soon as he said it, he wished he hadn't. What a dumb thing to say to a cop, even if the cop had been your friend twenty-five years ago. "I just mean, not that I should be a suspect. I mean, I didn't do anything wrong. But they fired me at the art gallery, and—well, they didn't *fire* me, but—"

Shelby laughed again. "It's okay, Larry. You'll be pleased to know you've been cleared. Your boss will probably be in touch with you soon, and, on a personal note, I'm sorry that any accusations made it into the paper. That shouldn't have happened. However, we've had some very recent developments, and you're no longer a person of interest. We had determined that one of the threatening calls came from your property on Montreal Street—"

"*Oh!*" Larry exclaimed, wishing they'd mentioned that part earlier. "But I don't live there."

"We know—now," said Shelby. "We weren't aware when we began the investigation that the property was being rented out, and we apologize for the inconvenience."

Larry felt so relieved he was almost dizzy. It was a little more than an inconvenience, wasn't it? "Well, thanks for coming by to tell me I'm not a person of interest. Not that I don't sometimes wish I *were* a person of interest." He grinned. "Joking," he said, just in case they didn't get it. "Like, I wish I were an interesting person—"

Shelby smiled amiably (she'd always been so kind, even back in high school), but her partner cut in. "We actually dropped by to ask you a few questions, Mr. Finley," she said. "About someone else."

"Benjamin?" He shouldn't have said that either. It was like a talent, how many wrong things he could say in a single conversation.

"No," said Shelby. "How much do you know about the three renters in your Montreal Street house?"

MAUDE DOES SOME UNAPPRECIATED SLEUTHING

Sunna

At first the sound was a tapping so quiet that Sunna thought it was the radiator or some kid outside bouncing a ball on the sidewalk. Then it became a knock, and before she could make it across the room, it was a full-on pounding, which made her reconsider answering it at all.

She peered through the peephole, and there was Maude, hands jammed into her coat pockets, shoulders up, a giant cloth grocery bag slung over her shoulder, and a ferocious look on her face.

Sunna had just come home from work. She wanted to take a nap before they went to the coffee shop. More importantly, she didn't want to spend more time talking to Maude than necessary. She began to tiptoe away from the door.

"Sunna! I know you're in there. I heard you singing! I saw you get home a few minutes ago!" A pause. More knocking, more squawking. "I heard the toilet flush *and* the sink run! Sunna!"

Sunna could pretend she had just left, that Maude had indeed heard all these things but that she was already gone again. She had no car to give her away. She kept tiptoeing.

"I can hear the floor creaking! I can *hear* you sneaking away from the door! Sunna!"

"I'm coming, Maude. Calm down." Sunna took her time opening the door.

"Hello, Sunna," said Maude solemnly. She looked like the grim reaper.

"Hey, Maude."

Maude pursed her lips. "May I come in?"

"Well, I'm kind of in a hurry."

"No, you're not."

Sunna frowned. "How would you know if I'm in a hurry or not?"

Maude moved into the suite, drifting forward almost imperceptibly, like a spirit. "You just got home from work, and you don't have any friends, and we don't leave for Paper Cup for at least an hour, so where in the world would you be going 'in a hurry'?"

"How would you know if I had any friends?"

"Oh, I don't know, maybe because I live in the same building as you. People who have friends invite them over sometimes. People who have friends go out in the evenings—and come home without takeout and grocery bags. They have their noses up against their phone screens all day every day—like Mackenzie. She's always on there, talking to her friends. *Mackenzie* has friends. I would believe *Mackenzie* if she were to tell me she was in a hurry."

"Well, then, you must not have any friends either."

"Of course I don't have any *friends*. But I'm also not trying to brush someone off saying I'm in a hurry when the only place I absolutely have to go today is the bathroom. Which"—Maude gestured—"you've just done. I heard the water running and all that. Besides, don't tell me you're not curious."

Sunna was not. "Should I be?"

"Yes. Absolutely. I don't like you, you don't like me, and yet, here I am, an hour before I have to be. Mackenzie, the person who keeps us from ripping each other's hair out, is absent. I have a tote bag." She widened her eyes and held up the grocery bag.

Sunna was still not curious but only because she didn't want Maude to be right. "So?"

Maude stepped past Sunna and headed for her kitchen table, which was still set with a cup of coffee and bowl of oatmeal. "Is there more coffee?"

"No." (There was.)

"Fine, okay, come see what I've got here."

Maude began spreading papers across the surface of the table. There was a loud bang above them, and both women looked at the ceiling. "You know," said Maude, "I only started hearing them when you conjured them up with your disbelief and bad attitude."

"What is this, Maude? It couldn't wait for this afternoon?"

"No, it couldn't. Mackenzie wouldn't like it."

"Why wouldn't Mackenzie . . . oh, *Maude*." Sunna only had to see one sentence, printed boldly across the top of one of the papers to know what Maude was up to.

"Exactly."

"Mackenzie asked you not to."

"No, she didn't. She said not to be entertained by it—which is an unfair thing to ask of someone. You can't go around controlling what people are entertained by. A kitten is entertained by a ball of string, and no one can tell it not to be. You could also tell the kitten not to play with the ball of string, but that would be ridiculous. No one tells a kitten what to do. You'd have to take the ball of string away from the kitten—"

"Maude."

"And why would you take a ball of string away from a kitten? A kitten doesn't have a lot of joys in life. Why would you take away something's one source of joy? Especially an adorable little kitten."

"This is crazy." Sunna didn't point out that Maude was neither adorable nor particularly kitten-like.

"You see what I'm saying, though? This is my ball of string. I am already entertained by it, endlessly fascinated with it, and you can't take it away from me. Because I know where there's more. I'm a *smart* kitten."

"Where did you get these?"

"Someplace." Maude went back to her papers, checking the dates at the top and lining them up in chronological order. Sunna wanted her gone, but she didn't know how to get her out, so she took a sip of her coffee and resigned herself—promising that she would never sing out loud in her apartment or walk on the floors or pee or open the door ever again. "It's all here, Sunna. And it's so much more interesting than Mackenzie made it sound. Also, Mackenzie's a liar. Also, the library."

"What?"

"I got these at the library. Microfiche! They let you print them now."

Sunna hated that she was curious. She kept her mouth shut. Maude kept bustling over the table, fluttering over the papers and clucking her tongue.

"Sunna, when I say Mackenzie's a liar, I don't mean she's a little-white-lie liar. This is a big red lie, Sunna. This is the biggest lie I think I've ever heard someone tell in person. Even bigger than when Richard . . ." Maude held up a hand and grunted, as though Sunna had been the one to say his name.

Sunna kept her eyes on the papers.

"Okay. So this first one is from the paper from almost a week after they went missing. She said it happened six-ish years ago; this paper is from . . . May eighth, 2014. That, at least, checks out."

Sunna raised her chin, as much interest as she could stand to express.

"Ah, good catch, Sunna. Yes, I *did* say *they*. Look at this headline."

Sunna couldn't help herself. She took the paper from Maude. The headline read TWIN SISTERS DISAPPEAR FROM BEDROOM.

Directly below, filling up half the page, a picture of two identical teenagers grinned in a black-and-white photo that washed out their features and made their teeth and eyeballs glow.

Maude smacked the table again, the way she had at the coffee shop the day before. "Twin sisters disappear! *Both* of them! Remember what Mackenzie said? Mackenzie said her sister—singular, *one* sister—disappeared from her bedroom in the middle of the night. She never mentioned that she was with her. She said she left in the night and she never saw her again. Lie *one*."

Sunna shook her head. "This article isn't about Mackenzie's sister, Maude. This is a different case."

Maude looked smug. "Why do you say that?"

"Because neither of these girls' names are Mackenzie. See? 'Late Sunday night, twin sisters Kate and Tanya Simons disappeared from their bedroom after a birthday celebration thrown by their parents.' This is a different case." She examined the paper for a moment, reading the rest of the article. "Oh. And like you said, this paper is from 2014. These girls were . . ." She checked the article again and did some quick math in her head. "Sixteen then. So they'd be twenty-two now. Mackenzie said she was nineteen. And those girls don't even look like Mackenzie."

Maude's smile was wide in her crepe paper face. "Of *course* they don't look like her. Like you said, this was six years ago. These girls aren't wearing heavy makeup, and they don't have short dyed hair. And they're *girls*. Mackenzie's an adult, a *woman*—legally, if nothing else. Maybe she *is* twenty-two—it's called lying. Lie *two*—lie three? Where are we? I'm losing count! But what are the chances of having *two* missing person cases in Saskatchewan that year, and only one appearing in the papers, and that they both involved sisters with the last name Simons—and one of whom is named *Kate*—who disappeared on their birthday? Either this is the same case, but Mackenzie is lying about a lot of details, or some weirdo out there has a Simons twin collection in their basement. In which case, Mackenzie should be worried, because she'd complete one of the sets." Maude laughed and assumed a pensive pose. "Hmm . . . maybe Mackenzie *is* worried about something. That would explain why she's lying about her name and age. She's in hiding. It would make sense. You'll see."

"You think she's lying about her name? Maude—"

"Not think. *Know.*" Maude pulled a sheaf of papers, held together by a paper clip, out of her tote bag and threw them dramatically on the table in front of Sunna. "Aha! Proof!"

Sunna picked them up and flipped through them. "What are these? Music articles? Album reviews?"

"I had to get the librarian to find those for me on her computer. She printed them off. Look at the picture at the bottom. The author biography."

Sunna did a double take. "Kate Weiss? What—" She was having a very hard time not appearing too invested. "What is this, Maude?"

"Look at the tattoo. Poppies. Recent picture, too, I'd say."

Sunna didn't say anything. She thought of the way Mackenzie touched her tattoo whenever she was nervous or distressed. It was, without question, the same girl.

"So you see, we have here twins named Kate and Tanya, and despite the fact that Mackenzie said Kate was missing, Mackenzie *is* Kate—which lines up with my research. I already knew she wasn't the other one."

Sunna conceded. "Go on."

"Okay, so. The local paper continued to cover the story. The information they had to go on was, like Mackenzie said, *very* minimal. The articles all said the same thing for a long time. Described what they'd been wearing at the party, described their physical characteristics, mentioned that the girls were close, that the family was longing for their safe return. Yada yada yada. They'd just vanished, and no one had any idea how or why or anything."

Sunna was glad Mackenzie was not there to hear Maude say 'Yada yada yada,' like she was recapping the boring part of a movie.

"But then!" Maude yelled loud enough that Mackenzie could probably hear. She was building to something. "Then!" she exclaimed again for good measure, or maybe because Sunna didn't look impressed enough. She picked two of the newspapers up and cleared her throat, wiggling her glasses with the other hand. "Okay, two things. First, this article"—she set one of the papers in front of Sunna and pointed to the fine print— "discloses the fact that *both twins* emptied their bank accounts the night before they disappeared and that they *stole* from their parents—jewelry and the like. They took their mother's *wedding ring* set."

Sunna said nothing, and Maude studied her. The silence began to feel like a challenge. Sunna wondered if she imagined these kinds of quiet standoffs; they happened to her all the time. She usually won. Maude, however, was a formidable opponent.

Sunna sipped her coffee and took a bite of her oatmeal. Maude stared steadily at the coffee cup. She didn't need a prop. She wasn't the one anxious to reclaim her apartment. She could sit there until Mackenzie showed up.

Sunna tried to think of a way to give in without sacrificing her pride. "You know you could've just looked all this up on the internet, right?"

"I don't have the internet. I don't even have a computer."

"You don't have a computer at all?"

"Why would I need a computer?"

"I don't know. To play solitaire when you're bored. To have the internet."

"Why would I need the internet?"

"To check the weather. To look up stuff you don't know."

"I could play solitaire with actual cards. I have those. I have a window for checking the weather. I have the entire *library* at my disposal. Why is your generation so opposed to actual things and places?"

"Why is your generation so opposed to convenience?" Sunna knew she was no longer winning. She was on the defense.

"My *generation isn't*," said Maude crossly. "I've met people much older than me who are very good with new technology. But . . ." She played with the corner of one of the papers, folding it forward into a little triangle and tearing it off. "It's like with anything new that comes along. You have to want it. If the old way works and you like it, you need a reason to want to switch over. And maybe someone to show you how."

Sunna felt her defenses wither. She nodded, acknowledging that Maude had won that round, and Maude looked surprised.

"And besides," Maude muttered, as though she had one more great point that she didn't want to waste even though she'd already won, "twenty newspapers are much easier to carry around in a tote bag than twenty computers."

Sunna looked down at the papers again, biting her tongue. "Is this all there is?"

"Oh no. This is just the beginning." Sunna thought she saw Maude smile a little as she selected the next paper. "This one is very interesting," she said. "Tanya's wallet showed up in a thrift store a month later. In *Florida*."

"How did they know the wallet belonged to her?"

"How do I know?" Maude said. "Oh, wait—" She scanned the article again. "Oh yes, I do know. Her driver's license was still in it. Along with an Aldo gift card."

Sunna couldn't help scanning the rest of the papers, but she tried not to lean in. She didn't want Maude thinking she was on her side just because she'd let her win a fight. "Just Tanya's? Not Mackenzie's? Or Kate's, I guess?"

"Ah, good catch," said Maude. "The owner of the thrift store said their clothes came from a donation bin next to a 7-Eleven, so someone probably tossed it in there as they were walking past, if I remember right . . ." Maude was flapping her arms again. "I can't remember. It's in there somewhere. There were vigils and search parties and everything.

Mackenzie made it sound like the police were playing canasta the whole time—canasta is another card game; it's better than solitaire, and you probably don't have it on your computer—but they were *very* involved."

"Well. To the family it probably felt like they were doing less than they should've. I'm sure if someone I loved went missing, I'd never think anyone's efforts were enough." Sunna felt superior to Maude. She was rational and empathic. She would give Mackenzie the benefit of the doubt. Strange, she thought, how someone you disliked could bring out the good in you but for the worst reasons.

"Yes, but you're forgetting—we're not talking about someone Mackenzie loved. We're talking about Mackenzie."

Sunna realized that their shoulders were touching as they hunched over, and the spell was broken. She moved away. "We shouldn't be doing this."

"Shouldn't be reading the newspaper? Oh, you're absolutely right—how *dare* we read the newspaper? Tsk tsk tsk. I'm appalled at us."

"Maude. Do you have to mock every single thing I say?"

"You say a lot of ridiculous things."

"You should go home."

Maude smirked. "You don't want to hear the most interesting part?"

Sunna couldn't help it. If none of this was the most interesting part, what was? She sighed. "Fine. What's the most interesting part?"

"In the end, after all of this, they didn't close the case because they decided Tanya ran away. According to this"—she picked up the last paper on the table and turned it so Sunna could see the headline—"Tanya's not a missing person. Tanya's dead. And the other twin—Kate? *Mackenzie?*—is still missing. And, in my mind, she's also the main suspect in the murder of Tanya Simons."

PEER PRESSURE

Mackenzie

It was late at night, and Mackenzie wasn't expecting anyone, so she wasn't going to answer the door. She didn't like answering doors—if she was expecting a package too big or valuable to be left on her doorstep, she let the deliveryman leave a slip and she picked it up at the depot. Her friends and family knew better than to show up unannounced. She never ordered pizza. Celeste had teased her about it once; she'd called her antisocial, and Mackenzie had accepted the title without cringing outwardly, but what she'd wanted to say was, "I'm not antisocial; I'm afraid." But then she'd have had to explain why she was afraid, so she'd just let it be. Some things were too hard to explain, even to the person who supposedly knew all your secrets.

The knock came again, and this time it was accompanied by a hiss. "Mack! Mack! It's Sunna! Come here, quick!"

Mackenzie moved the chair from under the handle and ran up the stairs, and sure enough, it was Sunna out in the vestibule, a sagging white sheet mask stuck on her face and her hair pulled back in a headband. Her eyes, peering out from inside the mask, were wide.

"What's wrong?"

"Did you hear it?" Sunna was still whispering.

"I didn't hear anything. It's midnight."

"Come with me." Sunna spun and ran up the stairs, and Mackenzie followed, her curiosity piqued.

"There! Listen!"

Above them was a loud scraping sound, followed by heavy footsteps. Sunna grabbed Mackenzie's arm. "Did you hear it?"

"Of course I heard it," Mackenzie said, looking upward. "I still hear it. What's she doing up there?"

"It's not Maude. I thought it was, too, but the other night she was down here, standing right in front of me, and I could still hear it. She said it was the ghosts."

The hallway's light bulb was dim, and Sunna looked fairly ghostly herself with the sheet mask hanging off her face. Mackenzie began to feel uneasy. "Maybe she has other people in there."

"Maude? Other people? Other people in Maude's apartment?"

"Could be."

"I'd sooner take up a belief in ghosts than believe Maude has friends."

"That's a little mean . . ."

Sunna was smirking; Mackenzie could tell even without seeing her mouth. "Is it mean if it's just factual? It was Maude who told me she has no friends." She tried the handle on Maude's door. It was locked, as usual. "Too bad."

"Sunna, what are you doing?"

"I want to go up there and see. Once and for all. This is driving me crazy; it happens almost every night."

"Yeah, but you can't just go into someone's house without their permission. And Maude's never going to invite you."

"I know. That's why I came and got you."

"You want me to go up and see if Maude has company?"

"No, of course not. I want you to get her down to your place. And I'll go up."

Mackenzie sighed. "Not doing that."

"Why?" Sunna had forgotten her whisper; her voice came out in a loud whine.

"Are you serious?"

"Okay, Mack." Sunna began peeling the mask from her face. "Listen to me. I wasn't going to tell you this . . ." She paused to pull the thin material from around her lips and then began folding the mask into a small square as she spoke. Bits of paper stuck to her cheeks and forehead. "But Maude kind of owes you one."

"What do you mean?"

"I mean she went digging into your weird missing-twin thing after you asked her not to. And when I say *digging*, I mean she went full-on Nancy Drew; she's studied every newspaper clipping, and she has all these theories and questions. She's got it all in this big grocery sack." Sunna looked down at her neatly folded face mask as she spoke, until she got to the end. Then she looked right into Mackenzie's eyes. "She snooped. You should snoop back."

Mackenzie felt her mouth drop open. Her face was hot, and she felt as though she might cry. "She what?"

"Yeah."

"Did you see them? The papers?"

"Uh . . ." Sunna clearly hadn't anticipated being part of the problem. "Maybe? Yeah? Like, some of them. Not . . . I didn't read them. Really. She showed up at my door, and I basically just told her to get lost."

Mackenzie wanted to feel relieved, but her throat was tight. "She had no right to do that."

"No. She didn't."

"It still doesn't give me the right to help you break into her apartment. What she did was awful, but at least it was *legal*—"

"Mackenzie!" Sunna threw her head back and breathed hard through her nose. She searched the ceiling for a moment. "Okay, listen.

Here's the thing. You and I both know there's nothing in her apartment. No flat-screen TVs, no stereo equipment, nothing of any value. No one wants that couch, or the cat, or her plastic salt and pepper shakers. Or all those *tapes*."

"So?"

"So you know I'm not taking anything. I'm not gonna rob her. It's not even really invading her privacy—we've seen it all before. We're her"—she faltered—"friends. In fact, I bet the noise is coming from the attic. I'm going to basically bypass her apartment and go see who, or what, I guess, is up there."

"I didn't say you were going to rob her. Breaking and entering isn't only bad if you rob someone. That's why those are two separate charges. I'll come up with you to see what's going on—you just have to do it the right way. Knock and ask if you can come in. Like a normal person."

Sunna sighed again. "Fine." She turned back to Maude's door and raised her fist.

"Wait, now?"

"Of course. There's no way Maude's asleep with that racket, even if she isn't the one making it. That's another thing. I don't believe her when she says she isn't noticing the sounds or that she didn't hear them until I did. Not possible. She either knows something, or she's just trying to make me mad—which, by the way, is working."

Mackenzie took a small step back. "It's midnight."

But Sunna was already knocking. After a minute, they heard steps and the slow unlocking of the door. Maude peered out. "What?"

Sunna pointed up. "That sound. What is going *on*, Maude?"

Maude narrowed her eyes. "Ghosts," she said and shut the door.

Sunna knocked again. "Maude. Maude!"

Maude called from behind the door without opening it. "If I know anything about ghosts, it's that you choose to either peacefully coexist or you move! Stop talking about them; stop knocking on my door—let us all alone!" Her footsteps receded until they couldn't be heard anymore. The scraping sound kept on.

"We definitely should've done it my way," said Sunna.

~

The next night, Mackenzie woke to Sunna standing in her bedroom, flicking on the overhead lights. She let out a scream before she realized who it was and clutched the covers around her, blinking frantically against the brightness.

"Sunna! I just about had a heart attack! What is *wrong* with you?"

"Come on! I can't believe I didn't think to try this before; the landlord is an idiot. Our locks are all the same. My key works in your door, so it probably works in Maude's too. PS, the chair below the handle thing? Doesn't work. Not effective at all."

Mackenzie cleared her throat and rubbed her eyes. "What time is it?"

"It's three. Maude's probably asleep. So let's go see what's going on up there—we'll just sneak through her hallway into the attic."

"I already told you—"

"Is it breaking and entering if you *have a key*?"

"Yep. I think."

"She owes you, Mack. And me. It's every single night, and I can't handle it anymore. I'm not getting any sleep, you know? It's not fair."

Mackenzie flopped forward in her bed. "You are exhausting, Sunna . . ."

"Come on. I'm not leaving until you come with me. I'll swing you over my shoulder and carry you up there if I have to."

Mackenzie obediently set her legs on the floor. "Why do you need me? You have a key; just go in."

"I need a lookout. Plus, I'm scared out of my brains."

"I feel like I'm babysitting you and Maude, sometimes."

"You're meaner at night, Mack. Come on. Let's go."

"Fine."

The women crept up the stairs, stopping in the drafty front entrance to unlock Maude's door.

"Huh," said Sunna as she turned the key in the lock.

"What?"

"It was already unlocked."

Sunna pushed the door open, and they stood just inside, listening for a moment. The rumbling sound above moved from left to right and back again, like a giant dragging his foot across the roof. Sunna pulled Mackenzie's elbow, urging her up the stairs.

The empty living room was eerie in the dark; their footsteps creaked no matter how carefully they walked. The heavy scraping sound paused, then carried on. Mackenzie thought it sounded angrier somehow. Sunna was right; the noise was coming from the attic.

"Do you even know where the attic door is?" Mackenzie whispered.

"I'd assume it's one of those." Sunna pointed at two narrow doors in the hallway. They tried the first; it was a closet containing a broom and dustpan, a soap refill, and a couple of towels. The second was locked, and Sunna's key didn't work to open it.

"Okay, let's go," said Mackenzie, relieved. Whatever dazed curiosity had enabled her to come this far had worn off, and now she was desperate to be back in her bedroom, covers pulled to her chin, dreaming about something else.

But Sunna was disappointed.

"This all feels like such a waste if we're gonna just turn around and leave," she said. She wiggled the doorknob again, and it rattled loudly.

Mackenzie shushed her.

"Oh, whatever," said Sunna. "Maude's old; she's probably half-deaf. And there's no such thing as ghosts. I'm not worried about *ghosts*."

Mackenzie expected the ghosts to seep out of the walls at this proclamation, or whatever was making the scraping sound above them to descend the stairs and bust through the locked door. She hadn't realized how much she believed in ghosts until now.

Sunna headed down the hallway toward the kitchen, and Mackenzie scuttled behind her, hissing like an angry teakettle. "Sunna! Sunna!"

Sunna ignored her. She probably understood by now that it would take a lot of time to talk Mackenzie into her plots, but if she just plowed ahead, Mackenzie would have no choice but to follow. It was much more efficient this way.

Sunna tiptoed through the kitchen and peered into the bedroom. Mackenzie hung back, ready to bolt. She watched with horror as Sunna stepped into the bedroom and flicked on the light.

"Sunna!" she gasped. "What—"

"She's not here." Sunna was in Maude's bedroom now, peering into the closet rather indignantly, like Maude owed it to them to be in her bed in the middle of the night.

"What?"

"Maude's not in her bed. Which means . . ."

"Uh, that she is . . . somewhere else? In the hospital? At a friend's? With the ghosts? None of our business?" Mackenzie had inched halfway across the kitchen; even though she knew that Maude wasn't anywhere in the house, she still couldn't bring herself to go nearer to the bedroom. It struck her that this was actually worse—if Maude arrived home at this point, they'd be trapped.

"Sunna, let's get out of here."

Sunna looked annoyed. "This just proves it. Maude's up there." She pointed at the ceiling, and they both realized at the same time that the terrible sound had stopped. "That proves it too," she said. She stalked toward the attic and began to bang on the locked door. Mackenzie wondered whether she should run back to the safety of her suite or stay to witness what would, no doubt, be an intense face-off between Maude and Sunna.

Before she could make up her mind, the ceiling began to thud with what seemed like the weight of an army jumping up and down in unison. The lights rattled, and the house shook. The attic door began to bang back at Sunna. Sunna backed away, staring at Mackenzie. "Maaaauuuude?" she whimpered.

"What's going on in here?"

Mackenzie gasped and spun, instinctively slapping Maude across the face. Maude looked even smaller and paler in the dark room, her mouth wide in shock, her bony hand pressed against her cheek. Something had fallen to her feet, and Mackenzie saw that it was a carton of cigarettes. Maude was wearing shoes and a jacket over her nightgown—she'd been smoking on the porch.

The banging continued, and Maude looked at the attic door, at Sunna, at Mackenzie. She was still holding her face.

Mackenzie mumbled an apology, fled down the stairs to her suite, and dead bolted the door behind her. She stood there shaking. She wished she'd run out the front door, away from this stupid, terrifying house, instead of into the basement. Why were her instincts always so wrong? Always. She was never, *never* right when she trusted her instincts. But she couldn't open the door now. Neither would she be able to turn her back to it or fall asleep again tonight for that matter. She would stand there until the sun came up.

And she would start apartment shopping tomorrow morning.

MAD MAUDE

Sunna

Maude wasn't there the next morning when Sunna opened her door—
which was, of course, a relief. Sunna couldn't stop picturing Maude's
shocked face the night before and feeling awful about it. Since the day
she met Maude, Sunna had intentionally provoked all kinds of Maude
faces—angry ones, irritated ones, offended ones—and she'd enjoyed it.
But the face last night just made Sunna sad.

She slung her purse over her shoulder so she had a free hand to
knock on the door. She had a pair of shoes clamped to her side with
her elbow—she'd found them under her bed that morning, and while
she couldn't fathom how they'd gotten so far into her apartment as to
be under her bed, she knew they had to be Mackenzie's missing pair.

Mackenzie, after all of her usual lock sliding and chair scraping,
opened the door. "Hey, Sunna," she said quietly. She looked like she
hadn't slept since the last time Sunna saw her.

"Hey. You okay?"

Mackenzie shook her head.

"Yeah, same." She cleared her throat. "Oh. Hey. Question: Are
these yours?"

Mackenzie brightened and gathered the shoes in her arms like they were a lost puppy. "Thank you! I was wondering where they'd gone." She gave Sunna a funny look. "Where'd you find them?"

"Um . . . well. Okay, so this is weird—"

She was interrupted by the sound of feet stomping down the stairs from Maude's apartment, a methodical BANG! BANG! BANG!— warning shots. Sunna instinctually turned to go back into her suite, but Maude's door flung open before she could get there.

"Where are they?" Maude said, seething.

Mackenzie had been staring down at her shoes in confusion, but now she looked up at Maude with the same expression. "What?" She held the shoes up tentatively, as though to say, *Here they are.*

"Not your stupid shoes," said Maude. "I'm not talking about your stupid shoes. I want to know where *they* are."

"Who?" Sunna had thought Maude might ask what they were doing in her apartment the night before or what they'd done to make the ghosts so angry. This question made no sense.

"You know very well what I mean. You know *very well.*"

Sunna looked at Mackenzie to see if she knew very well what Maude meant, but Mackenzie was looking at Sunna for the same answer. Sunna tried again. "Like, you mean where are the ghosts?"

"I mean where are my *rings*. I mean what did you do with my *rings*." The skin around Maude's mouth was twitching like electricity coursed through it, and she sounded like she was going to cry, an event for which Sunna was entirely unprepared. "I mean where are they, and what did you do with them. Where *are* they? And what did you *do* with them?"

She was so angry she was delirious. She only really had one thing to say, but she couldn't stop talking so she just said it over and over.

"Your rings?"

"*Yes*, my rings! What did you—"

153

Mackenzie dropped her shoes and stepped forward, speaking in her soft, motherly way, her voice controlled and comforting, like she was going to start stroking Maude's hair. "Maude, I am so, so incredibly sorry we came into your place last night, but we definitely didn't touch your rings . . ."

Maude, hands now trembling violently, shoved her purse into Mackenzie's hands. "Open it!" She screeched. "Open it and look in there!" When Mackenzie didn't open the bag right away, Maude pushed it into her belly, hard. "I said *open* it! Get the ring box!"

Obediently, Mackenzie unzipped the purse and retrieved the ring box Maude had shown them in the coffee shop.

"*Open* it!" Maude cried again, grabbing her bag back so quickly that Mackenzie almost dropped the box.

Mackenzie obeyed, cracking open the small gray box to reveal the three shiny rings. Maude's jaw dropped as though someone had reached out and unhinged it. She snatched the box from Mackenzie's hands and held it close to her face, unable to believe what she was seeing. "They . . . they were *gone* . . . ," she said. "Last night, they were gone." She searched Mackenzie's face and then Sunna's, her mouth still slack, her eyes still furious and wild. "How did you do this?" She was yelling now, waving the ring box around. The largest ring fell to the ground, and she scrambled to pick it up, like she was worried that Sunna or Mackenzie would dive after it. "How did you do this? Do you go into my house all the time? Do I have *any* privacy at *all*?"

Sunna realized that Mackenzie was looking to her for help, but she didn't know what to do either. "Just the once," she whispered.

Maude shoved the ring into the box, snapping it shut and pushing it back into her purse. "Oh good!" she cried. "Just the once! You just broke into my apartment and stole my wedding rings just the one time. That's great. So then tell me how you returned them? Hmm? You didn't have to break in again to do that?"

Sunna shook her head again; it was all she could think to do. Maude straightened up, folding her hands in front of her. "You may have returned the rings, but I saw you there last night, and it would be so stupid of you to pretend like I didn't. I know it was you, even if I don't know how, and my question is *why*? Why would you invade my privacy like that?"

"I'm sorry, Maude," said Sunna. "There was that noise again, and it was keeping me awake. I needed to know what it was. And you shouldn't get mad at Mack; she didn't even *want* to—"

Maude cut her off, staring at Mackenzie. "Not *wanting* to do something is not the same as not having *done* it in the first place, and I reserve every *right* to be *mad at Mack*." She turned her direct gaze back on Sunna. "And I have told you what that noise *was* and what it *is*, over and over, and if you're not going to believe me, that's *fine*. But it doesn't give you the right to come into my house when I'm not there. Or when I am there. Or ever."

"Why weren't *you* there?" asked Sunna. She knew she shouldn't say anything.

"*How?*" shouted Maude, droplets of spit visible in a beam of light shining through the window. "How, exactly, is that any of your business? How, Sunna? Tell me. You don't break into someone's house and then have the *gall* to ask where they were when you were breaking into their house!"

"We should go," said Mackenzie. "It's time to go."

"Oh, I'm not going anywhere with you two," said Maude. "I just came down to say this: stay out of my apartment, or I will call the police. I'm not even sure I'm not going to call the police about last night. I should. I want to. It honestly just . . . seems like . . . a lot of work . . . but I *am* getting a new lock on this door!" She started flinging her hands at them. "I hope the ghosts eat you, or haunt you, or cut you up, or whatever exactly it is that ghosts do to people they hate!" She turned and slammed her door; they heard the sound of the dead bolt and her feet marching to the top floor in muted exclamation points. Mackenzie and Sunna looked at each other.

"She was smoking," Mackenzie mumbled, rubbing her forehead.

"Just now?"

"No. Last night. When she came back in, she had her jacket over her nightgown and a carton of cigarettes."

"Oh. I guess I didn't notice. I was too busy being chased by a pack of ghosts and a crazy old woman. And I'm not even sure who was scarier," Sunna said. She felt stupid. Smoking. Obviously. And even if she hadn't been, Maude had a point. It really wasn't any of Sunna's business why a grown woman—a stranger, basically—wasn't in her bed in the middle of the night. Sunna wanted to pull her coat over her head. "You hit her," she said. Suddenly, this was hilarious.

"Yeah." Mackenzie covered her face with both hands, and at first Sunna thought she was crying. Her breath came out in muffled gasps. "I didn't mean to," she said. Her hands moved to her mouth, and Sunna saw that her eyes were full of tears. She was giggling hysterically.

Sunna started laughing, too, more at Mackenzie than at what Mackenzie had done. Poor Maude; hopefully she couldn't hear them. "I'm surprised she didn't say anything about that. I mean. Breaking and entering is one thing, but then add *assault*—"

"Sunna!" Mackenzie started hiccupping, still trying to suppress her laughter. "You're terrible." She covered her eyes again. "*I'm* terrible. Are you coming to the shop today?"

"I thought I might. I have a book to read, might as well. Especially after, you know . . ." They both looked up instinctually and then back at each other. Mackenzie nodded.

"Okay." Mackenzie shook her car keys. "Let's go, I guess."

MENDACIOUS
MACKENZIE

Sunna

The ride to the coffee shop was quiet without Maude. Mackenzie had
the radio tuned to the CBC, loud enough to hear bits of a satirical news
show but not loud enough to follow the segments. Sunna recognized
the voice of a man she'd known back in Toronto, a friend of a friend
she saw at parties every once in a while. He'd been so excited to land
this gig back then. Sunna had been mildly jealous but consoled herself
with the thought that one day she'd be part of more "important" things
than a half-hour comedy show on the CBC.

She changed the channel to a local country station, where a reporter
was talking about those stupid bomb threats again. She spun the volume dial down. Mackenzie glanced at her quizzically. "I knew that guy
back home," she said. "The one on the CBC."

"He was a jerk, or . . . ?"

"Yeah. Such a jerk."

But no one would ever describe him as a jerk. He was exactly as
he sounded on the radio—kind and funny. He was successful. Sunna
was bitter. That was all. She stared at the passing flagstaffs as they drove

over the Albert Memorial Bridge. The sky was blue. The weather was nice. Sunna was bitter.

A man was sitting on the sidewalk outside Paper Cup when they pulled up. He was grizzled and old with long scraggly facial hair, slumped over an ancient acoustic guitar. Only when Sunna opened the car door did she realize the man wasn't actually playing anything. He wore clumpy woolen mittens that would've made it impossible to play a guitar, but he moved his right hand up and down in a simulation of strumming and his left along the fretboard, back and forth, back and forth. He looked up at Sunna with a strange expression as she and Mackenzie approached his spot by the pay phone. He nodded as Sunna stepped onto the sidewalk. "Hello," he said to her. His voice was all used up and barely made a noise. "Lovely day, isn't it?"

"Yeah, it is," Sunna said nervously.

He scoffed at her. "No it's not," he said. And he went back to pretending to play his guitar.

~

The women found a table, and Mackenzie pulled out her phone.

"What're you up to?" asked Sunna, digging through her tote bag for a book.

"I'm kinda checking to see if there are other places available to rent in the area," Mackenzie said.

"Yeah? Had it with the ghost thing?"

"Is that a stupid reason to move? I don't even know if I believe in ghosts, but last night was so creepy. There *is* something up there, and I don't want to live with it. What're you reading?"

"This, I guess." Sunna held a book up, and Mackenzie briefly studied the cover, the way one does when they've asked a question to which they didn't actually care to know the answer. "Wait, what . . . look at this! This page has been torn right out!" Sunna leafed through a few pages until she found another half-missing page. "Someone's gone through and ripped out a bunch of pages! This is a library book—they better not charge me for this." She threw the book down on the table. "That sucks. I swear, if I have to pay fines . . ."

Mackenzie frowned sympathetically. "I'm sure they'll believe you if you tell them it was like that when you got it."

"I really hope so . . ." She put the book down in disgust and looked over at Mackenzie, who was back to scrolling through listings on her phone. She hadn't been able to stop thinking about her strange visit with Maude and all her outrageous theories. Mackenzie wasn't a murderer—that was obvious. Not that Sunna thought every murderer necessarily looked like a murderer. Mackenzie just looked—and more importantly, acted—emphatically *not* like a murderer. She was too easygoing and kind to be a killer. She spoke of her sister with such fondness. Besides, if she had killed her twin sister, why on earth would she bring the whole thing up in the first place? Why would she even link herself to that particular family?

But then, there were those newspaper articles. The picture of Mackenzie in those magazines with Kate's name in the byline. There were those twins who disappeared the same night, from the same town.

"So, Mack," she said, trying to act casual, "Maude thinks you, like, lied about your missing twin, or whatever."

Mackenzie's head snapped up, her face white. "What?"

"Yeah . . ." Sunna hadn't expected that reaction. She wasn't sure she'd expected any reaction, other than maybe incredulous laughter. Something to indicate that not only was Maude wrong, she was also ridiculous. Crazy. Delusional. But this reaction was baffling. Mackenzie seemed . . . caught.

"She said that?" Mackenzie's cheeks were red. "Why? Why would she think that?"

"Oh, I have no idea," said Sunna dismissively.

Mackenzie stared her down. "What did she say, Sunna? What's her big theory? You made it sound the other night like you didn't let her explain anything to you, like you just told her to take her papers and get lost, but you didn't, did you? What did she show you? What does she think happened?"

Sunna pressed her lips together. "Mackenzie, I d—I don't . . . I don't really remember, exactly."

Mackenzie shook her head and waited.

"Like. Okay, so she thinks you're someone named Kate? Kate Simons. Or Kate W—"

"Shut up, shut up."

Sunna flinched. "Mackenzie, I—"

"No, no, sorry." Mackenzie was distracted by someone who had just entered the coffee shop. "Look. I can't believe it." She chewed her thumbnail. "I can't believe he's here. It was him. I can't believe it was him. I don't think I wanted it to be him, after all."

There was a young guy standing by the door. He had a short neat haircut and a short neat beard. *He* was short and neat. He was holding hands with a female beardless version of himself—shorter still, and, arguably, a bit neater. She was telling a story, gesticulating without letting go of his hand, and he looked at her with shining eyes, throwing his head back in laughter. They look so . . . *neat*, Sunna thought. *Short.* They were a couple with no other adjectives.

He was taking in the space—the artwork on the back wall, the menu board, the baristas behind the counter. Then he froze; he'd seen Mackenzie, but he looked away quickly.

"What do I do, Sunna?"

"Is that what's-his-face?"

"Jared. I can't believe he's here. Does this mean he wrote the letter? Why would he bring *her*?"

"You know her?"

"No, I just mean . . . like, if he wrote the letter, if he wanted to talk to me and explain where he went, why would he bring along his girl-friend or whoever she is? Do I look sweaty?" She did, but Sunna shook her head. "What if he brought her as part of his explanation? Sunna!" Mackenzie grabbed Sunna's wrist. "What if he just comes over and is like, '*This* is why I ghosted on you.'" Mackenzie gestured beside her at an invisible girlfriend.

"Or," said Sunna quietly, sitting back in her seat so that her wrist glided out from under Mackenzie's hand, "he just lives in the same small city as you, and it's actually kind of amazing you haven't run into each other before this?"

"Maybe he didn't see me," said Mackenzie, shrinking into her seat.

"Nah, he did. I saw him see you."

"What do you mean? Like, he *looked* at me?" Mackenzie's voice was loud.

"Shh, yeah. Calm down. You should go over and say hi."

"What?"

"Well . . . what if he did write the letter? Or, you know, *so what* if he didn't? Either way, this is what we're here for. Closure. Maude's not get-ting hers; I'm probably not getting mine . . . it's all yours, Mack. Show me we haven't just wasted however-many days of our lives with this."

"That's way easier said than done."

"No, it's not. You're brave."

"Am not."

"Then act like you are. Pretend you're Maude. Channel Maude. Pretend you're stomping over there to tear a strip off of him. Pretend you're Maude and he's me." Sunna was cracking up, and Mackenzie couldn't help but smile back. "Go!" Sunna gave her a gentle shove, and Mackenzie was on her feet, shaking like a leaf.

THE DOCTOR FIANCÉE

Mackenzie

"Jared?" Mackenzie could not, in a million years, "channel Maude" as Sunna had suggested. But she did feel emboldened at the thought of Sunna watching from their table.

"Mackenzie!" Jared had the nerve to act surprised. "Is that actually you?"

Ugh.

"In the flesh," said Mackenzie, trying to stay cool. She was not the kind of person who normally said things like "in the flesh." This felt like such a big mistake. What was she doing? He hadn't come here to see her; it was blindingly obvious. He had come here to be alone with this girl whose hand he held. To *date* her. Mackenzie was interrupting her ex-boyfriend on his date. She tucked her hands into the kangaroo pouch on her sweatshirt and popped her knee to the side nonchalantly. She didn't want to channel mousey, disheveled Maude; she wanted to channel some A-list celebrity "caught" leaving the gym in sweatpants by the paparazzi but still looking 100 percent magazine ready. "Saw you come in and thought I should say hi. What're you doing in town?" She flashed a smile. *You have super nice teeth, Mackenzie! Show him your super nice teeth! He liked your smile; he said it a thousand times when you were dating.*

Then she thought about how she wouldn't like it if she were on a date with her boyfriend and his weird ex-girlfriend came around showing off her super nice teeth. She shut her mouth.

"Oh!" said Jared. "I live here now! I'm taking a business course." This kind of measured, forced enthusiasm was strange on Jared, who had been so confident and uninhibited when she'd known him before. But then, present-day Jared didn't seem to have much in common with the Jared she'd dated. That Jared had unruly hair and wore band T-shirts and ripped jeans. It was obvious that present-day Jared controlled everything: his excitement, his hair, his clothes. He had it all whipped into shape. Gelled. Ironed.

"Business? You're not . . . still doing the music thing?"

"Ha!" He looked embarrassed. He glanced sideways at the girl, who seemed surprised at Mackenzie's question. "Forgot about that. The band. Yeah, we broke up a long time ago. Cody got engaged, and his fiancé hated us."

The girl gave him a smile that said *I have so many questions*, and Mackenzie marveled at the fact that Jared, who had never been able to go more than five minutes without mentioning his band, had apparently stopped mentioning it altogether.

"Nah," he went on, "Lauren's still got a few more years of school left here, and then she'll have to go wherever they send her for her residency. She's gonna be a *doctor* . . ." He lifted her hand, still clasped in his, when he said her name, and gazed at her with admiration. It was as though he'd forgotten for a moment who he was talking to and then abruptly remembered again. He looked up at his discarded nondoctor, nonshort, nonneat nongirlfriend towering over him. "Oh, uh . . . have you actually met Lauren?"

Mackenzie shook her head. She wanted to say, "When and why and where and how would I have 'actually met Lauren,' Jared?" But she didn't say anything. Just shook her head. Just smiled with her lips closed.

"Oh, well then, Lauren, this is Mackenzie. We were friends in— when? High school? Sometime in high school. *Way* back." Jared pumped his head up and down like a moron, chewing on the inside of his lip. Mackenzie pictured Maude hovering over Jared's shoulder, saying, *You're all of twenty-two years old, stupid boy. You don't have a way* back. "And Mackenzie, this is Lauren. My fiancée. We're getting married."

The imaginary, hovering Maude said, *As most fiancées tend to do*, but Mackenzie was stunned. She looked at Lauren's left hand. Sure enough, there it was. It was huge and shiny, and Mackenzie briefly felt like using it to gouge out Jared's eyeballs. "Oh wow!" she said. "That's beautiful! Congrats. So exciting." *Slow down. Save some words for later.*

"Thanks," said Lauren. "And it's so nice to meet you. I keep running into people Jared knew from high school—I guess lots of people from there end up here for university, hey?"

Mackenzie nodded. "Pretty much all of us," she said, smiling.

"Same here," said Lauren. "I mean same with my town. I guess all the small towns around here just kind of funnel into the city. I don't have any friends who still live back home." Lauren was nice. Jared was acting ridiculously awkward, but of course he was. It was an awkward situation. He knew what he'd done—all the things he'd done—but it wasn't like he could apologize for them now, in front of his future doctor fiancée, who looked like she could be his younger sister.

That was it, then: this was a chance encounter and had nothing to do with the letter. Mackenzie would not be getting any closure after all; she would not know why he had disappeared. But she realized then that an explanation wouldn't help anything. That if Jared had not disappeared all at once, he would've disappeared bit by bit. This couple in front of her made sense in a way that she and Jared never had; you could tell by looking at them. Their feet and shoulders pointed toward each other. They were thrilled just to be in each other's presence. She tried to remember if Jared had ever seemed thrilled to be with her. Maybe at first? But not like this. She'd never made him laugh with his head back. He'd never introduced her to someone while naming her accomplishments, eyes shining at her like spotlights.

"So, maybe I'll see you two around," Mackenzie said, feeling shaky. "I come here all the time. Literally. I mean, I'm here every day." Was she warning Jared? *I'm here every day. Just in case you want to maybe go off and find another coffee shop to take your fiancée to.*

Jared looked relieved. "Cool," he said. "We probably will. Sometime. Nice to run into you, Kenz."

Mackenzie couldn't help but smirk at his lame attempt at casual familiarity; he'd never used that nickname before. It was a message: *We're just friends now. You have to let me go.* Condescending, but she understood.

"Cool, you too, *Jer.*" She had a message for him too. Then she turned her back on the couple and headed to the table where Sunna was pretending to be engrossed in her novel—but as soon as Mackenzie sat, she leaned in. "So? Did he write it?"

"Nope," said Mackenzie. "Turns out he's happily engaged. That's good. I'm happy for him." Her voice sounded funny; she hoped Sunna didn't notice.

"You're such a weird, good person, Mackenzie."

Mackenzie almost laughed. Her hands were still shaking, maybe even more than they had been before. Pressure was building behind her eyes, and she was sure her face was either white as paper or red as blood—was Sunna so self-absorbed that she didn't notice? She took in a big breath and slowly let it out through her nose.

"Huh. Now would you look at *this.*" Sunna pointed behind Mackenzie.

Maude was standing in the doorway, scanning the room. Something was wrong; her mouth was hanging open, her eyes huge, her forehead glistening with sweat. She looked desperate. But once she spotted

Mackenzie and Sunna, she began to barge through the coffee shop like someone cutting through a jungle with a machete.

Sunna braced for an onslaught of screeching and screaming, but when Maude arrived at their table, she said nothing, just stood over them, sweating and gasping for breath.

"Maude, are you okay?" asked Mackenzie. "What happened to you? You look—"

"Like I've seen a ghost?" said Maude.

Mackenzie paused. "Sure?"

"I have. It was in my kitchen."

Mackenzie looked at Sunna, waiting for her to burst out laughing. But she didn't.

Maude was growing impatient.

"I saw a ghost in my kitchen," said Maude.

"A ghost . . . ly person?" said Mackenzie.

"Not a *person*! Not a *ghostly* person! A ghost!" cried Maude. "A ghost! A *ghost*!" She was shrieking, and everyone in the coffee shop stared. Mackenzie realized with dismay that the staring didn't faze her anymore.

Maude sat and dropped her head into her outstretched hands. "Not a person," she mumbled into her fingers.

"How do you know it was . . . how do you know it wasn't . . ." Mackenzie was fickle on this subject, and she knew it; she believed in the ghosts except when she didn't. It was a belief based entirely on feelings. "Could someone have broken into our house? That would explain the noises in the attic. Or could we have something, you know, living in the attic? Like a wild animal? Raccoons? Do raccoons live in attics? Or . . . rabbits?"

"Rabbits?" said Sunna.

"I don't know," said Mackenzie. "Maybe? Something that jumps a lot . . . something that just sounds loud in the middle of the night or because of the acoustics of an old house or . . . I don't know." She felt stupid.

"It wasn't rabbits! It wasn't a person! I'm not a delusional old *lady*—I'm not *crazy*—I saw a *ghost*!" Veins pulsed in Maude's forehead as she spoke.

Much to Mackenzie's surprise, Sunna nodded and in a sincere tone said, "Okay, Maude, tell us everything."

KITCHEN GHOST

Mackenzie

"I went to my suite after you two left," said Maude. "And I made myself a piece of toast. For lunch." She stopped and looked at Sunna, as though Sunna might have something to say about having toast for lunch.

Sunna didn't.

"Then I went for a nap on the chesterfield. I don't know how long I was asleep—an hour? Maybe thirty minutes? I woke up and thought I'd heard something in the kitchen, but I figured I'd been imagining it, so I tried to get back to sleep. Then I heard this shuffling sound, a ripping sound, and then papers falling off my kitchen table. It made my blood run cold. It was so *loud.* You know how loud sounds are when you're in a completely empty house and you're not expecting . . . my heart started . . ." Maude laid a shaky hand on her chest and fluttered her fingers.

"So I stood up, trying not to make any noise. I thought it was an intruder. For the *life* of me, I didn't know what they'd be looking for in my apartment—you saw it yourselves. There's nothing in there! Which made me worried that they just wanted to *kill* somebody and had seen me sleeping on the chesterfield and knew I'd be easy to kill. And I would be. Especially since they'd done half the job just by throwing my mail on the floor.

"I walked to the kitchen doorway, quiet as I could. I was, my heart was still"—she fluttered her fingers again—"and then I saw *her. It.* Standing at the kitchen table, my mail on the floor at her feet. She'd ripped it up. The flyers. My, my, my g-g-grocery store flyers . . ."

"Saw who?"

"The ghost!" Maude yelled. "She was terrifying; she had gray skin and bright-white hair and angry, terrible eyes. She just stood there, staring at me." Maude had tears in her eyes. She was looking at the ceiling, like the ghost was up there now.

"What did you do?" asked Mackenzie, also looking at the ceiling, fully expecting, for a moment, to see something up there.

"I ran to the stairs. And then I had a moment of, of, I don't know, bravery or *insanity*, and I turned back to see if she was still there. She wasn't. She was just gone. I have to tell you, that was more frightening than if she'd still been there. Because then I expected to turn and see her blocking the doorway, like in a movie. But she wasn't there either. And before I knew what I was doing, I was running from room to room looking behind and underneath everything. But she was gone. *It. It* was gone. *Vanished.*" For someone who had been so adamant that there were ghosts in the old house, Maude seemed awfully surprised to have actually seen one.

"Okay," said Sunna. "So we have a weird old homeless lady living in the attic."

"*What?*" said Maude. "No, we do not. Were you even *listening* to what I was saying?"

"Maude," said Sunna, "it's not that I don't believe you saw something. I totally do. But I don't think it was a ghost. I know you believe in these things. I don't. I just don't. Whatever's up there freaks me out. It's scary to have anything in your house, even if it's something as benign as a spider. A whole person? Forget it. I'm glad I'm not living in your apartment; I can't imagine how much that must mess with your head. But ghosts aren't real, and that lady you saw is totally just some rando living in our attic. That's how she disappeared. She went up the stairs. Shut the door behind her. We should call the landlord. Or even the police. I don't know why we haven't already. Maybe because it hadn't occurred to me that it might be a person . . . I think I still thought it was you somehow. Or animals. In the middle of the night, the ghost thing seemed almost plausible. But now? Now I just think we should call Larry and tell him to clear out the attic."

"I'm not against calling Larry," Maude said. "But he's not going to find anything up there. He's not going to find a-a-a"—she gasped for breath—"a *rando*. We don't have *randos*; we have ghosts. And Larry is very hard to get ahold of. He rarely answers his phone."

Sunna tipped her head to the side. "Uh—"

Maude cut her off. "It was a ghost, Sunna. You know how I know? Because I *recognized* her. And she's dead."

"You *recognized* her?"

"Yes. I recognized her."

"From where?" Mackenzie had goose bumps on her bare arms. She wondered if ghosts stayed put when they haunted houses—or if this particular one had followed Maude to the coffee shop. Was she sitting at their table, listening? "You . . . you knew . . . *it*?" Mackenzie whispered.

"No." Maude turned her attention to Mackenzie, seemingly glad that someone was taking her seriously. "I didn't know her when she was alive, but I've seen her before. In the newspaper. In the *obituaries*."

"Maude." Sunna shook her head.

"It's true!"

"Well, I'm going to call the landlord at least," said Sunna, irritation creeping back into her voice. Mackenzie had wondered how long it would take for Sunna to lose patience with Maude. "I need to call him about a broken window in my place anyway. And he probably has a key to the attic. He can go see if someone is squatting up there. Or animals."

Maude grunted. "I know the difference between a woman—ghost or not—and a bunny rabbit."

"I know you do, Maude. But you said yourself you were sleeping right before you saw the woman in your kitchen. You might have heard a noise in the attic when you were half-asleep and 'seen' her before you'd fully woken up. Especially since she looked like someone you'd seen before, even if just in a newspaper picture. That's what I think. That makes sense. We have animals living in the attic, and you dreamt a lady in your kitchen."

Maude still looked frantic and afraid, but her face was now also pinched with anger. She grunted again. "Oh! But I can show you the ripped papers. And maybe it took my rings that night. If neither of you did."

Mackenzie remembered her missing shoes. "And my shoes," she said to Sunna. "Where did you say you found those again?"

Sunna started to reply, but then she stopped. "My books," she said under her breath. She picked the book up from the table and leafed through to one of the ripped pages. She pulled another book from her tote bag and flipped through. More torn pages. She shook her head. "I have the landlord's phone number in my phone, but what's his name again?"

"Larry," said Mackenzie.

"He doesn't *answer* his phone," said Maude. "I've just said that."

Larry answered on the first ring. Sunna spoke curtly into the phone, frowning at whatever he said. She walked away from the table and stuck a finger in her other ear to block out the noise from the café. When she came back, she flopped into her chair and rolled her eyes. "Had to basically twist his arm off, but he'll come over tonight around seven. He's kind of a weirdo, hey?"

"Be nice," said Mackenzie.

FACE TO "FACE" WITH A GHOST

Larry

Larry could hardly believe his luck when he answered the phone and heard Sunna's voice on the line. He'd been expecting Maude again, and Sunna's voice was like a reward. "Hi, Larry," she said. "This is Sunna. I live in one of your buildings."

Like she thought he was someone who might own more than one building. Like she thought he'd ever forget who she was even if he had a thousand tenants in a thousand buildings. He tried not to stutter.

"H-h-hi, Sunna. Uh, yeah, sure, I remember you. Uh. What, what can I do for you?"

"Okay, so I'm here with the other two tenants, and we've been hearing a lot of noise coming from the attic. We'd like you to come over and see if there's some kind of animal infestation or something. It's quite loud, and we're concerned. Maude—the lady on the top floor—she thinks there might be people up there. Or, well, she thought she saw a woman in her apartment anyway. I kind of"—she lowered her voice— "think she imagined it? But still. I can tell it's upsetting her. So."

The ghosts. The skin on his arms bubbled up. Would she think he was crazy if he told her it was ghosts? Probably. He didn't want that. Was he brave enough to go up there, after having been expressly forbidden in his aunt's will? *Nope.*

"Y-y-you know w-what, Sunna, I, uh, I actually don't have access to the, uh, attic."

"What do you mean, you don't have access? This is your house, isn't it?"

"Well. I mean. I don't have . . . the key? The door's—locked—there, and—"

"So get someone to come open it. Take the door off. Break it down. Pick the lock." She paused. "This is *your house*," she said again.

He laughed. He wanted to tell her: *This isn't my house or your house or any living person's house.* "Well," he began. "Yes, but actually . . ." He coughed. "So my aunt left me this house when she died, and in her will it specifically says I can't go into the attic."

"Why?"

"Well. It didn't say. It just says I can't. The will had a bunch of rules like that. Like, I can't, I can't plant, uh, flowers in the uh, the uh, the—"

"I'm sorry, Larry, but it's not like she's going to find out. She's dead. Who's going to tell on you? What's she gonna do about it?"

"That, uh, that's true, but . . ." How did you admit to someone—especially another adult, especially an adult you had a crush on—that you believed in ghosts? And not only that you believed in them but that you owned a house full of them and were too cowardly to disobey their rules? The answer: you didn't.

"I'm sorry, Sunna. I'll look into it." He wouldn't. But he would say he would, and then he would say he had. And then maybe he'd ask her out. Or maybe she'd ask him out—she seemed assertive and confident—at which point he would, of course, say yes.

"When?"

"Uh, today. Uh, seven."

"Okay."

She hung up without saying thank you or goodbye. He frowned at the phone. At first he'd thought maybe she was oblivious, that her flippant disregard for him came from shyness, like his, and she didn't know how she came across. But now he realized she was actually just rude. Disappointing.

~

Rude or not, Sunna was Larry's tenant. It was his responsibility to at least make her feel heard, to show up when she asked him to show up.

It was 7:10 p.m. He was late, as usual, but he showed. Sunna opened the door. Maude was there, too, as sour and shriveled as the last time he'd seen her. He felt awkward seeing these women. Did they know they were being investigated? Larry had been asked not to mention the visit from the officers, so maybe they didn't. They hadn't asked anything that gave him much of a sense of what was going on, just wanted to know if the women had jobs, where they hung out, that kind of thing. The police must have been having a hard time getting ahold of them.

The other girl, Mackenzie, was not with them, which was too bad. She was the nicest one. He smiled at the women; they did not smile back. "Hi," he said.

"Hello, Larry," Maude said. "You're late."

"I'm sorry," he said.

"It's fine," she said in a voice that also said "It's not fine" at the same time. "Follow me."

Maude creaked up the stairs, Larry followed obediently, and Sunna came last, her steps almost silent. Larry heard her, though, loud as crashing cymbals behind him. He'd decided earlier that he didn't much care for the rude woman in 2139B, beautiful or not, but now he was in her presence and thought he could give her another chance. After all, some people made terrible impressions one through three and ended up making a very good fourth impression. He'd heard of it happening.

They entered Maude's suite and stood in front of the locked attic door. The two women looked at Larry expectantly. He smiled and shrugged his lanky shoulders. "So, like I said, I don't, uh, I don't have a key or anything."

"We could try a credit card," said Sunna. She nodded at the door.

Larry felt stuck. What if a credit card was all it took? He hadn't thought they were going to watch him and had no idea what to do if it worked. There was no way he was going up there. His plan had been to stand in front of the door for a while, then *say* he'd gone up and found nothing. That plan would not work with these two women watching him.

He slid a card out of his wallet, cringing when he saw he'd chosen his Blockbuster card. He tried to obscure it in his palm so Sunna wouldn't see and made a pathetic attempt at sliding the card into the crack in the door. When nothing happened, he tried to look disappointed.

"What else did you bring?" said Sunna. "We could call a locksmith."

"Do you have a hex key?" asked Maude.

"What? A what? No. I don't . . . I don't think so?" said Larry.

Maude scowled.

"Whoa. Did you hear that?" Larry backed away from the door. *A footstep.* He looked at Maude and then Sunna. They both seemed uneasy, but neither moved.

Neither of them coughed, either, but he heard a cough nevertheless. "Did you hear *that*?" he asked in a low whisper.

Sunna nodded.

"That's not a rabbit," Maude whispered.

Larry couldn't help but snort. Of course it wasn't a rabbit. There was clearly a person just on the other side of the door, so close that if there hadn't been a door there, he could have reached out and touched them.

A person . . . or a ghost. Did ghosts cough? They probably couldn't *catch* colds, but maybe if they'd had one when they died, it just stuck around forever? Who knew how ghosts worked?

"Who's there?" yelled Sunna.

Larry felt the blood drain from his head.

"Seriously!" shouted Sunna. She leaned forward and thumped on the door once with a flat hand. "I'm calling the police, right now!" She wasn't bluffing; she was tapping away on her phone, dialing a number much longer than 911. He wanted to say, "You could just call 911," but he couldn't say anything. He felt like he'd swallowed his tongue.

The door began to heave toward them, as though it was being kicked from behind. Maude and Larry froze, but Sunna just looked annoyed. *"Stop that!"* she yelled. "Not kidding—I'm seriously calling the police, like, right now!" She held the phone up to her ear.

A thudding sound came from above, a unified stomp. Larry worried the roof would burst open and something supernatural would come flooding out. What would it look like? Would it be like bees pouring from a broken hive?

"Hello," yelled Sunna into her phone; Larry couldn't decide if she was actually irritated or if she was just masking her fear with irritation. "Yeah, can you hear that? That's in my house, in my attic . . . No, I don't know what it is . . . Yeah, I'd like for someone to come check it out. I think I have people living up there . . . Yeah—I mean, I'm renting. Yeah, he is here with me . . . He doesn't know what it is either . . ." She gave the address and her name and phone number and even engaged in a bit of small talk, much to Larry's chagrin. And then: "Thank you." She hung up, nodded, and screamed at the ceiling, "The police are coming!"

The pounding stopped, all at once. The three adults looked up at the ceiling. Larry wanted nothing more than to run out of the house and never look back. Let the house rot. He realized he'd wrapped his spindly arms around himself, gripping so hard his knuckles were white, in a silly-looking, self-comforting stance. He straightened his back and lowered his hands to his sides, a movement that took an extreme amount of effort.

"Aren't you supposed to stay on the line?"

"I don't know. They didn't say to. Maybe that's just with 911."

The trio was silent—Maude still staring upward, Sunna fiddling with her phone, Larry drumming his fingers against the sides of his legs. The situation had moved from terror to—to what? Comedy? It was a little funny. What was funny about it? Nothing. Nothing at all. And yet, Larry started to laugh. Sunna rolled her pretty eyes at him and then back to the screen of her phone, but Maude locked him in her piercing, hawklike gaze. "What," she spat, "is so funny?"

"Nothing," he said. But he had a hard time keeping errant giggles from escaping. He tried to smile at Sunna, but she gave him a cautioning look. He now understood that song about laughing at funerals. He understood the word *hysteria*. He worried he might start crying next, and if the laughing thing was any indication, he wouldn't be able to control that either.

There was a faint knocking sound, but this time it was coming from down the stairs instead of the attic. "The police!" he exclaimed, and there was more unwelcome giggling.

"Let them in," said Maude, and he could never remember afterward if she'd actually said *idiot!* out loud or just implied it so strongly that he thought he'd heard it spoken.

"Sure," said Larry. He practically fell down the stairs trying to get away from these rude, unhappy women and their spiritual cohabitants.

A pair of officers greeted him warily when he answered the door, and he realized that he was officially trapped. He'd have to show them upstairs and let them break that door down and stand by as they unleashed angry spirits on an otherwise very pleasant neighborhood.

"Thanks so much for coming," Larry said brightly, racking his brain for a way out. "I'm the landlord. My tenant called you. Called your people. Called your . . . uh . . . dis . . . patch . . . person?"

"May we come in?" the taller of the two asked.

"Abso-lutely, please do," he said, stepping to the side and motioning up the stairs. He heard Maude and Sunna greet the officers and made his way slowly after them. *Now what?*

Everyone was waiting for him when at last he stepped into Maude's suite.

"You don't have a key?" asked one of the policemen.

"No," he said. "Uh . . ." He cleared his throat. "So, in the will—oh, uh, okay, so I inherited this house from my aunt, first of all. And—" He had so much saliva all of a sudden. He tried to swallow but couldn't get it down his throat, which suddenly felt about as wide as a stir stick. He swallowed several times, uncomfortably, and was aware he looked incredibly guilty. Of what? Who knew at this point? Did these policemen know about the bomb threat investigation? Not that it concerned him. It was just another bizarre wrinkle in this strange visit. "I inherited it from my aunt, and in her will, she said I couldn't go into the attic. She didn't leave a key or anything. So." He nodded. "So. Locked up! Tight as a, uh, drum." He felt some of the stray saliva dribble out of his mouth, and embarrassed, he slurped it back in, wiping his face with the back of his hand. Maude and Sunna cast looks at each other, as though saying things about him telepathically. Terrible things.

"Can you break it down?" asked Sunna.

"Uh"—the policemen looked at Larry—"I'm as curious as anyone, but . . . well, she specifically said that if I wanted to keep the house—"

"Are you hiding something up there?" asked one of the officers.

"No!" said Larry. "No, I'm just as curious as anyone . . ." He trailed off. What if they found something awful up there? A body or something? Lots of bodies? One thing was certain: if he protested too much now, it would look bad for him later on. "Yeah, you can, uh, you can definitely break it down if you want. I mean, that would, uh, that would be good. Great. Definitely do that." He noticed Sunna looking at him with something like disgust. The way he had found it hard to stop giggling earlier, he now found it hard to stop talking. "In fact," he babbled, "I've kind of always wanted to see the police break down a door. Just like in the movies. Let's get this party started!"

Everyone was ignoring him now. The shorter officer stepped forward and pounded on the door. "Hello?" he called. "Is anyone up there? This is the police. If anyone is up there, you need to come down and unlock this door right now."

There was, of course, no answer. Larry waited for the pounding to start up again in the attic, but it didn't.

"You're quite sure you heard someone up there?" asked one of the officers.

All three nodded emphatically. Maude crossed her arms. "I'd venture to say we heard at least ten . . . people . . . up there."

"We'll go up and check it out for you," said the tall officer. The other one stepped forward and jiggled the handle. He leaned into it to see if it would give, but the lock was sturdy. He pulled a tool out of what seemed like midair and effortlessly jimmied the lock. Larry was impressed. The door swung inward.

THE UTTER HUMILIATION!

Mackenzie

"Thank ye, matey." Mackenzie mumbled her lines at the debit machine and adjusted her tricorn, trying not to make eye contact with the girl standing in front of her. "Kindly walk the plank to the pickup window and"—she sighed heavily—"*ahoy*, there yer pizza will be."

"Pardon?" said the girl, who was wearing a miniskirt and so much eyeliner that her little eyes looked like black cracks in the middle of her claylike face.

"Pickup window's over there." Mackenzie pointed.

The girl wandered off in that direction, looking confused.

"What ails ye, Boatswain?" Randall was in annoyingly high spirits today, standing too close to everyone and talking too loudly, his breath reeking of alcohol. "Ye look to be in Davy's grip! Please, lassie, don't ferget to talk like a buccaneer! It's in th' job descriptarrrrrr . . ." He surveyed his restaurant proudly like it was a ship. "And ye needs t' get t' work swabbing the poop. *Ahoy!*" He was gone as quickly as he'd come, sweeping flamboyantly into the kitchen, yelling happily at one of the line cooks in pirate gibberish. Mackenzie stared after him until she realized another customer was standing in front of her.

"Ahoy there, matey," said Mackenzie, sounding more like a sad robot than a pirate.

"Uh, ahoy," said a familiar voice.

Her head snapped up, and her cheeks turned bright red. "What can I get for you today?" she asked, abandoning her lines, lowering her voice so Randall wouldn't hear.

"Oh! Hey, Mackenzie! I didn't recognize you at first. You're all pirate-y." Jared stood before her, just as neat and clean looking as the last time, but without the doctor-fiancée affixed to his hand.

"Yep." She wanted to die. What was worse than running into an ex-boyfriend? Answer: running into an ex-boyfriend with a stuffed parrot Velcroed to your shoulder. There were no words for this kind of humiliation.

"I guess, you know, it's a small city. We'll probably run into each other a lot," said Jared.

Jared seemed perfectly fine with the prospect, but Mackenzie wasn't sure how to feel. It was one thing to have closure, however spotty or inadequate; it was another thing to have to see the person a lot afterward. Especially if she was going to be dressed like a pirate for some of the encounters. "Yep," she said. "Probably."

"So . . . cool." They stood there in awkward silence, and Mackenzie couldn't help but wish they had come to the restaurant together, and that she wasn't in a pirate costume, and that she was going to be a doctor someday. "Well. I just want a pepperoni pizza. A deep-dish one."

"Okay," said Mackenzie. She hid her hands behind the cash register so Jared wouldn't see they'd started shaking again. What was wrong with her?

"I think you mean pepp-*arrrr*-oni, young lad!" Randall's voice boomed from behind Mackenzie, and she was so frazzled that she jumped and banged her hip on the cash register, which jangled and beeped, spitting out the cash tray and spilling quarters on the floor. She stared down at the pile of change, clutching her hip, her face blazing.

Jared barely acknowledged the display. He was distracted by Randall, the swaggering pirate who swung one boot way up onto the counter and struck a buccaneer pose too stretched and unstable to look natural or comfortable. "Pick up those doubloons, matey! And get this lad his pepp-arrrrrrrrr-oni!" Randall clapped Mackenzie on the back and lowered his voice. "Did ye forget, lassie? Yer a buccaneer! Don't forget, or ye'll dance the hempen jig!" He staggered away, and Jared and Mackenzie raised their eyebrows at one another.

Mackenzie wished he wasn't watching her kneel to the floor to retrieve the coins. A memory from a long time ago wiggled to the surface, wormlike and uncomfortable: They'd been sitting on the floor in his kitchen late at night, backs against the cool wooden cabinets, eating leftovers out of Tupperware containers. Talking.

"Jared," she'd said, "were you dating her? When it happened?" She'd never asked him that before.

He'd played it cool and pretended to be stumped. "Who?"

"You know who."

He'd been quiet for long enough that he'd answered her question. "Isn't it kind of weird to ask your boyfriend questions about his exes?"

"I don't know. I've never had a boyfriend before. *Is* it weird?" But now he'd said it out loud, too. *Exes.*

"Yeah. It's weird. It's not your business."

"You're not my business? My *sister's* not my business?"

"Your sister's not here." He'd said it angrily; he'd gone from almost whispering to almost yelling.

"Whoa. Sorry. Jared, are—are you mad?"

"At her?"

Mackenzie had set her food down on the tile. "No. I meant me. Why would you be mad at *her*?"

"For getting herself killed. For leaving me like that."

"Are you kidding me?" Mackenzie's head had swum when he'd said that. In all the weeks and months since the night her sister had disappeared, she had not even once thought to lay the blame *there*.

Jared had softened then, just enough to reassure her—or for her to reassure herself, really—that he hadn't meant it like that. "I just don't want to talk about her," he'd said finally. "It sucks, what happened."

"Well, obviously I feel the same way, but I . . . I like talking about her."

He'd looked at her with a mix of frustration and anguish. "Yeah, well. Maybe it's not all about you."

"Dance the what?" asked Jared, snapping Mackenzie back into the present.

"Uh . . ." Mackenzie stood up, put the coins back in the register, dusted off her knees. She tried to regain her composure. "The, uh, the hempen jig. He says that all the time. It's piratespeak for hanging somebody. Hemp. Ropes. And, you know, people getting hung kind of look like they're . . . dancing."

"Yeah, got it."

"So anyway. Deep-dish pep—" She looked behind her for Randall. "Pepperoni pizza. Pop?"

"No, just a cup for water, please."

Mackenzie nodded. She wanted to go back down on the floor and stay there until Jared was gone. At one point in time, she had been in love with the person in front of her—but he'd never prioritized her, never opened up to her, certainly never looked at her with pride or bragged about her to anyone. And when he was done with her, he didn't even tell her. Was it just a high school rite of passage to be so utterly infatuated with someone who didn't care about you at all? Even more humiliating: Was she just the replacement sister? The one he settled for because the one he wanted was gone? *It's not all about you.* Maybe what he'd meant was, *It's not about you at all. Any of it.*

But she was also humiliated at her present-day self, who still wanted him. Still wanted to know why he'd left her, wanted to hear him say that he missed her and wanted her back. She wanted him to explain how he could be so hung up on Tanya, could be so angry at her for "leaving" him, and then turn around and do the exact same thing to Mackenzie.

"Here," she said, handing him an empty cup. "Pop machine's over there; handle on the left for water."

He hesitated. "Thanks." Then, "Hey, Mackenzie, sorry if that was weird the other day, with, uh, my . . ." He let out a breath. "I mean. It's not like we were serious, you and me, but I didn't know if I should—you know?—get into it right then. Because it was a long time ago, and it just would've been weird, right? For Lauren? To be like, 'Oh, by the way, Mackenzie and I . . .' Ha! Mackenzie and I, I don't even know what." He laughed, and she saw him relax. "Okay, anyway, I'm going to get my"—he looked around and then leaned in conspiratorially—"pep-arrrrrrr-oni pizza. Later, Mackenzie." He did a little drum fill on the counter with his pointer fingers, looking relieved to have said what he needed to. He didn't seem to mind, or even notice, that he hadn't given her a chance to say anything back.

She tried to take stock of her feelings, but there were too many, and she was still at work.

Grant appeared at her side, like she'd summoned him. "You okay?"

"Not so much," she said, grateful to be able to say it out loud.

"Need to take a break?"

"Nah, I'm good."

"Take your break," he said, patting her lightly on her shoulder. "I got this."

∼

Slowly, the stream of customers tapered off, and Randall staggered out the door, singing at the top of his lungs. Grant left his post at the pizza ovens and leaned against the counter beside Mackenzie.

"So, who was that guy?"

Mackenzie chewed her thumbnail. "Which one?"

"The guy who threw you off so badly."

"Ex."

"Ah. You okay?"

"Yeah. It's fine."

"Okay." He looked closely at her face like he was checking to make sure she wasn't lying and cleared his throat. "Here's an awkward, possibly inappropriate, segue. I was wondering if you'd go out with me sometime. A date."

She looked at him in surprise.

"I know this super gross place with no health codes and a drunk pirate," he continued.

She laughed weakly.

He scratched his head, looking embarrassed. "I'm sorry. That was terrible timing. I was just on my way over here to say that and didn't realize I'd be following up a visit from your ex . . . but then I had this emotional momentum . . ."

"No, it's all good. Sorry, it's just . . . you know. It's just been . . . a really crazy week. Really crazy. Family stuff—you know? And then, *him*. I think I just need some time, you know?"

"Totally. No worries." He gave her a genuine smile, but she could tell he was embarrassed. He, too, was wearing a parrot and a tricorn. "I'll work on my timing and ask again later? Maybe?"

She nodded. "I'd be okay with that." She glanced around the nearly empty restaurant. A shadowy figure sat in the farthest corner booth. It was wrapped in a long coat, collar up, covering its hair, hat pulled low over its face.

Grant followed her gaze. "That person's been here for an hour, at least," he said. "Hasn't ordered anything. I don't want to ask anyone to leave, especially if they've got nowhere else to go, but . . ."

Mackenzie shrugged. "It's not like people are clamoring for tables," she said. "I'll go see if they're okay."

"Good call," said Grant. "Thanks. And . . . again, I'm really sorry."

Mackenzie half wished now that she'd said yes to him. It was too bad that the best test for whether a guy was worth going out with was refusing to go out with him. "You have nothing to be sorry for," she said. "I'm just kind of in the middle of something."

"Totally," he said again.

She walked to the corner booth and sat across from the shriveled figure. "What are you doing?" she asked.

The figure sniffed. "It's perfectly within my rights to be at a pizza parlor."

"Well, sure, Maude, but you should probably buy something if you don't want to get kicked out for loitering."

Maude jerked her head up. "I was going to! Just haven't decided what I'm in the mood for." She took her hat off; her hair was matted and sweaty.

"Maude . . . did you not want me to know you were here?"

"Of course I wanted you to know I was here. How else was I going to order my pizza? I've been waiting for over an hour. The service in here is terrible."

"Then what's with all this? You're not even wearing your usual hat. You look like you're trying to be . . . discreet. And this is an order-at-the-counter kind of place."

"Well, I'm not trying to be discreet. I'm not trying to *be* anything. I'm just going out for pizza, and I was cold. And I thought it might rain. And I wanted to wear a different hat—sue me. And I didn't want people trying to talk to me. People try to talk to you much less when you dress in a way that tells them not to. But of course you already know that."

Mackenzie tried not to laugh. She felt strangely comforted by the older woman's presence. Jared's visit had ripped her into the past, and Maude was coaxing her back into the present. "Okay! Okay. Sorry, Maude. What can I bring you? What kind of pizza do you like?"

"Uh . . . cheese," said Maude.

"Just cheese?"

"That's what I said."

Mackenzie went into the kitchen and dished two slices of cheese pizza onto paper plates for her and Maude. "Grant," she said. "I'm going to sit with that lady. She's having a hard time. Randall's gone home, right?"

"Yep," said Grant, clearly impressed. "That's really nice of you. Take your time. Nothing to do back here."

She paused in the doorway. "Hey, Grant?"

"Yeah?"

"Do you want to go out sometime? With me?"

He grinned. "Yeah."

"Okay. Cool."

When she returned to Maude, the woman had taken off her jacket as well and was holding her shirt away from her chest, fanning her face with the other hand. "It's too hot in here," she complained when the pizza was set in front of her.

"Then why were you wearing that jacket?" asked Mackenzie.

Maude took a big bite of her pizza. When her mouth was half-full, she grunted at Mackenzie to signal that she had something important to say. "Mm," she said, "the police went into our attic tonight."

"Oh yeah," said Mackenzie. "Larry didn't come?"

"Well, he came. But he didn't have a key, and he was a big wuss about it. And then the ghosts started banging on the door, so Sunna called the police. *They* picked the lock." Maude took another bite of pizza, and Mackenzie wanted to smack her on the back of the head so it would come back out so Maude could finish telling the story.

Luckily, Maude didn't wait until her mouth was even close to empty before speaking. "They opened the door, and Larry just cowered in the hallway, shaking like a little puppy dog. It was pathetic. But the two officers went up, and Sunna and I followed them—there wasn't anything to see. We didn't even all fit; we had to stand on the stairs and look around. It was just an icky old attic. Tiny, empty, pitch black—no windows or anything, not even anything stored in there." She sniffed disdainfully. "Obviously we didn't see any ghosts. Obviously. If ghosts don't want you to see them, you don't."

"And nothing . . . else?" asked Mackenzie. "Like, animal droppings?"

Maude looked vaguely insulted. "No. We didn't find *animal droppings* because we didn't find *animals*. We didn't find a homeless gentleman in a sleeping bag or—what was Sunna's word—*Randalls*?"

"Randos."

"Sure. We didn't find anything or anyone, because ghosts are invisible. Unless they don't want to be."

"Weird," said Mackenzie.

"That ghosts are invisible?"

"No, that they didn't find anything in the attic . . . I thought for sure they'd find . . . something . . ." She shuddered.

Maude looked exasperated.

"So, does this little visit of yours have anything to do with what Sunna told me?" Mackenzie asked after they'd eaten in silence for a few minutes.

"I don't know what Sunna told you," said Maude, but she looked guilty. A clump of pizza fell out of her mouth onto her lap.

"She said you think I'm Kate."

Maude was clearly trying to look natural, but her eyes were now watching Mackenzie's hands instead of her face, and the corners of her mouth were pulled taut.

Mackenzie raised her eyebrows and leaned forward. She'd seen Maude and Sunna play this standoff game enough times that she knew how it worked. She smiled and waited.

"Well, are you?" asked Maude at last. Mackenzie was surprised at how easily she'd won. Did this mean she could beat Sunna as well?

"No," she said.

"Oh, for *Pete's* sake," said Maude.

"What?"

"I don't believe you. Also, I can't believe you think I'm so stupid. I saw your picture in magazines, and I read all the papers; I know everything."

Mackenzie was surprised at how calm she felt. Like she was watching other people have this conversation, like this conversation was about people she didn't know instead of her family. Part of it was, she figured, the fact that Maude clearly *didn't* know everything, didn't seem to even know half of it. "You don't, though, if you think I'm Kate Simons."

"I don't think you're Kate Simons. I think you're Kate Weiss."

Mackenzie felt her ears turn red. "Which magazine?"

"Uh . . . blade something. Muffin. Cake. Something baking related. *Blade Cake*? That's not it . . ."

"You read *Razorcake*, Maude?"

Maude looked down her nose at Mackenzie, which was difficult, almost impossible, as Mackenzie was so much bigger than her. "*Yes,*" she said primly. "I *do.*"

Mackenzie snorted. "Sure. Well, I'm sorry, Maude, but you're wrong. I'm not Kate, and you don't seem to actually know anything."

"I *read* the papers," Maude said again, her mouth full of pizza.

"Not carefully enough, apparently."

"Are you saying the papers were wrong?" asked Maude, as offended as if she had edited the papers herself.

"I didn't say that at all. I'm saying you probably didn't read every article to do with the case. And you clearly don't know anything about my family. You don't know the first thing about *me*. And that's all I'm going to say about that because I already asked you not to snoop around in my business." Mackenzie stood. "I have to get back to work. You can pay for your pizza at the counter. I was going to say it's on the house, but . . ." She shrugged again. "A good spy doesn't make their subject foot the bill. And I'm pretty done with you right now, to be honest." In spite of her firm words, Mackenzie felt her voice shake. She took a deep breath.

Maude looked deflated. She had cheese stuck to her right cheek, in the hollow below her eye. Everything about her sagged. Mackenzie sat back down. She couldn't help herself.

"Look," she said. "I'm sorry. I shouldn't have said that. We're just not going to talk about me anymore. There is one thing I've been meaning to say to you, and the fact that you researched my *life* and came to my place of employment to spy on me makes me feel like I have the right to be a little intrusive. Like Sunna says: fair. So I'm going to say it, and then I'm going back to work, okay?"

Maude somehow appeared to agree—or at least concede—without moving a single muscle.

"You should call that guy. Richard. Closure feels good. Maybe it would make you feel . . . better." She stood up. She thought of Jared, of what he'd said. *It's not like we were serious.* How stupid had she been to think he'd written that letter? He hadn't even thought they were *serious*.

Yeah, sure, Mackenzie. Closure feels great.

"Call him?" Maude scoffed. "Oh, I won't be doing that."

"Why?"

"Because I hate him. Because he doesn't deserve to hear from me."

"Maude. He might not deserve to hear from you, but you deserve to hear from him. You deserve closure. And who knows? Maybe it's not how you remember it."

"What do you mean? That I lied?"

"No. I mean that maybe you remember him leaving you at the altar, but there was something else about the situation that you don't remember or didn't understand at the time. Maybe he had . . . a reason? I don't know. That all sounds super patronizing, and I don't mean it to—I'm just saying maybe sometimes these things aren't as cut and dry as they seem."

"You're a little girl!" Maude burst out. "Who are you to give me relationship advice?"

Mackenzie bit the inside of her cheek. "I'm not giving you relationship advice. I know nothing about relationships, and I don't give out relationship advice. I'm giving you *post*relationship advice—all the credentials you need to divvy that out is postrelationship experience—which I do have."

Maude frowned. "I don't even know his phone number."

"So find it. It's 2020. You can find anyone." She flinched as she said the words, knowing firsthand they weren't true.

THE CASE OF THE ROGUE FLOPPY HAT

Sunna

When Sunna walked into her living room after work the next morning, it felt wrong again, and it only took her a moment to figure out why.

The curtains.

The curtains were open. And as she grasped them to slide them shut, she saw something even more unsettling: The tape was gone. The hole was gone. She second-guessed herself—this was the window through which she'd thrown her cell phone the other night, wasn't it? She checked every other window in her suite, and every one was intact. She felt like she was going crazy. Could you call the police to report a fixed window? Could you report *anything* the day after the police had been at your house to check for rabbits in the attic?

Legs shaking, she stumbled into the kitchen for a drink of water, and that was when she saw the parrot—Mackenzie's shoulder parrot from her Picaroon costume—perched on top of her refrigerator. Its glassy black eyes stared blankly at her, like it was confused about where it was and who she was. She stared back. It blinked. No, it didn't—a car had driven past and reflected light briefly into her kitchen and across those beady eyeballs, causing the illusion of movement.

She grabbed the parrot and slipped into the hallway, knocking softly on Mackenzie's door; for some reason she didn't want Maude to be part of this conversation. There was the usual sound of the chair being dragged away from the door, despite the fact that Mackenzie now knew it did nothing to keep anyone out. Sunna had never met someone with such a tough exterior who was also so noticeably paranoid. Footsteps traveled up the stairs, and the door clicked and opened. Mackenzie peered out, eyes wide. She relaxed when she saw Sunna standing there.

"Hey, Sunna, what's up?"

"Someone fixed my window," said Sunna.

"What? What window?"

"I threw . . . my . . ." Sunna didn't want Mackenzie to think she was psychotic. "I dropped a . . ."

Mackenzie waited patiently.

"I accidentally broke a window in my place a few days ago, and when I got home from work this morning, it was fixed."

"Larry?"

"Ugh . . ." Sunna hadn't thought of that. "Is he allowed to just come into our places like that?"

"Doubt it. Hope not. But who else—"

"Oh—*and* I found this on my fridge." Sunna held out the parrot.

Mackenzie frowned as she took the stuffed bird. "How . . . I was just wearing this last night." She looked down the stairs behind her. "But the chair was still under the doorknob when I woke up this morning . . ."

A shriek, a thud, and the sound of breaking glass from above caused them both to jump, and Sunna grabbed Mackenzie's shoulder. "What was that?"

Mackenzie shook her head. "Maude? Should we check to see if she's okay?"

Sunna knocked on the door. "Maude," she yelled, "you okay?"

They heard a shuffling sound above them, and then Maude screamed, "*Stop* it, Janet! Don't *eat* that!"

They looked at each other. *Janet?*

"Someone's up there with her," said Sunna. "She sounds like she's okay. Should we just leave her alone?"

Another thud, then,

"JAAAAAAANNNNNNET!"

Sunna knocked again. "Everything okay up there, Maude?"

"No!" Maude yelled back; she sounded hysterical. "There are artichoke hearts *everywhere!*" There was the sound of stomping feet and a crack like a baseball bat hitting the floor above their heads. "*Stop* that, Janet!"

"Can we come up?" Sunna called tentatively. She didn't want to go up. She hoped Maude would say no. But instead she heard the familiar clack of Maude's heels on the steps behind her door.

The door was flung open, and Maude stood there with a broom in her hands. "Can you hold Janet for me?" she pleaded. Her eyes were full of tears, and her wiry hair was sticking up so that she looked like a mad scientist.

"Who's Janet?" asked Mackenzie. She had backed up against her door and was clutching the knob, ready to escape to her basement at a moment's notice.

But Maude just turned and marched back up her stairs. Sunna and Mackenzie followed—what else could they do?

They found Maude in her kitchen, a broken jar on the floor. She was trying to mop something up with a sopping wet tea towel while using the broom to smack the floor beside her cat—Janet?—who was attempting to help her clean up the mess by eating it.

"What happened?" asked Mackenzie softly.

"I was making omelets. I was trying to open this jar of artichoke hearts," said Maude, sniffling hard, "but they don't make it so you can *open* jars these days. It's like they don't *want* you to open them. And when *Richard* was around, *Richard* could get into these jars *for* me, but"—she choked on a sob—"but *Richard* isn't here, is he? So I have to open the jars by *myself*. And I *can't*; they're so *stupid*. It's like he didn't *think* of that when he left me. It's like he wasn't even *thinking* about *jars*. It's like he wasn't *thinking* that *I might want some artichoke hearts*." Maude was weeping now, kneeling on the floor, waving her broom in the air. "Stop it, Janet!" she wailed. "Artichoke hearts aren't good for cats!"

Mackenzie stepped forward and picked Janet up. The cat stared at the parrot already in Mackenzie's arms. The parrot was still staring at Sunna.

"Do you have some paper towels?" Sunna asked, after a moment of silence.

"No," said Maude. She was starting to calm down, looking more embarrassed than angry now. "I have *this*. *This* is what I have." She wrung the tea towel into the sink, rinsed it out, and wrung it again.

"I'll go get some paper towels," said Sunna.

As she walked through Maude's empty living room, she heard Mackenzie say, "You okay, Maude?"

"Yes," said Maude. "I just don't like living alone."

"You don't live alone." Mackenzie's kind voice floated out after Sunna as she jogged down the stairs. "You live with Sunna and me."

~

The women cleaned up the artichokes and the broken glass. Maude gave Janet some cat food, admonishing her like she was a child.

They met again after lunch and drove to the coffee shop together and sat in their usual spot, being watched by the usual baristas, drinking their usual drinks. When Mackenzie got up to use the bathroom,

Maude leaned across the table and whispered conspiratorially to Sunna that she had been spying.

"Maude." Sunna shook her head disapprovingly. "You need to leave that girl alone. You need to leave *me* alone. Just leave everybody alone."

"That's what you want? Is that what everyone wants? Do you want me to *ghost* you?" Maude was sulking. Maude's sulking face was just her regular face with the chin tucked in.

"That's not what I meant."

"But it's what you said."

Sunna rolled her eyes. "I didn't say *that* at all. I meant you've gotta get back from people's business. Get out of their space. Don't, you know, *investigate* them. People don't like being investigated."

"When have I ever investigated you?"

"Well, you sure interrogate me a lot. That's either equal or worse. It's definitely not better."

"Well, I'm sorry."

Sunna tilted her head to the side. "You're *what* now?"

Maude didn't answer.

"Okay, I'm sorry, too, Maude. I shouldn't have said it like that, but I do mean it. You can't spy on Mackenzie. It's not right, and it's not fair. You need to mind your own business."

"Do you give this speech to police officers?" demanded Maude. "Do you say this to private investigators? Do you storm into courtrooms, railing against the judge and the jury that they mind their own business?"

"Obviously not," said Sunna. "This is those people's *jobs*. You aren't a police officer or a private investigator or a judge or a juror."

"What about Trixie Belden? Miss Marple? Jessica Fletcher?"

"Uh . . . they're fictitious characters and clearly don't hold any real weight in this discussion?" She ran her fingers through the ends of her hair. "Jessica Fletcher? Really, Maude?"

Mackenzie returned, and Maude sat back in her chair with a snarl.

Mackenzie eyed both with a knowing look. "You guys being nice?" she joked. Then she tilted her head at Maude. "Wait, Maude, where's your hat?"

Maude touched her head sadly. "The ghosts took it."

"This is getting ridiculous," said Mackenzie. "What now?"

"What now what?" asked Maude, her hand still resting atop her head like a substitute hat.

"What do we do about this? There's something up there, but there's nothing up there, but whatever it is, it's still stealing our stuff. Ripping it up. Misplacing it. I got a letter from the university the other day, and I had to email and ask them to resend it because all that was left of it was the return address."

The three women stared at each other. "Move out?" suggested Sunna.

"There's nowhere to *go*," said Mackenzie. "Larry didn't do his market research—rent at this place is, like, four hundred bucks cheaper than anywhere else. Especially this close to the U of R."

Maude and Sunna nodded.

"I don't feel *unsafe*, necessarily," Mackenzie added. "Especially with the two of you there. And if they are . . . ghosts . . . I don't think they're mean . . ."

"Mean spirited," said Maude without smiling. "Ha ha."

Mackenzie stared at her.

"Spirits. Mean spirited. A play on words."

"Yeah, got it. Sorry, Maude, I've just never heard you make a joke before."

"I'm very funny," said Maude, picking something out of her teeth. "Always been very funny."

Mackenzie smiled graciously and continued. "I'm not afraid, necessarily. It's just . . . unnerving. It's too weird."

This, they could all agree on, but no one knew what to do about it. Sunna picked up her book, and Maude went back to her newspaper.

"Ooh! Look at this," said Maude suddenly. "They have some new information about the bomb threats—they found *tunnels* underneath the art gallery!"

"Joined to existing tunnels," Mackenzie read from across the table. "We have existing tunnels?"

"Of *course* we have existing tunnels," said Maude indignantly. "They used to carry coal-fired heat from a power plant to lots of the bigger buildings downtown. Everyone knows *that*."

"I didn't," said Mackenzie. "That's cool. Says, 'A new tunnel was discovered beneath the gallery that led to a preexisting tunnel that connected various buildings in the city to a central power plant about two hundred meters south of the downtown area—' Huh, like you said, Maude. 'They left behind an acetylene oxygen tank, concrete cutting saws, ladders, and lighting equipment in the tunnel below the art gallery.' Oh, and check this out—nothing was stolen."

Maude's face drooped. "Disappointing," she said.

"Why are you disappointed, Maude?" Sunna was incredulous. "Why does everyone in this town love heists and bomb threats so much? Do you people *want* crime?"

"Well, no," said Mackenzie, looking sheepish. "Not like muggings and stabbings and stuff. But art heists and bomb scares just feel more . . . I don't know . . . exciting . . . cinematic."

"But you don't *have* art heists," Sunna huffed. "You have . . . you have whatever these are. People digging in basements and then running away. People making prank calls."

"I don't know, Maude." Mackenzie ignored Sunna's grumbling. "It's not like this is nothing. In a lot of ways, I think this is more interesting than a heist. Who would go to all that trouble for no reason? The tools it would take to dig into the basement of the art gallery wouldn't be cheap. You wouldn't do that for fun. And I think there have been, like, three or four bomb threats at this point—"

This cheered Maude considerably. "*Sixteen,* actually," she said. "According to the papers."

Sunna rolled her eyes. "Also, according to the news websites. And Twitter. And Reddit."

But Maude didn't hear her. She was frozen, eyes wide, mouth hanging open like she'd been shot in the back of the head.

"Maude?" Mackenzie looked concerned. "You okay?"

"Uh," said Maude. "Uh. I-I-I . . ." She was pointing at a picture at the bottom of the page. "It's . . ."

"You," said Mackenzie.

Sunna leaned over the table to see.

There was a smaller heading that read: HAVE YOU SEEN THIS WOMAN? Underneath was a picture of an older woman dressed all in black taken from security camera footage. Her face was blurry and mostly obscured by a black hat with a gothic prom-corsage monstrosity on the side of it.

"Your hat's in the paper," said Mackenzie.

"Maude," said Sunna, "did you . . . *is* this you?"

"Of course not!" Maude snapped. "*Context!* She's buying a *cell phone!*"

"Also making bomb threats," said Mackenzie.

"How dare they," said Maude.

"How dare they try to find the person who made bomb threats to an art gallery?"

"How dare they print my picture!"

"So . . . it *is* you?"

"Of course not!"

"It really does look like you."

Sunna watched the back-and-forth with amusement.

"That's absolutely my hat, but it's not me. I'm being *framed.* How *dare* they," Maude said again, with even more conviction. "Who would do that?"

"An enemy?" said Sunna.

Maude scoffed. "I don't have enemies. I don't even have—" She stopped, contemplated what she had been about to say, and looked at the women across the table, her eyes settling on Mackenzie. "I don't have enemies," she said.

"Don't worry about it, Maude," Sunna said. "Me and Mack will be your alibis."

Maude looked like she was going to cry. "Really?"

"Of course," Mackenzie said. "We know where you are basically all the time, except when you sneak out to smoke on the porch. And no offense, Maude, but you're not exactly a high-profile figure. No one's going to look at this picture and go, 'It's Maude!' Except me. And Sunna."

Maude looked doubtful.

"Okay. We'll figure this all out. It'll be okay. You'll be okay. But in the meantime, and because we don't know how long until you're arrested and have completely missed your chance . . ." Mackenzie laughed at her own joke and pulled out her cell phone and a piece of paper and slid them across the table to Maude.

"What's this?" asked Maude suspiciously.

"Richard Payne's phone number. Lucky for you, this is a small city, and there's only one listed. He still lives here."

"Shall I also tell him I'm being investigated by the police for making bomb threats to one of our city's most-treasured institutions?"

But Mackenzie held up a hand. "No, Maude. First of all: you're not being investigated. Your ex-*hat* is being investigated. Let it go for now. Secondly: you owe me. You know you do. *And* you owe yourself. You don't have to be nice to him, just ask what happened." She took her phone back and dialed the number from the paper, then passed it across the table again to Maude.

The phone rang for what seemed like forever before they heard a man's voice on the other end. Maude looked to Mackenzie for help, but Mackenzie just raised her eyebrows. "Richard?" Maude said.

The voice mumbled.

"This is Maude."

There was no mumbling for a very long time.

Then there was a lot of mumbling. Endless mumbling. Maude's face remained stoic. She didn't look at Mackenzie for any more help.

"I see," she said after a while.

Then she said, "Okay."

Then she said, "Yes, that's fine. But not at your house, and not at mine. Do you know the coffee shop near the airport—on Hill?" Sunna heard a faint *no*. "It's across from that gas station—in between the crematorium and the tattoo parlor. It's called Paper Cup . . . Yes, that's fine. Thursday. I'll be there at one."

LARRY DISCOVERS HE IS AN OLD FOGEY

Larry

"Hello, Larry. Maude here. I just wanted to tell you that things have been continuing to disappear from my place—not that I *have* many *things*. But now I have even less! My mop is gone, and a few days ago I went to get myself a drink of milk from the fridge, and the fridge was completely *empty*! Again! They only left an apple and an onion. What am I supposed to make myself for supper that involves only an apple and an onion? This is *preposterous*!

"I have been locking both the door handle and the dead bolt, and you and I both saw that there is nothing in the attic, but I know *for a fact* that the girls downstairs can get in here with their keys. I think it's Sunna, actually, who's doing all this. I don't know what she's up to, but you can't let her get away with this crap just because you're all goo-eyed over her—I can tell. I'm perceptive about these things. I'm not saying you need to evict her—in fact, I don't think you should; I don't know where she'd go. She doesn't seem bright enough to fend for herself, so maybe it's best she's here with me, but *at least* change the locks on my door. And call me back; this is—"

A beep, and Maude's voice was snuffed out. There was no more room in Larry's message in-box.

"Thank goodness," he mumbled to the ceiling.

Maybe now she'd take a break for a few minutes so he could use his own phone for an outbound call.

He typed in the number on his rental paperwork, and it rang a few times before Mackenzie picked up.

"Hello?" He could tell she didn't have his number programmed into her phone. That, or she was very perplexed about receiving an out-of-the-blue phone call from her landlord.

"Hi, Mackenzie, it's Larry. Your landlord." He probably didn't need to specify. How many Larrys could a teenager possibly know?

"Oh, hi, Larry."

"Hi." He was talking in an extra-businessy voice, like he was about to ask her if she had enough life insurance. "I was wondering if you would, uh, go for coffee with me?"

He had planned, when he made this phone call, to launch straight into an explanation from the invitation, so that she wouldn't think he was asking her *out*. But then he got a tickle in his throat and had to clear it, and that gave her enough time to say, "Oh, Larry, I'm actually seeing someone . . ."

No. No no no. He didn't want to be the creepy landlord. *Business!* "Oh," he said, trying to sound even more professional. "No no no no no no no no." That didn't sound as professional as he'd hoped. "Ha ha." Maybe it would be best to lighten the mood? "Ha! No. No no."

This was a disaster.

"No, no. Let me start over. But first, let me just say that I don't want to go on a date with you. Ha. Ha ha. No." He needed to stop saying *ha* and *no*. "Not in a rude way, right, just in a—well, I'm pretty old, kind of way. Compared to you. I was actually calling because I saw your article in *Razorcake*, or, at least, I think it's you? Assuming Kate Weiss is . . ."

"A pen name," Mackenzie said, still sounding very confused and a little defensive.

"Yeah, yeah, and I would like to, uh, also? Write for *Razorcake*? Or, actually, any magazine or newspaper or website or . . . yeah, anything music related? I would like to write about music. Like you do. And so . . ." Larry lurched through his prepared speech like a fifteen-year-old trying to learn how to drive stick. Was he making sense? Was he freaking her out?

"*Oh.*" Mackenzie got it now; he could tell. "I'm so sorry, Larry, of course. You want some pointers? About submitting your work to publications?"

"*Yes!*" The relief flooding through him was palpable. "Yes. I would. And I'd pay you for your time. And I'd buy your coffee. But not in a creepy way."

Mackenzie laughed. "Larry. I think that would be really fun. Honestly. I like talking about that stuff. You wouldn't have to pay me—but I'll let you buy the coffee."

"Well, good—great! Okay, then." This was something that he'd always noticed old people said at the end of conversations. *Okay, then.* Old fogey, he was.

"I actually hang out at a coffee shop every afternoon these days—Paper Cup? By the airport? You could just meet me there; I'm generally there from one until five. So just, you know, whenever works . . . ?"

"Cool. How about Thursday?"

"Sounds great."

Larry resumed his business voice. "Thank you, Mackenzie. I look forward to it."

A LOSER WHO SITS AT HOME WITH HER SECRETS

Mackenzie

"You can wear any of those," said Celeste from the computer screen on Mackenzie's bed. "They're the same. They're all black. Everything's black. This is the most ridiculous thing to stress over."

"They're not the same at all. This one's a V-neck. This one's short; those are long. This one's got this lace piece here." Mackenzie pointed, her voice rising. "This one has *buttons*."

"You are the most extra," said Celeste. "At work, you're both in pirate costumes. He's going to see you in literally anything other than a pirate costume and go, *Oh! Wow! She's not a pirate, and that's, like, so great!*"

"He sees me at university all the time. He knows I'm not a pirate."

"I know he knows you're not a pirate, Kenz. Just making a joke. Lighten up."

Mackenzie threw the one with buttons on the bed and covered her eyes. "I don't know how to date. Help meeee . . ."

"Kenz. You're going to be fine. Grant sounds amazing. And you see him, like, every day; this is the furthest thing from a blind date. It's not even a first date—you had that group date the other night!"

Mackenzie sat on the floor, eye level with her laptop. "It wasn't a group date. It was just a group."

"Shut up. It was a group date. And it went well. You said. So I don't know why you're nervous. You're not wearing a parrot on your shoulder, and you're not dressed like a pirate, and you don't smell like Picaroon."

"Except . . ."

Celeste leaned into her laptop, her concerned face taking up the whole screen. "What's wrong, Kenzie?"

Mackenzie debated whether she should tell the truth or not. She picked the fresh nail polish off of her thumb. "I didn't actually go."

"Didn't go where?"

"On the date. Or the group date. Or whatever it was. I stayed home."

Celeste sat so still that Mackenzie thought the FaceTime app was frozen. "You lied about going on a date?"

"Yeah."

"To *me*?"

"Yeah." Mackenzie climbed onto the bed, and several black shirts fell to the floor at her feet. If Celeste only knew all the things Mackenzie had lied about.

"Why?"

Mackenzie fought the urge to shut the laptop. "Because I didn't want you to think I was a loser who sits at home by myself all the time."

"Are you a loser who sits at home by yourself all the time?"

"Yeah."

"Aw, Kenz . . ." Celeste never stayed mad. This was why their friendship was so easy—neither of them ever stayed mad. It had probably been more of an inherent character trait for one of them, but, like so many other traits and quirks and even physical mannerisms, they had spent so much time together growing up that it had rubbed off on the other. "Why? You were so excited to finally be out of your parents' house and away from that ridiculously oppressive curfew. You wanted to be free, remember? You wanted to actually leave your house after seven p.m. You wanted to go to movies. To parties. On *dates*."

"I know. I did. And now that I'm actually here . . . I don't."

"It actually sounds like you do but can't. Or won't. Or something."

"Celeste." Mackenzie moved the computer over so she could lie down. "It's just this weird thing. It's like I've been living in a cage my whole life, but now the door is open, and I can't go out there. It's *scary*."

"But . . . you're going tonight?"

Mackenzie nodded. "Planning on it. Also, kind of planning on faking sick and canceling last minute."

"Pick me up."

"What?"

"Pick me up, so I'm right in front of you. I want to talk straight to your face."

Mackenzie sat up obediently and held the laptop in front of her. Celeste's face was full screen again, her thick black eyebrows forming two straight, stern lines across her forehead.

"You need to go tonight. You have to. If I were there, I'd promise to sneakily follow you in my car and watch over you, but I'm in Edmonton—which, I realize now, was an awful decision, and please forgive me—and you're just going to have to go on your own, and it will, I promise, feel so good to have done it, and I'll never forgive you if you don't."

"You'll forgive me in, like, two seconds, Celeste."

"Not this time. This time I will just stay mad until I die."

"I miss you so much, Celeste." Mackenzie put Celeste down so she could blow her nose.

"So you're going?"

"I'm going to try to go." Mackenzie picked up one of the black shirts. "Okay, so—"

"Is that your phone?"

"Huh?"

"I think I can hear your phone ringing."

Mackenzie dropped the shirt. "What if it's him? What if *he's* canceling?"

"Just answer it, Kenz."

Mackenzie sighed with relief when she saw her mother's number on the screen. "Hey, Mom."

"Hi, baby. I just wanted to update you on the situation."

"There's an update? Already?" The first time they'd gone through all this, they'd gotten used to going months without hearing anything, and the updates had always been fairly insignificant and meaningless—until, of course, the final update, which had been about as insignificant and meaningless as an atomic bomb. She'd learned, in that time, that it did no good to feel joy about the investigation going well—or, in this case, going at all—because that didn't mean it was going to end well. It did no good to feel despair about the investigation going poorly either.

"Well, yes, actually. A fairly big one. Are you out in public? Is it loud where you are? Can you hear me?"

Mackenzie wanted to claw at her face. How, after all these years, were her parents still so bad at sharing news? "Mom! Yes. I can hear you. I'm home, in my bedroom. I would tell you if I couldn't hear you. Just talk."

Celeste burst into muffled laughter on the computer screen. She knew about Mackenzie's parents.

"Sorry. So, when they announced that they were reopening the case because they had received an anonymous tip, it apparently spooked someone into coming forward to confess that they had lied when they were questioned the first time."

"What?" Mackenzie's heart beat louder than her mother's voice. She swallowed and wiped her forehead with the back of her hand. Her body registered agitation before she was even aware of the feeling. The pounding in her chest sounded like a word, a name. *Jared. Jared. Jared.* She moved out of Celeste's line of sight. "Who was it?" She knew she should ask. Was it considered lying to ask questions you already knew the answers to?

"Jared Hall. Do you remember him? Tanya's friend? When they questioned him the first time, he said he was home watching TV that night, and his parents backed him up. Now he's saying he was with them."

Mackenzie breathed in deeply, trying to sound surprised. At least surprise and guilt didn't sound much different. "Jared? Yeah, I . . . think . . . I remember him . . ." She tried to say it quietly. Celeste knew that she'd kept her relationship with Jared a secret from her parents, but it still felt weird lying in front of someone who knew you were lying. "Why did he lie the first time?"

Mackenzie's mother sighed heavily. "He was covering for his parents. They supplied the alcohol for a small party that happened that night just outside of town—and he's saying that's the last place he saw . . ." Her voice slid up an octave. "To think he and his family were more afraid of the repercussions for hosting that party than they were for our daughters' safety. To think that they, that all of those kids who were there, were more afraid of getting in trouble for underage *drinking* . . . than . . ." She composed herself. "Everyone just thought, you know, *It's a small town where nothing bad has ever happened. They ran away. They'll turn up.* And then by the time anyone realized what a big deal it was, they felt that they couldn't take it back—they'd already lied to the police. To think of the guilt they've probably been living with for all these years—and rightfully so—"

Mackenzie couldn't listen to this anymore. "Will they be in trouble? Jared and his family?"

"I'm guessing they will." Her mother's voice was hard and angry, more of a wish than a guess.

"So they know what happened? Have they said anything yet other than . . ."

"Jared has given a statement. The police are looking into things," said her mother. This was the first time anyone had uttered these words since that night. Until that point it had always been, *No one seems to know anything,* or *If anyone knows something, they're not saying.* That second one had always killed Mackenzie, because she knew of a few people who knew something they weren't saying. She was one of them.

FIRST FIRST DATE

Mackenzie

The doorbell rang, and Mackenzie realized she'd never heard it before. Because the only people who ever came to see her were Maude and Sunna, and they were already in the house. How long had she lived here now? How long had she been going to this university, mingling with other students and working with people at Picaroon? Was it pathetic that this was the first time she'd heard the doorbell?

If she had to hazard a guess: *Yeah. Pretty pathetic.*

She took a breath, locked her door behind her, and marched up the stairs.

When she opened the front door, the sight of Grant caught her off guard, even though she'd been expecting him. He looked out of place on her porch. It was weird—in a good way—that he'd come to her house, just to see her. Any other time they'd been together, they'd had reasons to be in the same room that had nothing to do with each other. Now he was on her porch purely because it was her porch. It felt like such an immature thing to be processing it all so consciously, but Mackenzie had only ever dated Jared, and that had been a big secret, and she had never felt quite certain that *she* was the reason he was with her.

"Hey," said Grant. "This house is really cool. It's got character."

"Yeah, doesn't it?" said Mackenzie, so glad he hadn't opened by telling her she looked nice or giving her flowers. Jared had done those things because those were easy, generic things to do.

"It looks like it's haunted," said Grant.

Mackenzie smiled in spite of the chill that shot up her back. "Why do you say that?"

"It's just got that, like, old-school ghost-house thing."

"Well," said Mackenzie, "you'll be happy to know that it *is* haunted. There was a suicide in the attic? Or something?"

Grant looked like he wasn't sure if Mackenzie was joking or not, but he also looked like he didn't mind one way or the other. "Whoa," he said. "Freaky."

"You have no idea," Mackenzie said sincerely. "Shall we?"

"Definitely."

She stepped onto the porch and locked the front door behind her just as nonchalantly as if she did this every night—as though this was not, in fact, the first time she'd ever gone out on a real date. She felt like she was doing something brave and extreme and extraordinary, but she didn't want Grant to know she felt like that, so she smiled at him and asked, "Where do you want to go?"

He looked like he wasn't completely sure of what he was about to suggest but was also very excited about it. "So there's this thing at the RPL they do sometimes where they play old kids' movies—*Beethoven, Air Bud, Big Green,* stuff like that"—he drew in a breath and squinted at her, like he was about to jam a nail into his own foot—"with the sound off. And they have a local improv team come in and do funny voice-overs. It's . . . it's awesome. I don't know if it's technically first-date material, but . . ."

"That sounds amazing," she said. "And I don't think there are rules about first-date material anymore. Are we going to drive?"

"Can, if you don't like walking. Or we can walk if you don't like driving. Or we can do whichever one you hate less. Or whichever one you like more. Either way's good." He was talking faster than usual.

"Are you nervous, Grant?"

"Yeah."

That made Mackenzie feel a bit better. "Don't be. It's just me. Let's walk, then. If there's time?"

"Yeah, the RPL isn't far from here. If we were going to drive, I was going to say we could stop for ice cream first at Dessart, but this way we'll make it just in time; we can go for ice cream after. Show's at seven thirty."

Mackenzie felt short of breath. Either way's good. Walk or drive. Whatever. This way or that way. She was walking off into the evening with a guy she barely knew. They had very loose plans, nothing in writing. No work schedule for police to consult later, no eyewitness accounts from other employees that she had or hadn't shown up. No *"She was supposed to be at Picaroon at eight, so she would've left the house at seven forty-five."* No *"She left work early because she wasn't feeling well, and here's a detailed description of the suspicious-looking man who followed her to her car."*

She could vanish without a trace or a clue, and for some reason the thought of that didn't scare her for her own sake. It scared her for the people she might leave behind.

"Either way's good," she said. "Should we . . . should I just . . ."

He looked at her with concern, and she thought she probably looked like she was about to pass out.

"Grant, I—I feel like I'm going to be sick."

And she ran to the side of the porch and puked over the railing onto the lawn below, hating the sound she made and the way she convulsed as she emptied out.

When she was finished, she stood and wiped her mouth. "I think I need to go back to bed," she said hoarsely, without turning to look at him. "I'm so sorry, Grant. You should leave so you don't catch this."

DEATH KITS IN MANILA

Sunna

"Did you know that you can buy death kits in Manila?" asked Maude.

Sunna was confused. Death kits? What time was it? Why was Maude here, in her bedroom? It was dark. So dark, in fact, that Sunna couldn't even see Maude's outline; she was just a voice that came out of nowhere. A disembodied sound. Words that didn't make sense.

"Maude," she said, "what are you doing in my bedroom? What time is it? What are you talking—"

"*Death kits,*" said Maude. Her voice was wandering around. "In the *Philippines*. Sunna, I'm trying to find your light switch and—oh."

The overhead light came on, and Sunna screeched, pulling the covers over her face.

"Sunna. Just close your eyes for a moment and let them adjust; I'm going to trip over something and break my hip if I keep wandering around your place in the dark."

Sunna lowered the sheets, squinting against the light. "So your solution is to turn the light on instead of to stop wandering around my place in the dark."

"Sunna, I need to borrow your Google."

"You need to borrow my what? My Google? Like you mean you want to borrow my phone?"

"Is there a Google on your phone?"

"Well, yeah."

"Then yes. As soon as possible. Do you keep it in your bedroom?"

Sunna was too tired to be angry. "What time is it?"

"One o'clock. I'm sorry, but this couldn't wait, and I figured you'd be up. This is about the time you usually go prowling around *other* people's apartments, isn't it?"

"I'm sleeping, Maude. Get out."

"Aren't you listening to me? *Death kits!*"

"Aren't you listening to *me*? *I'm sleeping.*"

Maude sat down on Sunna's bed. "Remember when you told Mackenzie that I owed her because I was spying on her, and that gave her free rein to break into my apartment?" Sunna tried to emulate a blank look. "She told me you said that to her. Frankly, I really, *really* don't see how this is any different. You owe me because you broke into my apartment. That's much worse than using the microfiche at the library. One is illegal, and one—"

Sunna was fully awake now, and furious—and yet, she couldn't argue with this logic. She waved her hand in front of her face like Maude was a gnat. "Fine, fine, Maude. Fine. My phone is on the nightstand. It's unlocked."

"*Unlocked.* What does that mean?"

"It means I don't have a pass code on it."

"What's a *pass code*? Like a combination lock?" Maude looked confounded.

"Yeah."

"Why would you put a combination lock on your phone? So that if someone else is in an emergency situation and they need to call for help, they *can't*?"

"Yep," said Sunna, turning over and burying her face in her pillow.

Maude picked up the phone and stared at it. "How does it work?" she asked. She squinted at the black screen. "Can *you* get Google on it?"

Sunna grabbed the phone out of Maude's hands. "Okay, Maude, here I am; I'm awake. How about you tell me why you want to google *death kids*, and then if you have a good enough reason, I'll do it for you."

"Death *kits*," said Maude. "Not death kids."

Sunna probably looked like she was going to kill Maude, because Maude began nodding.

"Okay, so. I was at the library, and I was talking to a young man there about Mackenzie."

"Really, Maude? She asked you not to look into it at all, and now you're talking to strangers about it?"

"He asked!"

"Oh really? He asked? A stranger walked up to you in a library and said, 'Oh, excuse me, do you know anything about this cold case from six years ago—'"

"No. He saw me looking at the microfiche."

Sunna cocked her head to the side. "Maude. I thought you got everything you needed off the microfiche?"

"Mackenzie told me that if I thought she was Kate, then I hadn't seen everything or I was missing information. She told me, quite emphatically, that she was *not* Kate. And you know what, I believed her. Because she looked so arrogant. I could tell that I was wrong. It was like she was *challenging* me." Maude was looking around Sunna's bedroom, her eyes lingering judgmentally on anything that looked out of place. "I took that as *permission*."

"You would. Maude, is there a chance that all this snooping is just you trying to distract yourself from the Richard thing?"

Maude went off into a coughing fit and flapped her hands at Sunna. When she'd recovered, she cleared her throat a few times and cast a disdainful glance at the other woman. "*The Richard thing?* You mean our meeting next Thursday? Why would I try to distract myself from *that*? I feel great about it."

"You feel great about it."

"Yes. I look forward to getting to the bottom of it. I like getting to the bottom of things. Which is why I want to get to the bottom of *this*."

Sunna shrugged. "'Kay."

"So you saw the picture in that *Cake Blade* magazine. The girl in that picture had the same tattoo as Mackenzie and the same face as Mackenzie and the same hair as Mackenzie, so I thought it was Mackenzie. Rookie mistake. They're twins; they have matching tattoos and faces and hair. Of course they do. It's obvious, and I don't know why it didn't cross my mind sooner. People probably get sister tattoos all the time. And why would she change her last name but not her first? Marriage. The magazine articles are recent, so Kate Weiss née Simons is very much alive—but according to the newspaper, like I said before, still technically *missing*. Why? She went missing but is somehow still publishing music articles? Interesting. And Tanya's dead, right, according to those old newspaper articles, but we also have this mysterious third person—Mackenzie Simons, who isn't mentioned anywhere but has the same face as Kate and, presumably, Tanya. And here's something, Sunna: I asked the librarian if she had any way to find a list of people who had graduated from the high school in Mackenzie's hometown, and she got right on *her* Google for me and searched—she told me small-town newspapers often have a picture of that year's graduating class with a little write-up and list of graduates—and she couldn't find one single Mackenzie Simons in the last ten years in any of the newspaper archives. Not one. Anyway. I was trying to find what I'd missed, and this young man asked me to show him how to use the microfiche machine. He saw what I was looking up and said it looked interesting, and *of course* it was interesting, so I explained the whole thing to him, about how there were these twins and one is dead and one is still missing, but I've sort of located the missing one and somehow also got an extra one living in my basement—it's like a riddle! And I told him how I thought Mackenzie was Kate but that I had been wrong, so I was coming back to see what I could possibly have gotten wrong, and *he* says to me, 'Are you sure she's not *Tanya?*' and I say that no, of course she's not Tanya because Tanya is dead, and they have the body and they had a funeral and all that, and *he* says, 'Google *death kits.*' Then I asked him what in the world he was talking about, and he was telling me about how you can buy a body and a death certificate and even eyewitnesses to say they *saw you die*, and he said something about how maybe Tanya—Mackenzie—purchased a death kit and faked her own death, and then he looked at the clock on the wall by the door and said he had to go and thanked me for the microfiche lesson. Isn't that all so bizarre? And now do you see why I need your Google? I don't feel like I should ask a librarian to search for death kits on hers."

Sunna glared at Maude. "Maude, if you don't get out of my room right now, I am going to buy *you* a death kit."

~

Sunna couldn't fall back asleep after Maude left. She grabbed the phone off the nightstand, pulled up Facebook, and typed in *Mackenzie Simons*. She clicked through several profiles belonging to women with that name, but found no one who looked like the girl living in the basement suite. She tried *Mackenzie Weiss*, then *Kate Weiss*. No luck. She tried the same combinations on Twitter, Instagram, Snapchat. *Nothing. Nothing. Nothing.*

But Mackenzie was nineteen. She was probably on some other social media network Sunna had never heard of. One last-ditch effort: she googled her.

Again, nothing under Mackenzie's name. Kate Weiss had a very nice portfolio of music essays and reviews, but no social media accounts, nothing personal. What nineteen-year-old didn't have a digital footprint?

Sunna glanced at the door. She was sandwiched between some seriously troubling people right now. One of them a suspect in a police investigation and one who seemed like maybe she didn't exist.

She pulled up Facebook again and typed another name: *Tanya Simons.*

This search rewarded her with one account belonging to someone in Saskatchewan, but this page was different from a regular Facebook account. Sunna had never seen a memorialized account before. The profile picture was a tiny faraway shot of a group of teenagers, one of whom was presumably Tanya Simons. The friends list was still there, and some basic profile information, but the page was largely a place where loved ones left messages, as though the girl had a laptop and reliable Wi-Fi with her in her grave.

One read: *Tanya, my baby girl was born today, right on her due date. I named her after you so part of you will be with me every day. It might be my imagination, but I feel like she has your eyes. Miss you so much, Angel.*

Depressing.

Sunna clicked on the profile picture, wanting to see a clearer picture than the grainy one printed over and over in the newspaper articles. She didn't see a Mackenzie look-alike in the group shot, so she looked at the next one. Something was off, if this was, indeed, Tanya Simons: she looked nothing at all like Mackenzie—not in a twin way or even a sister way. Where Mackenzie was tall and tan and dark eyed, this girl was tiny and pale, with frizzy red curls and freckles all over her face and shoulders.

She typed *Kate Simons*, ignoring her shame as she pictured herself reprimanding Maude for doing this very thing. *Can't help it. I'm just like my dad.*

This account, too, was memorialized; the notes were similar to the ones on Tanya's account, only they had the occasional note of hope (*I still believe you're out there somewhere, Kate. Come home to us!*). The only picture of Kate Simons confused Sunna even more. She looked *exactly* like Tanya. Maude was right—hard as it was to admit, Mackenzie was lying to them. But Maude was wrong about a lot of things; this was also blatantly obvious. Kate and Tanya were identical twin sisters, and they were both gone: one dead, one missing. So who was Mackenzie? And why would she pretend to be the dead twin sister of someone who had gone missing? And who was Kate *Weiss*?

Sunna was tired of wondering why someone had done something or what they were thinking; it was exhausting. Mackenzie's actions were strange, but Sunna wasn't going to run all over the city, visiting libraries and talking to strangers about death kits to get her answers.

She would just ask Mackenzie.

DO GHOSTS
HAVE FEET?

Mackenzie

Mackenzie vaguely registered the sound of knocking, but it spliced itself into the dream she was having so neatly that for a few moments she thought she was being steadily, painlessly beat over the head with a two-by-four. Her heart quickened as she realized the sound was coming from her door. She tried to push the thought of ghosts away.

She tiptoed to the door, moved the chair, jogged silently up the stairs to the next door, and tried to see through the crack underneath—were there human feet there or—horrors—nothing?

Feet. Did ghosts have feet? These feet were bare, which meant, barring the supernatural, that it was most likely either Maude or Sunna. Or a barefoot Grant, come back for a second helping of abject humiliation for everybody?

"Yes?" she whispered cautiously.

"Mack, it's Sunna."

Mackenzie breathed a sigh of relief and opened the door.

"Hey. What time is it?"

"Huh." Sunna popped her hip out and clucked her tongue. "I am *so* sorry; I just got mad at Maude for coming to my place in the middle of the night, and then I did the same to you . . . although, Mack, I woke up to her *in my bedroom*. Sitting on my bed."

"But . . . what time is it?" Mackenzie heard her voice crack and self-consciously pulled on the bottom of her oversize sleeping shirt.

"Right. Sorry. I actually don't . . . know . . . like, twoish?"

"Wait, she was on your bed?"

"Well, not at first. But yeah. I woke up to her *in my bedroom*. Honestly, Mack, I almost wished it was a ghost."

"And what are *you* doing *here*? *Now?*"

"Uh . . . can I come in?"

"Sure."

Mackenzie led the way to the table and slumped into one of the chairs, rubbing the sleep out of her eyes. "What's up?"

"Oh man. Where do I even start . . ." Sunna sat, too; she looked awkward and apologetic.

"I don't know," said Mackenzie, feeling uneasy. This would have to do with Kate and Tanya, for sure. Sunna was acting too weird for it be anything else.

"So . . ." Sunna searched Mackenzie's kitchen, moving her eyes along the countertops and the tops of the cupboards. "I snooped. Like Maude. I'm sorry. I couldn't help myself; I was on Facebook—you know how easy it is to snoop around when you're on social media. It's too easy, you know? You almost can't blame people."

Mackenzie sat across from Sunna, holding as still as she could. She did know. It was easy. But that didn't mean you had to. It wasn't *impossible* not to snoop if you exercised some self-control. These nosy women. Why couldn't they leave it all alone?

"I shouldn't have, but I searched for them on Facebook," Sunna continued. "I saw a picture—like, a clearer one than in the papers. And Maude's completely wrong—*neither* of them are you."

"True," said Mackenzie. "I never said either of them were."

"You said your twin sister went missing. And Kate and Tanya Simons are the names of the twins who went missing on their birthday. But I saw their pictures, and you look nothing like them. At all. Not in a blown-out newspaper article or a clear Facebook profile picture."

"I never said my twin sister went missing. What are you talking about?"

"I—" Sunna looked lost. She lowered her head onto the table. "I don't know, Mack," she said, her voice muffled. "I think I'm getting the things you said confused with the things Maude said. She found these articles about Kate and Tanya Simons, these missing twins . . . I think she filled in some blanks."

"Maude? Fill in blanks? That's ridiculous, Sunna."

Sunna lifted her head to see if Mackenzie was kidding. Maybe also to see if Mackenzie making jokes equaled Mackenzie not being angry.

(She was, but it didn't.)

"Anyway, yes. Kate and Tanya are my sisters. They're the twins, and I'm the perpetual third wheel."

Sunna sat up. "Okay. And who's the one you think wrote the letter? Tanya?"

Mackenzie felt a laugh climb her throat, but it was the kind that comes when your body knows there are too many emotions inside, and it needs to get rid of some very quickly. "No. Tanya didn't write the letter because Tanya's *dead*. We have her body; it's in a box, in a hole. Covered with dirt. Tanya's not writing letters or asking to meet up with me in a coffee shop because she's super, super dead. I *do* have maybe a fraction of a dream that the writer of that letter is Kate. But, I'm pretty sure she's . . . you know. Not writing letters anymore either."

Sunna waited a respectful amount of time to speak again, an unspoken moment of silence for each of the dead girls.

"Who's Kate Weiss?" she said finally.

"Me. It's my pen name. Kate—because, obviously—and Weiss, the last name of the lead singer of one of my favorite bands. I like to write but I started pretty young, and my parents wouldn't let me, so I picked a pen name and did it anyway."

"Okay, but then who are you?"

"What do you mean, who am I? I'm Mackenzie Simons. The accused."

"I looked you up. On social media. I couldn't find you anywhere."

"Welcome to the world of a kid whose older sisters disappeared into thin air. You think my parents were going to let me have social media accounts? You think my parents were even going to let me finish high school in peace? They pulled me that week. Bam. Homeschooled. Good thing I had Celeste, or I would've died. It was the worst. That's why they don't even mention me in the newspaper articles; my parents didn't know if the kidnapper—or whoever—was going to come back for me, so they asked for a publication ban on me. It was like they thought if no one knew I existed, I'd be safe. Real great way to grow up. You have no idea what a huge deal it is that I'm even living here, in a house in a city this far from home. I fought for it. I fought for it so hard, and now that I'm here, I just think about going home every single day. I'm petrified twenty-four seven because I'm pretty sure fear is just imprinted into my DNA at this point, but I'm here. Do you want to know something else? I've never even gone out on a real date. Or to a movie. Or anything. I have not—since that night my sisters went missing—left the house after supper, besides to work. Because I just have it in my head that if I go out at night and I disappear, they won't have enough clues to be able to find me. Or there'll be, like, one person who saw me last, and the entire investigation will hinge on that one person's testimony—which, can you imagine the toll that would take on a person?" Mackenzie was talking too fast. She took a breath. "Any other questions? Did you want to know why I don't look anything like them?"

Sunna looked like she was deciding whether Mackenzie was actually giving her permission. If she'd looked uncomfortable before, now she looked like she was scoping the apartment for places to hide. Like she might actually attempt to climb into Mackenzie's fridge. Mackenzie felt okay about letting Sunna marinate in her embarrassment. Maybe it would teach her a lesson.

But curiosity won. "Do you guys have different dads, or moms, or . . ."

Mackenzie sat back in her chair, disappointed in Sunna. "Yeah."

"Different dads?"

"Different dads and moms."

"So, then you're not even sisters?"

"No, we are sisters. We just have different parents. Different biological parents."

"Oh. Adopted."

Mackenzie nodded. "They are."

"Okay," said Sunna. "Why didn't you just say that? In the beginning?"

"I didn't see why I needed to." Mackenzie was just beginning to fully appreciate how odd this trio was—Sunna, Maude, herself. They were the kind of close where they demanded extremely personal information from each other though they had just met and didn't even know the basics about one another yet.

"I'm really, *really* sorry, Mack. I shouldn't have snooped. I shouldn't have asked so many questions; it's none of my business. The frustrating thing is that I've been giving Maude this exact lecture over and over, thinking I was so much better than her, and then I did the exact same thing."

"No. I get it. I catch myself thinking like that a lot too. That I'm better than Maude." Mackenzie hadn't realized she felt like that until she said it out loud, and then she wished she hadn't admitted it. "We should be nicer to her," she mumbled.

"By *we*, you mean me."

"No, I mean we. We've been alive about a third of the time she has, and we treat her like she's two. That's not fair. She's not dumb—she's just fed up with everything. And I bet it didn't help, getting stood up for her own wedding." Poor Maude. Maybe having something like that happen to you made it so you stopped seeing anything good in yourself. Maybe Maude just hated having to exist in front of other people, and that was what made her mean. "I bet all this 'investigative' stuff is just her trying to distract herself from the Richard thing," Mackenzie said, feeling worse by the second.

Sunna slammed the table like Maude always did. "That's exactly what I said! Maude says no, though. She says she's excited about the meeting with him."

"Excited?"

Sunna shrugged. "That's what she said."

Mackenzie's phone buzzed on the counter, and she sighed. "This is going to be something," she mumbled, leaving her phone right where it was.

"What do you mean?"

"I mean that I'm going to answer this phone call, and it's going to be something. I'm—what'd Maude say? One of *those* people."

She grabbed the phone and hit the green circle without checking to see whose name was on the screen.

"Mackenzie?" It was her father. His voice was cautious and creaky. "We've heard from the police."

There was a whooshing sound, like a washing machine, and she observed, with some interest but no alarm or sense of personal involvement, that it was the sound of blood rushing around in her head, as though her heart were in her ears, and suddenly she was thinking about the summer she turned nine.

She'd gone to a baseball tournament in a neighboring town. Her team had just played their first game, and she, along with a small group of teammates, was headed to the snack bar to buy a hot dog. They'd been walking past a game in progress, and someone had yelled, "Heads!"

Mackenzie had known this meant she should look up and around, that she should put her hands up to cover her face. But as she glanced up, something in the sky caught her attention, and time slowed as she wondered what the thing was. She stared straight at it. Right as she realized what the small white thing was, it knocked her out. But there had been a fraction of a second in which she understood everything with horrible clarity, in which she knew that it was a baseball, that it was going to hit her in the face, and that it was going to hurt. A moment between comprehension and pain.

Why were they having this conversation here, in this haunted house, with all the ghosts? She wanted to be in her living room, sitting on the couch between her parents. She wanted to have her head on her dad's chest when he told her this news. She knew what it was; she just wasn't ready for it to land yet.

"I'm on my way home, Dad," she blurted before he could say anything more.

"Now?" He sounded relieved.

"Yeah, right now. I'll be there in an hour and a half."

"Okay," he said. "Love you, Mack."

"Love you, Dad."

Sunna, who was sitting close enough to hear the whole thing, seemed to magically understand what neither Mackenzie nor her dad had said out loud. "Want some company?" she asked.

Mackenzie couldn't speak, but she nodded gratefully.

SUNNA'S FIRST NIGHT SKY

Sunna

Sunna stared out the window as they passed the town where Mackenzie grew up. The houses were old, the lawns overgrown, the grain elevator standing guard at the entrance like an old man who was tired of his job. Mackenzie seemed not to notice how dilapidated it all was. She pointed out the tiny school building, the church, the bank, the post office, the gas station, and the bar, all visible from the highway, lined up like a ghost town on a TV set. "That's basically it," Mackenzie said. The town disappeared in the rearview mirror as quickly as it had appeared in front of them. "There's a hall and a senior citizen's center, too, and a big hole where there used to be a swimming pool. Before I was born. Kids used to climb into it and do drugs."

The sparse streetlights were the last of the town to vanish, and they were back in the country again, beneath the enormous black sky.

Sunna was mesmerized by it.

An incredible thing—an almost unbelievable thing—was that this was her first time seeing an unobstructed night sky. She'd grown up in Toronto. Her family, when they still called themselves a family, anyway, didn't camp—they vacationed in other cities. Montreal. Vancouver. New York. Seattle. Boston. Wherever her dad's work took him, Sunna and her mother followed along and called it family vacation, though they never saw him. If she had ever been out from under the canopy of city lights at night, she couldn't recall it. And she *would* recall something like this. Endless night—filled with stars. Speckled, like someone had flicked a paintbrush at a large dark canvas.

"I've never seen anything like this before," she said.

Mackenzie looked shocked, as though she'd forgotten Sunna was in the car with her. But then Sunna realized it wasn't that she'd spoken—it was what she'd said that had surprised Mackenzie.

"Huh? Seen anything like what?"

"That sky," said Sunna. "I've never seen anything like it before."

"You've . . . you've never seen the *sky*?"

Sunna laughed. "No. Grew up in the city, stayed in the city . . . and Regina's small, but . . . I mean, it's still got streetlights. When I first got there, I remember getting up at five a.m. for a class—and it was late summer still, so it wasn't pitch black like this—but I still remember thinking, *Whoa, the sky is so big out here.* But this . . ."

Mackenzie slammed on the brakes and swerved into an empty approach that seemed invisible from the road. She threw the car into park and got out.

Sunna followed, confused. "What are you doing, Mack?"

Mackenzie climbed up onto the car's hood. The night was dark enough that you could see every star, but the stars were bright enough that the women could see each other, as though they were in town under the glow of streetlights. "I just need a minute," she said. "To rest my eyes and . . ."

Sunna waited for her to finish the sentence, then realized she wasn't going to. Sunna climbed onto the hood of the car, too, pulling her jacket across her chest.

"I can't believe you've never seen this. It's amazing, hey?" Mackenzie tipped her head back and stared straight up. "When I first got my license, I used to do this all the time on my way home from town, especially if I was upset. I'd pull off the road and lie on my car and just look up. It's so big. It's familiar to me, but it's one of those familiar things that stays amazing. Really—how many familiar things stay amazing?"

Sunna thought about it. She didn't feel amazed by much lately. Was that just part of getting older, or was it more like a muscle that atrophied if you didn't move it for a long time? She tried to pick a square section of the sky and count just the stars inside of it but couldn't. It *was* amazing. She heard a sniffle from beside her and tried not to turn her head, to let Mackenzie have some semblance of privacy. "Are you nervous?"

"About what?"

"About finding out what happened."

"No." Mackenzie sniffled again.

"Oh." Sunna didn't know what to say to that.

Mackenzie was quiet for a long time. "I'm not nervous to find out what happened because I already know what happened."

Mackenzie looked sideways at Sunna, then quickly away.

"You mean, like, you can guess?"

"No. I mean I *know* what happened. And yeah, if you're wondering, that does mean I lied to the police and to my parents and to everyone." She had her head tipped back now, like she was confessing her sins to God, and it seemed probable out here that he was very close, listening. Sunna felt like, if she jumped high enough, she could brush her fingers against the sky and some of the stars would rub off like glitter. It had moved closer to them while they sat there, she thought. Like Maude did when she was talking to you, drifting closer and closer without you noticing.

"My parents don't know. That I know, I mean. I caught Kate and Tanya sneaking out the window that night, and Tanya made me promise not to tell on them. I read their email all the time back then—they never signed out of their accounts, just left them open on their laptops in their bedroom. That's how I found out they were looking for their biological family. They'd go on these forums where adoptees entered personal information, like, what hospital they were born in, birth dates, anything they knew about their birth parents, whatever."

"You didn't like that they were on those forums?" Sunna could tell.

"I didn't. I hated that they wanted other family. They came to my parents as babies, so they were already there when I came along, and I felt like if they were enough for me, I should be enough for them. I didn't understand that they weren't looking for *extra* people—do you know what I mean? I didn't get it, and I didn't try to get it. Which was really unfair." She was talking upward again, confessing. "I didn't know what it was like to not know where someone is, someone who's intrinsically a part of you; I didn't know how much a person would want to know where that person was and why they weren't with you. I didn't get that you could love the people you were with while still agonizing over the unanswered questions about the ones you weren't with. And the worst part of all of this is that now I get it, and now I would be so sympathetic to them, and I would help them find their bio family because I get it. But I only get it because they're not here."

Mackenzie drew in a long, shaky breath.

"They found this guy named Owen on one of the forums. He convinced them that he was their older brother, and after a few months of emailing back and forth with them, he had this story about his house burning to the ground and needing money for a plane ticket to California. He said he had a hunch that's where their birth mother was. He asked for money and promised to repay them as soon as he could, and he said that if he found their mother, he'd try to convince her to come back with him and meet them. That's where they went that night. To meet Owen and give him all their money."

"And your mom's wedding rings."

Mackenzie seemed not to hear this, and Sunna was glad. She'd never had someone confess something so huge to her before and it was hard to hear it without trying to reply to it.

"So it was me." Mackenzie's voice rose, like she'd only just realized no one would overhear her. It must have felt good, not only to unburden herself but also to do it so loudly. "The anonymous tip that made them reopen the case. I called it in on a pay phone. I gave them the forum and their username and password. Something I should've done a long time ago."

Sunna was speechless. Which was probably good, because she knew if she were to speak, she'd say the wrong thing. There were no right things to say about something like that.

"I know you're probably judging me so hard right now," said Mackenzie, and Sunna cringed. She was; she couldn't help it. She didn't want to be. "I was *thirteen*. I was so mad at them for leaving me behind on our birthday, but I also didn't want them to hate me for ratting them out. I didn't know"—Mackenzie's voice rose and wavered—"that not ratting them out would mean I'd never see them again. I was pretty sheltered, and it honestly didn't cross my mind that this was what was going to happen. I thought—I honestly thought this, Sunna—that what had happened to them happened before they met up with Owen. That me giving that information to the police didn't matter because it was unrelated. Isn't that so, *so stupid*?" Then Mackenzie had to stop talking for a few minutes and Sunna kept quiet too.

Mackenzie was quiet for so long that it startled Sunna when she spoke again. She'd gone her whole life without absolute silence, and then gotten used to it in ten minutes.

"This is part of it too, though," said Mackenzie slowly. "Jared also knew. He was the one who drove them there. He was Tanya's friend then, not mine. I always thought they were dating when she disappeared, but he was never straight with me about it."

"How do you know he knew?"

"He came by the next day. My parents were driving around all over the place looking for my sisters, and I was supposed to stay home and answer the phone in case they called. My mom had gone by his house to see if my sisters were there—or Tanya, at least—and he told her he'd been home the previous evening and hadn't seen them. But I'd seen them all leave that night, and I'd thrown this big fit about being left behind. He knew I knew.

"He was really jumpy and agitated. He said Kate and Tanya left the party early. He didn't know when, or with who, just that at one point he'd looked around and they were both gone. He said he never saw the guy they were supposed to meet. But he wasn't worried about them; they'd probably just gone to someone's house and slept over. He was annoyed that my parents were worried, and was acting like it was this huge inconvenience that he had to come over to my place. But he told me"—Mackenzie paused and shifted in the darkness—"that I couldn't tell anyone about it. Turns out he was covering for his parents, who hosted the party. Can you believe that? That parents would ask their kid to lie for them? And then ask me to lie for them too? And here's the biggest, stupidest part: I had a crush on him. So I promised him I wouldn't say anything. A crush, Sunna. I—"

Mackenzie studied the big black cavern above them.

"I didn't tell anyone what I knew. I think I even believed him at first that it was no big deal, that my sisters were probably at another friend's place. And then by the time the police started asking questions, I'd already lied to my parents, told them I'd gone to sleep right after the party and didn't hear them leave. I was so naive. It all felt irreversible. And scary. I was scared of them thinking I was guilty of something horrible because I'd lied. I was scared of my parents thinking my sisters could've been saved if I hadn't lied—and I was really, *really* scared that was true. Still am, honestly . . ." She laughed weakly. "I was—I realize now—even scared of Jared, which got even more complicated when he and I started dating. Secretly dating, because my parents . . . Sunna, it was all just . . ."

"No, I get it. You don't have to make excuses. I get being scared."

"And now it's just . . . you know? I can't ever tell them."

"Mack. They'd understand. You were *thirteen*. People make terrible decisions when they're thirteen. You'd feel better."

"No. You should've heard my mom on the phone the other day, talking about 'those people who cared more about not getting into trouble than about her daughters.' And *I'm* one of those people. They'd never forgive me. And they can't afford that; they've already lost two daughters, you know? So. Today I'll go home, and my parents will tell us that they found out about 'Owen' and that the police caught him, and it'll all just go away. Apparently Jared told his side of the story, too, so, *good*. That's it. It's over."

Sunna shook her head. She knew what happened to relationships if you ignored things instead of working through them. She'd seen what happened between her parents. What had happened with her and her mother, her and her father, her and Brett. What had happened to the sidewalk in front of their house when the tree roots began to grow through it. "Stuff like that doesn't just go away, Mack."

Mackenzie frowned, but she didn't say anything more. A spectral howling sound filled the air, and Sunna grabbed Mackenzie's arm.

"It's just coyotes," said Mackenzie calmly. But then she laughed. "They sound like ghosts, don't they?"

LARRY GOES TO A SHOW

Larry

Larry was dressed in his favorite outfit, sourced from a thrift store in 1990—gray, XXL pin-striped dress pants his sister, Glenda, had altered in her tenth-grade home economics class to fit him. Old black-and-white chucks with holes in both heels. A teeny-tiny, impossibly tight black T-shirt—had he gotten it in the kids' section?—with a giant smiley face. A small rip by the right armpit was held together with safety pins. He'd been caught in a tough place in his teens: he loved punk fashion—the colorful hair, the plaid, the big boots and patches and dog collars and leather jackets—but then there was the whole antifashion punk movement, and he wanted to be part of that, too, because it sounded right (the music!—it was only ever about the music!). But also, he lived in Regina, Saskatchewan, where a lot of the politics and statements that drove punk in other regions were often ignored. So in the end, he found himself somewhere in the middle. A toned-down version of the English punks, an amped-up version of the antifashion crowd.

And tonight, he was back. He felt young again! His clothes still fit! He was going to a punk show!

He had a notepad in his pocket; he was going to write a review of the show and send it to a few local publications. It was time.

It would be dark in the venue; he'd blend right in with the kids. He'd stand in the back and feel the bass vibrating up his spine; he could reclaim that *feeling*. Maybe he'd get something pierced. Maybe he'd see a girl across the room, and she'd walk over. They wouldn't be able to talk during the show—it would be way too loud—but afterward, he'd say, "Hey, I don't feel like going home yet. You want to go to Smitty's with me?" Did people still do that? He chided himself. Didn't matter what kids did now. She would be older, like him. She would remember the scene the way he did. The kids would see them standing in the back and feel impressed. Respectful. Awed, even.

He locked the apartment door, watched his legs walk down the stairs, satisfied with his pin-striped pants. He caught his reflection in the car window as he leaned down to unlock the door. He looked a little like Guy Picciotto. He *felt* like Guy Picciotto.

In less than fifteen minutes, he went from Guy Picciotto to Mr. Rogers.

He was, for one thing, the first to arrive. The website said the band would start at seven, so he was there at quarter to. This part of things, to be fair, was foreign to him. He'd never been to a show at the Exchange. At house shows, they started when they started; no one ever put a time on it. But he wanted to make sure he didn't come in after the band had started playing. What if the stage was by the door, and everyone watched him come in? He wanted to plant himself against a wall somewhere so he could observe without being observed, at least until he was ready to be revered. So he needed to be there with plenty of time.

Turned out, he *was* there with plenty of time—a whopping forty-five minutes before anyone else showed up. For the first five, he leaned against a wall until his knees began to ache and he wished he was wearing his orthopedic shoes. He stood up again and straightened his shoulders, his back stiff and sore; he'd pay for those few moments of slouching for the next month or so. Glenda kept telling him to go to her chiropractor, but he was only forty-three! Now he thought he should change that *only* to an *already* and get himself in to see her guy.

The kid at the door was wearing jeans and a T-shirt. He was young—maybe thirty—and didn't have any tattoos or piercings; his hair was brown, and it sat on the top of his head in a style that would not look out of place in an office setting. He was drinking a beer and looked bored with his job and wary of the scrawny middle-aged man standing against the wall at the back of the room. The house lights were on. *Not right,* Larry thought grumpily—not unlike, he realized with dismay, a cantankerous old man. *None of this is right.*

At exactly 7:45 p.m., the band came in. Larry knew they were the band only because one of the guys had a bright-red electric guitar slung over his shoulder. They didn't look right, either; they looked like little kids on their way to some kind of weird dress-up party. A couple of the guys had their jeans tucked into their socks; they were wearing basketball jerseys and polo shirts. They looked preppy or athletic or some strange combination; not one of them looked like they played in a punk band, not even the punk band in his *Razorcake* with their tongues out. They didn't exude any kind of self-confidence or conviction or obstinance. Despite his own lack of confidence and conviction, Larry found himself irritated by their apparent nervousness.

Then the crowd began to filter in, and that was when it went from *Not right* to *Hey you kids, get off my lawn.*

Children! *Babies!* Walking in with their braces and acne and preppy clothing. Everyone was laughing, jumping around like idiots, showing off for each other. Why were they shrieking? This wasn't a theme park.

It was a punk show. Or . . . it was supposed to be, according to the website.

Larry wished the houselights would go down so he could fade into the corner.

"Larry!"

People looked in his direction, and Larry wished that whoever was shouting his name would stop shouting his name.

Wait.

"Sunna?"

MACKENZIE AND SUNNA GO TO A SHOW TOO! EVERYONE GOES TO A SHOW!

Mackenzie

It felt like a few days had passed, but it had only been that morning that Sunna had gone with Mackenzie to her childhood home and sat with her across from her mother and father in their outdated living room as they tearfully filled her in on everything she'd already explained to Sunna on the hood of her car a few minutes before. As she sat there, trying to appear shocked at all the right moments, Mackenzie realized that Sunna was right: it wasn't going to go away just because they knew what had happened. A bad decision she'd made when she was thirteen was going to be with her forever, whether or not she told her parents about it now. She'd made the decision to keep quiet when she was thirteen, and maybe Sunna was right that no one would hold that against her, but she'd doubled down on that decision when she was fourteen, and fifteen, and sixteen, and seventeen, and eighteen, and nineteen. At some point in there, she was certain, she had forfeited her right to mercy.

Her parents had only one piece of information that Mackenzie didn't already know: the police had been able to track down and arrest Owen—whose name was, of course, not Owen—and there was going to be a trial. Owen-who-was-not-Owen was being charged with two murders, though Kate's body was still missing.

And now, Sunna and Mackenzie were taking the exit off the high-way back into the city. Sunna had surely noticed that it was the wrong exit, that Mackenzie wasn't headed back to their place, but she wasn't saying anything about it; after all, she was not the one who had just been told that her sister's missing person case was closed because there was no longer a missing person, only a most-likely-dead one.

To say Mackenzie wasn't feeling like herself tonight would be an understatement. She felt reckless for the first time in years. She'd spent so much of her life terrified that she was going to end up missing like her sisters, taking care to make sure that her whereabouts were not only known but written down somewhere—on a work schedule, on an attendance page—but tonight she kept thinking about how going missing might not be the worst thing. It suddenly felt like the better alternative to having to face her parents anymore. It would be better for them to have another daughter disappear altogether than to have to find out that she might've been able to save their other two in the first place.

"Where are we going?" Sunna said in a cautious voice. "Home?"

"No," Mackenzie said, squinting at a street sign, trying to remember how many blocks past Broad she needed to go. "House is too quiet. I want to be somewhere loud."

"Oh. I get that. Well . . . the mall is loud? And I'm pretty sure it's open until nine . . ."

"No, I mean *really* loud. I don't want to be able to hear myself think."

"Oh." Sunna was quiet for a moment. "I don't really know this city yet—"

"No." Mackenzie was going somewhere she'd never been before, but she had the address memorized. "I actually have a place in mind."

"Oh."

"Is that okay? I can drop you off at home first. I'm sorry, Sunna, I just started driving this way. I should've asked—"

"It's cool," said Sunna, and she sounded like it was, mostly. "Where are we going?"

"The Exchange," said Mackenzie.

"And that is . . . a bar?"

"A venue."

"Oh. Live music?"

"Is that okay?"

Sunna didn't say yes, but she didn't say no either. "Do you know who's playing tonight?"

"Nope. But it's Friday, so chances are good that *someone's* playing, and that's all I care about. I just want . . ." Mackenzie inhaled and suddenly felt dizzy. It was something like jet lag, like she'd been traveling for days and hadn't slept and hadn't felt all *that* tired, and then her body realized, in a millisecond, that it needed to shut down immediately. "I just . . . I want . . ."

She pulled in front of the old warehouse and put the car into park with a shaking hand, thankful she'd arrived before she crashed the car.

"You okay, Mack?"

Mackenzie nodded, resting her forehead on the steering wheel, deliberately pushing all the air out of her lungs and then dragging it back in. "I just want *noise.*"

"Okay. Let's go get you some noise."

~

A group of teenagers hung around the entrance of the Exchange. They ignored Mackenzie and Sunna as they walked up the rickety wooden ramp to the door.

The band hadn't started yet, but tinny emo music blared from the house speakers. The guy who took their money at the door looked old and bored and out of place in his baggy jeans, like a parent chaperone at a high school dance. The Exchange looked just like every picture she'd ever seen of it, every video Celeste had shown her. Celeste had come here all the time in high school with her friends; Mackenzie had only dreamed of it. Obsessed over it. She'd written whole concert reviews of shows she'd only seen snippets of online, imagining she'd been there too. Standing here now was like finding out that a recurring dream you'd been having for your whole life was about a place that existed and then going there.

"Is that . . . Larry?" Sunna pointed at a figure slouched in the corner of the room like a wilting sunflower. "He looks super dismal."

Mackenzie laughed, surprising both of them. "He does. Wow."

"What's he doing here, I wonder?"

"Oh." Mackenzie thought maybe he'd taken her up on her invitation. "I uh . . . I told him about it."

"You?"

"Well, yeah. He was at our house that day when you locked yourself out. He said he liked punk music. Lots of punk bands play here, so I figured . . ."

"Oh. Nice of you. Well . . . should we . . ."

"Go say hi?"

"I was going to say . . . not that." Sunna glanced furtively at Larry, who hadn't noticed them yet. "I was thinking maybe . . . we could stand over there." She gestured at the open area by the bar, where they would be hidden behind the sound booth.

"Sunna."

"What? You want to talk to him?"

"Well. Not *want*. But like, he's here alone. And I was the one who told him about it. And what if he sees us and realizes we're avoiding him?" Mackenzie felt emotion thicken in her throat. She knew it wasn't *for* Larry, but the people it *was* for weren't around anymore, so Larry could have it. It was like the day they'd found Tanya's body—the first thing Mackenzie did was go into Tanya's room and find the gift she'd given her for that last birthday. She'd walked out the front door, past her sobbing parents and the police officers, who hadn't even left yet, and she'd gone to the house four doors down where one of Tanya's friends lived. There, she'd stuffed the gift—a record—into the mailbox and run back home. For some reason the thought of that record sitting in Tanya's room, still wrapped in its cellophane, was all-consuming. She'd wanted to clean out Tanya's whole room, redistribute her things to anyone who would have them. It was just awful to think of something she'd given to her sister, with so much care, just sitting there unused. Wasted. She hadn't understood why then, and she didn't fully understand now, either, but maybe it was about the energy, the emotional work. If you put that kind of work or energy or—love?—into something for another person, and they didn't use it or receive it, where did it go? And if you didn't redirect it, would it just dissipate, not matter anymore?

Sunna nodded. "Right. Maybe." She stretched an arm around Mackenzie's shoulders and pulled her into a side hug. "Let's go say hi."

"Thanks."

"Larry!" Sunna began to weave through the small crowd, pulling Mackenzie along behind her. Larry spotted them, looking exactly as surprised as Mackenzie thought he would.

"Sunna?"

Sunna forced a smile. "Hi, Larry. You're here to see . . ." She looked back at Mackenzie, who shrugged. Neither of them had even glanced at the posters plastered all over the wall on their way in.

Larry nodded, his eyes shining like he was talking to a celebrity. "Yeah," he said enthusiastically. "They're really great."

"Oh good," said Sunna. "So—who is it? Who's playing, I mean?"

Larry looked mortified. "Uh . . . you know, I . . . don't remember"—he emitted a nervous laugh that made Mackenzie want to start crying again—"their name. I just, I just meant I heard they were good . . . from the . . . the kid at the door." He motioned at the "kid," who was now counting the money in the cashbox and looking more angry than bored. Maybe angry about being bored.

Sunna was really trying to be a good sport, Mackenzie could tell. "Cool," she said, looking at Mackenzie for help.

Then, something happened that felt like a miracle at first simply because it was a distraction. It was, however, incredibly unlucky and the exact opposite of a miracle: Jared walked in. He had an arm draped loosely around the neck of his doctor fiancée, his hand resting on her shoulder. She put her own hand over his, and they surveyed the room, the kids, the three adults standing in one corner. Mackenzie barely had time to hope he wouldn't see her before he saw her.

"Hey, Mackenzie!" he called, pulling his future wife along with him. "Where's your parrot?"

"You have a parrot?" Larry looked concerned. "Uhhh, in the house you have a parrot? Uhhh, not to sound like a—"

"No, no." Mackenzie felt strangely thankful for Larry in this moment. "No, a stuffed one—part of my work uniform."

"Oh good. Good. Because, you know, the pet thing—in your contract—"

"Oh yeah, no worries, Larry."

Jared still had his arm over Lauren's shoulder, their fingers interlaced. His eyes were glassy, and his breath reeked. "Wait, you all here to see the band?"

Sunna, Larry, and Mackenzie nodded in unison, and Jared laughed. "Huh. Okay."

Mackenzie shifted uncomfortably. "You're . . . not?"

He snorted. "It's Lauren's little brother's band. We *had* to come. Which is why *I*"—he pointed at the bar and made a clicking sound with his tongue as he dug in his pocket for his wallet—"am gonna head over to . . ." He turned to go, but then turned back, looking more sober. "Oh, hey, Mackenzie, I heard about all the new stuff with your sister's case. Sorry, man."

Sorry, man.

How about, *I am so sorry to hear that, Mackenzie.*

How about, *I couldn't believe it.*

How about, *Are you okay?*

Maybe even, *I'm sorry I didn't say anything. I'm sorry I made you go along with me.*

She swallowed, but she had no saliva in her mouth and had to clear her throat. "How did you find out?"

"It's been on the news. Glad they caught that guy; what a creep." His fiancée was looking at him in confusion, so he elaborated for her. "Guy killed Mackenzie's sisters. One was just missing for a while, but they're pretty sure she's dead now. There's going to be a trial." He noticed everyone staring at him and added, "Sad, real sad. Sucks." *Sucks.* "Anyway. But. I just . . . like, I guess I'm just a little relieved. I'm off the hook now that they know who did it, you know?" His eyes narrowed at her, and even though the stupid smile stayed on his face, she realized he was upset. "What's the matter, Mackenzie? Are you mad that your 'anonymous tip' didn't get me into big trouble?" He reached out and tugged at Mackenzie's shirtsleeve. She stepped backward, and he howled. "What? You didn't think I'd know it was you? As soon as they said there'd been a tip, I knew it was you. And I knew exactly what you told them."

"I didn't say anything about you," she said.

"*Right,*" said Jared. He wasn't smiling at all now. "I don't know why, but for some reason I don't believe you. Hmm. Maybe because you *lie* sometimes?"

Mackenzie shook her head, willing herself not to burst into tears. "I didn't. And this isn't a great time, Jared. I just got back from my parents' house—"

"And straight out for a night on the town? That's weird." Jared looked around the circle, and his eyes landed on Larry. "Well? Isn't it weird? If my sister *died*, I doubt I'd be *here* . . ."

Sunna's mouth hung open. Lauren was staring at her shoes. Larry's face was now completely devoid of that anxious, pleading, please-like-me puppy-dog look. He was mad. Suddenly, he didn't look ridiculous and out of place here; everyone else in the whole room did. He shook his head, his arms crossed tightly, his hands in his armpits.

"Kid," he said, "maybe you should go hang out somewhere else."

Jared's face turned red. "I'm not a kid, and maybe you shouldn't tell other people what to do."

Larry stepped closer to Jared. "I'm not trying to tell you what to do, but you're obviously a little drunk—Mackenzie's had a rough day from the sounds of it, and she can handle it however she wants to, and I just think you should knock it off."

"Sure, I'll knock it off." Jared took a swing at Larry's head. He looked like a five-year-old going at a piñata with a blindfold on. The element of surprise still prevailed, and Larry, though he hadn't been hit all that hard, fell over. But, because the precedent had been set, and because she'd wanted to for a while now, and because she wasn't in a very good mood that night to begin with, and, last but not least, because she was feeling reckless, Mackenzie didn't have to think twice about taking a swing herself.

Jared went down.

Sunna and Lauren stood looking at each other. Lauren gaped at her fiancé on the floor and then turned and left the building without a word to anyone.

Jared scrambled to his feet and went after her without looking at Mackenzie or Larry. Larry stood, too, and his shoulders sagged forward. "Sorry, Mackenzie—"

"Don't be, Larry. That was really nice. He's . . . completely awful."

"Did that feel good?" Sunna asked.

"No," said Mackenzie.

After a moment, Sunna said, "Well, it felt good for me."

"Same," said Larry. "I'm glad you did it, even if you're not. I wanted to myself."

"Oh, I'm not sorry I did it," said Mackenzie, examining the back of her hand. "It just didn't feel good. Faces are a lot harder than you'd expect."

Larry was nodding again, the way he usually did. Nodding, nodding, nodding. "Looks like the band's getting ready to start," he said, and sure enough, some little kids were on the stage. The crowd was fairly disinterested.

"Hi," said the one in the front. He looked petrified and held his guitar like it was an alligator. "Thanks for coming out. We're going to get started here."

Larry shook his head. "We're going to get started here," he mimicked, but he was smiling. "Was it like this when I was this age? Am I remembering it wrong?" Mackenzie wasn't sure if he was talking to her or not, so she pretended not to hear him.

The band started into their first song, and Larry pulled out a notebook. Mackenzie shut her eyes. The music was terrible, but it was loud enough, and she was at her first live show, and no one knew where she was, and if she went missing, the police would have absolutely nothing to go off of, and for the first time in her life she didn't care about that. She was free and sad and excited and weightless and so, so, *so* unbearably heavy.

THE WIDOW'S WALK

Sunna

"Maude, you're going to spill your coffee. And mine." Sunna restrained herself from reaching across the table and holding Maude down.

"This is a terrible idea." Maude's whole body vibrated. She was dressed up; she wore a necklace and makeup. She had obviously fussed with her hair, too, but it still clung to her head like a stubborn little animal. Her lipstick made the dryness of her lips more apparent. Most of the mascara she'd applied now rested in the wrinkles and creases beneath her eyes in heavy lines. Altogether, she looked desperate and pathetic, and it made Sunna feel sad.

"No, it isn't," Mackenzie said. "You've been letting this Richard thing consume you because you think it serves him right not to hear from you ever again. But what about you? Closure is a unicorn. Sunna and I aren't getting it, but you have the opportunity. Now you don't want it? That's stupid. Take it, Maude."

Sunna nodded. "Bravo, Mack. Well said."

Maude grumbled something Mackenzie couldn't hear, but Mackenzie didn't seem to care.

Sunna leaned over the table. "To take your mind off it, Maude— because you still have at least five minutes, and if you just sit there shaking, your brain will be completely scrambled by the time he gets here—could you please tell me what you were up to last night? Eleven p.m.? Were you . . . *square dancing?*"

Maude threw herself back in her chair. "Sunna! How many times do I have to tell you? I do nothing up there. I go to bed way before eleven p.m. Sometimes I can't sleep, so I go out and have a smoke. Although I'm a little bit afraid to do that now because last time I did, I was robbed and assaulted. That's it, that's all. You saw the attic—there's nobody up there. You either need to move or get used to a few harmless noises. And I do think they're harmless. If we leave them alone." Maude seemed less confident on this point today.

"I heard it too," said Mackenzie, frowning. "It really did sound like square dancing. I even thought I heard music. And . . ."

"And?" Maude coaxed.

"Did . . . did you guys leave flowers . . . on my kitchen table?"

Maude shook her head. "Wasn't me. Was it your boyfriend?"

Mackenzie blanched. "I don't have a boyfriend."

"Don't lie to me, Mackenzie. I saw him at your work. I saw you with him. Flirting. I saw him watching you. I saw you watching him. I saw—"

"Maude." Sunna shook her head. "What did I tell you—"

"Oh, come off it, Sunna. This was before you told me to stop spying on people. And look!" She held her arms out and lifted her chin. "I have. So calm down." Sunna gave her a look, and Maude clucked her tongue the way she always did. But then she seemed to have some kind of internal conversation and cleared her throat. "No, you're right, Sunna. You're right about this—you're right about Richard. I'm sorry for coming into your room when you were sleeping, Sunna. And Mackenzie, I'm even more sorry to you. I'm sorry I invaded your privacy and . . . called you a murderer."

Mackenzie smiled and shook her head. "It's all good, Maude. We're cool."

Sunna felt as though she'd just witnessed a sleight of hand trick. Did it work like that? Could you just apologize for calling someone a murderer? She'd called Brett all kinds of things but never once implied she was capable of killing her sister, and yet her apology hadn't been at all effective.

"Wait." Sunna squinted at Mackenzie. "Someone put flowers in your kitchen?"

Mackenzie nodded. "They were there this morning when I woke up. They had a little card attached that said *Sorry for your loss*. They weren't there last night when I went to bed. And the only people who have keys to my place are . . . well, you guys and . . ."

"Larry," said Sunna.

"But he wouldn't do that," said Mackenzie. "I don't think."

Sunna shrugged. "Maybe your boyfriend got Larry to let him into your place. That makes the most sense. Also, I didn't know you had a boyfriend."

"Because I don't," said Mackenzie, suddenly unable to make eye contact.

"Okay," said Sunna. She took a drink of her coffee. "But yeah, Maude, it really did sound like you were dancing up there. So creepy. I thought I would feel better after seeing the attic, but I definitely feel worse. There's not even enough room up there for a person to fully stand up. Like, I know ghosts as a concept aren't constrained by physical spaces, but how am I hearing noises directly above me when there isn't even attic directly above me?"

"What do you mean?" asked Mackenzie.

"I mean—oh, I guess you didn't see the attic. It was a tiny little crawl space. It doesn't extend across the length or width of the entire house, not even close. I'm hearing sound where there isn't *space*. How is that possible? Are the ghosts dancing on the roof?"

Mackenzie sat up. "You guys!" She half stood in her excitement. "There's a widow's walk!"

"A what?"

"A widow's walk! On the top of our house. A widow's walk."

"I don't know what that is," said Sunna dryly. She didn't watch those shows on cable about house renovations and interior design. Those, she thought, were probably interesting for people who owned or wanted to own a house. Sunna had only ever wanted a small apartment, a place to crash between flights to other places.

Maude sniffed. "A widow's walk is that little patio on the roof with the, uh"—she snapped her fingers, looking for the word—"the railing around the outside? A lot of older houses have them."

"My mom is obsessed with them," Mackenzie said. "She noticed it right away when she saw the pictures in the rental listing. She said it's usually more of a coastal home feature, that you don't really see it here on the prairies all that much—so maybe the builder was a bit eccentric. The story behind them is something about women whose husbands were lost at sea; they'd go out on the roof and watch for their beloveds. And then it just sort of became a trend in home building."

Maude nodded. "Rich people liked how it looked. But what . . . ?" She looked at Mackenzie quizzically, and Sunna felt herself do the same.

"How would someone get up there? Is there a staircase on the outside of the house?"

Maude shook her head. "No, I don't think so."

"And did you see a way to get onto the roof from inside the attic?"

"I didn't look very closely," said Sunna. "There were a lot of us looking in there all at once. But no, I didn't see a door or a ladder or anything."

"I don't know much about house construction," said Mackenzie, "but I feel like if the home builder went to the trouble of building a widow's walk, they wouldn't have closed it off. And a house that size really should have a large attic anyway."

"But it doesn't," said Sunna. "I saw it."

"But maybe you didn't see the whole thing? I want to go look," said Mackenzie. "Did they lock the door again after they left? The police?"

"I haven't checked," said Maude, "but I don't think so. Let's go now."

"Maude." Mackenzie laughed. "You can't. You have an appointment."

Maude sighed. "I don't want to have an appointment. This was a terrible idea." She started trembling again.

The bell over the coffee shop door tinkled. He was one minute early.

~

Richard, presumably Richard, as Maude hadn't positively identified him yet, just stood at the entrance, and people filed around him as though he were a turnstile. He had a large head, a heavy-looking nose, and a substantial mouth. He wore a suit jacket and tugged at the sleeves as though he wasn't used to such attire. He kept touching his hair and face, patting them like they were brand new. His shoulders rounded, and he looked as though he was practicing saying *Sorry* in his head. That was how Sunna knew it was the right person.

"Do you want us to leave you alone with him?" asked Sunna.

Maude's little head swiveled around on her neck, craning to see Richard. She spotted him standing just inside the door and ducked her head.

"No!" she whispered fiercely. "Do *not* leave me alone."

Mackenzie shifted in her chair. "Maude . . . that's just going to be super awkward. For *everyone*."

"Not for me," said Maude. "I'm going for closure, as you said, not comfort. And I *definitely* don't care if he feels awkward. He *should*. I *want* him to."

Sunna shot a panicked look at Mackenzie, who returned it with equal weight. Neither of them wanted to be privy to such an intimate discussion.

Still, they sat.

"Well?" Sunna said to Maude after a few moments. "How's he going to know it's you?"

"Sunna. It's only been a few years. I've lost a few pounds, but I look the same; he'll know it's me."

"Of course."

But he didn't seem to, and Sunna wasn't sure if she should point it out or not. He was scanning the room, looking more anxious by the minute. Once or twice, Sunna saw his eyes pass their table, but his gaze didn't even slow down as it swept over Maude.

"I think you're going to need to go over there and get him," Sunna said.

She expected Maude to start screeching at her to mind her own business, but Maude did a shocking thing instead: she clasped Sunna's hand with both of hers and leaned in with shining eyes. "Will you go get him for me?" she pleaded. "Please? I can't."

"What? No!" Sunna gave her an exasperated look, but it was getting harder and harder to treat Maude poorly, and this was most likely a good thing. The more time she spent around Mackenzie, the more she wanted to be like her. *"Oh, all right."*

She walked toward the man at the door, who now looked like he was about to leave. He saw her approaching, but she could tell he didn't think she was approaching *him*. When at last she stood right in front of him, he still didn't seem to think she wanted to talk to him. He looked over her, around her, not rudely, but like he was self-aware enough to know that a young woman would never approach him in a coffee shop.

"Excuse me," she said.

He looked over his shoulder, his expression guarded and uncertain.

"Yes?" he said tentatively. "Can I help you?"

"Yeah," she said, feeling sorry for him and slightly amused. "So, I'm here with Maude . . . ?"

"Oh!" He smiled, looking more terrified but less confused. "She's here?"

"Yeah," said Sunna. "That table, there."

Richard's gaze followed her finger. He blinked at the vulturelike figure that had once been his fiancée.

"Oh," he said. "I didn't . . . I didn't recognize her." He looked like he might cry. "She . . ." He began to scratch his neck, leaving red lines. "But you're right—that's her," he said now. "That's Maude. I didn't recognize her. Her hair used to be—" He nodded at Sunna, catching himself. "I suppose she's told you all about me."

Sunna laughed, unsure how to reply. "I . . . well, yeah?"

He shrugged and started scratching his neck again. "That's fair," he said. He cleared his throat. "But. Well. I should probably . . . go over there." He smiled, as if to leave her and go to Maude, not realizing that she would be following right after him, sitting down beside him.

Poor Richard.

THE WIDOWER'S WALK

Mackenzie

Mackenzie watched Richard approach. In the space between the door and the table, he slowed down and sped up twice. Maude held still, her eyes fixed on Mackenzie, full of trepidation. She must have heard him stop behind her chair, but still she didn't move, and he just stood there staring at the back of her head. Sunna couldn't get past him to sit in her seat, so she waited. The three of them were frozen in that moment, staggered, staring at Mackenzie, waiting for her to do something.

Mackenzie didn't know where to look or what to say. She wanted to take her backpack and leave, but she couldn't do that to Maude. "Hi," she said to Richard. It felt like a safe bet. And it forced Maude to turn and look at him. He, in turn, self-consciously took a step backward, right into Sunna, who was then able to apologize and squeeze past him, plunking herself back into her seat and making a hilarious expression at Mackenzie, who was about to burst out laughing at the ridiculousness of it all. And then everyone—except Maude—looked like they might laugh, but no one did.

Maude spoke crisply. "Hello" and "Please sit down, Richard." Like he was there for a job interview. Or to be fired.

This was when Richard seemed to realize that Mackenzie and Sunna were not leaving. He looked at Maude. Maude looked up at the ceiling, lips pursed, waiting for him to sit. He had no choice. He sat.

"Hi, Maude," he said. He looked at his hands. He nodded at Mackenzie too. "Oh, hi. I'm Richard." Maybe he thought that if he introduced himself, they would leave. He was going to be disappointed.

"Mackenzie."

He shook her hand and then Sunna's. "We've met already—sorry, didn't catch your name."

"Sunna."

"Oh!" he said. "That's an interesting name. You're from . . . ?"

"Toronto," she said.

He smiled at all of them like he was in a great deal of pain, and Maude let him suffer for a long time before Mackenzie nudged her under the table. "I hope you won't mind if my friends join us," she said to Richard, glowering at Mackenzie.

He shrugged. "If that's what you need," he said. "But I have to say, I wouldn't mind having a word alone with you at some point."

"That won't be possible," said Maude.

Richard seemed shocked at this. It was the second or third time he'd been shocked since he walked into the coffee shop, and he had to be wishing he hadn't showed up at all at this point. To his credit, he kept trying to make eye contact with Maude, kept trying to smile at Sunna and Mackenzie. Kept not leaving.

"Well," he said, "I can't say I blame you, Maude. I acted very poorly." Mackenzie peeked at Maude to see what kind of effect this had on her, but Maude just sat there, picking at her cuticles and blinking like she had fleas in her eyes. "However," said Richard after a beat, "I am glad you called me. I've thought of calling you many times and just assumed you'd never hear me out."

Still, Maude didn't raise her head.

He sighed, tugged at his sleeves, rolled his shoulders. "Come on, Maude. *You* called *me*, remember? Are you just trying to punish me? Because I gotta say, it's working. I'm not really sure . . ." Richard trailed off. His hands were out in front of him in surrender, and his heels jittered against the tile floor. He looked helplessly at Mackenzie and then at Sunna.

Maude's punishing all of us right now. Mackenzie wondered if they would all sit there until the coffee shop closed, and then Maude would smirk at the people seated around her and say something about how they all deserved these five miserable hours, and then stand and triumphantly stalk out of the shop.

But Maude was punishing herself too. She appeared more agitated by the second, working hard to keep it together. Mackenzie reached under the table and rested a hand on the older woman's knee. Maude blinked at her gratefully. Or at least, Mackenzie thought it was a grateful look. Maude was still so hard to read.

"No, you're right. I called you," Maude said at last.

Richard relaxed just a little. He nodded. "What . . . did you want to talk about?" He cast looks at Sunna and Mackenzie as though maybe they didn't understand what was going on and would leave if they did.

Poor Richard. Mackenzie settled back in her chair to let him know he shouldn't get his hopes up. Somehow, she and Sunna had become loyal to the sharp old lady.

Suddenly, Maude slammed both palms down on the table—her signature move—and Richard jumped. Mackenzie and Sunna didn't even flinch. "Oh *come* on, Richard! You *know* what I want to talk about. I want to talk about why a person would propose to another person and then get drunk out of his big stupid brains on his wedding day. I want to talk about why he would tell someone he loved her and then do something so *awful*, something that any empathetic person with half a big stupid brain would know not to do—because if he did have a brain—or a *heart!*—he'd know how much it would hurt her, how it would practically *kill* her." It was alarming, the amount of precipitation coming off Maude's face. Sweat from her forehead, tears from her eyes, spit from her mouth. "And then," she said, her voice quaking, "we could talk about how cowardly a person would have to be to never *speak* to that woman again. To never even think he owed her an *explanation*. How much could he have loved her if he did all of *that*? Let's talk about *that*. He must not have loved her very much at all. I would even say that he must have *hated* her. Because *I* would never do *any* of that—let alone *all* of it—to someone if I even kind of *tolerated* them."

At some point during this speech, Richard's large head fell into the palms of his hands, and he began making uncomfortable squeaking noises. Mackenzie was mortified. She had not been prepared for grown-man tears. Sunna began mouthing things at her that she couldn't understand. She mouthed back that she had no idea what Sunna was trying to tell her. Sunna gestured at Maude and mouthed something else, and then Mackenzie became aware that both Richard and Maude were watching them mouth things back and forth to each other and clamped her mouth shut.

Look at the time, she wished she could say. *I should get home to bed.* Alas, it was the middle of the afternoon. What other reasons did people give for leaving places? She couldn't think of a single one.

Richard leaned toward Maude, his voice barely above a whisper, as though they could have this conversation in front of Mackenzie and Sunna without actually involving them in it. "Maude," he said. "Oh, Maude." His eyes were red, and his mouth was moving a lot in between words. "I did love you. I'm so sorry. You have no idea."

Maude's tears dried up as soon as she saw his. She sat tall with her neck outstretched, like she was trying to look down on him. "That's not enough," she said. "I'm not here to give you a second chance, just so you know. I only want to know why you did all of that."

Richard seemed to have thought that a second chance was exactly what he would be getting that day. "Oh," he said, crestfallen. "That's fair. Okay." He sniffed and tried to compose himself. "Well, first of all, I think . . ." He looked at Mackenzie and then back at Maude. "Well, I was afraid—"

Sunna snorted, and everyone turned to look at her. She raised her eyebrows. "What?" she said. "I've just heard that line so many times. Everybody's afraid. That's not a good excuse. Next."

Richard looked like he wanted to tattle on Sunna to someone, but upon looking around the table he was sorely reminded that this table was squarely Team Maude. He nodded again. "True. That's true," he said. "It's not an excuse. It—it is a reason. It is the truth"—he shot a look at Sunna—"but it definitely doesn't excuse what I did. So. Here, let me start at the beginning. When I met you, Maude, I fell in love with you right away. You were so funny, and so easy to be with. But our relationship, it really caught me off guard. Everything happened so fast. We went on that first date, and all of a sudden we were engaged—"

"You proposed," said Sunna. She was taking her role as moderator very seriously.

"Pardon?" said Richard. "That's what I said."

"No, you didn't at all. You said, 'We were engaged.' You should have said, 'I proposed to you.' You didn't just *become* engaged by sneezing on her at a speed dating thing," said Sunna, pointing to various places on the table like she had a map of their relationship laid out in front of her. She jabbed her finger down on an imagined point A and dragged it to point B. "You *proposed* to Maude. You *asked* her to become engaged. It just sounds very passive the way you said it, like something that happened to you, as opposed to an action you took." She smiled at him, didn't even try to cover up her condescension. "Just thought that was an important clarification."

Sunna was ruthless. Sunna was amazing. *She should talk to Jared next.*

Maude seemed to think Sunna was amazing too. She nodded in agreement with the speech.

"Okay," said Richard, who, to his credit, corrected himself and carried on. "We went on that first date, and before very long, I proposed to you. Because I wanted to marry you. And because you wanted to be married so badly."

"Interesting," said Sunna.

Richard looked down at his hands, and a vein popped out on his forehead. "What's interesting, Su, uh—" He looked up at her.

"Sunna," she said. "I just think it's interesting that you phrased it that way. You wanted to marry *her*, but she just wanted to *be married*. To anybody? Is that what you meant? That you felt as though she would've married anyone, didn't matter if it was you?"

"Well, no—"

"Oh, because that's what you said."

"Well." Richard tugged on his sleeves, and then his collar, and then the knees of his pants. "I'm not saying that; I'm not speaking for her. But I have to admit, it felt like that, a little." He looked across the table at Maude.

"That's ridiculous," said Maude. "Ridiculous."

Sunna gently steered the conversation away. "We'll get to feelings later. Especially speculated ones. Your explanation shouldn't involve what you thought Maude was thinking, just what you were thinking and what you did. Keep going. So you proposed . . ."

Richard took another deep breath. "I proposed. And she—you—agreed to marry me. And everything was great, and then the day of the wedding came—"

"Oh," said Mackenzie, without meaning to. Everyone looked at her, and she blushed.

"What now?" asked Richard, who had moved, in one conversation, through embarrassment, exasperation, confusion, grief, shame, and annoyance and now appeared to have resigned himself to this strange meeting with some level of humility and openness. Mackenzie couldn't help but give him points for that.

"Well." Mackenzie couldn't believe she was speaking. She'd wanted to stay as much out of this as she could, considering the present situation, but Sunna's boldness must have rubbed off on her. "It feels like you skipped something. If everything was great, and then the wedding came—and the wedding was the day you left her . . ."

Richard blinked at Mackenzie, then at Sunna. He placed both hands on the table. "I'm sorry, who *are* you? Maude, is this really necessary?"

But Maude glared at him until he quieted and said, "They're friends of mine. And I thought that was a good point, Mackenzie. Thank you. I would also like to know what happened in between us meeting and our wedding day that put you off marrying me."

"Hi, Mackenzie!" Larry appeared at the side of the table then, balancing on his heels and bending his neck so that his head hovered over their table like a desk lamp. "Oh, hey, Maude. And Sunna's here too. Wow!" Larry nodded at Richard and held out a hand. "Hi, I'm Larry. You're a friend of . . . ?" When Richard didn't answer, Larry gestured at Maude. Maude shook her head, and Larry shrank a bit.

Richard looked like he was going to fall out of his chair. He looked at Maude incredulously.

"Larry!" Mackenzie had forgotten about the coffee date she'd set with Larry to go over his writing stuff. Could the timing have been any worse? "You came!"

"Yep," said Larry proudly. "I'm really excited about this."

Richard was mortified. "Excited . . . ?"

"Me too," said Mackenzie.

"Pull up a chair, Larry," said Maude, who could not possibly have known why he was there but was obviously more than pleased to add to Richard's discomfort.

So Larry dragged a chair from another table to theirs, and the legs screeched loudly across the floor like fingernails, like even an inanimate object could tell that the tension at the table was too thick and awkward to go into willingly. Larry, however, was oblivious.

"I did a little write-up about that show at the Exchange, and I brought it along as kind of a sample piece," he said to Mackenzie, flashing her a goofy grin. "I know you said you didn't want payment for this, but I just appreciate it so much—"

Richard cleared his throat. "Do you two want to continue this conversation at another table maybe?"

"Richard!" Maude clucked her tongue. Mackenzie pictured a slightly younger version of this couple in a relationship, him saying something inappropriate, her admonishing him and rolling her eyes, smiling in spite of herself.

Larry's mouth dropped open. "Oh," he said. "I'm interrupting something."

"No," said Maude.

"Yes," said Richard.

"Sorry," said Mackenzie. "This is my bad. Larry, let's move over—"

"No, no, Mackenzie," said Maude. "I still need you here for a minute. Larry, you're fine where you are."

Larry nodded. Dark circles were already forming under his armpits.

"Maude," whined Richard, "I know I deserve this . . . whatever this is. I know. I was awful. It's just so hard to form a sentence with three women . . . a-a-and"—he looked at Larry—"staring me down . . ."

"Maybe he's right, Maude," Mackenzie began, but Maude gave a single shake of her head that said *no* louder and more definitively than if she'd shouted. Mackenzie sat back and gave Richard an apologetic look.

"So?" Maude said. "What was it? The thing that happened between the engagement and the wedding?"

Larry leaned forward.

Richard looked her square in the eye. "Nothing. But that's just the thing, Maude. There was no time for anything to happen. We were engaged for all of a month!"

Sunna and Mackenzie swung their heads toward Maude in unison. "A month! No, Richard, it was at least three," Maude said, throwing her hands in the air.

"No, I met you in October, and we were engaged in November and married—er, almost, er . . . in December." He cleared his throat. "It was October for sure when we met. It was a Halloween-themed speed dating, uh, thing."

"No, I met you in February. It was a Valentine's Day speed dating event." She rolled her eyes. "*Halloween* speed dating? Why in the world would the library throw a speed dating event for *Halloween*? We met on Valentine's Day, and we were engaged in March, and our wedding was set for June. It was summer, Richard—you know how I know? Because I was the one standing in the *park* in a wedding dress. I would have known, Richard, if it were December! I would've died of hypothermia before you had a chance to break my heart!"

It seemed to dawn on Richard then that he was wrong. He spent a long time perusing an internal catalog for the appropriate response. "Right," he said finally, and it must have seemed like a good choice because he repeated himself. "Right."

"So three months," said Maude, tipping her head toward Mackenzie, "from the time *you* asked *me*"—she glanced at Sunna—"to marry you. What happened?"

Richard's jaw seemed to collapse. He sighed. "Honestly, Maude, nothing. The time between the engagement and the wedding flew by for me. I loved every minute of it—"

"Then, what?" Maude pleaded. "You woke up on the morning of the wedding and realized you didn't love me all of a sudden?"

"No!" cried Richard. "I woke up on the morning of the wedding and realized that I loved you too much!"

Sunna groaned. "Aw, Richard! I was starting to root for you. Get out of here with that."

This confused the man. He had, perhaps, thought his impassioned words would win the hearts of his strange audience. Although he seemed to resent the fact that he had these spectators, Richard now looked to Sunna for help. "I . . . I don't . . . what's wrong with . . ."

"What's wrong with what you just said?"

He nodded. Mackenzie felt sorry for him. He looked so lost.

"Poor lamb," said Sunna, and Larry laughed but was quickly silenced by a dark look from Richard. "You don't leave someone standing at the altar because you love them too much. You just don't. You said that because you thought it would make her feel better, but it's not going to because it's not the truth, and she's not dumb enough to believe it is. You don't get to waltz back into her life spewing this schmaltzy crap and expecting her to eat it up. She's smarter than that."

"Thank you, Sunna," said Maude.

"So what you need to say, at this point," said Sunna, "is what happened that morning that caused you to get blasted and miss your own wedding. And you need to leave out the flattery, the rom-com-speak, and give it to her straight. If you thought she was too ugly for you, you say that. If you couldn't stand the way she chews her food with her mouth open, you say that. If you were in love with someone else, you say that. That is how explanations work. They *explain*. They do not assuage your guilty conscience. This is the trial, not the community service, and you're not allowed to be your own character witness."

"I missed something," Larry announced.

"Mackenzie will get you all caught up," Sunna said calmly. "After. Now, Richard, please do tell us about the morning of the wedding."

Richard sat stiff and straight as a brick wall. He was sweating profusely. "Okay," he said. "Well, I don't know if Maude told you this, but I'm a widower. I woke up the morning of the wedding, and I couldn't help it, I started thinking about the first time I'd done the whole marriage thing. It wasn't that I hadn't thought of my first wife before that point in our relationship, but I think the excitement of meeting someone and falling in love was enough to distract me. Until all of a sudden, I was standing in my bedroom—in the bedroom I'd shared with Sheila for thirty years—and feeling so *guilty*. I just began to panic. I think I would've still gone through with the wedding, but then I started thinking about sitting with Sheila as she lay dying of cancer, and I remembered how much it had hurt to say goodbye. I didn't think I could go through all of that again. And I know this might sound hard to believe . . ." He stopped to take a breath. He was directing all of this to Sunna, but Maude didn't notice; she was staring at her lap, expressionless.

Larry stood up. "Guys," he said, "this has been so nice, but I just remembered that I have to go home. So, Mackenzie, we will do that stuff another time?"

She nodded, Larry collected his things, and Richard let out a long breath that almost—almost—sounded like a growl.

"This might sound hard to believe," he began again when Larry was gone, "but I took the first drink just to calm myself down. And I don't remember how it progressed from there. I was a mess, Maude." He was still looking at Sunna, and Maude was still not looking at him, but when he said her name, she flinched like he'd reached out and plucked a hair from her head.

"I don't remember anything else about that day. I honestly don't. I just knew when I woke up the next morning that I couldn't ever face you again—and even if I could, what would I say? Our whole wedding day had passed without a single word from me."

"A single word? You don't remember the phone call?" whispered Maude.

"There was a phone call? I called you? That day? But you didn't have a phone . . ."

"I called you," said Maude. "Pay phone. But it doesn't really matter now."

"Actually, it does," said Mackenzie, surprised again to hear her own voice in this bizarre conversation, especially to hear how bold and angry it sounded. "It all matters. Richard may have been dealing with a lot that day, but you didn't know any of it. You deserved to know, to make your own decision about whether to give him another chance or not instead of him making it for you. This is all very sad, Richard, and I'm sorry, but you still should've told her. Maude deserved to know."

"Yes," said Maude, "that's right. I did."

"Yes," Richard agreed. "You did."

Maude stood up, digging in her purse. "Here, Richard," she said, selecting his wedding band from the little box and setting it gently on the table. "This is yours, and I'm sorry I've kept it for all these years. You understand."

He nodded. "I'm really sorry, Maude."

Maude pursed her lips. "Yes, well," she said, "I am too."

JANE EYRE VIBES

Mackenzie

"Did I do the right thing? Was that the right thing?" Maude was curled over in the passenger seat, freaking out like a teenager.

"I think so," said Mackenzie uncertainly.

"Absolutely!" called Sunna from the back seat. "Do you feel better, Maude?"

Maude had to think about it. "Yes," she said, "and no. I'm glad to finally know what happened, but instead of resolving it, it's like it's now split into two more problems."

"What problems?" said Sunna. "You have closure! You're one of the lucky few who got to confront and ask questions without getting sucked back in or condescended to. You got to hear him out but also let him know how much he hurt you. You even got to yell at him and pound your fists on the table. What more could a girl ask for?"

"Well," said Maude, "for one thing, it would've been nice if his reason for leaving me at the altar was, for example, that he got shot in the head during a home invasion. Not that he got sad about his first wife and selfishly drank himself into oblivion."

"Fair," said Sunna, nodding grimly.

"And secondly, I know I shouldn't, but seeing him again made me wish that I could just forgive him and give him another chance."

Sunna rolled her eyes; Mackenzie saw it in the rearview mirror and was glad Maude hadn't. "You're right," said Sunna. "You shouldn't. That would be such a bad idea."

"Why?" Maude had given up on twisting around; she leaned her head back on the headrest and cast her eyes in Sunna's general direction.

"Maude, remember? You hate him! *Remember?*"

"You met him, Sunna. Wasn't he sweet? And so humble. And so handsome. And even though you were so mean to him, he just sat there and took it."

"*I* was mean? You too, Maude. You were ruthless."

"But I was engaged to him. And he did leave me at the altar. I had . . . a bit more *license.*"

"Well, anyway," said Sunna. "You did the right thing, and now you never have to worry about Richard again. You can move on with your life."

Maude seemed to shrink in front of Mackenzie's eyes. "Yes," she said softly. "What's left of it." They all sat there quietly for a moment, and then Maude added, "It's very hard to meet men like Richard at my age. They're all married or coming out of marriages—divorces—with children and *baggage*. They all have baggage. Richard's not the only one with baggage, either—now *I* have baggage. And—and maybe if we *all* have baggage, then baggage isn't a good reason not to love someone."

Mackenzie considered this. She looked in the rearview mirror. Sunna's head was bowed.

"Well," said Sunna. "We're here."

"Yep," said Mackenzie. "I guess we should do this. Do you need just another minute, Maude? I don't want to rush you."

"Do what? Oh! Right, the attic! The ghosts! Yes, actually, that will be good. Something to take my mind off of Richard."

"Okay," said Mackenzie, shivering. "I'm going to run down and put my backpack away, and then I guess . . ."

"Okay. Let's do it," said Sunna.

~

They were lucky; the door had not been locked again after the police left. It swung open easily, and Sunna was the first one up the stairs, using the flashlight on her phone to illuminate the crawl space.

This amazed Maude. "That thing is a phone *and* a Google *and* a flashlight? That's incredible."

Sunna smirked. "That's just the tip of the iceberg, my dear Maudikins."

Maude didn't seem to appreciate being called Maudikins, but her scowl was not nearly so severe as it had once been, and all she said was, "You and your *nicknames*."

Mackenzie and Maude waited on the stairs as Sunna crept on ahead. "Hmm," they heard from above. "Interesting."

"What? What's interesting?" Maude was impatient.

They heard several quick thumping noises as Sunna pounded on the walls with her fists, and then her head appeared again in the opening. "Mack, can you shine your light up here too?"

"You have a flashlight phone, too, Mackenzie?" Maude asked.

Mackenzie smiled. "Yep." She hopped up a step, nervous about getting closer to the haunted attic but anxious to get the whole thing over with. She turned her light on and shined it into the crawl space.

Sunna was in a corner. She pushed on one wall and then on the other. "Check it out." She pointed at the floor. "It looks like there's been traffic here, right? I mean, other than me. I guess now you can't really tell the difference. But anyway, these walls aren't budging. The way that it looked when I first came here, it was like someone came back here and scuffled around a bit. But . . ."

"Did you push on the ceiling?" Mackenzie asked.

"Oh. Ha! I didn't even think of that. Duh." Sunna pushed up, then let out a gasp when the roof gave way. She let it fall back down again with a soft crack. Her eyes grew wide in the glow of the flashlight. "I found something," she whispered. "I think."

Mackenzie felt a thrill run up her neck. She doubled over, suddenly out of breath. "What do you mean," she managed. "Like you found a . . . an . . . you found . . ."

"You were right, Mack." Sunna pushed on the wooden panel above her head again, a little harder this time. "This panel is on hinges. It's like a door on the ceiling. Minus the knob." Mackenzie watched, transfixed, as Sunna opened the little door. "Mack!" she called. "Get over here. You have to see this. Get Maude too. Or tell her to call Larry." She thought about this for a minute. "Or the police? I don't know! I don't know. Um . . ."

"What's up there?" Mackenzie asked, alarmed.

But something had apparently made Sunna change her mind. She was now scrambling toward Mackenzie, shooing her down the stairs.

"Go, go, go!"

Mackenzie didn't need much convincing; she turned and all but pushed Maude to the bottom, and the three of them tumbled back into the hallway, shutting the attic door just as the familiar stomping started up with even more ferocity than usual. Sunna pulled her phone out and shakily tapped in her access code. "What happened up there? What did you do to make them so mad?" Maude asked. "I told you! I told you it was ghosts. Did you see them?"

"Shh!"

Sunna's fingers froze, and so did Mackenzie's hand on the knob and Maude's mouth mid-admonition.

Each woman thought—or hoped—she was imagining it at first, the sound that began like fork tines dragging across a porcelain plate, culminating in an anguished, guttural scream. It died away and rose again, swelling and subsiding in waves as the ceiling thudded like something was trying to break through.

"What did you *do*?" whispered Maude, but Sunna just whimpered. The sound carried on through her head and, it felt like, down into her legs, where it sat so heavy she couldn't move her feet.

Then: a muffled click and a faraway voice in a heavy southern drawl. "911, what is your emergency?"

"2139," said Sunna, "uh, uh . . ." She looked frantically at Maude, who was still frozen, then Mackenzie, who just shook her head. Was it the fear or the noise that made them all forget which street they lived on, or were ghosts able to scramble brain waves?

"Ma'am?" The voice of the 911 operator sounded loud, and it was only then that Mackenzie realized the screaming had stopped.

Sunna blushed and almost dropped the phone. "I'm sorry," she said, so quietly that Mackenzie could barely hear her. "There's someone in my house. In the attic."

AGING SPIRITS

Sunna

Sunna hoped Maude wouldn't say anything to the police about ghosts in the attic. She wanted them to take her seriously at least long enough to go up there.

Sunna ran down the stairs to wait on the porch and jumped up to greet the officers as they walked up the steps.

"Afternoon," said one of the officers, a smiling woman with her hair pulled tightly into a bun at her neck. "I'm Officer Seales, and this is Officer Bulawayo. We're looking for Maude Mitch. Is she home?"

Sunna frowned. "Yeah, but I'm the one who made the call," she said.

Officer Seales looked genuinely shocked. "You made the calls?" she said.

"Yeah," said Sunna, disconcerted. "I did."

The officers seemed in no hurry to follow her into the house. What part of 911 didn't they understand?

"Ma'am," said Officer Bulawayo, "you do realize this is a serious offense?"

"Yeah," said Sunna. *That's why I called 911.*

The officers furrowed their brows and exchanged glances.

A second police car pulled up.

The male officers who had come to the house the last time emerged, and they were in no hurry either.

"Hey, Shelby. Eva. You guys got this one?"

"Yeah, we came to talk to Ms. Mitch about the bomb threats, but this lady says it was her all along."

All four officers stared at Sunna, who suddenly felt sure she was dreaming. As though this day had not already felt like one weird, long dream. "I, no—what? I called 911. About the attic. I have people in my attic. I called 911. Not—I didn't make any threats. *Ever.*"

"Oh, I see," said Officer Seales. "So you two—" She stepped aside so the other officers could get past. "Well, we still need to talk to Ms. Mitch. Is she . . . ?"

"Come on up," said Sunna. "She's upstairs. Everyone's upstairs."

Mackenzie was still standing in exactly the same place as when the screaming started. Maude stood by the attic door.

"Maude," said Sunna. "These officers are here to see you."

"Good," said Maude. "So just up these stairs—"

"Maude Mitch?" said Shelby Seales.

Maude nodded. "Yes, so just up these stairs—"

"Ma'am, we have reason to believe you've been calling in bomb threats—"

Suddenly, Maude seemed to understand what was happening and began to panic. "But *I'm* not the janitor! And that hat was stolen!"

"Pardon? No one said you were the janitor, ma'am."

Mackenzie pointed at the attic, her face serious. "I think you have your calls mixed up. We're the ones with the ghosts."

The officers all looked at each other.

"That would be us?" said one of the men, looking skeptical.

"Okay," said Shelby, "but we're here to talk to Ms. Mitch."

"For sure," said Mackenzie, "but we called 911 because there's something freaky going on in our attic. Can we deal with that first?"

Shelby shrugged. "That's fine." She moved to stand beside Maude and motioned for the men to carry on with their business.

Sunna pointed to the door. "Up there," she said to the officers. "There's a crawl space, but it has a trapdoor in the ceiling. You have to crawl to the farthest corner and then push up. It opens into"—she realized she hadn't told Maude and Mackenzie what she'd seen—"a living room. With a couch and chairs and pictures on the walls and these deep-red rugs on the floor and—just, it's *lived in*," she told them. "Just like—" She motioned toward Maude's living room, though that room still only had a couch. "No, not like that," she said, almost laughing. "*More* lived in. And there were paintings everywhere. *Everywhere.* And there was a fireplace," she said. Then she shuddered. "There was a fire burning in the fireplace. And . . . there were people."

"You saw someone?" Mackenzie swayed slightly, like the top of a skyscraper.

"Yeah," Sunna said. Did she believe in ghosts? What if they went up there and the living room Sunna had seen was just a dusty old attic full of trunks and cobwebs and bare floors, and what she had seen was some kind of glimpse into—into what? The ghosts' world?

Was that how it worked?

She didn't watch enough horror movies to know.

"Well," said the officer, "this might surprise you ladies, but this does happen from time to time. People sneak into attics, knowing the owner of the house doesn't go up there much, and they just move right in. Free rent. Sometimes they have some kind of reason for choosing a particular home, but often it's just a place to stay."

"Okay," said Sunna, "I believe that, but . . . how *many* people are we talking? And do they usually furnish these attics? Do they hang pictures on the walls? Install fireplaces? Just . . . go look."

The men nodded; one of them stepped forward and knocked on the attic door. "Hello," he called. "This is the police. If there's anyone up there, I'm going to need to ask you to come down. Otherwise we will be coming up in a moment."

He waited.

The officers nodded again, then clomped up the stairs one after the other. She heard muffled footsteps as their heavy shoes crossed the floor above. Sunna shivered and wished there were more officers. Maude and Mackenzie had moved close enough that she could reach out and put an arm around each of them. That was comforting. She sneaked a peek at Maude, wondering what she would do if Sunna put an arm around her. Or hugged her, for that matter. Probably die of shock.

But then, Sunna thought, hugging Maude wouldn't be the worst thing. And if Maude hugged back, it would be sincere. No doubt about that. This was the thing about Maude: she didn't pretend. And a hug that really, for sure meant something would be quite a beautiful thing. Sunna suddenly kind of wished that Maude would actually hug her.

Shouts and a couple of loud thuds came from the attic—people falling? The sound of running—lots of running. The officers, probably, but there were more footsteps than just theirs.

Lots more.

Shouting. Scuffling.

A bang—a gunshot? No, the trapdoor slamming against the floor. A voice, authoritative. "I have a gun! Stop or I'll shoot!"

The scuffling stopped.

"Uh . . . so someone has a gun out," Sunna said, sounding infinitely calmer than she felt. "Should we run? What do we do?"

Maude's eyes twitched in the direction of the door, but she backed up instead. "If they're coming down, maybe we'll be safer if we're not in their way. Maybe they'll all just run out the front door."

A good thought: whatever was in the attic was being flushed out.

"It's not ghosts." Mackenzie sounded oddly disappointed.

Maude shook her head, her face ashen and her hands shaking. Sunna could tell she was much more afraid of this tangible thing than she'd ever been of ghosts. Maybe Maude had never really believed in ghosts. Maybe she used them as an excuse so she didn't have to think about this other possibility. And now she was probably thinking about how someone had been living just up the flight of stairs, creeping through her apartment when she was asleep, taking the rings from her purse . . . Sunna placed a hand on her shoulder, and Maude blinked at her. Smiled.

The three women backed toward the kitchen, their breath caught in a collective inhale. What would come out of the attic? No, that wasn't right anymore. *Who. Who* had been living above them all this time?

The door opened, and one of the officers emerged, red faced but calm. Sunna and Mackenzie exchanged glances.

The man called up the stairs. "Okay, guys. Come down nice and easy. I don't want any trouble from anyone. Uh . . ." He looked flustered. "Does . . . does anyone need help coming down?"

"I'm okee." A strange hillbilly voice. "Giv'n me *time*, boy. I kin only go so fast."

"It's fine," said the policeman. "Take your time. Don't need to deal with broken hips today on top of all this."

He looked at Sunna and Maude and Mackenzie linked together like an absurd paper chain. Sunna's hand still rested on Maude's shoulder and her other around Mackenzie's. "Is your mom okay?" he asked, addressing Sunna and Mackenzie. "Do you need to sit down?" he asked Maude.

"I'm okay," croaked Maude. Her eyes were suddenly watery.

"Well you might need to sit down when you see what's been going on in your attic," he said, adjusting his hat and, Sunna thought, trying not to laugh.

The bottom stair creaked. Sunna anticipated some kind of hardened criminal. Or a ghoul. It was hard not to dismiss that thought completely. She'd only seen feet in her quick glimpse of the secret attic room.

"Oh," said Mackenzie, looking, as she often did, like she hadn't meant to say anything.

A tiny old man, who mostly consisted of rambling white facial hair, hobbled out into the hallway, breathing hard and glaring at the police officer. His legs were spindly and spiderlike, and his feet stuck out to the sides at a strange angle. "I ain't come down these sters in ten yers," he said, mumbling around the pipe in his mouth. "Giv'n me jis one mer'n you coulda curried me oot'n a body bag."

The room went completely still as the man stopped next to the officer, coughing and sighing like being arrested was a huge inconvenience.

The three housemates stared at him, unsure how to feel at this revelation. The officer handcuffed him and read him his rights. The man just rolled his eyes and issued a steady stream of complaints.

Soon another figure appeared in the doorway—it was, much to everyone's surprise, another elderly man, also bearded and spidery, blinking and grumbling his way into the brightly lit hallway. He wore a plaid flannel shirt and looked only slightly more kempt than the first man, as though he actually left the attic from time to time. He nodded at Maude, winked at Sunna, ignored Mackenzie.

On his heels was another old man, but this one had a surprise on his arm: a stunning ancient lady, all done up in bright-pink lipstick and blue eyeshadow and diamond earrings. She was smiling like she was the queen and everyone here had come to look at her.

The couple leaned on each other and shuffled forward.

The last person in this odd procession was a stately old woman who held her chin so high Sunna worried she might trip over her feet. Atop her head was Maude's saucer-shaped hat. She was followed closely by the other policeman, who did, indeed, have a gun.

Maude gasped. "It's her," she whispered to Sunna, "the ghost in my kitchen! The woman from the obituary! And she has my *hat*!"

The woman cast a glance in their direction, and when she saw Maude, she smiled. Not a rude or unpleasant smile. Not a sheepish one either.

It was *knowing*. She recognized Maude too.

It was the same look the busker had given Sunna the other day in front of Paper Cup. This realization hit Sunna like ice water, and her eyes darted to the old man who'd winked at her. Sure enough, he held her gaze now with that same recognition. The man from downtown on the day of the bomb threats. The busker. The fellow who walked in circles around and around and around their house and, as it turned out, lived just up the stairs behind that locked door.

THE SECOND LAST WILL AND TESTAMENT OF REBECCA FINLEY

Larry

Larry was a music reviewer now. He had one gig—but it was a gig, a paid writing gig!—and he was working on a piece to send to *Razorcake* (a now-and-then kind of essay on how the punk scene had changed over the past thirty years). He was going to wait to send that one off until he had a chance to sit down with Mackenzie again and pick her brain—sometime when she wasn't doing freelance marriage counseling or whatever weird thing he'd stumbled upon the other day—maybe see if she could give him a referral. He felt very optimistic about the whole thing. He felt cool.

He felt cool, but he did not look cool. He stood in front of the small mirror in his bathroom, turning his head and examining his chin-length mud-brown hair. It was stringy and greasy and streaked with grays. It made him look conspicuously middle aged. Everything made him feel middle aged lately, and he hated it. Would his old hair help? Larry missed his mohawk.

Almost without considering it at all, he retrieved his razor from the vanity drawer and shaved the area above his right ear. A cartilage piercing he'd sort of forgotten about sprang out at him. He liked it. He grinned and shaved another stripe. And then, purely because this was the worst moment for something else to demand his attention, the phone rang.

Sunna again. He didn't even care very much this time. He cared so little he almost didn't care at all. Almost.

"Hi, Larry," she said.

"Hi," he said in his best not-caring voice, which was a bit breathier than he would've liked, maybe too high—did he sound desperate?

"Are you busy right now?"

He looked at the small mound of hair on the counter. *I don't care. I don't care at all.* "Yeah," he said. "I am busy." He felt proud of himself. He didn't need a pointless crush on a woman who didn't care about him—especially someone so . . . *mainstream.* Wasn't that what the entire punk scene was about? Rejecting the mainstream? Individuality and nonconformity and brash, bold self-confidence, flying in the face of what society perceived to be beautiful? He looked into the mirror again and lifted his chin.

"Okay," said Sunna, "well, I just wanted to let you know that the police are here arresting all the old people who were living in that secret apartment in your attic."

"Okay," he said.

"Hmm," he said.

"Wait, say that part again," he said.

"Which part?"

"Just, all of it," said Larry. He must have misheard her. "Start at *Hi, Larry.*"

~

281

Within minutes he was on his way to his house. He had owned it for three months now, and more than ever he wished it was a 1974 Lincoln Continental—*told you, Glenda.*

He had to make his way through a maze of onlookers and police cars. The women stood on the porch looking dazed and talking to a policeman. Mackenzie waved him over. "This is the landlord," she told the policeman. "Larry. Larry, you will not believe—"

"I told him," said Sunna. "On the phone."

"Yeah, about the old folks' home he's running in the attic, but did you tell him about his aunt?"

"Oh. No, I didn't tell him that."

"Sunna!" Mackenzie laughed. "That's kind of the most important part."

"Aunty?" Larry interjected, then caught himself, looking quickly at Sunna. Suddenly, he remembered the bald patch above his ear. He reached up to cover it, though it was certainly much too late. "My aunt? What about my aunt?"

"She's in that police car over there," said Mackenzie.

Larry laughed politely. "Oh, then it's not *my* aunt," he said. "My aunt passed away recently. Actually, funny thing: she's the one who left me this house—"

"Sir," said the police officer, "it would appear we have quite the situation on our hands. Your aunt is very much alive and is, in fact, sitting in that police cruiser. She's been living in the attic along with her husband and—"

"Her husband?" Larry forgot all about his bald spot. "No, that can't be right, either; Uncle Garnet's been dead for well over—"

"*Uncle Garnet,*" the officer interrupted, "is in that cruiser . . . there." He pointed toward the car with the flannel-shirted man.

Larry stared at the officer as though he'd just asserted that Uncle Garnet had been reincarnated as a jelly bean.

"Wait. What did you just say? Uncle Garnet and Aunt Rebecca have been *living* . . . in the attic?"

Everyone nodded with matching enthusiasm.

"But what about the ghosts?" Even as he said it, he understood why his aunt had wanted him to stay out of the attic. That it was Uncle Garnet who hated Celine Dion and liked sports.

The officer seemed to be enjoying himself. "Mr., uh—"

"Finley."

"Ah, you're a Finley, too, okay. So, Mr. Finley. I have quite the fantastic little family history lesson for you here. Your uncle Garnet"—he snorted—"is an artist."

"*Was* an artist," corrected Larry stubbornly.

"When he 'died' back in, what? '07? '08?"

"'08."

"Yes, '08. When he 'died' in '08, your aunt was in charge of his body of work. She waited a few years and then tried to sell his paintings—the two of them thought the paintings would gain value because the artist was dead. People tend to think that's how it works."

"That's not how it works?" Maude interjected.

"No," said the officer. "If no one knows who you are before you die, they just seem to keep on not knowing who you are after. So he 'died' for no good reason. And then, because faking your own death comes with a lot of . . . well, legal baggage, he just stayed 'dead.'"

"But . . . no, he *was* dead. Actual dead. Real dead. There was a body. They cremated him—"

"Death kits!" hollered Maude, causing Larry to jump. "Did he buy a death kit?"

The officer stared at her. "I . . . I don't know," he said. "We'll have to look into it."

Maude nodded smugly at Sunna. "Probably," she said to the officer. "Because you *can* buy death kits. In Manila."

"I'm sure you can," said the officer, looking a bit concerned. "There's quite the underground market for—well, all kinds of crazy stuff. Lots of ways to fake your own death."

"Okay," said Larry impatiently. "Go on."

"So he moved into the attic, and your aunt lived in the house as normal. Tried to sell his work but couldn't. That's why they hatched this guerilla art exhibit plan. They were going to dig up into the building and put his work up in an empty gallery. One last shot at fame and fortune—your cousin Jim was in on it too. Your aunt left him quite the body of work in her will; he was going to sell it, split the money with them, and then they were going to 'retire' to"—he pulled out his notepad and read—"'somewhere hot but not annoying and much bigger than that thar attic.'"

"Your *aunt*," said Maude, "almost got me *arrested*. She wore my hat and used my credit card when she went to buy a new *burner phone*. She was making her calls from our attic, so on their computer thing it looked like they were coming from *me*. I was really lucky she was here when the police came to arrest me. And that she still had my hat and my credit card and the cell phone they *thought* was mine." She looked at everyone in the little circle meaningfully. "It wasn't mine," she added.

"But you said five people," said Larry. He felt upset. Very upset. He was a quiet kind of guy; he didn't ask for trouble. This felt like a lot of trouble. He wanted to set the whole house on fire and just walk away—although that would just get him into more trouble. He was not half as punk as he wished. "She said five. Five people. In the attic . . ." He was whining like a middle-aged woman who'd been cut in front of in line at Costco.

"Yes, she did," said the officer. "We're sorting it all out. At this point, all I can tell you is that there were five people—including your aunt and uncle—living in that house, but mostly that attic, for about a decade. They had a fully furnished suite up there. They were quite comfortable. Your uncle moved in first. He had a friend, a notorious bank robber from Alberta, who also moved in at some point. His wife joined them. And then one of his buddies from the States. Not sure they all faked their deaths—maybe. Don't know yet. And then when they'd decided enough time had passed, your aunt joined them *up there*." The officer looked up reverently, as though he was referring to heaven and not the attic.

"Why are they being arrested? Is it a crime to fake your own death?"

"No. Well. There are certain ways to do it that are, surprisingly, not illegal. But it does need to be investigated because there are also certain ways to do it that are very illegal. Squatting, however, is illegal."

"Is it squatting when you own the house?"

The officer stared at Larry dumbly.

"Because," said Larry, "if the owners of this house are both alive, this isn't my house, is it?"

"Afraid not," said the officer, but then he clicked his tongue and frowned. "Actually. I don't know—maybe it is. I can't say's I've ever seen someone come back from the dead to reclaim what they've left to others in their will. This is *quite* the situation."

Larry pulled out his key ring. He slipped off the house key and handed it to the officer. "Well, I'll save everyone the trouble," he said. "I'm not going to put up a fight. You just give that to my aunt Rebecca." He held both of his hands up and started backing away from the group. "Tell her I've already said my goodbyes. To both her and Uncle Garnet. At their *funerals*. Funerals are for saying goodbye. You say goodbye, and then that's it. You don't say hello after that." He ran his hand along the bare skin on his head. "Okay. I have to . . . go . . . finish . . . doing my . . . hair."

He nodded at his tenants—his tenants? His aunt's tenants?—and stalked back to his car, trying not to look into the patrol cars.

TAKING THE HOUSE BACK

Sunna

"What do you figure?" Mackenzie was sitting on the curb, looking up at their house. Though it was now decidedly "ghost-free," it was an even more terrifying place now. It had broken trust with them—what else was hiding in there? It was easy to imagine that the curtains were moving, that wherever she looked, something had just floated by.

"What do you mean?" Sunna asked.

"I mean, are you sleeping here tonight?"

"Hadn't really thought about it. I don't really have any other options. I don't know anyone else here other than people at the gym." Sunna squinted at the attic windows. "But I think we're on the same page. I don't want to sleep here tonight either."

Maude was confused. "What's wrong with you two? The house is cleared of ghosts and robbers. For the first time since we all moved in. This is the first night I actually feel safe staying here."

"What are you talking about, Maude?" Sunna smiled. "You were the only one who wasn't afraid of the ghosts."

"No," Maude corrected her. "I was petrified. I just . . . I just never said so. To you. I'm not scared anymore—it's safe now."

"But it's so *creepy*," said Mackenzie. "It's creepy knowing that the whole time we've lived in this house, there have been five other people living here too. And that they could just go wherever they wanted, whenever. I think they had secret passageways. They came into my apartment more than once without ever moving the chair."

"And they knew us," said Sunna, thinking of the busker. "They *recognized* us. They played pranks on us. They took my library books."

"They took my shoes," said Mackenzie, shivering.

"Well, that's true, but they also left you flowers," said Maude. "They took food out of my fridge. Which was terribly rude. Speaking of that . . . I'm sorry for accusing you two of stealing my rings. I should have known you wouldn't do that." She said this more into her shoulder than to the other two women.

Sunna and Mackenzie nodded.

"It's all good," said Mackenzie. "I'm just glad it's sorted out."

"It's *all* good," echoed Maude, like she thought this was a funny thing to say.

"Same," said Sunna. "And you know, you're both welcome to sleep over at my place tonight, if you want. I mean, no pressure, but if—"

"Yes, please," said Mackenzie. "I'd rather not be alone tonight. Maude?"

Maude was distracted, staring at someone in the diminishing crowd of gawkers and police officers. He wasn't coming toward them, but they could all tell he was watching Maude out of the corner of his eye. He was rocking back on his heels and toes with his hands in his pockets, perhaps trying to appear nonchalant but failing miserably.

Sunna put a hand on Maude's elbow. "Hey, Maude?"

"What?" Maude snapped.

Sunna was surprised, even though it hadn't been all that long since Maude had spoken to her that way.

"Are you going to tell me to slap him across the face and ask him to leave me alone? File a restraining order? Are you going to tell me I can't talk to him, like you know what's best for me and I don't? Because why? Because no one takes me seriously anymore? Or is it because he messed up? Well, *I* mess up sometimes too! And if everyone stopped loving me every time I messed up, *no one* would love me. Oh, *wait*—"

"Maude," Sunna said. "I'm sorry. I'm really sorry. I was only going to say that, in the car earlier, I could tell you didn't think you'd done the right thing."

Maude relaxed, just a little. She stared at Sunna's hand, still on her elbow. "That's true," she said. "I don't think I did the right thing. But what would have been right? *Is* there a right thing?"

Sunna laughed. "No," she said. "This isn't exactly a moral dilemma. It's just . . . whether you believe him and accept his apology or not, and whether you *want* him or not. I think I was trying to answer those questions for you. And I'm sorry I did that. I shouldn't have."

Maude considered this. "It's—*all* good," she said. Sunna thought it seemed like she was trying to emulate Mackenzie this time, not mock her. "And you're right. If you don't *give* a second chance, you don't *get* one either. Right?"

"True," said Sunna.

They all looked at Richard, who was still rocking on his feet, back and forth and back and forth, pretending to look at the house or at the police cars, anything but Maude. He was very much looking at Maude.

~

"That's good," said Mackenzie as they watched Maude cross the street.

"I guess so."

"What, you don't like love? You don't think it's cute—Maude and Richard?"

"Nah. It's good. You're right. What about you?"

"Me? What about me?"

They watched as Maude leaned into Richard and he put his arms around her. Mackenzie grinned.

"Jared," said Sunna. "Does watching them make you wish you'd asked him more questions? Gotten more answers? Or was a punch in the face enough?"

Mackenzie's smile faded, and she shook her head. "I think that's part of being an adult, you know? Your life is just frayed at the edges, and you have whole haunted cities full of people who owe you explanations and apologies. Cities full of ghosts. The end."

"That's depressing." Sunna leaned back on her elbows and sprawled out on the cement. "Okay, but here's a question: Where do ghosts come from?"

"What do you mean?"

"I mean where do ghosts come from?"

Mackenzie shrugged. "Uh . . . dead . . . people?"

Sunna shook her head.

"'Kay . . . um . . . cemeteries."

"Nope."

"Out of thin air? Um . . . attics . . . I don't know, Sunna. I think the actual question is whether ghosts exist in the first place."

Sunna began to nod vigorously. "Exactly. *Exactly*, Mack. If ghosts do exist, I don't know where they come from. But I feel like they don't. Call me a skeptic, whatever, I just don't think they exist. And if ghosts don't exist, this question actually has a super easy answer. So. Mack. Where do they come from?"

Mackenzie was lost. "Uh . . . your . . . imagination?"

"Right. Exactly. You're talking about cities full of ghosts, and I say those ghosts all only exist in your imagination. Like, take Richard and Maudikins over there. He was her ghost, and he haunted her for years. It changed her, to the point where he didn't even recognize her when he saw her again. But really, she could've just called him the day after their 'wedding.' Not to beg him to come back even, just to ask where he'd gone. Or she could've let him go without even involving him in the process. You know what I mean? Same with me and Brett. I *let* her be my ghost. I conjured her spirit up and let it haunt me all this time. But my obsessing over her like that never made her real, didn't impact her reality at all. She's off living the dream, maybe thinking about me, *probably* not, while I'm stuck living this haunted life, miserable. And you and Jared, same thing."

"But not Kate and Tanya," said Mackenzie. "That's different."

"No," said Sunna, getting excited. "I mean, it's different, but it's also the same. The ghost isn't the person; it's the feelings attached to the person. It's like, my ghost wasn't Brett. My ghost was the hurt I felt that someone I considered family could desert me like that and the worry that that was going to be the story of my life. Forever. With you and Kate and Tanya, your ghosts are guilt and fear. And you're hanging on to them because you're afraid the truth will hurt your relationship with your parents. And you know what: it already has, whether they're aware of it or not. But hurt relationships can be fixed. Exhibit A." She pointed at Maude and Richard again. Still hugging. She rolled her eyes—though she was smiling at them.

Mackenzie stared at them, too, unconvinced. "But then: closure . . . is *it* real?"

"Totally. And it's way easier than we thought. Because you don't need the other person. What we're looking at right now, with Maude and Richard, that's not closure. I think I was right after all. She got closure back there in the coffee shop. That's why this can happen now. She told her ghost to get lost, and now there's room for Richard again."

Mackenzie still looked doubtful.

"Mack!" Sunna cried. "You, of all people, know how much it sucks to live in fear of ghosts only to find out they're just five cantankerous but harmless old people with broken dentures and white hair. Take your house back."

So it wasn't a perfect metaphor, but it was good enough for Sunna. For the first time in years, she felt decidedly unhaunted.

MAUDE'S WEDDING (A FEW MONTHS LATER)

Maude and Richard

It was Maude's wedding day, and she looked awful in her dress—even worse, objectively speaking, than she had the first time she'd worn it. She looked in the mirror on the back of Sunna's bedroom door. Her face was pinched and sharp and hollow and sagging and grayish and whiskery. She made her mouth smile, and the skin around her eyes bunched up like sweatpants with the drawstring pulled tight. She sighed. More bunching on the forehead.

She thought about mirrors. A mirror was designed so a person could see their own face. A face, with its eyes and nose and mouth and ears on the side, was designed to perceive the world, not to perceive itself. And what did people do? They made a thing that would block the world in front of them and replace that view with their own reflection. There was nothing *wrong* with mirrors. They were, Maude thought, just unhelpful. She decided to look at this face for one more minute, only to make sure there wasn't lipstick on the teeth or mascara on the cheekbones. She would look objectively, like she was looking at a stranger; then she would turn away and think about all the things that were actually important about this day.

This time she saw the face differently.

It was the face of a woman who was sharply aware that her wedding day could take any number of tragic turns, that she could end up alone in the end, again, but it wasn't a face that *expected* to. It was not a face without fear, but it was not without hope either. It was a face entering into marriage with reverence and solemnity and, still, joy. It was a *human* face, beautiful in its intricacy and emotion. She had compassion for it, and she understood, suddenly, why Richard touched this face when he said *I love you*. Until now, she'd thought maybe he was trying to make her feel good, or that it was a gesture he'd seen on enough romantic movies that he did because he thought he was supposed to. Now she realized he'd been saying it because he meant it and he'd been touching her face because it belonged to *her*. Simple as that.

"You ready, Maudikins?" asked Sunna, peeking around the bedroom door. "Wow. You look really beautiful."

"Thank you," said Maude, blinking furiously.

"Are you . . . are you okay?" Sunna took a step forward cautiously. "Did something happen?"

"No," said Maude. "Well. Yes."

Sunna looked around the bedroom, as though Richard might be hidden somewhere. She raised an eyebrow.

"Just something internal," said Maude, trying to dab her eyes without wrecking Sunna's careful makeup application. "Just one of those moments, you know, where you have no new information, but your brain rearranges all of what you *do* have and it suddenly makes sense."

Sunna nodded, her eyes wide. "Okay? Like . . . about . . . like about *today*? Or . . ."

Maude gave a short laugh. "Yes. I suppose it is about today." Sunna was still nodding, blatantly uncomprehending. "It's just that when Richard left me that first time, I didn't think it was for any one reason—I thought it was all of them. Every time I found a flaw in myself after that, I just added it to the list of Reasons Richard Left Me. It was my face and my body and my mind and my sense of humor and my hair . . . all of the things that made me *me*. And do you know what I did? I ghosted *myself*. Or—" She frowned at Sunna. "Ghosted *on* myself? Not so sure of the grammar around that word just yet." She sat on Sunna's bed, plucking a Kleenex from the box on the night table. She began to get weepy again. "Does that make sense to you, though? I was perfectly fine with myself until he left, and then I began to just hate every single thing, and before I knew it, I'd shrugged it all off and become someone who just sat in her apartment and watched old detective shows on VHS."

Sunna nodded, as though *she* could relate to what Maude was saying. It was nice of her to display some empathy, Maude thought. "Not that there's anything *wrong* with those old shows, but it was the *principle* of it, Sunna. It was the fact that I would so quickly abandon my own life, betray my own self, disappear without a trace like that, just because I thought that my completely irrational reasons for doing so trumped all else. You and Mackenzie and I have all been so livid that other people did those things to us, but I did those things to *myself*, Sunna."

Sunna wasn't nodding anymore. She sat on her bed beside Maude and stared at her fingernails.

"And you know what," Maude went on, "I feel dumb for taking this long to figure out that I don't have to be any particular way that I wasn't already before he fell in love with me. That just because someone leaves you, that doesn't mean that you are not still perfectly fine and valuable, and it definitely doesn't mean you should leave yourself. This is a lesson for a *teenager*, and"—she picked the heavy skirt of her dress up and let it fall—"this is a dress for a twenty-*five*-year-old, and here I am. Learning *that* lesson in *this* dress. It's *embarrassing*."

Sunna put her hand on Maude's shoulder. "Nah," she said. "It's great. It's the perfect lesson to learn on the first day of your married life. And even if you *had* learned it as a teenager, you'd just have to learn it again and again between then and now, like the rest of us. Like me. I mean, I just learned it again right now. From you. So . . . thanks."

They smiled at each other.

"I think you're in your BLZ, Maude," said Sunna.

Maude blinked at her. "I don't know what that means," she said.

"I love that about you," said Sunna, "and I'm going to miss having you upstairs."

"No, you're not," said Maude, sniffling again. "You're just going to miss sneaking into my house and stealing my takeout."

There was a knock on the door, and Richard poked his head into the room. He looked startled when he saw Sunna. "Oh, sorry, am I interrupting?"

Sunna stood up. "Nope! I should actually go see what I can do to help. I think Mack's making lunch for after the ceremony."

∼

Mackenzie and Grant

Sunna found Mackenzie in the kitchen, but she wasn't making lunch. She was sitting on the counter holding her phone in the palms of her hands like she was weighing it.

"What're you doing, Mack?"

"I don't know. Just waiting for stuff to start."

"Like . . . the wedding, you mean?"

"Yeah, yeah, the wedding." She gave Sunna a look like, *Of course the wedding, what else?*

"Oh. I just thought you were being, sort of, melodramatic or something. Like, *Just sitting here waiting for my life to start,* or whatever."

Mackenzie laughed. "That, too, I guess. I do kind of get like that at weddings."

"How so?" Sunna hopped up on the counter beside her.

"Well, you know. The whole point of this day is that we're all here just watching someone 'arrive.' Marriage is, like, a *conclusion*. And I guess it just makes me think about all my loose ends . . ."

"Jared."

"No. No, not Jared. No." Mackenzie laughed again, harder this time. "Ugh. Though now that you mention it, I wonder how that poor Lauren girl is doing."

"Mm. Like you worry they broke up after that whole thing at the Exchange?"

"No, like I worry they're still together. Poor girl."

"Oh. Gotcha. Yeah. So . . . who, then?"

"Grant. A guy I worked with."

"Oh. Someone you dated?"

"No. Almost. I threw up when he came to pick me up for our first date, and that was right before everything went down with my sister and the trial and all that—when I quit at Picaroon. And I haven't actually really gotten a chance to talk to him since."

"He hasn't called or texted?"

"No, *he* has . . ." Mackenzie leaned forward and put her head in her hands on top of the phone. "Sunna, you're going to just hate me for this . . ."

"You ghosted *him*."

"Yep."

Sunna shrugged. "Okay. So that was a bad move. Call him."

"I can't now. It's been too long."

"Is that what you would've said if the letter had been from Jared or Kate? Do you think that's what I would've said if it had been from Brett? Mack. Think about whose wedding we're at *right now*."

Mackenzie considered this. "But what do I say?"

"Everything. Just say everything. Say what you wish Jared would've said to you. Say what Richard finally said to Maude. Explain, explain, explain. Apologize. Own it. You were a jerk; ghosting is rude. If he gives you a second chance . . ." She nodded at the window that looked out into the backyard, where an arch and twenty white chairs were set up.

"I marry him?"

"*No!* Mack!" Sunna rolled her eyes. "You take the second chance. See what happens. Like Richard."

Richard appeared in the doorway of the kitchen, a millisecond too late to hear his name spoken. "Oh Sunna! There you are. Change of plans: it's just too cold out there for this backyard wedding business; we're going to do the ceremony inside. Maude finally relented. That lady is more stubborn than this prairie weather, but we finally got her to break." He smiled. "The photographer says the lighting is terrible in the living room, though—and besides, the reception is all set up in there already—so we're going to do it"—he paused for dramatic effect—"right here!"

"You're getting married in my kitchen?" They couldn't tell if he was joking or not.

"I'm getting married in your kitchen! By this big window! Maude just wants a nice picture of us saying 'I do'—for over the fireplace. The photographer wants lots of natural light." He hooked his arm through the air in front of him like an old-timey entertainer holding an invisible cane and turned to leave. "Pass the word on to everyone you see!"

They watched him scurry out into the hallway, as effervescent a man as either of them had ever seen. It was almost surprising that he didn't jump into the air and click his heels as he rounded the corner.

"See?" said Sunna. "You could make Grant *that* happy."

"Or maybe he's gone out and got himself a friend like you who's going to put me through the wringer and then tell me to get lost."

"Hopefully. It would serve you right, Mack."

Mackenzie laughed in spite of herself. Then she pulled out her phone and typed, *Hey.*

~

Sunna

Sunna was in charge of answering the door and directing people to the kitchen. Not that there were many people to direct: the pastor and his wife and their eight-year-old son. Maude's sister, Linda, and Linda's husband, Harv, who was very short (they flew in from Ontario). Two of Richard's friends and his father, Edward, who was in a wheelchair, which was why they were not getting married in Maude's kitchen upstairs. Larry. And the photographer, the son of a friend of Richard's, who everyone was just calling Photographer, like it was an inside joke.

It was not a big crowd for a wedding, but it was a big crowd for a kitchen. It was a big kitchen for cooking—but not a big kitchen for, say, marrying.

The pastor stood in front of the fridge, Maude and Richard stood in front of the pastor, the photographer in front of Maude and Richard. The pastor's wife and son stood in the back, beside the stove. His father sat at the table, and Harv and Linda and one of Richard's friends took the three chairs; the other friend stood in the back by the pastor's son. Mackenzie sat on the countertop by the sink. Larry stood in the corner with his hands in the pockets of some strange, terribly altered pinstriped pants. Sunna stood in the doorway.

"Well? You ready, Maudikins?"

Maude sniffed. *"Maudikins,"* she said under her breath. Richard, chuckling, opened his mouth to speak, but Maude jabbed him in the ribs. "No. Only Sunna gets to call me that." She nodded to the pastor. "Okay, Kevin. We're ready."

The pastor smiled. He was one of those relaxed pastors who was okay being called Kevin instead of Pastor Kevin or Father Kevin or whatever. "All right," he said, "let's get this show on the road. Maude. Richard. We're gathered here today, in front of this lovely stainless steel Frigidaire, in the presence of all of your—"

The doorbell rang.

"Who rings a doorbell in the middle of a wedding ceremony?" Maude looked annoyed.

"I'll get it," said Sunna.

She opened the door to a stranger. A woman with chin-length neon-purple hair poking out from under a knit hat and large brown eyes, her face decorated all over with tiny silver hoops and studs. She was wearing a large winter jacket, open despite the chill, over ripped black jeans and a white T-shirt that had *Fugazi* scrawled on the front in fading black Sharpie. Not the kind of thing you'd normally wear to a wedding.

"Oh," the woman squeaked, stepping into the small interior landing and stomping on the welcome mat to get the snow off her boots. "It's *you*."

Sunna frowned. "Yeah," she said. "It is."

The woman must have realized she wasn't recognized back. "I used to see you at the Cup, like, all the time. I go there on my coffee breaks. I work at the crematorium next door."

Sunna realized then that it had never occurred to her once in her whole life that people worked at crematoriums, same as people worked at gyms and flower shops and pizza parlors. "Oh," she said. "Yeah. I saw you out front. I thought you were there for . . . you know. Because somebody close to you had—"

"I have kind of a weird question for you." The woman interrupted Sunna, and Sunna was thankful for it. There was a muffled but distinct clinking sound, and Sunna realized it was a tongue piercing moving against the woman's teeth. "Is there a guy who lives in this house who's, like, tall, and has a goatee, and he has, um . . . a lot of piercings." She pointed at her own face. "And like, he's got longish hair—I don't—this is super embarrassing—I don't remember his name, but when I met him, he was telling someone how he'd just inherited a big house on this street . . ." She couldn't stop touching her face, playing with her hair.

Sunna smiled kindly at the woman. "Yeah," she said. "I mean, yeah, I know who you're talking about, but he doesn't live here. He's the landlord. Funny story, actually: He inherited the house from his dead aunt, and then she ended up being alive so he *un*inherited it, but then she went to jail, so it's his again. Until she gets out, I think. And then . . . I actually don't know what happens then." She laughed. "It's been a bit of a trip. You looking for a place? I don't know how much longer it'll be available, depending on what happens with Larry's aunt."

The woman looked surprised. "Oh, no! No, I'm not . . . I actually met him at the grocery store in the summer. He asked for my number, and then he was gone before I could give it to him . . ." She looked up and stopped short. "Oh. You've got a lot of company."

Richard and Mackenzie had followed Maude into the hallway, and Richard's two friends peered curiously from the doorway. The photographer snapped a picture.

The woman with the purple hair cleared her throat, wary of the large group. "I did leave him a note in the mailbox, but . . . maybe he didn't ever get it, if he doesn't even live here . . ." She began to laugh but trailed off and bit her lip, looking embarrassed. "I probably seem like a creep, but also . . . I kind of laughed at him when he asked for my number, and I've felt really stupid about it—I wasn't laughing at *him*, you know?—I was just nervous. I just thought . . ."

"Oh," said Sunna, who had just turned to call Larry from the kitchen. She froze. "It was *you*."

"Yeah. This was a really weird thing to do, come here. I should just—" She motioned at the porch steps and began to back toward them.

But by this point, Larry had found his way into the hallway, and when he saw who was standing in the entryway, his face stretched into a grin that made him look like some kind of stupid bird.

"Hey!" The woman let out a relieved laugh when she saw him. "Hey," she said again. "Um. Hi. I'm Nikki. I actually don't know your name—"

"Larry!" Larry said over Richard's shoulder. "Larry Finley!"

"No way!" Nikki called back. "As in the music reviewer from the *Gopher*?"

"Yeah!" Larry was beside himself. "Yeah, that's me!"

"I *love* your column!" Nikki said. "It's refreshing to have someone who knows what they're talking about doing that gig."

Maude cut in. "I'm sorry," she snipped in a voice reminiscent of the Maude Sunna had met on the porch a few months ago. "I'm getting *married*."

"Oh!" Nikki grimaced. "I'm in your way—"

"No," said Maude. "I'm getting married in *here*. You can come; you can be Larry's date, but you need to hurry it up."

Richard winked at Nikki as they all shuffled back into the kitchen and took up their places once again. "Yes, hurry it up! We have a reception we need to get to in the living room," he said.

"Oh stop, Richard," Maude mumbled, but she was smiling.

Richard put his arm around her. "What's the rush, Maude?" he said into her hair. "We have the rest of our lives. Actually, that's, uh—Kevin, can we hurry this up? I'm seventy-two."

Maude burst out laughing, and unbeknownst to her, the photographer snapped a picture at that exact moment. He'd been right about the light from the window over the kitchen sink; it was perfect. (A month later, when she saw the picture—Richard looking at her with shining eyes, her with her eyes shut, accentuating her laugh lines, her head bowed so that her double chin bulged out like she'd swallowed a pillow, mascara traveling up onto the drooping skin above her eyes—even she couldn't say it wasn't a beautiful shot, and she would hang it above the fireplace.)

Kevin led the couple in exchanging vows and rings and pronounced them husband and wife, and then the group moved to the living room for the meal. When that was done, Sunna asked if they were having a dance, and Maude said they weren't, but Sunna started moving the rented tables anyway. "One dance," she said. "You at least need to do the first-dance-as-husband-and-wife thing. Just that."

Maude begrudgingly agreed.

Sunna ran into her bedroom and brought out a Bluetooth speaker. Maude and Richard stood in the middle of the floor like a couple of teenagers at their first prom, shy about performing in front of the small crowd. "What will you be dancing to?" asked Sunna, wiggling her eyebrows.

"I don't know," said Maude. "Just pick something."

"How about *My Heart Will Go On*?"

"Oh, isn't that by Celine Dion?" Larry blurted loudly. "I don't think—"

Everyone looked at him, and he blushed.

"Ha! Nothing. Never mind," he said, laughing. But then he couldn't stop laughing, even when the dance had begun, and he kept looking up at the ceiling.

Sunna watched him and Nikki sitting in the corner, Larry constantly looking upward at every creak, real and imagined, her gazing at him adoringly. Mackenzie hunched over her phone texting with someone—Grant? Hopefully. Maude and Richard, awkwardly but sweetly clutching each other's shoulders and swaying back and forth. She thought about relationships and friendships and social media influencers. About ideal lives and real lives and BLZs and expectations and unexpected friendships and aging and plastic surgery and how Richard looked at Maude like she was beautiful. She thought about what Maude had said about ghosting herself. And she thought about how she *would* miss Maude living just upstairs from her. She was kind of like Brett in that unapologetic, speak-your-truth, no-holds-barred kind of way. She was kind of like family.

The last notes of the song died away, and everyone clapped politely. Richard pulled Maude into a hug. The ceiling popped loudly, and it was probably just the wood expanding as the weather shifted, but everyone jumped.

"That woman," said Larry gravely, "is caterwauling like a banshee." He'd probably meant to say it quietly, an inside joke with only himself, but it hung in the air for everyone to consider. And then, because it made so little sense, everyone laughed like it was the funniest thing they'd ever heard.

BOOK CLUB QUESTIONS

1. Have you ever had an important relationship end suddenly and without explanation? Do you relate to the way any of the characters in this book reacted to this situation?

2. Have you ever been the one who "ghosted" someone else? Did you feel frustrated with Mackenzie that she ghosted Grant even though she knew how terrible it would feel?

3. Do you agree with Sunna that you "don't need the other person" in order to have closure? Or do you think she should've called Brett and attempted to figure out what happened?

4. Which character did you hope the letter was for?

5. What marks the turning point in the women's relationship, where they become actual friends and not just housemates?

6. Could you relate to the characters' struggles with aging, physical appearance, and how their exteriors didn't quite match how they felt on the inside? What did you think of Maude's final thoughts on all of that in the last chapter?

7. Would you have given Richard a second chance if you were Maude? Would you have given Mackenzie a second chance if you were Grant? Would you have given Brett a

second chance (if she'd asked for one) if you were Sunna? In these kinds of relationships and situations, what kinds of things are unforgivable (or is anything truly unforgivable)? Or are there cases where it's fine to tell someone—even someone very important to you—that you just need to move on from them?

8. The adopted sisters story line highlights the fact that some adoptees, though in a happy family situation, still long to know where they came from and will go to great lengths to do so—even to the point of substantial risk, as with Tanya and Kate. Mackenzie says, "I didn't know what it was like to not know where someone is, someone who's intrinsically a part of you; I didn't know how much a person would want to know where that person was and why they weren't with you. I didn't get that you could love the people you were with while still agonizing over the unanswered questions about the ones you weren't with. And the worst part of all of this is that now I get it, and now I would be so sympathetic to them, and I would help them find their bio family because I get it. But I only get it because they're not here." Did it surprise you that Tanya and Kate would take such a big risk, or did it make sense to you?

9. Like Larry, do you have something from your teenage years (a hobby, a passion, a subculture) that you can't quite let go of? Have you found a way as an adult to still be involved with that thing (like Larry did with his album reviews)?

ACKNOWLEDGMENTS

Thanks to Barclay, Sully, and Scarlett for taking care of each other while I write and for welcoming me back into the real world so enthusiastically when I'm done. I love you all so much.

And thanks to Victoria for being so supportive and helpful in this process. I'm really, *really* glad you're my agent.

And thanks to Alicia, Laura, and all the incredible people at Lake Union for all the time and hard work you've put into this book. I love being part of this team.

And to the cover designer, Liz Casal, for the gorgeous artwork.

To Rachel for taking my picture.

To the authors I've met through this process who have become my friends.

To the book bloggers—many who have also become friends. (Writing a book is a great way to make friends.)

To Marty for watching the kids on Thursday mornings so I could go get some work done. You're a great gramps.

To Kiersten and Kaeli for watching my kids that one morning as I frantically attempted to meet a deadline (I did!).

To Kaeli and Kate for the writing dates.

To Kate and Sarah for the early edits.

To Hannah for telling me about Conor Oberst's new band that one day when I had writer's block. That album cured me.

To my friends and family, who are so wonderful and supportive.

To the Regina Public Library and all the various coffee shops that were my offices this past year.

And to all my own ghosts, without whom I would not have thought to write this book. (Feel free to email me and tell me what happened.)

ABOUT THE AUTHOR

Photo © 2019 Rachel Buhr

Suzy Krause is the author of *Valencia and Valentine*. She spends her days with her kids and writes when they sleep. She still occasionally finds time to blog just for fun at www.suzykrause.com. She lives in Regina, Saskatchewan.